Praise for Em

'Funny and sexy - I loved
magical world is the per
adventurous romantic comedy'
HELEN HAWKINS

'An engaging and magical tale, full of humour
and warmth. Loved it
JENNI KEER

'Fun, sweet and sexy'
SARAH HAWLEY

'What a gorgeous, fun and sexy romance!
I loved every word. Emma's stories just keep
getting better. More please!'
CARRIE ELKS

'This is the perfect witchy comfort read'
LAURA WOOD

'The sparks really fly in this bewitching
enemies-to-lovers tale, packed with magical characters
who aren't always what they seem'
SARA DOWNING

'Another enchanting delight from Emma Jackson. A cosy,
magical treat of a book that charmed my socks off!'
M.A. KUZNIAR

'A deliciously fun rom-com full of hilarity, sweetness, and
a swoonworthy romance. I loved every moment of it!'
STEPHANIE BURGIS

'I love this series! The world-building is so charming
and the love story sparkles with chemistry'
LEONIE MACK

Emma Jackson has been a devoted bookworm and secret-story-scribbler since she was 6 years old. Her bestselling debut novel, *A Mistletoe Miracle*, was published in 2019 and a contender for the Joan Hessayon Award.

When she's not running around after her two daughters and trying to complete her current work-in-progress, Emma loves to read, bake, catch up on binge-watching TV programmes with her partner and plan lots of craft projects that will inevitably end up unfinished. Emma also hosts the *SFFRomCast*, a podcast dedicated to sharing the love for fantasy and sci-fi romance novels, with fellow writer, Jessica Haines.

You can sign up to Emma's monthly newsletter at www.esjackson.co.uk or follow her via social media https://linktr.ee/ESJackson

Careful What You Witch For

EMMA JACKSON

ORION

An Orion paperback

First published in Great Britain in 2024
by Orion Fiction,
an imprint of The Orion Publishing Group Ltd,
Carmelite House, 50 Victoria Embankment
London EC4Y 0DZ

An Hachette UK company

1 3 5 7 9 10 8 6 4 2

A CIP catalogue record for this book
is available from the British Library.

ISBN (Mass Market Paperback) 978 1 3987 1798 5
ISBN (eBook) 978 1 3987 1797 8

Typeset by Born Group

Printed in Great Britain by Clays Ltd, Elcograf S.p.A.

MIX
Paper | Supporting
responsible forestry
FSC® C104740

www.orionbooks.co.uk

For Lily and Penny, I've finally finished it!
You two are my world and you make me so proud.

Chapter One

BECCA

There was a commonly held belief that 'the witching hour' took place from midnight to 1 a.m. Becca Ashworth wished that were true. It *actually* took place between 2.45 and 3.30 a.m. (depending on the sunrise), and reality was short-changing witches by fifteen minutes. But, as someone who liked sleep, Becca didn't mind prioritising efficiency and getting back to her bed sooner rather than later. Preferably with the answers that would make all her family's problems go away.

Still, it was a tight and fairly disorientating timeframe to be trying to get serious magic done. And it was only 'serious' magic that necessitated an atmosphere as close to utter stillness as the modern world was capable of.

She stifled a yawn and shifted on the freezing bare-stone floor of Ashworth Hall's cellar, just enough so that blood flowed into her right butt cheek again. As she lifted her hand directly over a thick white pillar candle, fingers poised to click and light it with a spark of magic, she glanced over at Kay – her cousin Harry's girlfriend – who was sitting outside the chalk pentacle at the point opposite and to the left of her.

'Everything good, Kay?' It seemed to take an extra-special effort to break through the bubble of quiet – as if the air were charged, heavy with expectation of the spell they were about to cast. The only other noise was the soft scrape of chalk as Harry drew runes directly onto the floor as part of the pentacle. But, since Kay was gnawing on her thumbnail, a frown etched across her brow, Becca figured it was worth making the effort to speak up and check.

'I just . . .' Kay pressed her lips together and tapped her thumb against them before continuing, her words pouring out like commuters exiting the London Underground during rush hour. 'Are we definitely, absolutely, one hundred per cent sure about this?'

Harry set down the chalk and dusted off his fingers against his shirt, before he reached across to catch Kay's hand – presumably to prevent her losing an entire finger to the nervous nibbling.

'We can't ever be "definitely, absolutely, one hundred per cent sure" about anything in life.' Then he paused and asked, with genuine curiosity: 'Can we?'

Kay's hand tightened around his. 'I think you're right but . . . but technically this is *death*. Not life,' she pointed out, her tone a touch sardonic. 'So I feel like we should be even *more* conscientious about the possible consequences.'

Becca sighed. These two. They were hopelessly adorable. The hopeless bit being more annoying on some days than others . . . like today. Or tonight. This morning? Whatever.

She understood their reservations – she really did – despite being a witch not taken to second-guessing herself. She worked to a simple yet effective system: assess a problem, identify a solution, get on with fixing it. That being said, even within the witching community, summoning the spirits of ancestors past was not exactly encouraged.

OK. Fine. There was *literally* a Worldwide Witching Tenet forbidding 'unnecessary communion with, and/or manifestation of, spirits', which had been in place since the very unfortunate seance frenzy in the Victorian era.

Increasingly stringent UK Witches Council by-laws, fines and prosecutions of the last decade aside, Becca knew the prohibition was there for a very good reason. But this was not 'unnecessary'.

Whether the Witches Council would agree with that or not was another matter and, given their frosty relationship with Becca's family, it wasn't worth asking them for permission. There was too much at stake to risk inviting the Council's notice or censure, so, what they didn't know wouldn't hex them. This was a last resort, for the sake of Becca's family and, ultimately, the whole of Biddicote village.

She knew she didn't need to remind Kay and Harry of that. They were just conflicted. Kay was not a natural law-breaker – not to mention she'd been working for the Council for less than a year – and Harry was gravitated towards feelings of guilt at any given opportunity, regardless of the fact that he was one of the most generous and kind people Becca had ever known. So . . . hopelessly adorable. Prone to heartfelt deconstructions of their personal morals, magical ethics and their interplay within witching society or the world as a whole. Something they did *not* have time for. Becca might permanently damage the nerve-endings in her derrière.

She snapped her fingers, harnessing the friction between her digits with a wordless magical intention to create a flame, which she transferred to the wick of the candle. The lovebirds both jumped and tore their gazes away from each other to look at her.

'Don't start tying yourself up in knots again, please,' Becca said, lightly but firmly, withdrawing her hand from the candle as its light flickered and grew strangely long. The pentacle was doing its job already – she could feel the air thinning around her. The tip of her nose getting cold. 'You'll just end up at the same conclusion as before and all we'll have gained are numb backsides and summer colds from sitting in the damp longer than we had to. You know why it's come down to this. We're not doing it lightly or without good reason. Right?'

Becca could almost see the chain of events that had led the three of them to this moment running through their minds like a training montage in an action movie. Or maybe that was just her. It was possible she was a little delirious from lack of sleep.

The sequence would begin with Uncle Adrian – Harry's dad – growing sicker and sicker over the last few years from the mysterious respiratory illness that no healer or doctor could figure out the origin of, or – most importantly – a cure for.

Cut to Harry returning to live at Ashworth Hall to help his mum – Becca's Aunt Elenor – look after his dad and alleviate the demands on the Ashworth family from the larger-than-average population of witches in Biddicote. At first, this meant simply being the person they came to if they noticed one of the wards, charms or runes the Ashworth ancestors had built into the village causing any issues or weakening in power. It was that very network of spells, woven to protect witches from discovery and allowing them to live alongside non-magical neighbours, which had enticed so many to make Biddicote their home – even if they didn't know exactly how deep the magic went, how it all worked together, or that the Ashworth heir was a physical lynchpin. Or rather, magical anchor.

That had been the next stage: Harry having the anchor tattoo of the Ashworth heir – a closely guarded secret – permanently inked onto his chest, in a bid to relieve the drain on Uncle Adrian's already low reserves of energy. Becca's father accusing Harry of taking advantage of the situation to ensure he inherited the Hall, while doing *nothing* to help as usual, just adding to the stress and pain and guilt when Harry's tattoo didn't activate and they watched Uncle Adrian deteriorate to the point where they knew he didn't have long left.

Cue momentary uplifting music as, last Samhain, it *did* finally work, and the draw of the anchor split between father and son. Uncle Adrian rallying from his death bed, regaining his voice, his life . . . albeit weakened, but the improvement had been undeniable.

The chord changing to minor again as *Harry* started to show signs of a different illness. Dizzy spells and heart palpitations whenever there was a large gathering for the witching festivals, which they'd – prematurely, as it turned out – reintroduced. And it becoming obvious that it was due to the increased demand on the protective magic woven throughout Biddicote, and therefore on the anchors. The tattoo wasn't just exacerbating an existing illness, it was *causing* the illnesses in the first place, weakening the centre of magic for the witch it was inked onto.

The realisation was followed by confusion and panic, because the tattoos had *never* made any heir to Ashworth Hall ill in the past. They'd gone through every book in the extensive family library *again* – since they'd already picked over each precious grimoire looking for notes on the runes that made up the tattoo – trying to figure out what might have been missed from the tattoo ritual, when it hadn't immediately activated on Harry. But it was all such a hallowed family secret that none of their ancestors had written down helpful details about what all the symbols meant, exactly how it worked or the precise method of implementing it. They'd relied on oral history, and the only logical conclusion was that at *some* point down the line of inheritance, someone *must* have forgotten something. Leaving them with only one option: speaking to a witch in the family who was alive *before* someone in the chain screwed it up.

Which brought them right here to this moment. Sitting in the cellar, getting ready to break several witching by-laws without special dispensation because Becca was *not* going to watch her baby cousin (yes, he was about to turn twenty-nine, but he was still a baby to her) or her uncle wither away, closely followed by the entire legacy of her family.

They needed answers, and if they needed to get them from beyond the grave, so be it.

As though they could see the renewed determination in her eyes, the set of her jaw and the strengthening of her spine, Harry and Kay nodded.

'Right,' she repeated, this time softened by relief that they were still in agreement over this course of action and she wasn't going to have to convince them all over again. 'So . . . do you want to crack on with those runes, Harry? It'll be easier to call the spirits if my teeth aren't chattering.'

'It's thirty degrees outside, Becs. We're in the middle of a heatwave.' Harry rolled his eyes, but, after kissing Kay tenderly on the cheek, he rested back on his haunches and picked up the chalk again.

'I can't help it if I'm a cold-blooded creature.' Becca gave an exaggerated shiver.

'That explains the scales,' he teased, even as he concentrated on drawing the next rune.

'And the forked tongue,' Kay joined in.

'You know turtles are cold-blooded. So are honeybees. You could have compared me to one of those . . . or any of the many other *cute* animals that can't regulate their own temperature. But no, you two bullies have to go with a snake.' Becca feigned a wounded sigh.

'Oh, I wasn't thinking of a snake,' Harry said, glancing over at her, his mouth hitching up at the side in his familiar mischievous smile.

'No? What then?'

'Komodo dragon,' both Harry and Kay answered simultaneously.

Becca let her jaw drop. 'Look, I'd accept the dragon part, but Komodos have more bacteria in their mouths than a bachelor's bed sheets, so I'm sticking with calling you both out as bullies. Weirdly synchronous bullies, too. Tweedledum and Tweedledummer.'

Kay snorted and Harry shook his head, laughing: 'Stop – I'm trying to concentrate,' he implored.

Becca bit her tongue on another retort, holding up her hands in surrender, and they all settled down as Harry finished off drawing the runes around the pentacle.

'There.' After a few minutes, he flicked the last line with his natural artistic flare and sat back in his spot. He pushed his coppery hair back from his forehead, rubbing away the perspiration dotted at his hairline with the heel of his hand.

Becca's smile faded and when Kay's eyes met hers, she knew the concern in them was mirrored in her own. Regardless of the heatwave, it was not the temperature in the cellar making Harry sweat – it was exertion . . . and that wasn't proportionate to the magic he'd just worked. Not for him anyway. Runes were very old, extremely tricky magic that few witches could use effectively, but the handful he'd just drawn would never even have registered on him this time last year. He'd been capable of

7

recharging the entirety of Biddicote's charms and wards when he was trying to stop the anchor from draining his dad too much – it had exhausted him, but he could do it. Now the intermittent demands of the anchor seemed to be gradually eroding Harry's natural magical stamina. How long before it affected his health *all* the time, in the same way that it had with Uncle Adrian? Before both he and his dad were bedridden?

She folded her hands in her lap and took a deep breath, making an effort not to let her voice betray her worry. 'Can you light your candle for us, Kay?'

'Sure.'

There was another snap and more light crept into the room, pushing the shadows further back towards the old boxes and fragile pieces of ancient furniture they stored down there instead of wine. *That* cellar was in another part of the house near the 'new' kitchen. But this being one of the original and therefore oldest parts of the Hall was exactly why they were using it.

They could have gone outside to the cave on the grounds, where their ancestor Biddi had first lived before she married William Ashworth and founded the village, a few hundred years ago. Her disappearance from the cave instigated the carefully planted rumour, which had turned into folklore, that 'the devil' had already taken the witch, deterring the Witchfinder General from poking around in the area for too long.

Without a doubt the depth of magic would have been even stronger in the cave, but they'd all agreed they weren't quite ready to try to summon such a legendary witch, even if they were related to her. Even if Becca was the first person in their family since Biddi to have the same primary gift as her – the ability to find lost objects for people. Her own father thought she wasn't living up to the responsibility of *that* privilege, so Goddess knew what Biddi would make of her.

Still, if Biddi turned up, she turned up. It wasn't like Becca had a supernatural phonebook to make sure she dialled the right ancestor. All she could do was reach out and see who, if anyone, responded.

Being a medium was Becca's secondary gift, but between her mum (the only other medium Becca had met) passing away before Becca's gifts had manifested fully at fifteen and the tightening shackles of the Witches Council, she'd never put anything into *practice*. She knew from living with her mum and, later, recognising the sensations in herself that she could feel it if she was in a place where many or strong spirits lingered. And she knew that her presence alone could help the strongest of those spirits become more visible or capable of communication – if they were so inclined – but she had no control over it. Had not been taught any spells or rituals first-hand for summoning or exorcism. It was all theory from books, which the Witches Council was probably dying to confiscate from the Ashworth family library. Here's hoping they didn't have good reason and Becca wasn't about to turn Ashworth Hall into something from *The Shining*.

She took a deep breath. 'Let's do this.'

Both Harry and Kay nodded again, and mirrored her cross-legged position, hands on their knees, silent. Becca was at the 'top' of the pentacle, with two empty points on either side of her, while Kay and Harry sat at the points next to each other. Ideally, they would have had two other people at the empty points, and she didn't want to think too much about the consequences of that, but it had just been too complicated to find anyone else to join them.

The older generations of their family were either not well enough, at odds with each other, or would disapprove. Getting them involved would only have delayed things. And none of them had wanted to rope any of their other friends or family into what was technically illegal magic. That was why they'd had to wait until Uncle Adrian and Aunt Elenor had gone away for a restorative ten-day break at the coast.

On the plus side, three was always a good number for magic and, between them, they had a broad mix of useful gifts. Harry's ability to influence through art gave him the magical edge needed to draw the runes, invoking varying degrees of protection, security and good will. Kay – when she wasn't wearing her magically charmed glasses – could see the emotional bonds between people. They didn't actually have any idea whether it would work on a ghost, since Kay had never seen one, but on the off-chance it did, it would only be a bonus to have a heads-up on whether whichever spirit of Ashworth past happened to answer the call had any instinctive, protective familial feelings towards them. And then, of course, there was her. Becca. The untried and untested medium.

Time to do her 'stuff'.

She closed her eyes and focused. Just like with the tugging pressure she felt when she was locating lost things, when she was accessing her gift as a medium her awareness usually started in her head. A tingle at the base of her skull, before snaking down her spine and spreading out over her skin like goosebumps. Ashworth Hall had always made her skin feel slightly more 'awake', so she knew spirits were here – but they were never oppressive or demanding so she had been able to coexist with them quite happily without disturbing them or herself.

And she was almost 99.9 per cent sure that she wouldn't summon her mum. They hadn't lived at Ashworth Hall, and she'd never sensed her mum's spirit here – she was sure she would have felt something different . . . The only place Becca had ever felt her mum's presence since she died was in her heart – her chest hitched a little at the thought, but she pushed it away. She knew it was for the best. Because as much as it would be a sharp, fierce joy to see her mum again . . . knowing she couldn't keep her would be devastating.

Clear your mind, breathe deep, she instructed herself, and when she felt a chill in the air settling over her like a blanket of dew, she opened her eyes again. Harry was looking at her like he wanted to say something, but she gave her head a slight shake to stop him and a small smile to try to reassure him.

She lifted her hands and pulled a long, old-fashioned hair pin from the messy bun of her hair. She'd found it in one of the spare rooms in the Hall when she was a teenager and had worn it for years, so it served the double purpose of being old, connected to an ancestor most likely, and being something she owned, which was perfect for the next step.

Holding the base of the pillar candle, she stared into the bright flame, the darkness everywhere else deepening by contrast, and then slowly, carefully, pushed the pin through the candle as she spoke, calm and quiet.

''Tis not only this candle I mean to stick, but a spirit's ears I mean to prick. If someone is listening, please answer to me, but only if you are part of the Ashworth family. We three seek the knowledge to help Biddicote village. We ask kindly for this boon, by the light of the moon.'

As she spoke the last word, the candlelight flared, the flame turning silvery pale and inexplicably round. It grew, wavering, and the heat touched her face, in stark contrast to the cool air in the cellar. The sensation of tingling across her skin intensified, making her want to either giggle or scrub at her arms, but she stayed as still as possible.

Kay let out a little squeak, but Becca couldn't see her or Harry. The light from their candles was doing the same, growing and thinning as the flames stretched towards each other, almost like bubbles being blown by children.

Becca's heart clenched for a moment, wondering if the distance would be too far for the light to cross, if they should have put two more candles down, despite them not having the witches to sit by them, or maybe they *should* have got her aunt and her dad in to help, regardless of the days of arguing that it probably would have necessitated—

And then a man's head popped into sight, floating above them and the glow of light in the centre of the pentacle. He had a mess of blond curls, with a side parting so far over it was almost at his left ear, and the biggest, most impressive sideburns Becca had ever seen.

The head twisted around, seemingly taking in the dim corners of the room as the candlelight eased back and more of his body came into view. He was wearing a long, white . . . nightshirt? And nothing else. When he looked down and realised he let out an enormous groan.

'What in the blazes? Where are my dratted inexpressibles?' He tipped his head back and pressed a palm to his forehead. 'And in the presence of ladies, too.'

Becca blinked as the ghost heaved an enormous sigh. 'Umm . . . hello. Thank you for joining us.' She winced – why was she talking to him as if this were a Zoom meeting? Although, she supposed, it wasn't too different. Even the underwear bit wasn't unheard of . . . Admittedly, the whole being *dead* thing was less common. 'Honestly, don't worry about the clothes.'

'My sincerest apologies,' he continued, as though he hadn't heard her speak, shaking his head and dragging his hand down to cover his face. 'I'm afraid I had no way of realising that, when I heard you and went towards the light, I would appear in the same apparel I died in. Honestly, where is the dignity?'

Harry cleared his throat. 'Please, like Becca said, don't worry about it. You can't be held accountable.'

The ghost dropped his hand immediately at the sound of Harry's voice, and turned to him with a relieved smile. 'Kind of you to say, my dear fellow.'

Ah. So, he'd needed some male approval to stop him fretting. Becca had forgotten someone from an earlier time period would probably assume another man was in charge. It still happened in the twenty-first century; what could she expect of someone born in the . . . nineteenth? She was guessing.

'And you are?' the ghost continued, talking to Harry.

'Harrison Ashworth.'

'Heir to Ashworth Hall,' Becca added, because it seemed like something the ghost would have respect for, but Harry never wanted to volunteer that kind of information.

Again, there was no acknowledgement she'd spoken. Maybe those sideburns were so big they deflected female speech patterns?

'Indeed? A descendant! Not directly of mine, obviously – I sadly died before I had any issue . . . but a relation.'

'Yes. As is my cousin, Rebecca Ashworth.' Harry nodded towards Becca and the man glanced over at her.

'Charmed, I'm sure, Miss Ashworth.' He grasped at the side of his nightgown and sketched a short bow, now they had been formally introduced.

'Likewise, sir,' Becca said, trying not to laugh. Maybe the use of her magic was making her light-headed. 'Might I enquire as to your name?' They'd all be auditioning for parts on *Bridgerton* at this rate.

'Oh, but of course. I'm Horatio William Albert Ashworth.' He bowed again and as he returned his attention to Harry, Becca tilted her head, throwing a questioning look at Kay and Harry. Both of them were shaking their heads slightly, to indicate that they couldn't place the name from the family trees or diaries or grimoires they'd all studied. Perhaps the Witches Council would be less covetous of the Ashworth family library if they knew how poorly the records had been kept?

'I say,' Horatio said as he noticed Kay. 'Is your hair *blue*, young lady? Or has the afterlife done something wayward to my vision?' He rubbed his eyes, the motion lifting his nightshirt; Becca swiftly averted her gaze because she had no clue if the Victorians had worn underwear to bed. 'And by the by, you are all dressed *extremely* strangely.'

Kay let out a short laugh at that but covered it up with a cough.

'Things are a bit different now,' Harry, king of the understatement, said. 'It's the twenty-first century.'

'Twenty . . .?' Horatio trailed off and stared around him again, like he had when he'd first appeared. Then he shook his head. 'Well, my goodness . . . this calls for some investigation.'

And with that he stepped out of the pentacle and made for the stairs, floating up them, and disappearing through the locked door at the top.

'Cernunnos's balls!' Becca stared after him. 'That wasn't supposed to happen.'

Chapter Two

CONNOR

One week later

Connor Lynch ran his finger along the inside of his shirt collar, separating it from his neck, and attempted to scoot the cumbersome armchair he was wedged into further away from the window.

How did a chair manage to be the size of a grizzly bear while simultaneously being too small to sit in comfortably? The charm it had been infused with when it was magically crafted rolled straight over him, telling him that if he'd been even slightly susceptible to influential magic, he would have found it the perfect blend of supportive and deliciously soft – *taunting* him, in fact, as his kidneys were pummelled by upholstery, which was seemingly stuffed with rocks.

The stumps that passed for the chair's feet squeaked over the tiles and the witch working on the far side of the office/antechamber fumbled with her stapler, sending it clattering over her desk and onto the floor, little metal staples skittering out like miniature shrapnel.

Connor sighed and resisted the impulse to be helpful and levitate both it and the contents back up into her hands. It would only make her more nervous to see him using his own magic. As his boss, Warren Barraclough's, secretary, Priscilla was one of the very small handful of people, mostly made up of Tenet Enforcers, who were under one of the Witches Council's anonymity charms and therefore permitted to know both his role and true identity. Connor rarely saw her in person, though.

Warren was the United Kingdom's PR Councillor, which meant the overseeing of non-magical relations and media control. He split his time between this Reigate office, which was mainly given over to heritage, artefacts and historical research, and the technical centre in Portsmouth. Connor reported in to him at least every other month, if he wasn't on another continent or the far side of the country. But this morning he'd received a very rare request to drop in to the office. During the *day*.

Connor was familiar with the building's layout. He knew the reference and research departments, which spread over the first floor. He'd sometimes needed to visit the heritage and archaeology department, with its archives for magical artefacts tucked in the basement, alongside the still-rooms to test old spells that had been rediscovered, but when he was visiting he spent most of his time in Warren's corner office, here on the top floor, near the kitchen and the meeting rooms. Just the two of them. When he'd entered the reception ten minutes earlier and had to wait – because his ability to pass through wards was as closely guarded a secret as his identity – then been collected by Priscilla and got to walk through the offices and see it populated by people, it had been a nice, if overwhelming, change. Like when a zombie movie flicked from the stark, post-apocalyptic narrative to a scene of the 'good times', which were full of chatter and warm lighting, people going about their everyday lives, blissfully unaware of the calamity approaching them.

But Priscilla and her flying stapler was an excellent reminder of why he usually came after hours and interacted with the bare minimum of staff. It avoided questions about who he was from people who didn't know . . . and why his presence alone terrified the people who did.

Priscilla hurried out from behind her desk, heels clicking, to retrieve the stationery, and backed away again as if he were pointing a gun towards her. Connor averted his eyes and resigned himself to being roasted. You'd have thought that a building full of witches would have benefited from charmed glass, but perhaps other people enjoyed being shrivelled up into pieces of magical jerky.

He glanced out of the window, watching as dozens of non-magical people passed by without any clue that there was an entire building of witches right there, sandwiched between a jeweller's and a picture framer's. The Witches Council of the UK had offices all over England, Scotland, Northern Ireland and Wales, and they were utterly nondescript. Never any bigger or more intriguing than the average small accountancy firm, they blended in seamlessly with the neighbouring commercial properties without a single sign outside to entice a non-magical person to venture in.

The sound of a door opening drew Connor's attention back into the room, and a male witch around his age, with slicked-down blond hair, stepped out of Warren's office.

'Fecking hell,' Connor muttered under his breath as Edward Cochrane did a double-take and his narrow face tightened into a rigid mask. Edward was another person who 'knew' who Connor was – but not only because he worked at the Witches Council for Warren in the mythology and folklore verification department. He and Connor were old schoolmates.

Well, 'mate' was *entirely* the wrong word. 'Nemesis' was perhaps also too strong. It implied that there had been some kind of wilful rivalry on both sides. Connor had never wanted to achieve anything more from Dentwood, the witching boarding school they'd both spent their teen years at, than getting *through* it. He'd never entertained ambitions of coming top of his class or beating Edward and his gaggle of cronies at sporting activities or in the magical competitions. All Connor had wanted was to adjust to the reality of being a witch, when he'd never known such a thing truly existed. Not until he was thirteen and managed to set fire to a hay bale without touching it, instigating a blaze that ended up being reported on the local news.

And the worst part was that causing an incident big enough to attract the Witches Council's attention and have him removed from Ireland and packed off to Dentwood in northern England wasn't even the *most* damage he'd ever done with his magic. Something that Edward was well aware of because he'd been a witness when Connor's gift had fully manifested two years later.

'Warren said to tell you that you can send in his next meeting,' Edward told Priscilla, in that same insufferable, self-important tone Connor remembered well. By the time Priscilla finished reloading her stapler and nodded, Edward was already out of the door and into the hallway.

Priscilla looked over at Connor, in the same way a person who'd been told they could go pet a dog with rabies might, a few wisps of grey hair curling out from her neat up-do and spoiling her otherwise orderly appearance. He was literally making her hair stand on end. Grand.

'Don't worry. I heard,' Connor said, saving her the trouble of finding her voice, and stood, arching his spine ever so slightly to ensure the chair hadn't permanently compressed anything vital. He tried not to walk too fast towards her, lest she scream and dive underneath her desk.

Warren was sitting at his desk, scribbling notes on a tablet, but he glanced up as Connor entered, the corner of his mouth lifting in a smirk. 'Didn't want to linger for a catch-up with the charming Edward?'

Connor rolled his eyes and shut the door behind him with a wave of magic. Before Warren became Connor's boss, part of his duties had included working as Educational Liaison at Dentwood and then Connor's personal mentor when his gift manifested. He knew there was no love lost between Connor and Edward and didn't even blame Connor. Warren could commiserate, having confessed to being an outsider at Dentwood himself, ostracised when a change in policy left his parents' business on the wrong side of a by-law. His own miserable experience had prompted him to volunteer as Educational Liaison in the first place, to help students like himself who were snubbed.

'If "charm" and "Edward" go together in the same sentence, it's not one that makes sense to me,' Connor commented, dryly.

Warren snorted. 'Spare a thought for us poor souls who have to work with him.'

Connor sent him an apologetic look, knowing that Warren had basically had to promise Edward a position way above entry level within the Witches Council as soon as he left school because it was the only way to guarantee he would keep his mouth shut about knowing Connor – or, more specifically, knowing what his gift was. A minor could not legally agree to be part of an anonymity charm, or have an influencer attempt to convince them to 'forget' something – which was almost impossible anyway, because it needed a high level of susceptibility to suggestion, some willingness from the subject, and no strong reminders to jog the memory. And using influence in that way was considered entirely unethical to try to do to anyone, not just minors. So Warren had to resort to good old-fashioned bribery. Apparently, the future prospect of inheriting Mummy and Daddy's golf course and spa resort hadn't been enough for Edward, and he eagerly snapped up a job at the Witches Council at eighteen that others would have had to pay many years of dues to achieve. All he'd had to do was keep his mouth shut and agree to the anonymity charm as soon as he was legally an adult.

Warren waved the matter away, along with his stylus and tablet. 'Anyway – enough about him. We have *other* insufferable and over-privileged witches to fry. Don't hover. Come and sit down.'

Connor took a seat in a slightly more comfortable, though still magically crafted, chair and Warren magicked open the filing cabinet to the right of him. A manila folder the depth of the *Lord of the Rings* trilogy stacked together floated out and landed on the desk in front of Connor.

'Holy grimoire.' Connor frowned. 'So, what's this?'

'Your next assignment.' Warren tapped the front of the file and the front cover peeled back to reveal a page of photocopied reference cards, which had been lined up next to each other to fit the sheet.

'Is it a dangerous witch you've been tracking?' Connor touched the edge of the uppermost report and felt the binding of a privacy enchantment wrapped around the whole file. The only place he'd come across restrictions like that was in the archives . . . but this was definitely not an archive file. He could feel the deliberation of Warren's magical signature.

'Possibly a whole family of them.' Warren linked his fingers and scooted his chair closer under the desk, leaning over his arms to pin Connor with a look that was both concerned and yet, somehow, oddly excited. 'I've been gathering notes on the Ashworth family and activities in Biddicote for . . . oh, about a decade, I suppose?'

Connor's eyebrows rose involuntarily. He knew the name and had heard of the place, of course – what witch hadn't? But it was a twee little village as far as he was aware. He'd never even had to go there to deal with a hexed object or to unravel spells left by an elderly witch who'd passed away – the most innocent of the cases he dealt with. Which . . . was a wee bit odd, now he came to think of it, for a place with, reportedly, the highest density of witches in the UK. 'Why have you been keeping tabs on them? What's the story?'

'I'm still not sure. But something, definitely.' Warren dug a finger inside the file, flipping the stack of papers over manually to review something similar to the assignment sheets Connor usually received, but older and incomplete. 'Back then, I was working for Beckett Kirby, before he retired. We were getting called out there more and more for fringe slip-ups and sightings. Adrian Ashworth constantly stonewalled us and "dealt with things". Kirby was happy to trust them, always keen to appease such an old witching family.' Warren curled his lip and continued: 'But Ashworth *hated* us being there, questioning him. Or even the merest suggestion that the Witches Council should step in to look into the problems. His deepest desire whenever the Witches Council was there was for us to leave, immediately. So – alarm bells.'

Connor nodded a little. By his own admission, Warren was not an especially powerful witch, and he had no sought-after gifts like influencers or seers or healers. But he *was* an empath who could read what a person wanted most, an ability which came in handy when assessing the threat level of a dangerous witch, mostly as additional evidence during a trial, and to help the jury decide upon a suitable sentence if found guilty. A witch whose deepest desire was to be hugged by their father would be dealt with differently from a witch who dreamt of enslaving all of non-magical kind. Intention was the backbone of magic, after all. It was just a shame Warren's gift, or something like it, couldn't be utilised to somehow flag dangerous witches *before* they caused people harm and Connor was called in.

He curled his hands into loose fists, leaning back and resting them on his thighs. 'But that was a while ago. Are they still having problems?'

'No. Not with the protective magic in Biddicote, anyway. They closed their doors for a while when Adrian Ashworth got ill and his son, Harrison, came home. Apparently last year Ashworth almost succumbed, but they've recently started to hold festivities again, and his health has improved.' Warren tapped his linked hands against his mouth. 'And I could have been persuaded to write it off – their hostility towards the Witches Council, I mean. It could just have been a symptom of their arrogance. They are one of the oldest witching families, to the point where they actually pre-date the forming of the Council – so they hate having to answer to us. But then, Harrison's girlfriend, Kayla Hendrix, started working here, around six to seven months ago . . .' His eyes jumped to Connor's, their light blue as arresting as jumping in an ice-pool. 'And she's been a naughty witch. Rifling in our restricted records. Looking up spells that are prohibited. Trying to find out what information we have on the Ashworths . . . They're worried about something again, and this time *I'm* in charge and I'm not going to let it slide.'

'You don't think she could be up to something independently, trying to scam them?'

Warren shook his head. 'Having seen her deepest desires, no. I won't divulge them at this stage for the sake of her privacy, but I can say that her feelings for Harrison are genuine. I fear it is more likely *she's* the one being used for her access to our records. It's why I want to tread carefully with this. If I go in too soon, it will just have to be a disciplinary slap on the wrist and the opportunity to pull back the curtain on the Ashworths will be lost.'

'OK . . . so, your plan is . . .?' Maybe Connor had been in the sun too long, but he couldn't figure out why *any* of this necessitated him being called in at short notice.

'Well, I'm too high up to approach her. It won't set her at ease, especially if the Ashworths get wind of my involvement. And I can't bring any enforcers in either; the Ashworths have worked their PR image to perfection, "the benevolent protectors of Biddicote".' Warren rolled his eyes. 'I can't trust them to go in and not be starstruck.'

'What about her manager?'

'Same applies. Plus, she's friends with Kayla's father. You, on the other hand, I know are not swayed by the kudos of an old witching name. You'll be impartial and thorough.'

Connor's mouth opened and closed a couple of times before he could articulate any words. Because if 'Edward' and 'charm' didn't make sense in the same sentence, neither did 'Connor' and 'tread carefully'. 'You want *me* to do an investigation?'

'Yes.' Warren gave him a small smile. 'This is a very unique set of circumstances, so it makes sense to take a unique approach. And it won't be an investigation in the usual sense, of course. I was thinking, in the first instance, you could pop by Ashworth Hall to talk to Kayla. Give her a friendly warning.'

Connor's eyebrows drew together. That made even less sense to him. Especially because it sounded suspiciously like it required *social* skills. 'D'you not think the "friendliness" of the warning will be somewhat undermined with it coming from me?'

Warren laughed, slapping his hand on the stack of papers in front of him. 'I'm not expecting you to tell her you're the Abrogator! She doesn't know, you've never met, so just . . . your name and that you work for me in enforcement should suffice. And while you're having a nice, civilised chat over a cup of tea—' He raised his eyebrows, indicating that he expected Connor to fill in the blanks. Which he did. Relieved to finally be catching on.

'I can nose around at whatever magical signatures are on the place. What spells have been recently cast.'

'Precisely. Take a peek behind the veil of the Ashworths' perfect façade, as only you are able to do.'

'You don't think it'll seem strange, visiting her at home, rather than her having a meeting with her boss?' Connor pinched the seam of his trouser leg, worrying at it as he shifted on his seat.

'I imagine she'll take it as proof of your intention to keep it off the record. Hopefully it will encourage her to open up more about what is going on. Besides, she's taken the afternoon off, and told her line manager it was for an emergency at home, so timing-wise, it just makes sense.' Warren closed the folder and levitated it over to Connor. It dropped onto his lap, making him flinch and sit up. 'It only takes about an hour to get to Biddicote from here. Address is in there. If you leave soon, you'll be there by 2 p.m. Call me afterwards with an update.'

'Right.' Connor stood up, tucking the folder under his arm, hesitating for a moment.

'Is there an issue?'

'No. I . . . I suppose it's a little outside of my wheel-house, is all.'

Warren sent him a gentle smile. 'I wouldn't trust this to anyone except you, Connor. You can do this. And, surely, it will be a nice change of pace for you? The last year has been relentless, hasn't it?'

Connor couldn't argue with that. He hadn't been back to Ireland since the funeral of his cousin Rory's wife. Every time he booked a ticket, another assignment cropped up that took him halfway across the world. Which reminded him. 'Oh, I meant to ask you for some advice? My cousin's eldest daughter is—'

Warren's mobile phone began ringing and he picked it up, pausing just a second before he answered. 'I'm really sorry, I have to get this. I'll speak to you later this afternoon.'

Connor nodded. It was only a question about a birthday present, since Warren's daughter was eight years old, too. It could wait. He left Warren to his call, doing his best to slip through the halls quickly before anyone noticed him.

Chapter Three

BECCA

If Becca hadn't been so frustrated, she might have found a week-long game of supernatural hide-and-seek between her, Kay, Harry and Horatio fun. They knew Horatio was lurking there – he was tethered to the property. Unfortunately (in this instance), Ashworth Hall was an extremely *large* property. Rooms upon rooms, corridors and attics, and then of course there were the gardens. It was a lot of ground to cover, and the more they chased Horatio, the more skittish he became.

OK, maybe it was still a *little* bit fun – watching a grown man in a nightshirt shriek and disappear through a wall whenever they happened upon him was inherently absurd. Maybe if grown-ups played kids games more often, she'd have been able to control the way it tickled her funny bone. Football carried over already, obviously. But group skipping, hopscotch, tag – if the gym offered a class with *those*, she might be more inclined to go. And what about playing horsies? Actually, she'd heard there were adults who played that but in a very different way, with bridles and whips and everything.

She was not one to call other people out on their kinks, though. Especially when she had a weakness for tall men, which was just stupid, patriarchal indoctrination. So they had a long torso or legs . . . or, in the case of Drew, her ex, an abnormally big head. It really didn't make them superior

– or inferior – in any particular way. Just a different body shape. The next man she dated was going to be the same height as her. Or *shorter*. Because she was an enlightened, modern woman, Goddess-dammit.

She'd been working at Biddicote Primary School earlier that day, taking the Year 6 leavers' photographs, which was the reason her brain was yo-yoing between childhood nostalgia and boyfriends she regretted – Drew was a TA at the school. Things had definitely been simpler when she used to spend all her lunchbreak giddy-upping around the playground with a friend . . . whose name escaped her now. How bad was that? All she could remember was the bounce of a strawberry-blond ponytail ahead of her as they clip-clopped, surrounded by the shouts and screams and giggles of the playground.

The sound of kids at playtime was surely a form of magic. She wondered if there was a witch somewhere with the ability to bottle it. It didn't fit in with her understanding of the workings of magical energy, but you never knew.

'"*There are more things in heaven and earth, Horatio,*"' she whispered as she walked casually down the first-floor corridor. Her phone buzzed and Becca pulled it out of the back pocket of her cropped trousers. Becca was in charge of checking the first floor, Kay the second, and Harry had taken the attic. They were communicating through text message, so if one of them spotted their quarry they could quietly mobilise into a pincer movement to ambush him, like a pack of lionesses.

Harry: No sign of him up here. But I'll check inside the old trunks and closets.

This was the problem. Now she had an image of Horatio curled up in a trunk full of old toys because he was so

27

desperate not to be found. She pressed her lips together to contain her laughter.

No. It wasn't really funny. Horatio was probably disorientated, trying to adjust to his old home and the world nearly two centuries later. Giving him some time would have been kinder . . . however, if they *didn't* track him down, Becca was going to have to figure out how to exorcise him. She didn't *want* to, and not just because they hadn't got any answers from him – it felt wrong to drag a spirit in and out of the corporeal world at whim. But she doubted her aunt and uncle would be happy that she'd inflicted a permanent house guest upon them. They'd always maintained that the Hall was as much hers as theirs and Harry's; she had a key and was welcome to come and go as she pleased. They might draw a line at her summoning ghosts into it, though, and she could hardly blame them for it.

All in all, the summoning idea had not paid dividends. Yet.

She stepped into the largest bedroom on the first floor. It was a guest room, with sage green and cream decor, a four-poster bed and dressing tables. Becca hadn't been in there since Kay's brother had got married at the Hall, last Samhain. The bride-to-be, Sandy, and her bridesmaids had used it to get ready and Becca had been their photographer, getting candid shots of them as their hair was curled and they drank champagne and laughed.

Her scalp tingled as she walked through the room. This space had made her feel off-kilter for as long as she could remember. An unsettled sense of something bittersweet. She'd figured maybe someone had died young in there . . . and since Horatio didn't exactly appear old, maybe this had been his room?

But it was empty. She checked the massive wardrobe and the en-suite bathroom for good measure and heaved a sigh. She was about to message Kay and Harry to tell them the green guest room was all clear but then the movement of something pale caught her eye out of the window.

'Gotcha.'

CONNOR

Connor had never really been able to shake the feeling of claustrophobia that spending a prolonged period of time in a small village brought him. He knew it was mostly a prejudice born from the first thirteen years of his life growing up in one, tucked deep in the Irish countryside, feeling like the entire population all knew him and his private business. The sad shakes of the head and tuts of pity that followed him because his mother had left him, and his father, when he was nine. A short note with an apology and the claim that she'd 'tried', propped up against the fruit bowl.

But there was more to the feeling than prejudice when it came to the village of Biddicote, in Surrey, where the Ashworths lived. He was almost a mile away when he felt the magical signature of it.

Other witches could only feel the hum or tickle of magical resonance if it happened to be a very old or powerful spell that had been placed on an object or location, but Connor was *always* aware of it. Like cobwebs trailing over his face or, in the instance of Biddicote, like being caught up in a fishing net. Nearly every thatched cottage, white-washed pub or clay-bricked shop, and much

29

of the flora and fauna spilling across the fields, woods and gardens, had been built or grown with magic. Wards and charms were wrapped all around it.

It was dizzying and he had to pull over for a moment by the green to settle himself into the sensation. As he crossed his arms on the steering wheel, he could see the hairs rising along his skin. Non-magical people sometimes talked about how low-resonance sounds could affect even those who couldn't hear them, causing headaches, nausea, uneasiness, sleeplessness, and this was somewhat akin to that. Connor was feeling decidedly twitchy.

But he could get used to it. He'd got used to a lot more unpleasant situations and learned to grit his teeth and hold in there until it was over.

He stared out of the window at the seemingly idyllic prettiness of the bright blue sky, sun shining relentlessly and gilding the ripples of the duck pond on the green. Some people were sitting on the grass on a blanket, soaking up the UV rays, while they had a picnic. Colourful flowers burst out of window boxes and plant pots, as if they wanted to spread and take over everything with their insistent brilliance – just a touch too perfect for them to be completely free of magical manipulation.

Connor shivered and it was nothing to do with the cool air he was blasting out of the vents in his car. This village was a magical island and non-magical people would never know. Even if Warren hadn't warned him about the way the Ashworths lorded it over the village, keeping their secrets and the Witches Council out, he would have got *Wicker Man* vibes. It was all too idyllic, and his skin fair crackled with the electricity of it – like the approach of a thunderstorm; that very specific, oppressive threat, even while it still looked like a beautiful summer's day.

He took a deep breath and wiped his hand down his face, reminding himself why he was there. Warren needed him to check that nothing untoward was going on. His job was to walk *towards* the witches who were dangerous, so that no one else had to.

He checked the satellite navigation once more and restarted the car.

If Biddicote village felt like driving through a net of magic, Ashworth Hall was like a Faraday cage settled in the heart of it, the magical charms and wards layered and nestled so closely the manor house actually appeared to have a halo of energy – something Connor had only ever witnessed at the hiding places of rogue witches, though even then, not to this degree.

A series of faded runes etched into the stone gatehouse at the bottom of the drive had swept along him, seeking to know his intentions upon entering the property. If he'd been able to stop and touch them, he would have been able to tell if and how they directed their findings. Did the message go anywhere still, and if so, what would happen in reaction if his intentions weren't good? What did they class as good or bad intentions?

The driveway continued uphill, the leaves of tall trees glowing bright green in the sunshine at the top but providing welcome shade below. The paranoia from the overload of magical energy and all of Warren's suspicions about the Ashworths gave him the feeling he was about to encounter a family of serial killers and would never leave Biddicote alive. But he reminded himself that he was meant to be going in there with a friendly warning, and taking the opportunity to poke around. He wasn't used to being around witches until the verdict was in or their hostility was confirmed – he needed to shake at least 50 per cent of his tension, or hide it at least, if he was going to pull this off.

And when he reached the top of the driveway and the house came into view, even he couldn't see the sinister side in it. Made of similar brickwork as some of the houses in the village but stretching across with wings and a multitude of windows, there wasn't a creepy gargoyle or Gothic spire to be seen. It was like Mr Darcy's house, whatever that was called.

Suddenly, the realisation hit him that, if Kayla's boyfriend Harrison was home too, he would have to deal with the upper classes, and he was as keen on *that* as having someone chase him through the woods with a chainsaw. The very significant downside of being allowed to attend a boarding school because he'd had no one magical in his family to guide him, was that he'd been surrounded by peers with long witching lineages. Old witching families with money, power and position. And they never let him forget it.

He got out of the car, wincing as a wave of heat assaulted him. Fecking summer. It had just increased his irritability by the power of one hundred. So much for shaking off his tension and paranoia.

A huge mature rowan tree sat in the centre of the circular driveway. It must have been nearly eighteen metres tall, its boughs spread wide, clusters of white flowers overhead. Connor went over to it, aware that he might have been procrastinating, but also drawn to it. The grey bark was warm and smooth against his palm as he pressed his hand to it, and . . . there was not a single spell or enchantment on it. No witch had coaxed this to grow or charmed it to repel disease.

And yet it still didn't seem entirely natural. It was larger, older, than any rowan tree he'd ever seen before. Perhaps the overwhelming nature of all the magic surrounding him was making it hard for him to focus? If the spell was really old – something the witch who'd planted the tree had fed into the roots and soil hundreds of years ago – he might not be able to pick it up as easily. Rowan trees were linked to protection, so it might be that its own inherent nature had been complemented by the magic. A reciprocal bargain, perhaps?

There was a loud rustle from above him and he stepped back quickly. Maybe it had a booby trap of some kind? Designed to draw in visitors. A *Little Shop of Horrors* tree that was going to eat him for daring to come and investigate the Ashworths. Or a bobcat would drop down and claw his eyes out.

He shook his head – he really was getting paranoid.

'It's really not dignified for a young woman to climb trees. Especially in *breeches*. What must your parents think.' An extremely posh man's voice carried down from the tree, with an oddly distant quality to it. As if the words were being caught by the wind – even though there hadn't been a breath of the stuff for eons during this Goddess-forsaken heatwave.

'I wouldn't be up a tree at all if you'd just come back inside and talk to us,' a young woman replied, her words clearer, the mix of exasperation and pleading in them obvious.

'And then be banished once you'd got your answers? I think not.'

Connor frowned and moved closer to the trunk again, peering up into the thick green-and-white foliage. A man and a woman were up there, at least two metres above his head. The man appeared to be wearing a long nightshirt, which he was clutching tightly at his sides, and therefore not holding on to anything in the tree whatsoever. He was . . . floating, and there was the odd glimpse of the leaves behind him, when he should have been solidly opaque.

The woman was very much holding on – one hand on a thin limb, her feet on two different ones below her, struggling for purchase, while her other hand reached ineffectually for another branch to steady herself. Her arms weren't long enough. She was dressed far more normally, in a pair of cropped trousers and a sleeveless top.

'Well, hello, good sir, welcome to Ashworth Hall. Please excuse my relation's unseemly manners.'

The woman looked down sharply as the ghost addressed Connor, the movement making her lean too far forward and sway precariously.

'Oh, hi there.' Her voice lifted, most likely to try to sound welcoming as she wobbled in place. 'Don't mind me – I'm . . . err . . . just checking on a birds' nest. You can go on up and knock on the front door if you like.'

'Worse and *worse*,' the ghost tutted. 'You really are a disgrace to the Ashworth name, young miss. Is that truly how they've taught you to greet visitors? I surely can't be related to such a reprehensible character.' At that, the man let go of his nightdress, giving Connor a fleeting glimpse of his private parts from an angle that no one could have argued was aesthetically pleasing, and then shot across the tree and straight through the young woman.

She shrieked and let go of the branch to shield herself in a natural, if misguided, move. The ghost sailed straight through her and out of the branches without so much as rustling them, and the woman fell out of the tree half a second later . . . landing right on top of Connor.

There was no time to react with any kind of spell to soften or deflect the blow. The woman's shoulder hit him flush in the chest, propelling him down and backwards, so he collided with the ground with the unfortunate luck that his head stuck out over the circle of grass surrounding the tree and hit the gravel.

He let out a huge, involuntary grunt as the weight of her drove all the air from his chest. Her elbow was still in his stomach, and it dug in deeper as she attempted to lift herself.

Despite the additional pain in the back of his skull, he wasn't actually seeing stars. What he *was* seeing was one of the prettiest women he'd ever met, and her face was close to his. Unnervingly close, since the side of her head had narrowly avoided connecting with his nose. Her auburn hair spilled over his cheek and down his neck like warm silk, and his heart thumped even harder as she groaned and looked down at him with large brown eyes.

'I am *so* sorry! The – err . . . I must have slipped. Are you OK?' she gasped, pink lips parted so her breath touched his chin, and it was the last straw.

His nerve-endings screamed at him with the overload of sensation. Neither his brain nor his body could cope with the heat, the intensity of the magic surrounding them, a ghost *flashing* him and now the shock of being felled by a tiny, gorgeous woman. His back and head throbbed, and he couldn't breathe or move. He needed air and space. Immediately.

He harnessed a current of air and pushed her unceremoniously off from her resting place along his chest and hip and – dear Goddess – groin.

'*Ooff*. Guess that clears up the question of whether you're a witch,' she muttered, rolling messily onto the grass and resisting his crude application of magic so she could sit up. 'There's no need to be like that. I said I was sorry, and if you hadn't been loitering by our tree, I never would've fallen on you.'

Her thick hair was tousled around her head with small bits of leaf and berries decorating it, like some kind of faerie queen, and he groaned again, trying to get some more oxygen into his lungs and calm the struggling beat of his heart.

'I wasn't *loitering*,' he retorted through gritted teeth, as he performed a sharp and painful sit-up – even though he had, in fact, been loitering. 'I'd just arrived and heard voices coming from the tree. What were you doing *up* there? Because it wasn't checking on a birds' nest.'

Her cheeks flushed but she scrambled to her feet, brushing herself off with hurried motions before stepping slightly closer again and offering him her hand to help him stand. 'Since you said "voices" rather than "voice", I'm guessing you *know* what I was doing. Talking to a ghost,' she said, as if it were the most normal thing in the world.

He frowned at her hand, then turned away from her to get up without her assistance. He wanted to crawl back into the quiet, cool containment of his car. Reset and start this visit all over again. But no, he couldn't even get through the front door of Ashworth Hall without a paranormal incident.

It definitely wasn't the first time he'd ever seen a ghost, but he knew they were never that solid or audible unless they were around a medium. So she was probably the medium. And an Ashworth, according to the ghost. That would make her Rebecca Ashworth, cousin to Harrison Ashworth, if he remembered the file notes he'd skimmed through while he was eating a sandwich from the petrol station earlier.

As he stood, arching his spine, what sounded almost like a gurgle of indignation came from behind him, but he was too busy making sure all his vertebrae were intact and accounted for to concentrate on it.

The large double doors of Ashworth Hall swung open and a man appeared, followed by a young woman with blue hair – who looked strangely familiar – both wearing matching looks of horror and concern.

Warren was right, something strange was *definitely* going on here, and Connor was going to do his best to find out what.

Chapter Four

BECCA

Becca didn't know who she was most annoyed at: Horatio for being so rude and making her fall out of a tree; *herself* for thinking that chasing a spirit up a tree was a smart thing to do, or the moody witch who had shaken her off him as if she were a piece of dirty toilet paper stuck to his shoe, all the while looking like the gorgeous, unearthly love interest from a special-edition dust jacket of one of Kay's romantasy novels. Or herself, for the immediate biological reaction she'd had to Mr Tall, Dark and Grumpy.

Yes, she knew that was two things she was annoyed at herself for, but honestly, the way her male-radar had gone on high alert as he stood up was horrendously irritating. Hadn't she *just* vowed to stop being attracted to tall men? Being over six foot tall didn't excuse a bad attitude. And nor did short, glossy black curls or a scalpel-sharp bone structure, for that matter.

'Are you OK, Becs? What happened?' Harry ran across the gravel to her. 'Who is this?'

That was a really good question. Judging from the way Kay was staring at the man with a creeping look of recognition, she figured her cousin's girlfriend knew him.

'I'm fine—' Becca started, eager to get back to tracking Horatio down, but Harry interrupted.

'You're bleeding.' He indicated to her elbow.

'I am?' She raised it for inspection, feeling the sting now that she could see the thin streak of blood making its way down her forearm. She must have landed on a bit of stray gravel when 'pushy-pants' had removed her from her unfortunate position, draped over him. 'Ah, 'tis but a flesh wound.'

When she lifted her gaze from it, she found that the man had turned towards her again, his mouth pinched in the weirdest expression. Did his eyebrows ever lift? Even when she was sprawled over him on the ground they'd been narrowed down over his closed eyes, and she couldn't help observing that his eyelashes were long and completely straight, like the bristles of a chimney sweep's broom.

Wait – how was that relevant? It wasn't. She'd just been so close it had been impossible not to notice. Now she had some distance, and knowledge of what a grump he was, she could archive that little detail and focus on more pressing issues – like where that Goddess-damned ghost had floated off to. Again.

Harry handed Becca a clean, folded-up tissue from his pocket for her bleeding elbow and stepped between her and the man, squaring his shoulders. There wasn't much between their height – her cousin being another specimen who had the tall gene switched on – but Harry's coppery hair and freckles contrasted with the stranger's dark colouring, so they were like fire and smoke.

Something instinctive in the back of Becca's mind reminded her that you often succumbed to the smoke first.

'Listen, I don't want to seem inhospitable,' Harry began, in the closest Becca had ever heard him come to an 'icy' tone. 'But I just heard my cousin scream and came out to find her bleeding, and a strange man on my driveway. I'd appreciate an explanation as to who you are and what you're doing here.'

After a long, slow look, which travelled over each member of Becca's family, the man settled his sombre gaze back on Harry. 'My name is Connor Lynch, and I came here to speak to Kayla Hendrix,' he answered quietly, his voice deep and soft, and his accent, if Becca's judgement was correct, Irish.

Kay had been living at Ashworth Hall for nearly two months now, so it wasn't odd that she was getting visitors. What *was* odd was how Kay's face had paled and her lips had parted in what looked like a gasp.

'Kay?' Harry lifted his eyebrows, his concern now focused on his girlfriend and her reaction. 'Do you know him?'

'Yes . . . well . . . sort of.' Kay swallowed. 'We met once.'

'We did?' For the first time Connor Lynch's expression fluctuated away from grim annoyance to something a touch off-guard.

'There was a – a hexed antique, and my boss, Cheryl, was off, so I brought it in at the end of the day . . .' Kay's voice trailed away as if her words had dried up.

'So, you work together?' Harry sounded anything but relieved at the short-term mystery being solved, and Becca couldn't blame him. *Or* Kay for acting like the Krampus had just turned up for her on Christmas Eve.

Connor Lynch was from the Witches Council. And Becca had just admitted to chatting to a ghost and then flattened him. *Awesome.*

But ghosts weren't illegal – she could talk to ghosts if she wanted to; it was just the summoning that was prohibited, and he didn't *know* she was the one who'd summoned the ghost. Horatio could have lived here for years.

The bit where she'd flattened him might be trickier to smooth over, although she had immediately apologised.

He sighed and placed his hands on his hips and Becca forced her eyes to focus on the spot of scarlet seeping through the white tissue she had pressed to her elbow – rather than his narrow waist and the way his shirt tightened across his shoulders. 'Can I come inside?' he asked, weirdly sounding as though it were the last thing he wanted to do.

'Erm . . . sure?' Kay didn't appear even slightly sure as she glanced at Harry, her mouth twisted ruefully and eyes seeking his with an intensity of concern that only the other one seemed to be able to alleviate.

Much as Becca's aunt and uncle hadn't been enthusiastic when Harry had started dating someone from the Witches Council, that had been months ago. Harry had fought Kay's corner, she'd been welcomed into Ashworth Hall without question and they'd all come to appreciate the way it had opened up their minds a little more to what actually went on at the Council. That the majority of staff there were just witches doing day jobs to help the community run smoothly – the bureaucracy was largely out of their hands. But Kay didn't seem to trust this Connor Lynch and the dynamic was beyond strange. They knew each other but didn't know each other? What was he doing here?

'Maybe use the blue drawing room? It keeps nice and cool in there,' Harry said, finally moving away from the tree to go to Kay's side. He put his arm around her waist and gave her a reassuring smile.

The blue drawing room didn't actually keep noticeably cooler than any of the other rooms in the house because they had the magical equivalent of air-conditioning, but no doubt Harry was thinking about how it was one of the most recent additions to the building, far away from the entrance to the basement where the pentacle was still chalked onto the floor, and the library, stuffed full of precious books.

Before Kay could reply, Connor answered Harry himself. 'You might as well join us. And *you* definitely should, given what I just witnessed.' Steely grey eyes met Becca's, making it clear that he was referring to her as well.

Becca didn't need to have telepathic magic to know that she, Kay and Harry had now moved out of the 'worried' zone and were inching towards 'unnerved'. It was definitely not just a friendly work catch-up going on here.

'What are you talking about?' Harry asked. 'What happened?'

'Your cousin was talking to a ghost—'

'But that's not against the tenets—' Becca interjected.

'It is when you summoned him without permission—'

Her mouth went dry. How did he know that? He couldn't know that. 'I didn't—'

He folded his arms across his chest. 'I heard him say that you wanted information from him and would send him away once you were done with him. That implies you got him here in the first place.'

Her breath caught in her throat as she stood there, in the shadow of this scowling man who had unravelled everything within seconds of meeting her, making snap – and unfortunately correct – assumptions like an Irish Sherlock Holmes.

'An implication is not proof,' she said, as evenly as possible.

'No. It isn't. But I can get proof. All I need is a warrant, which will take one short phone call.'

'Warrants take at least two weeks to process.' She crossed her arms over her chest, too, scrunching the tissue into a tight ball within her fist.

'Not for me it won't.'

Ugh, another man with an over-inflated sense of his own importance. She raised an eyebrow at him in challenge:

42

'And what makes *you* such a singular sorcerer that you can bend the rules—'

'Becca—' Kay's voice was shrill as she interjected, sounding desperate. 'Just – let's do as he asks.'

'Kay, I know you're Witches Council, too, but they still have to follow their own protocol—'

'I know, but this *is* different. It's different with *him*.'

There was something so fatalistic in her tone that Becca had to pause. She noted the seismic increase to Connor Lynch's frown, as well.

'Why?' she asked again, this time quietly, carefully, the tiny tingle of premonition she sometimes got hinting that the answer to this question was going to be very significant to her life.

Kay leaned more of her weight on Harry and took a wobbly breath: 'Because he's the Abrogator.'

Silence. Heavy, choking silence. Until Becca couldn't help but half laugh in what might have been a kind of hysteria. 'You're kidding. She's kidding, right?' She looked over at Connor and he shook his head slowly, his mouth a thin line.

Becca just couldn't compute it. It was like one of those videos of a dog trying to get through a garden gate when it was carrying a stick the length of a car. Over and over, access denied. The fact just didn't seem to fit in her brain.

There were some fears – some threats to health and happiness – which were just too big to hold in your mind on a daily basis. There was no way to function if you thought about them too much. The likelihood of being hit by a car. The statistical probability of cancer. And, for witches, the Abrogator removing every vestige of your magic permanently.

Nullifying powers was not a new punishment or preventative measure for dangerous witches, but the majority of the time throughout history it had been done by draining potions, regularly administered, or specially hexed objects cuffed to the witch. The magic was never gone forever, even if the witch was sentenced to never be able to use their powers again.

But an *Abrogator* could take away other witches' magic . . . for good. The ability to siphon magic only appeared once a century on average. It hadn't even been a decade since the Worldwide Witching Council had announced there was a new Abrogator, and the stories began to be whispered, every few months, that another witch, somewhere in the world, was technically a witch no more.

And he was standing here, on the driveway of Ashworth Hall. Holy grimoire, she'd just called him a 'singular sorcerer' – a name reserved for uppity witch kids who needed taking down a peg or two.

'Let's go inside.' How Harry found his voice – and it wasn't even shaking – Becca did not know. He pulled his arm from around Kay's waist and motioned both her and Becca in front of him. 'After you, ladies.' Right, he was going into protection mode.

Becca lurched forwards, linked arms with Kay (because she was still looking like she might fall over) and led the way to the front doors. Connor followed them, his footsteps steady on the gravel, Harry at the back.

Was this it? Had their tightrope walk with the Witches Council finally come to an end?

CONNOR

None of this was going as planned. Kay was not supposed to know who Connor was. How was he going to set anyone at ease when all of them knew he was the Abrogator?

Admittedly, he had already threatened Becca with a warrant before that, caught off balance by . . . something about her. A combination of big eyes and a quick mouth and the way she'd given him a concussion, perhaps? But Kay's announcement was definitely the final nail in the coffin.

He still felt decidedly off balance as he walked into Ashworth Hall, though for different – or maybe it would be more honest to say additional – reasons. The entrance was wide and filled with golden light. There was a table in the centre, with an enormous jug bursting with colourful flowers, which should have been wilting in the heat but had obviously been charmed to survive.

There were charms *everywhere*. It was like he'd been sucked into a massive bowl of spaghetti, with strands of magic trailing all over him. His head was pounding. The power surrounding him was deep-rooted and strong, and having his skull cracked against the driveway by that mercurial little witch hadn't helped.

The grumpy refrain had barely entered his head when the image of a bloody tissue joined it – his conscience pointing out that she hadn't come out of the encounter unscathed either. Had *he* done that when he'd pushed Becca off him? It was stupid that it was bothering him so much. She'd fallen on top of *him*. But it didn't stop him from feeling bad, because he hadn't needed to be so rough, had he?

Another reason why he'd ruined his chances of coming across as 'friendly' before they'd even found out he was the Abrogator.

His thoughts were going round and round in a circle. He needed a moment to pull himself together, so, before they got to the 'blue drawing room', he asked to use the bathroom.

Imagine having so many fecking rooms you had to colour-code them.

Harrison showed him to a bathroom down one corridor, while Kay and Becca continued on. The memory of their expressions when Kay had announced who he was followed him inside the neat little water closet, so it was their faces he saw in the mirror rather than his own. Kay had looked like she was going to faint, and all of Becca's feistiness had abruptly evaporated.

He twisted the tap on and scooped up cold water to wash his face and cool the back of his neck. He needed to get focused. Pulling his phone out of his pocket, he quickly messaged Warren.

Connor: Am at the Ashworth's but there's been a couple of developments. Kay and I have met before. And she knows who I am???!!

Warren replied almost immediately.

Warren: She does? When did you meet?

Connor: Maybe a couple of months ago? I came in late to remove a hex from an old clock. But we never spoke. She brought me the clock and left. Someone must have told her.

Warren: No one can tell anyone else unless they've also been brought in on the anonymity charm. You know that. Are you sure you didn't talk? She's a pretty young woman. I wouldn't blame you, if you had.

Connor rubbed a finger across his eyebrow in an effort to stop his frown from splitting his head in two. Talk? He never talked to *anyone* at the Witches Council other than Warren, and the bare minimum of courtesy that was required if someone like Priscilla was forced to interact with him. Even if he *had*, what did Warren imagine he'd have talked to Kay about? His previous assignment? Just

46

before the clock, he'd been in Australia, siphoning the magic from a witch who'd been using his influential gift to gain more support for his race-hate gang. He wasn't likely to lead with that for a chat-up line, if he'd been so inclined. Which he hadn't.

Connor: I'm sure. And now Ashworth and his cousin know too. Should I leave? Or wait around until you can come and cast the charm with them?

The ellipsis popped up and down, up and down, on the phone screen until Connor thought he might just be hallucinating it because of the head injury. Then finally:

Warren: Don't worry about that for now. I'll deal with it once we've got a better picture of what's going on. You mentioned 'developments' plural. What else has happened?

Connor: Most likely an unauthorised summoning. Shall I get the evidence, and file a report with the Tenet Enforcers?

He set his phone down beside the sink and took the soft white hand towel from the ring so he could dry his face. As he was raking his hands back through his hair, dislodging bits of damned gravel from his scalp, it vibrated with an answer.

Warren: No! Like I said, we want them to have their guards lowered for as long as possible.

Connor: You don't think that ship sailed when Kay announced who I am?

Warren: Possibly. But we won't know if you go straight in for the kill. Try to play the situation to your advantage. You might find you are good at it. Remember, the threat of getting into trouble will be better lubrication than the reality of a simple wrist slap, which is likely all they'd get for the summoning. They hold too much sway, so our case will have to be extensive and watertight once we lodge it for trial.

The case for what, though?

Connor shook his head. That was why he was here. To find out what shady stuff the Ashworths were getting away with simply because they had an old name and lots of money.

He took a deep breath and let it out slowly. Tactics were not his forte. But . . . sometimes he did get tired of being a blunt instrument. Maybe if he handled this right, he could talk to Warren about being involved in the investigation side of the enforcement cases. And if he understood first-hand how the witches had come to be sentenced for nullification, it might help him process it all a little more quickly than simply reading the reports.

Connor: I'll do my best.

Warren: Good man.

Chapter Five

BECCA

As they'd walked inside, Becca had glanced back at Connor
Lynch and found him examining the entrance to Ashworth
Hall as though he expected the walls to start moving in
and crush him. As though *he* was as on edge as they were.
That was . . . well, it didn't match up with any ideas she
might have had about what the Abrogator was really like.

There were never any photos of the Abrogator. No one
was meant to know what they looked like or what their real
identity was while they were alive, the same way execu-
tioners in the UK were afforded anonymity when capital
punishment was still a thing. And, of course, that allowed
the imagination to run wild. Had she visualised someone
silent and grim? Yes. But young? Handsome? Cranky? No.

He even asked if he could use the bathroom – as if he
were a normal human with basic bodily functions – and
Becca found her adrenaline easing off just enough that she
could think straight again. When Harry showed Connor
the nearest toilet and indicated that he would prioritise
standing as guard, despite his obvious desire to talk to
them, Becca took the opportunity to hurry Kay down
the corridor to the drawing room, so at least two of them
could confer in private.

'What, in all the elements . . .?' Becca whispered as soon
as she and Kay got inside and closed the door. Sunlight
painted the room in lines of gold and blue as it reflected

off the light pine furniture with its pin-striped upholstery. 'I never realised you were in on the Abrogator's identity?'

'I'm not. I mean, I'm not *technically* supposed to know. Someone told me after that hexed-object incident I mentioned. It was the end of the day. Cheryl left at short notice because her daughter had an accident at school and they suspected a broken arm. So when *her* boss asked me to fill in, I just hung around for an extra hour, did some filing and took the artefact in to this special room we have when it was time and he was waiting in there. I didn't think much of it, except that it was weird that I wasn't meant to stay to put the artefact away again after. The next day I was making tea in the staff kitchen, telling people about Cheryl still being off and what I'd had to do the day before, and this guy from the folklore subdivision pulled me aside and told me I'd met the Abrogator.' Kay shook her head and her mouth compressed. 'He said he was surprised they'd let me go in on my own, and if I ever had to fill in again and the appointment in the diary was with "Connor Lynch", to make sure I had someone with me.'

Becca wondered if she should feel concerned that gossip trumped red tape, even when it came to something as confidential as the Abrogator. Not exactly a mark in favour of the Witches Council's diligence. She tossed the crumpled tissue she'd been using on her elbow into the nearest wastepaper basket. 'Have you got *any* idea why he wants to talk to you now?'

Kay's hand went to her face to push up the glasses she wasn't actually wearing – a nervous habit. 'It's – it's possible that I've been caught out poking around in the records.'

Becca blinked, and again an incredulous laugh sneaked out of her. 'Kay, if I weren't freaking out so much right now, I'd be impressed. I thought you were too strait-laced to do something like that . . . otherwise I would have asked.' She was only half joking. If the records were about the Ashworths, it couldn't be wrong to want to know what was in them.

A weak smile lifted Kay's lips but quickly faded. 'I was just so desperate . . . I started with spells for mediums, and then I was trying to find references to Horatio, but so many files on the Ashworths had been pulled and before I knew it, I was trying to find something – *anything* – to help. Harry had another dizzy spell the other evening. He tried to make light of it – you know how he does – but I found him sitting on the kitchen floor—'

Becca caught Kay's hands as her eyes turned glassy. 'I know. I know. It's OK. Don't worry. We'll get through this.'

At the end of the day, even if Connor Lynch *was* the Abrogator, he wasn't the first member of the Witches Council to come through the doors of Ashworth Hall with the intention of poking about. But that's *all* he could do, and that intention hadn't been enough to set off the protective wards around the Hall, so he couldn't mean harm to them. No matter the intensity of his power, he was not a loose cannon . . . more a firing squad. Which didn't sound masses better, admittedly.

But magic was not removed from witches without either a trial or very serious extenuating circumstances that proved, without a shadow of a doubt, that the number-one Worldwide Witching Tenet – 'Never use magic to do harm' – had been broken. As much as the Witches Council in the UK had tensions with her family, they couldn't go *that* far. Not without evidence. And what could they prove when her family had never done anything to harm anyone?

Perhaps they were growing suspicious simply because her family had been keeping them at arm's length. Once, her uncle had been happy – or, if not happy, reconciled – to inviting members of the Council to their festivals, which they'd stopped holding when he got sick. And, OK, since they reintroduced the celebrations, they hadn't invited them again – but the landscape had definitely changed within the Witches Council over the last decade. Many of the older council members had retired, Uncle Adrian hadn't been able to develop any significant new contacts, what with being ill, and schmoozing had never been Harry's favourite pastime.

Her cousin was charming and extremely personable, but he was uncomfortable with politics. He knew what to do, when he had to, but he never sought it out – another thing Becca's dad had criticised him for, arguing that he wasn't the right choice as heir, resurrecting an old grievance for a new generation, while doing nothing to prove that *he* should have been the choice when Becca's nan named his younger brother, Uncle Adrian, heir to Ashworth Hall.

But the point was, *all* the Ashworths knew about this dance, because it had been done ever since the Witches Council formed. They'd been keeping the secret of the anchor tattoo for even longer than that. There must have been tight spots before, and they'd managed to wriggle out of them. They'd manage this time, too. She just had to think about the best way to approach it.

CONNOR

When Connor emerged from the bathroom, Harrison Ashworth was sitting on the corner of a wooden side table a little further down the hallway, rubbing the centre of his chest slowly and frowning at a painting of a dog hanging on the wall, but with a distant look in his eye that said he probably wasn't really seeing it. He dropped his hand and stood up almost immediately when he noticed Connor coming out, indicating with a tilt of his head for Connor to follow him.

The blue drawing room was blessedly cool and ludicrously large. Connor took the proffered seat of a butter-soft armchair – no magical charms required – and Harrison fetched him a tall glass of water with lemon and ice. Connor couldn't help checking it for a hex because he'd expected the upper classes to have servants to bring tea – why else would an Ashworth be serving drinks himself? But no – it was clean, and he was relieved to be able to take several long, refreshing gulps of it.

Over the rim of the glass, he watched as Harrison sat down on the sofa opposite, next to Kay. The couple automatically settled into each other's space. Not in an overt display of affection, just aligning themselves and reaching for each other's hands without even checking to see whether the other would accept the gesture. They were in tune in a way that spoke of a long relationship. Nothing in the way they'd interacted up until now gave him the impression either one was taking advantage of the other, but then . . . what did he really know about relationships?

As he put the glass down on the end table beside him, Connor caught Becca's gaze. As if she'd been observing *him*, observing *them*. She'd taken the armchair diagonally across from him, and slipped off her shoes, tucking her feet in next to her, utterly at home in Ashworth Hall, although Connor knew from the notes in the file that she didn't currently, and had never officially, lived there.

He wiped a water droplet from the edge of his lip and she blinked, straightening her spine.

'Before you tell us why you're here, I should apologise,' she said. 'I mean, I think I already did, outside, when I fell out of the tree and landed on top of you, but it probably wasn't a great apology, given the shock of it all. So . . . sorry again. I would have used a levitating spell, but I didn't know if you were a witch until it was too late.'

He wanted to shift in his seat, because her big brown eyes were really, uncomfortably, pretty. He didn't know why they were making him feel . . . something. Why did some eyes do that and others didn't? Kay had perfectly attractive eyes, too, but they didn't make him feel like someone had pointed a floodlight right at him. Maybe it was just because she was actually looking directly at him? Not at the floor, or a spot over the top of his head, as though fearful he could laser-beam his power at her through his eyeballs.

'Apology accepted,' Connor said gruffly. He wanted to apologise, too – for pushing her off and hurting her elbow – but somehow acknowledging that he'd done that would make it unbearable for him not to do something more to *fix* it. And his touch wasn't a healing one, nor would she want it anywhere near her.

'And, with regard to the ghost . . .' She tilted her chin up a little, still focused unwaveringly on him. 'It was a silly mistake. I was a bit frustrated with the by-laws and never being able to use my abilities, so I gave it a go. I know I shouldn't have, and I never will again, but it really wasn't a big deal.'

'Becca, what are you saying?' Harrison leaned forward, his eyes wide at her confession.

'Just telling the truth, Harry.' She looked at her cousin and gave him a very determined, sunny smile. Connor could almost hear the words she was silently trying to communicate to him. Almost. He wasn't quite sure what this game was but, without a doubt, Becca and Kay would have conspired while he was in the bathroom and something new was motivating her confession. Outside, she'd been ready to put every legal loophole forward to avoid his accusation, and now she was admitting to everything? It was almost like she'd read the text-message exchange between him and Warren and realised that saying 'it's a fair cop, guv' would leave him with nothing else to pursue.

Kay ran her hand down Harry's arm, tugging him back into position beside her with a little nod, and he relaxed back slowly as though that was all he needed to understand what was going on. Connor wished it were as easy for him.

'So, anyway, yes. I'm sorry.' Becca directed that smile towards Connor, only proving that it wasn't genuine. 'I just had a few drinks and behaved stupidly. *Irresponsibly.* I won't do it again.'

He felt one of his eyebrows lifting almost of its own accord, despite the ripples of tension it sent across his head. If this burning supernova of a witch had done anything, it certainly hadn't been in a fit of alcohol-driven lunacy. It just didn't sit right with him. Did she really think it was going to be that easy to wriggle out of this?

'I'd like to talk to the ghost,' Connor said, finally.

'Er . . .' Becca, Harry and Kay all looked at each other and Connor clenched the armrests of his chair more tightly, as though he could brace himself against the way their silent communication excluded him. Stop him from feeling that familiar shrinking down inside when his outsider status was underlined in bold strokes. It was probably just a reaction to all the magic, making him sensitive, and much as he wanted to turn tail and drive away from this migraine-inducing place, he had a job to do.

'What about?' Harry asked. The words themselves could have come across as rude or challenging, but his husky voice was mild in tone.

'The circumstances of the summoning.'

'But I've admitted to you what happened—' Becca started.

Connor waved a hand as he cut her off. 'Yes, yes. You were stocious. *Apparently.*' Was it wrong that he liked the way her dark eyes flashed when he said that word? 'I only have your say-so for that, though. Not that it's any excuse, but I'd still like to get the facts straight with an objective witness, and he seems ideal.'

'Objective seems a stretch for Horatio,' she muttered, and then took a deep breath and gave him a seemingly rueful smile. 'That's easier said than done, anyway, isn't it?'

'Is it? You're the medium. Pull him here.'

'How?'

'You don't know how to contain him?'

Her eyes flicked up as though she wanted to roll them but was suppressing the urge. 'I would hardly have been climbing trees, trying to talk to him, if I knew how to call him to me.'

That was a fair point.

'So, I'm sorry,' she continued with a big shrug. 'But unless *you* know how to do it, we're just going to have to accept—'

'As it happens . . .' Connor stood up, pushing his already rolled-up sleeves higher towards his elbows. 'I'll need you to do it, but I can talk you through it.'

Her mouth fell open. 'Is this a trick? If I do this, are you going to add it to my rap sheet?'

He paused. Finally, an opportunity to play good cop. In the back and forth with her, he'd kind of forgotten he was meant to be doing that. Again. It was such a novelty having someone know he was the Abrogator and not lose the power of speech around him. 'No. You've got my permission – for this bit.'

Her lips pressed together. Strange, considering that should have been a relief. But the Ashworths were definitely used to being the authority around here. She probably didn't like him giving her permission to do something. If that was how she was feeling, she managed to swallow it and stood up to face him. 'What do we need?'

'The five staples.'

Harry made to get up, but Kay held out her hand to stop him. 'You stay there, I'll grab them.'

'I'm fine.'

'Humour me.' She dropped a kiss on his head and hurried out of the room.

Becca was looking at her cousin, a concerned frown creasing her brow, and Harry was making a point of avoiding her look this time. There was so much subtext to their interactions, *Connor* felt like the ghost around them.

'You'll need a space on the floor?' Harry asked, standing up.

'Yes,' Connor confirmed, though it was largely a rhetorical question when it came to using the five magical staples.

'Rug?' Becca said. Harry nodded and lifted the furniture – which included one sofa, three armchairs, a coffee table and the end table with a lamp and Connor's glass of water on it – magically with a simple scoop of his hand. The sweep of the spell brushed against Connor and he noted that Harry Ashworth's magic was warm and seeking, with a flourish, like it would have curlicues if it was visible.

Becca gave a quick flick of her index finger and the large rug spread across the centre of the wooden floor began to roll up neatly. She jumped over it as it rolled up to her, feet twisted to the side, with a little smile as if she were remembering days in the playground skipping, and sent what looked like a genuine smile this time to Harry. Such an odd little moment of joy on her face, given the tension in the room. Connor was so distracted by the dimple it revealed in her cheek, he almost forgot to move out of the way himself and stumbled back a step.

Just as Harry let go of the furniture, allowing it to settle back on the floor with a soft squeak, Kay returned holding a neat box, unadorned in a way that extremely expensive things often were. She brought it over to Becca and joined Harry again.

'What now?' Becca opened the box and the gentle scent of sage wafted out.

'Draw a lemniscate in chalk,' Connor instructed her. 'Large enough for you to stand or sit in one section. Surround it with a circle of salt. Sit in one of the loops and burn some sage over the candle and then call your ghost to you.'

'It's that easy?' The bright interest in her brown eyes zapped him, like a cattle prod.

'Should be. If you do it right. He'll appear in the other half of the lemniscate and he won't be able to leave until you do.'

'You've seen this done before?'

'A few times,' he answered, before wondering if he should be admitting that.

She nodded, looking at the space on the floor. 'Well, there you go then.' There was a pinch to her mouth again that spoke of irritation, but she gave her head a little shake and then set to work.

Harry and Kay sat down again, this time both leaning forward, but Connor stayed standing, checking the evenness of the lemniscate. It wasn't the easiest to draw because a large figure of eight required you to lean over where you'd already drawn part of the symbol – and you had to actually draw it, not use magic to move the chalk. Becca wasn't the tallest of witches, so it was a stretch for her, but she didn't hesitate, her line continuous and smooth, balancing on one hand and her bare toes, as if she were playing a game of Twister. She let go of the chalk once she was done and it floated back to the box, obviously charmed to return there. She grabbed a handful of salt and walked backwards in a circle around the symbol, dropping it steadily.

'Candle in the centre?'

He nodded at her, and she placed it on the lines of chalk where they crossed, lighting it with a rub of her fingers and holding the sage stick over the top so a wisp of smoke curled out and began to filter out into the room. When half of it was gone, she closed her eyes and took a deep breath.

'How do I call him?'

'Just find his presence and if you know his name, call him.'

'Horatio. Horatio. Would you——?'

'Don't ask him. Tell him,' he interrupted.

'OK. Horatio William Albert Ashworth, come here. Your presence is required.'

Connor refused to examine the shiver that went down his spine at the way she didn't hesitate to use an authoritative voice. He crossed his arms, ready to wait, but almost instantly the ghost from outside in the tree popped into the other side of the lemniscate.

He shouldn't have been surprised about the power of a witch from such an old bloodline, but it was still impressive how quickly the summoning had worked, considering she'd never practised her medium skills before. *If* she was telling the truth.

'You again!' The ghost whined and immediately turned, trying to push his way out of the bounds of the chalk. 'This is truly beyond the pale. Disturbing my peace in the hereafter and then *hounding* me in this infernal manner. You, sir,' he addressed Harry. 'You need to get this young lady in your care under control.'

'Becca isn't "in my care"—' Harry started to object, but before he could continue, Horatio, in all his nightgowned glory, turned to Connor.

'Then you. Are you her husband? Her intended? Is she answerable to you?'

Connor blinked at the man. He knew on one level that obviously this man was from the past when attitudes were different, but it was still quite something to witness such unashamedly sexist behaviour.

'Only in so much as she's a witch and I'm a member of the Witches Council.'

Horatio turned back to look at Harry. 'They're allowing the Irish into the Witches Council, now?'

'Oh, holy grimoire.' Harry groaned and rubbed his hand across his eyes before looking around the apparition to Connor. 'I'm so sorry.'

'I think there was a reason why we didn't find any mention of him on the family tree,' Kay muttered next to him.

'Regardless of your opinions on whether *you* should be beholden to a woman or an Irishman, the reality for you, Horatio, is that, unless you do as we ask, you're going to spend the rest of eternity in the middle of this drawing room.' Becca stood up opposite her ghostly ancestor and pushed her hair back from her face. There were still bits of leaf and berry in it. 'So, what did you want to ask him, Mr Lynch?'

'I'd like to hear the circumstances of the summoning. And . . . Connor is fine,' he added, telling himself it was because he was trying to come across as friendly – not because he wanted to hear her say his given name.

Becca's lips parted slightly, but Horatio interrupted before she could respond – if she was going to.

'It's none of your business.' Horatio crossed his arms over his chest. 'Ashworths don't kowtow to the Witches Council.'

Connor filed away the chagrin on the living Ashworths' faces for later, along with the way Becca had lied to the ghost about being stuck in the lemniscate. She'd have to move soon enough and then Horatio would be free, but the ghost clearly didn't know that, and using it as leverage wasn't actually a bad idea. 'Did you not hear the bit about spending eternity in one square metre of parquet flooring?'

Horatio's overgrown sideburns twisted as his lips pursed in irritation. 'Fine. *Obviously* she summoned me,' he admitted.

'And what state was she in?'

'I beg your pardon? What are you suggesting? I've heard stories about more primitive witchcraft methods in your neck of the woods, but in the *civilised* society of England, we practise magic fully clothed.'

'Goddess forgive me, I summoned the Nigel Farage of ancestors,' Becca lamented with a wince.

Connor chewed on the inside of his cheek for a moment, before trying again with a level of patience that should have earned him a trophy, given the circumstances. 'I was referring to whether she was drunk.'

'How should I know?' Horatio scoffed. 'Most likely, though – that would at least account for some of her indecorous behaviour.'

Connor was starting to think having this man haunting Ashworth Hall was going to be punishment enough for the summoning. But, of course, that wasn't the whole story or the reason he was here. It was, in fact, partly a distraction. It occurred to him that Becca had swooped in with her confession and it had side-lined the conversation he needed to have with Kay.

'Why are you so determined to get away from her?' Connor asked. 'You said something in the tree about her wanting information from you? And that when she gets it, she'll banish you. What information does she want?'

'You would have to ask her that.'

Connor looked over at Becca with a raised eyebrow. She was chewing her lip, but when she caught his eye, she stopped and put on an innocent face again. 'Well? *Is* there any information you want from him? Or are you ready to exorcise him now?'

He hadn't thought it was possible for a ghost to pale, but Horatio's colour and expression definitely drained. He supposed that was a bit of a heavy-handed threat. He wasn't very good at softening blows – it was, in fact, the opposite of what he did normally.

'Please. Not yet.' Horatio turned to Becca and addressed her for the first time in a tone that wasn't derisive. 'I died so young and there's so much I want to see.'

Becca pressed her lips together and then asked Connor, 'We don't *have* to do that, do we?'

'You're really considering having this great tool floating around your fancy house, permanently?'

'Hmm . . . good point, that is the flip side of the coin, and I don't live here.' Becca looked at Harry and Kay. 'How do you feel about that? If I don't exorcise him?'

Harry rubbed the back of his neck and eyed the ghost. 'Eh.'

'Harrison, please. I'm family.' Horatio moved to step closer to him and came up against the warding of the spell. He wrung his hands. 'And I haven't even helped you yet.'

'So you *were* summoned to help with something.' Connor tilted his head. 'Go on, you might as well ask him now. Give him a chance to convince you he won't be a complete arse-ache around the house.'

Silence as they all did more of their shifty-eyed communicating. Maybe he shouldn't have suggested them all being together – he might have been better off dividing and conquering. Too late now, and besides, he couldn't see any of them standing for that once they found out he was the Abrogator.

'Well . . . Horatio, would you be willing to answer a question for us?' Becca cleared her throat. 'About an old Ashworth spell?'

'Which spell?' Horatio was all attentiveness.

Becca's eyes darted at Connor and then she looked back to the ghost. She was trying to communicate silently with *the spectre* now. Even though Horatio had been unfailingly rude to her and only decided to change his tune because he faced going poof. But, of course, it didn't matter how detestable the old guard was to each other, they would always close ranks.

'The one which gives us a – a boost to help Biddicote with its protective magic.'

'Oh, the one for the—' The ghost broke off as she widened her eyes, and quickly stopped himself from saying more. 'Which the heir is privy to?'

Connor took a seat quietly, vainly hoping that they would forget he was there and slip up in their careful dancing around the truth. They must be exhausted. He was.

'Yes. That one.' Becca glanced briefly at Harry. 'Something's not quite working with it, and we can't find out why. Was there a particular grimoire it was written down in, because we've only ever known it via oral history.'

'Hmmm.' Horatio crossed his arms and rubbed his chin with his index finger and thumb. Now that he had accepted his fate and taken on the mantle of bastion of knowledge, he appeared to be milking it. 'That has always been the way it was passed on. I, myself, was not actually privy to the, ah, *application* of the spell, but I know the materials involved were just as important as the words and runes.'

'Of course.' Becca wet her lips. 'Maybe it would be easiest to explain to you how it's going wrong. The overall outcome of the spell, the goal, is being achieved, but there are some detrimental side effects.'

'*Dangerous* side effects?' Connor asked, forgetting that he was supposed to be getting them to ignore his presence.

'Not to other people,' Kay quickly interjected.

'Then who to?'

'The spell-caster,' Harry said quietly. 'It appears to be targeting the centre of magic.'

'Sounds like a power issue. Overstretching yourself,' Connor observed. Not all witches had the same level of power, just as not all people had the same energy levels or health – sometimes practice, regular use and the mastering of techniques could improve it, but if a spell was too ambitious or just surpassed the witch's genetics, the spell wouldn't work or the witch would end up drained and unfit for further magic until they'd recuperated.

'That's very possible,' Harry agreed. 'But it's never happened before with this particular spell, so we're trying to understand why.'

'Perhaps the problem is with the amplifier?' Horatio said.

Becca shook her head. 'The amplifier rune was definitely cast correctly. We've triple-checked it.'

'No, not the rune – the actual external amplifier.'

The three young witches looked at each other, as though they'd just heard that aliens had landed in their back garden and were having a picnic.

'There is no external amplifier that we are aware of,' Harry said, slowly. 'What does it need to be? Quartz or citrine?'

Horatio was shaking his head now. 'No. It's not just a random amplifier. It's specific for this spell. Dragon-eye stones that are alchemically fused. There was a box full in Papa's study. Locked away, of course. We weren't ever to touch them on pain of death. You're saying you've never seen or heard of them?'

'No. Never. Could you show me where they were kept?' Harry asked.

'Miss Ashworth will have to release me.'

'Right, of course.' Becca's strangely excited tone broke Connor from his contemplation of what was happening. 'So, how do I do that?'

'Blow out the candle,' he responded, 'and break the chalk and salt lines.'

She didn't even hesitate, which he thought was quite brave considering how unhelpful Horatio had been before, but her faith seemed to have been placed correctly, as Horatio followed Harry out of the room as promised.

'So, that's what you've been after?' Connor asked. 'Still holding to your story about being drunk?'

'Sure,' Becca said easily but without looking at him, concentrating on lifting and gathering the salt and chalk from the floor to put back inside the box. 'It's been really bugging us, so I got a bit tipsy and it made me break the rules, and I'm very, very sorry.'

She didn't look sorry. As she plopped herself back in the armchair and tucked her feet up again, she looked like she was barely containing an enormous grin of triumph.

'Was that why you were rifling through the records at the office?' he asked Kay abruptly, and she actually jumped.

She glanced at Becca, who gave her a little nod that she probably thought was too subtle for him to notice.

'Yes,' Kay admitted. 'Is that what you came here to talk to me about?'

'It was. But why didn't you just ask for access? Why do it unauthorised? Same when it comes to your summoning?' He looked over at Becca. 'That's exactly the type of circumstance the Witches Council gives isolated exemptions for, if they're warranted.' And now he'd witnessed this whole farce play out, he was going to have to tell Warren there didn't appear to be any other angles to cover.

Becca shifted on her armchair. 'I guess we didn't want to risk being told "no".'

'Or because, like your esteemed ancestor said, the Ashworths don't kowtow to the Council?'

She let out an irritated breath. 'No, but it does rankle when the information at the Council is actually about *us*, and the powers I wanted to use are *mine*.'

'Becca,' Kay said, in a chastising tone. 'It was poor judgement. And I definitely don't usually subscribe to the opinion that we shouldn't be held accountable for our actions. We were just . . . worried.'

'How bad *is* the reaction the spell-caster has?' Connor asked.

Before they had a chance to answer, Harry and Horatio came back into the room.

'Any joy?' Becca asked, jumping up from her seat again.

66

'No. No sign of it anywhere.' Harry shook his head.

'They're gone,' Horatio exclaimed. 'Quite gone. You never would have been able to miss them. The box was about yay big.' He held his hands out in front of him to show a length of about a foot and a half. 'Covered in warding runes to keep sticky fingers out.'

'I've never seen anything like that, anywhere in the house.' Harry rubbed at his forehead as though he was trying to remove his freckles. 'How could they have gone missing and the knowledge of them with it?'

'It doesn't matter,' Becca smiled. 'I never thought my gift would work on someone dead – no offence, Horatio – but it does. I can feel he has the sense of having lost them. It's . . .' She closed her eyes and lifted a hand, wavering it in front of her. 'This way. South-west.' She strode over to the corner of the room where a small bookcase was situated next to a card table. Pulling out a large A-to-Z, she flipped through the pages methodically, sometimes pausing with her hand over the page before flipping onwards again.

'Here.' She stabbed her finger into the page. 'Cornwall. Do we have any branches of the family down there?'

Harry shook his head. 'No. None.'

'So they've been stolen?'

'That's a leap,' Harry said. 'We should talk to our parents. Find out if they have any recollection of it.'

Becca shook her head. 'They would have told us if they knew of them, surely? *You* can talk to them if you want, but I'm getting in the car and getting my butt down to Cornwall, asap.'

'Slow down, Becs.' Harry held out his hands, as if he were actually going to need to block her from running out of the door. 'You can't race off when we have no clue what's happened to make the stones end up down there.'

'Why not? We need them back.'

Harry sent an imploring look to Kay. Perhaps it was a regular occurrence that they had to team up to rein Becca back in.

'Well . . .' Kay said. 'Maybe the stones were given away or sold and don't truly belong to the family any more? Or, if someone *has* stolen them, it's most likely to be a witch, right? Because who else would be interested or be able to get past the wards? And they're likely going to be powerful if they have. Maybe dangerous.'

Dangerous witches. That was definitely Connor's remit. So perhaps his involvement in this wasn't over? He didn't have time to call Warren and talk the matter through with him, but surely he would agree that if there was the possibility that a dangerous witch was in possession of a powerful magical artefact, the Witches Council should be involved?

'I do hear what you're saying.' Becca put her hands on her hips. 'But waiting isn't an option. We can do a three-pronged attack. Harry – you have to stay here, at least until your mum and dad are home, but you can speak to them to see if they have any recollection of the amplifier. Kay – you can do your research thing in the library again, now we have a better idea of what we're looking for. And in the meantime, I'll just drive down to Cornwall and get the lay of the land. At the very least it will stop the nagging of my gift from driving me to distraction.'

Connor could see from Harry's and Kay's dubious expressions that they didn't believe in the slightest that Becca would be satisfied with simply getting 'the lay of the land', and the idea of her approaching a dangerous witch, on her own, made Connor's chest tight. Even with *his* abilities, it wasn't always easy to subdue a rogue witch. He had to get close enough to touch them if he was going to nullify their powers, and magic meant there were lots of ways a witch could defend themselves from a distance. The thought of the malevolent spells and magically propelled objects he'd sometimes faced being directed at *Becca's* small, stubborn figure—

'No.' He stood up, noting the oddness of them double-taking over his presence. They were so het up, they'd actually momentarily forgotten that the Abrogator was in their midst. 'If an alchemist truly fused dragon-eye stones, this amplifier will increase the thief's power. And if they stole it, it's doubtful they have good intentions. The Witches Council needs to be involved . . . I'll come with you.'

Chapter Six

BECCA

Becca did not have 'drive down to Cornwall with the Abrogator to retrieve a magical artefact' on her bingo card for that day. Or any day in her existence. But she wasn't going to knock it. This could be playing out a lot worse.

She and Kay had confessed to indiscretions (to put it lightly) and yet they'd still managed to get the exact information they'd needed from Horatio without telling the Abrogator anything particularly secret, and he'd said nothing about punishments. Yet.

She wasn't silly enough to rule out the possibility that he was just waiting until she'd led him to the amplifier – he'd barely batted an eyelid at suggesting that they exorcise Horatio; whether that was because he knew the threat would get answers, or because he just judged the ghost superfluous to requirements, was a mystery but it suggested a touch of ruthlessness she wasn't going to dismiss. She might even grudgingly respect it.

Regardless, there were still more reasons why his accompaniment was a good thing than a bad. First, the amplifier *could* be with a dangerous witch, and while Becca was fairly confident in her abilities, she wasn't arrogant enough to assume that meant she could deal with an aggressive magic-wielder better than the Abrogator could. Second, if he was with *her*, then he wasn't sniffing around Harry and Biddicote. Third, it meant she could get on with retrieving the amplifier immediately, rather than waiting for Uncle Adrian to get home and relieve Harry of the Ashworth-heir duties so he could join her like he wanted to.

Her cousin seriously had enough on his plate between the threatening illness, the secret anchor tattoo and being the face in the community people turned to when there was any magical mishap, alongside his own work as a children's book illustrator. He was a busy man who needed to learn when to let other people help *him*.

Becca, on the other hand, had a full week clear, other than processing the school photos. She was about to be booked out back-to-back on weddings and christenings throughout the summer, so this couldn't have happened at a better time. The only real problem she had was Michael Kitten, but she could beg a favour for some cat-watching from her best friend for a few days.

Honestly, Becca could have floated down to Cornwall and dealt with this for the family, she was so relieved that this might actually be it. *The answer.* She'd have travelled to the South Pole if it meant getting to fix things.

'You don't have to rush off tonight – it's been a busy day and it's a long drive. Why don't you go in the morning?' Harry said as they stood on the doorstep.

'Sooner the better.' She tapped a finger to the centre of her forehead, where the tugging sensation was faint but insistent. It was different when she was far away from the lost object – it didn't shout as loudly, thankfully, but it was still there – like a song she couldn't get out of her head, playing in the background whenever her mind went quiet. And she knew even the mild discomfort it caused her would be enough to make Harry feel bad for asking her to delay.

He, predictably, sighed and nodded. She hugged both him and Kay goodbye and went back out onto the driveway where Connor was waiting – under the rowan tree. Maybe to remind her of the original scene of the crime.

'So, how long until we can leave?' she asked as she stepped into the shade of the tree alongside him.

He frowned down at her. She had a feeling she was going to have to get used to that slightly irritated/slightly bemused expression on his face when he looked at her. 'I can leave now.'

'You can? You don't have any weekend plans to change, bags to pack?'

There was a pause as he shook his head. 'I'm used to travelling where I'm needed at short notice. I have everything I need with me.'

Becca raised her eyebrows. 'Right, well, I *do* need to make a couple of arrangements, so shall I pick you up from somewhere, meet you on the way, or do you want to follow me now?'

'Or I could drive us to your place. You can grab your stuff and then we'll hit the road.'

'*Or* you could grab *your* bags and walk with me. It's only a few minutes away and we're going to be stuck in the car for hours – I'd prefer to get some fresh air and exercise while I can.' Becca was suddenly very curious to see how a low-stakes negotiation with him was going to go. Did he expect his word to be law?

'But I'll still need my car.'

'What for?'

'To drive down to Cornwall,' he said with barely concealed exasperation. Not-at-all-concealed exasperation, actually. Becca had to bite down on a smile as it hit her once again that his grumpiness made him seem so . . . normal. The mysterious Abrogator conjured an image of someone untouched by the small concerns of ordinary people, but Connor wasn't like that at all. It still might not be smart to wind him up, though – her excitement at finally getting a useful answer to the anchor problem was maybe affecting her judgement.

'Yeah, about that. You never even questioned what was happening once – when I was figuring out where the dragon-eye stones are. You already knew what my gifts were, didn't you? Before coming here.'

He tilted his head. 'Your family is famous – I expect most people know what your gifts are.'

'Hmm.' Maybe that was true, or maybe the Witches Council had compiled dossiers on them all. 'Well, anyway – I'm going to need to do the driving since I'll be the one figuring out where we're going, so we'll take my van.'

'*Just* your van? Why? Why not drive separately?'

'Because I might have to make a sudden turning. Or double-back. It's not like I can programme the location into a GPS right now. It gets more precise the closer I get. Not to mention, separate vehicles means twice the amount of fossil fuels used and no company.'

He blinked rapidly as though it was the most outlandish thing in the world for someone to want company on a four-to-five-hour drive. 'But we'd be reliant on each other.'

'We're reliant on each other anyway, right? You need me to lead you to this possibly dangerous witch thief, and I need you to protect me from being hexed *by* the possibly dangerous witch thief. We're a team now. Might as well start getting used to it.'

The silence rivalled that of the witching hour. Then he heaved a sigh and turned towards his car, muttering, 'I'll fetch my stuff.'

Becca pressed her lips together again. Well, that answered that question. Connor Lynch *was* flexible – all that remained to be seen was *why*, when he obviously didn't want to be.

The quickest way to Becca's house was through the woods that were part of the grounds of Ashworth Hall, but since she was hoping to catch Zeynep to ask her if she could cat-sit for her, she decided to take the long way, down the drive and through the centre of the village. Connor was one step behind her, looming and silent, a little like how she imagined a bodyguard would follow her around if she was actually famous.

Opposite the duck pond, the pub was busy already, with people outside on the picnic benches, large tubs of roses surrounding them and striped umbrellas shielding them from the hot sun as they sipped their cool beers and icy glasses of white wine alongside snacks and early dinners.

'Becca,' Cathy, who ran the newsagent's opposite the pub, called out as she drew closer. 'How are you doing, sweetheart? Work busy?'

Becca stopped by Cathy's table with a smile, while Connor loitered as far away as he could without standing in the road. 'About to be. Wedding season. How are things for you?'

'Good, thanks. I popped by your dad's yesterday because I haven't seen him in the newsagent's recently. I think he was in but didn't hear the door – everything all right with him?'

Becca's cheeks grew warm. That was Cathy's very polite way of saying Becca's dad had ignored her knocking because he was as sociable as a bear during winter. And he probably hadn't paid his newspaper delivery account. It wasn't that he couldn't afford it. Of course not. Even though he had estranged himself from Uncle Adrian and wasn't heir to Ashworth Hall, he still had ownership of the game-keeper's cottage and a sizeable inheritance. He just didn't think it was important enough to rouse himself from his hermetic tendencies. Even though it was Cathy's livelihood.

'He's fine. Just . . . er . . . think he's been wearing himself out with the gardening.' Becca cleared her throat and did her best not to look back at Connor to see if he was listening in.

'Oh, of course, all the plants have bloomed with this lovely sunshine we've been having. You were out in the garden for hours last weekend, weren't you, Kev?' Cathy addressed her husband, who nodded along, both of them graciously accepting Becca's excuse for her dad's rude behaviour.

Becca rifled through her handbag and pulled out her purse. 'Is it his newspaper account you were hoping to speak to him about?'

'It was, but no, no, you put that away.' Cathy raised her hand to stop Becca handing over the money she'd taken out. 'I'm sure he'll come by next week.'

'It's fine. Honestly. I'm about to go see him myself, so he'll pay me straight back. How much is it?'

Cathy reluctantly told her and Becca handed her the notes. 'Is Zeynep inside by any chance?' she asked, changing the subject once they were done.

'No. Sorry. Haven't seen her yet, sweetheart.'

'Hey, Becca,' someone else called and she leaned to the side to see Desiree, a dentist who lived over the grocer's, at the table behind. 'We were just talking about the summer fayre. Is your aunt going to be baking those amazing little bread figures again?'

'I'm not sure. But I can always check in with Harry next time I speak to him about how the plans are going and mention it.'

There was some more conversation about the fayre, but Becca excused herself as quickly as she could. She could practically feel Connor vibrating with impatience behind her – and the longer they lingered, the more likely it was someone would ask her who he was. She already knew there was going to be a bit of gossip – it was a small village – and she hardly minded if a rumour got back to Drew that she'd been seen with someone who looked as jaw-dropping as Connor, but she doubted *he'd* like being pulled into the conversation.

His face was as inscrutable as usual when she stepped back to the pavement and led him out of the main high street, down the roads that led to the fields, with odd cottages dotted about, including the game-keeper's cottage. Her dad had moved there mostly in protest before Becca was even born. Neither her late grandparents nor Uncle Adrian had ever said that he had to leave Ashworth Hall, as far as she could gather. She expected they'd been relieved to have his broody, resentful presence removed, all the same.

Despite living so close, she limited her own visits with him as much as her guilty conscience would allow. There was only so much negative energy one witch could take. But, given the news about the amplifier and the – extremely faint – possibility that maybe he *wasn't* doing so well, she figured she should drop in before she went to Cornwall.

'I'm just going to call in at my dad's,' she said to Connor as they reached the gate. 'I won't be long.' Perhaps he could read the sincerity of that in her expression because he offered no objection, gave a brief nod and then leaned against the gate post.

It was a full-height green gate and as she pushed it open, she ghosted her fingertips over the flowers her mother had painted on it during one of Becca's first days at primary school to surprise her when she got home. The paint was flaking and fading away because, even though Harry had offered to renew it, using a special charm he knew, which would replenish the images following the strokes before – a much sought-after spell for restorers of artworks – her dad had refused. Poor Harry, he only ever offered to help from the goodness of his heart, and all her dad did was resent his nephew's position as heir to the Ashworth legacy.

He'd always been adamant that Becca, with her primary gift mirroring Biddi's, should be the heir. The inheritance of the Hall wasn't a direct line, patriarchal, matriarchal or otherwise; it was simply about who the ascended heir felt best fitted the responsibility within the family. That was why Uncle Adrian had inherited it over his elder brother, George, Becca's dad. He'd borne the decision with little grace – which might well have been part of the reason why his own mother made the choice in the first place. But when Uncle Adrian had picked his own son, with what George considered 'inferior' gifts compared to Becca's, to be the next heir, his bitterness had increased threefold.

Becca had never been tempted to join him in the resentment. Her mother – when she was alive – had taught her that what was for you would not pass you by. Being heir was not for her and she completely understood why Harry had been picked. He had influencer abilities and he could do difficult rune magic; those skills, coupled with his unfailing generosity of spirit, made him the right person for the job. Being an Ashworth without the responsibilities of being heir was simply a privilege that she was never less than grateful for. Why her dad couldn't appreciate that, even when the anchor tattoo was literally making his brother and nephew ill and would have been doing the same to her if she'd been picked, she couldn't glimpse through the twisted brambles of his mind.

Her mother had always been more sympathetic. Her dad's gift was in the seer designation, but it was minimal – he caught small snippets of the future at random, and telling people their future was a double-edged sword. People only really liked it if it was good news. But that was natural in her opinion – he didn't have to take it so personally. Or act like it put him at liberty to tell people where they were going wrong with their life choices.

'Dad, it's me,' she called as she banged on the front door. Part of her was hoping he would ignore her like he had Cathy. And that thought made her snigger, as the image of being at the window, coupled with the name 'Cathy', brought about *Wuthering Heights* vibes, with a middle-aged newsagent squeaking her palms down the cottage windows while her dad watched the football inside.

Her dad answered the door just as she was about to give up. 'So, what brings you here?' He retreated into the compact kitchen to continue chopping tomatoes at the counter by the window. So he would have seen her coming up the path.

Becca pushed the door closed behind her and leaned her shoulder against the archway leading to the kitchen as she explained recent developments. He shook his head repeatedly throughout her monologue – sometimes in disapproval (the summoning), sometimes in answer (if he had any recollection of a dragon-eye stone amplifier). He was the opposite of a nodding dog.

He put the knife down when she was finished and picked up a tea towel to wipe his hands, smearing red all over its pale-green waffle material. 'And now you're off down there to save the day, I suppose? You'll get no thanks for it. Mark my words.' Another of her dad's specialities was making prophecies that sounded like they were derived from his gift but were actually pure cynicism.

'I will definitely be thanked,' she disagreed lightly, in a carefree tone she had perfected over the years. 'But even if I'm not, it would be thanks enough to have this problem fixed, right? To know they'll be well again.'

He rolled his eyes and picked up the chopping board, sliding the tomatoes into a bowl and seasoning them with salt and pepper. 'I've told you all before, I *know* they'll be fine. I've seen it.'

'Seeing Uncle Adrian fixing Harry's cravat on his wedding day isn't a guarantee of that. Harry's so smitten with Kay, I bet he's already got a ring picked out.' She hoped it was the case, though. With every ounce of magic in her soul.

'Of course you think my gift is useless and unhelpful. Just like they always have. Go on, run off on their errands again. Even as kind-hearted as your mother was, she'd be disappointed in the way you act like *they're* your immediate family, rather than me.' He dumped the empty chopping board and knife in the sink with a clatter.

Despite the sting, Becca bit her tongue on lashing back with a hurtful retort or denial. Because even though she knew her mum wouldn't have been disappointed in her, she *was* closer to Harry, Uncle Adrian and Aunt Elenor, and maybe that did upset him. But never enough for him to try harder with her.

'Much as that is an enticing conversational gambit, Dad,' she said, with dry humour that she knew he would ignore but at least made *her* feel better, 'I do need to go.' She pushed herself away from the wall and summoned a smile. 'Oh, and you put the potato peeler in the wrong drawer, if you've been looking for it. Try the one on the left.'

Chapter Seven

CONNOR

Becca really hadn't been long inside with her dad, so Connor was glad he hadn't taken the opportunity to ring Warren. He'd barely had time enough to examine each flower in the flaky paint on the gate. That might be because he was trying to figure out what game she was playing – he'd expected a lot more resistance to his insistence on going to Cornwall with her. Not her suggesting they were a team and that they should travel together.

Maybe the Ashworths *were* serial killers and she was going to drive him off into a dark forest and try to do away with him.

She threw him a quick smile as she emerged from her dad's house and marched past him, leading him further down the road. Within a minute they were turning up a dirt track and heading for a wide farm gate. Her whole family lived within walking distance of each other, the same way it had been for him growing up. The difference for her was the way all the villagers wanted to stop and chit-chat with her. Must be a nightmare.

Behind the gate was a generous front garden, with a green lawn and flowerbeds and a gravel path that led up to, and surrounded, what looked at first glance to be a little tower from a fairy tale about a princess. But if Becca were the princess, he couldn't see a knight getting a chance to save her from a dragon. She'd have tamed it and taken up riding before a sword could even be pulled from the scabbard.

As he latched the gate behind them, he had a moment of wondering if there was a Mr or Mrs Becca waiting for her, who would be concerned about where she was heading off to with some strange man. Not that it was relevant to anything, apart from the possibility that the conversation might cause another delay . . .

A bright-pink van was parked in front of the tower – or what he now guessed was actually a renovated oast house, as it bore a sign saying 'Oast of the Town' by the door.

'D'you want to come in?' she asked as she passed her hand over the door handle and he heard the lock click open as a magical ward recognised her.

'No. Thank you,' he added, belatedly remembering his manners. 'I need to make a call.'

She nodded and went inside, leaving it open for him in a way that seemed to suggest he'd be welcome to go in after. He retreated to the other side of her van and called Warren.

'You've absolutely done the right thing,' Warren confirmed, once Connor had explained as briefly and quietly as he could what had happened at the Hall. 'This is exactly the kind of activity I'm talking about. All these secrets, and now it turns out they could have a dangerous artefact that they're using to help control the magic on a whole village.'

'You think the *amplifier* might be dangerous?'

'It certainly could be, if the magic to create it was crude. But without a doubt, *anything* that can amplify magic to the power of multiple dragon-eye stones is a dangerous thing to have out there, unsanctioned by the Witches Council.'

Connor couldn't refute that. If the amplifier got into the wrong hands . . .

'Did you get any traces of the spell they need it for?' Warren continued.

'No. There's so much magic here, and a lot of it is so old, it's like trying to pick one voice out in a stadium full of people shouting. Unless I know exactly what to put my hands to, it's hard to read.' As he'd driven in earlier, he'd felt the general tenor of the magical spells, certain notes that repeated – particularly around the primary school – to influence non-magical people to overlook accidental displays of magic or deter people with bad intentions. But nothing he could unpick with any accuracy, unless he could touch it.

'Hmm,' Warren made a disappointed noise. 'Still, this lead is the closest we've ever come to an answer.' The fact that the Ashworths were central to the protective magic over Biddicote had never been in question, but *how* they held it all together – so much magic and power spread across the whole village – wasn't something that was known. And from the notes Connor had seen in the file, it was one of the things Warren was most suspicious about.

Connor *could* eventually give him the answer, if he was to walk around every building and piece of land and create a whole new grimoire documenting them, one by one, doing his best to interpret the old magic. But it would probably take months. Possibly a year. And it would be highly conspicuous – especially when he needed access to people's properties. So he knew why Warren had never asked him to do anything like that before.

'You'd think they'd be aware—'

Connor was distracted from the rest of what Warren was saying by the arrival of a young woman, dressed in a smart skirt and blouse, and with a long, dark braid trailing over one of her shoulders. She let herself in through the gate and cocked her head in curiosity at him but carried on straight into the oast house.

82

Probably a friend. Nothing for him to worry about. And he could get straight in there if he needed to. Or, of course, that might be Mrs Becca—

'Are you listening, Connor?'

'Sorry.' He pulled his attention away from the doorway. 'What did you say?'

'I was saying that they probably think they are getting this situation to work to their advantage. Let them think that. The downside to coasting through life with things handed to you easily is arrogance and complacency. They probably don't think it's possible for someone to be one step ahead of them. Just keep doing what you're doing and keep me informed.'

Connor made a non-committal noise, because he'd truly never felt *less* like he knew what he was doing.

BECCA

After Becca had texted Zeynep, she spied on Connor as he hung around outside her home, curious to see if he really was going to call someone or if it was just an excuse not to come inside. When not conducting Witches Council business, he didn't appear to be much of a talker. But she could only see the top of his head over the van so results on her spying were inconclusive.

Michael Kitten was asleep on the bed, curled up in his favourite spot by her stuffed-lion toy, so she put her open suitcase on the floor ready to start spelling different items of clothing neatly into it. Of course, he immediately woke up and came to sit in the middle of it.

She picked him up, nuzzling his black fur and explaining to him that she'd have to go away for a little while, but she'd make sure to get him some company – if Zeynep couldn't, she'd ask Harry or Kay to pop down – and he seemed satisfied with that, so he draped himself across her shoulders while she finished her packing.

'Becca, your saviour has arrived,' Zeynep's voice called up to her, just as she was zipping her case shut.

Becca picked up her bag and hurried down the spiral staircase leading into her circular living room to find her friend throwing herself onto the sofa. 'That was quick.'

'I was heading this way anyway. I come bearing gifts.'

'Ooh, this gets better and better.' She left her case at the foot of the stairs and went over to lean on the back of the sofa, looking down on Zeynep as she stretched out along the patchwork cushions. 'Didn't fancy the pub today?'

Most Fridays Zeynep and some of the other staff from the primary school went to the pub in the village to wind down and celebrate another week survived in the English education system. Zeynep didn't drink alcohol, but the landlord carried a stock of Aunt Elenor's influenced drinks – dandelion cordial and elderberry tonic, which relaxed you, energised you or allowed you to shake off the negative that little bit more easily. Becca often chose one of those herself if she joined them – all the good vibes, none of the toxins for your liver to deal with the next morning.

'I might go later. I had to talk to a parent and then – well, I've had enough of being around a certain TA.' A very un-Zeynep-like growl came out of her generous mouth.

Becca let out a soft laugh as she realised Zeynep was referring to Drew, Becca's recent ex. 'You can say his name. Drew Herman, Drew Herman, Drew Herman. You won't summon him from a mirror and there's no warding spell on the house that will eject you.'

'Maybe there should be,' Zeynep said, putting one hand to her forehead, pushing tendrils of dark hair back from her face. 'I still can't believe I set you up with him. You should revoke my best-friend card.'

'Never! Besides, the break-up is probably harder on you than it has been on me. You're the one stuck working with him. Is he being unprofessional?'

'No, but *I'm* finding it very difficult not to swap his Earl Grey teabags in the staff room for a special blend infused with laxative properties.'

Zeynep's magical designation fell under healing, her gift the ability to blend teas with magic to help with minor illnesses and ailments. Becca had never known her to use it for harm. Even if it hadn't been breaking Worldwide Witching Tenet Number One, Zeynep just wasn't that kind of person, despite how cross she was about the character assassination he'd done on Becca when he dumped her two months ago.

'And he will never appreciate your restraint,' Becca gave a wistful sigh. She'd dated Drew for about four months, but Becca had never been tempted to tell him she was a witch. Although public displays of magic were strictly prohibited, it wasn't forbidden to tell non-magical people about magic, but it was reserved only for those you were very, very sure were going to be a part of your life forever more. As much as any person could be sure of that. People you were planning to marry, or cohabit with, or your absolutely closest friends.

She had never been under the delusion that Drew fell into any of those categories, luckily, so the pain of his dumping was minimal, despite him seeming to try to make it hurt as much as possible. Among other ego-deflating things, apparently he'd felt that she was far too sure of herself. So it was a good job they'd never got to the point where she'd opened up to him about being a witch. If he was threatened so badly by a woman knowing her own capabilities, how would he have coped with that woman literally having magical powers?

Zeynep groaned and rolled onto her side to find something in her handbag, pulling out a handful of rainbow glitter that appeared to have some cardboard stuck to it. 'Here. This is yours. For the rescue of Bun Bun.'

'Oh!' Becca's heart leapt pleasantly in her chest. 'Little Aisha made this for me?'

'Yes. You are now the proud owner of half of my arts-and-crafts budget.'

Becca took it, her grin stretching wide. As a photographer, Becca frequented local schools fairly regularly to take individual and class photos, and she loved that part of her job as much as wedding photography and family celebrations. But schools were a minefield for a witch with Becca's particular gift for finding lost belongings, because kids *leaked* possessions. Cardigans, coats, hairbands, backpacks, water bottles, lunchboxes, Pokémon cards, shoes (?!) and basically anything that wasn't physically welded to their person. When Becca had finished with the Year 6 portraits earlier that day and was packing up her equipment, she'd heard a little girl crying about losing her stuffed bunny, and – *bam* – her gift had sprung to attention.

Finding it had been the easy part, as usual. Retrieving it, slightly trickier. It had been in the gutter of the music huts (Zeynep had suspected an accidental wind from a kid who came from a witching family with the elemental designation in their blood). No one had been able to physically *see* it with their eyes – there was not so much as a tuft of tail or the curve of an ear visible – so Becca hadn't been able to explain *how* she knew. And she might have been tempted to use a little magic to attract Bun Bun to her . . . if it hadn't been playtime with a crowd already gathering behind her.

There were charms woven through the school, runes secretly etched onto the head teacher's office and spells infused within the actual brickwork of the newer parts of the school and around the perimeter fences. All crafted to protect the children and deflect attention from slip-ups with magic, which could happen with younger witches. Specific gifts didn't come in until puberty, and with it, more power, but small children could carry out very simple spells or – more often – have an accidental outburst. But Becca wasn't sure those charms would activate when an adult witch used magic, since it wouldn't be accidental, and she was reluctant to activate any of them anyway, knowing that they all linked back and called upon her cousin's and uncle's well of power. They didn't need any additional demand on the magical anchor tattoo they both carried.

In the end, Drew had been fetched by a helpful girl in Year 4. He was obviously the go-to at the school for anything out of reach because he was six foot two, and he added an inch to that with the way he gelled his light-brown hair to flick up at the front. It made Becca think of that social-media trend from a few years back. 'Is he hot or is he just . . .' and when it came to Drew she could fill it in with 'tall', because now, for all the magic in her, she could not imagine what she'd ever seen in him.

Still, facing him and dealing with his scepticism about how she could just 'know' the soft toy was up there was worth it to see Aisha reunited with her favourite cuddly. What kind of person would she be if she left a five-year-old crying when she had the skills to solve the problem?

Becca went into her kitchen and fastened the . . . card to her fridge with a big magnet. She'd worry about the probable food contamination issue later.

When Becca came back in, ineffectually rubbing glitter off her hands against her top, Zeynep was sitting up again, her arm resting along the back of the sofa and her chin on top of that. Her dark eyes were wide and fixed Becca with a shrewd look. 'Now. You need to tell *me* what is going on. You said you needed emergency cat-sitting? Which is absolutely not a problem. But is that because you are off on a dirty weekend? Because, if so, we need to talk about your classification of an emergency. A dirty weekend is *not* one . . . unless you have been having an epic dry spell, and I know for a fact that you had sex just a couple of months ago.'

'It doesn't count unless you're getting orgasms from it.' Becca waved her hand, stopping herself from getting distracted. She didn't want to think or talk about Drew any more. 'Anyway, I'm not off on a dirty weekend.'

'So why is there an incredibly hot man waiting by your van as you pack?'

'It's a heatwave – of course he's hot. Plus, I don't think he owns shorts.' Why else would Connor be wearing suit trousers and a long-sleeved shirt in a heatwave? It was no wonder he looked like he wanted to murder the sun.

'You know that's not what I mean.' Zeynep's eyebrow quirked. 'I mean hot as in attractive, handsome, fit, fu—'

'Shhh,' Becca hissed in panic, and it was that, rather than all the walking around she'd done in the last fifteen minutes, which finally unsettled Michael Kitten so he flew off her shoulders and out of the front door, which was still open – hence her panic.

'So, who is he and where are you going?' Zeynep persisted.

Before Becca could answer, Connor approached the doorway with one large hand wrapped around Michael Kitten's body, his arm outstretched as if he were holding a bomb. 'Is it an indoor cat?' he asked gruffly.

Becca couldn't decide whether to be disturbed by Connor's apparent discomfort at holding her soft, cuddly cat, or touched that he'd even thought about whether Michael was an escape artist and pushed himself to pick him up and return him, just in case.

Doubly strange was that Michael Kitten seemed perfectly content to be dangled by Connor at Becca's head height. He gave Becca a meow of greeting but wasn't even scrabbling his back paws to try to get a purchase and get down.

'Err . . . he's not. But thank you for rescuing him anyway.' She reached out to take Michael, her fingers brushing against Connor's hand, and he dropped the cat into her grasp as though the feline had suddenly turned into a hedgehog and started prickling him. 'I'm almost ready,' she told him. 'D'you want something to eat here or shall we stop on the way?'

'We can stop on the way. Shall I put this in the back of the van for you?' He pointed to her bag.

'Oh, oh! Wait a minute. You're going to need your tea. Have you got your tea?' Zeynep asked, standing up and heading into the kitchen.

Becca raised her eyebrows. Huh. Interesting. Zeynep had made Becca a few blends. One for pre-menstrual cramps. One for achy muscles – photography could mean a lot of time on the feet. And one for when Becca hadn't been able to return a lost object to its owner and her gift was nagging at her.

'Is she a seer?' Connor asked.

'Only when it comes to her healing teas. She'll get a sense of when people need them sometimes.'

He nodded but didn't say anything else and then Zeynep came bustling out of the kitchen with a tin she'd appropriated from Becca's kitchen cupboard.

'So,' Zeynep said. 'Who is he if you're not shagging him?'

Becca snorted, unable to feel any embarrassment herself when presented with the utterly baffled expression on Connor's face. Zeynep was testing him – which meant she still didn't believe Becca when she said she wasn't going on a dirty weekend.

'This is Connor Lynch,' she said, fighting a laugh. 'He's going to be helping me in Cornwall while I track down a lost object for my family.'

'Ah, gotcha.' At this point Zeynep knew that if Becca was being vague about something to do with her family, it meant she *couldn't* tell her anything, so she didn't bother asking questions. Although everyone respected the Ashworth family and looked to them as the heart of the community, the ones who took responsibility for the upkeep of all the protective magic surrounding Biddicote, no one knew about the direct links of active magic, and they never really questioned it either. Which was a *little* odd. Kay was convinced there was something in the protective magic that made residents, both magical and non-magical, let go of any deeper questions they had about how the Ashworths were linked to the magic of the village. Probably a hangover from the witch-hunter days when things were even more precautionary, but they hadn't been able to find anything concrete about that either while doing their research and it was not exactly a priority. Plus, it worked in their favour to keep the anchor a secret.

Although they weren't doing harm to anyone else, technically the tattoo could be seen as doing harm to the *Ashworth* it was inked onto – and if the Witches Council found out, they could use it as an excuse to stop the Ashworths protecting the village. The tattoo couldn't be removed but the runes etched around the village could be if it all came to light. The community would crumble; the concentration of witches there needed that level of power to keep them safe – otherwise they'd be forced to uproot their lives and spread out across the country. Not to mention the ones who had grown so used to being relaxed around non-magical people that they would end up breaking tenets left and right . . . and being punished for it.

'And, Connor,' Becca forced herself to continue, pushing past the bleak sequence of events she'd just imagined – it would do her no good to focus on that while she had to make this trip with the actual Abrogator – 'this radiant being is Zeynep Kemal, best friend, amazing witch, favourite reception teacher at Biddicote Primary and occasional cat-sitter.'

'Aww.' Zeynep laid her head on Becca's shoulder and stroked her hair, which immediately soothed Becca's tension – as though her best friend had picked up on it – and prompted Michael Kitten to press his paw to Zeynep's cheek. 'You are such a suck-up when you want a favour.'

'Of course.' Becca laughed. 'You catch more mice with cheese than poison.'

'That's not how that saying goes,' Connor muttered.

'Is that so?' She shrugged. 'The only time I have problems with mice is when Michael brings them in.'

'Michael?' He looked around warily as though he expected someone to be lurking in the corner.

Becca lifted her beloved pet. 'Michael Kitten.'

Connor's gaze narrowed down on the cat.

'Ask her why she called him that,' Zeynep instructed and then went to carry on with the story, but Connor bent down and picked up Becca's bag and then backed a couple of steps away from the door.

'Maybe she can tell me on the way. It's a long drive.'

Becca's and Zeynep's eyes met over the head of her now purring cat. 'Guess that's my cue to go.'

'OK, Rebecca Ashworth, stay safe,' Zeynep said, the ring of a magical charm in her words.

Becca gave her a kiss on the cheek, then kissed the top of Michael's head, and swapped the cat for the tin of tea. 'You too, gorgeous. There are batch-cooked meals in the freezer, and a bottle of my aunt's dandelion cordial in the fridge.'

She slipped on her shoes, grabbed her handbag and dropped the tea into it, and then stepped back out into the sunshine, just in time to see Connor closing the doors to the van. She hadn't given him the key, but obviously that wouldn't stop a witch if they knew the right spells.

The golden light of the field behind him glowed, so she could hardly see his face as he straightened up and turned to look at her. He was like a shadow. A long, dark presence she would have to accept alongside her over the next few days. But she wasn't going to let that worry her. She hitched her bag higher on her shoulder and went out to meet him.

A shadow wasn't something to fear, after all. It was just a sign that the light was waiting around the corner.

Chapter Eight

CONNOR

Considering Becca had been all about getting down to Cornwall as soon as possible, they'd already stopped three times and she'd just put the indicator on in the van to pull over again. He barely stifled a frustrated moan.

She looked over at him and raised her eyebrows. OK, he hadn't stifled it at all. 'Problem?'

'Why are we stopping again?'

'Photographer's prerogative.'

Neither of those two words made sense to him in this context. 'What?'

She pulled the car over to the lay-by at the top of the hill, which was about to drop down into Lyme Regis. Climbing out, she opened the back door to the van and rummaged around and then slammed the door again.

Goddess give him strength. Forget her having any intentions of pushing him off a cliff; maybe her tactic was as simple as driving him to despair, so he voluntarily left her alone? But no matter how frustrating she was, he couldn't leave her to walk into a dangerous situation, nor could he let them recover a possibly unprecedented amplifier without understanding what it had been and would be used for. She was stuck with him. And he was stuck with her.

He watched her walk over to the metal barrier at the side of the lay-by. On the other side, the hill fell away sharply. She hooked a leg over the barrier and he near threw himself out of the van door to hurry over to her. 'What are you thinking?'

'Calm down.' She glanced over at him in surprise as she sat down on the barrier. 'I won't fall – I've cast a net.'

He looked in front of her and realised he could feel the criss-cross of magically cushioned air. Reaching out, he could run his fingers through the air and pick up each strand of the invisible net, like links in a playground fence. He could feel her magical signature, too. Bright and vibrant.

'Can you see it?' she asked, shock in her voice.

'No.' He pulled his hand back. He wasn't lying but he wasn't being totally truthful either, and he had the sudden realisation that it might become difficult to hide some of the aspects of his specific magical gift from her, while they had to spend so much time together. 'But you can't blame me for thinking you might be about to pitch yourself off the hill in a fit of clumsiness – you fell out of a tree within sixty seconds of us meeting.'

She shivered. 'Don't remind me. Having a ghost pass through you is a distinctly icky feeling. Have you ever experienced it?'

'Yes. But I just felt cold.'

'Hmm . . . maybe it's worse if you're a medium.'

'Maybe so.' He folded his arms across his chest. 'So, what's happening?'

'Sunset. Photographer's prerogative,' she said, repeating the phrase from earlier, and lifted the large camera that was now secured by a wide strap draped around her neck. 'I can't miss the opportunity.'

She removed the lens cover and snapped a couple of photos of the sea, ablaze with pinks and crimson and lilac as the sun set. Some of her thick hair was caught beneath her camera strap and the golden light brought out the red tones.

He forced his attention away to the grey of the barrier. 'I thought you were in a hurry.'

'This is five minutes. It's always worth taking five minutes to remember why it's wonderful to be alive.'

He rolled his eyes.

'I swear I just *heard* you roll your eyes at that.' She half laughed, her eye still pressed to the viewfinder of her camera, her hand deftly twisting the lens manually to adjust something. 'D'you never find it strange that non-magical people can go about their lives thinking there's no possibility of magic, when nature is this amazing and right in front of them?' She lowered the camera and tilted her head. 'Like, surely they can feel the energy of it?'

'Witches are very good at keeping secrets. And technology helps explain anything that slips through the cracks,' he said dryly, wondering how stupid she'd think *him* for not having believed in magic as a child, when he actually *had* it.

He didn't wait for her response, he just stalked back to the van but then couldn't even get inside, because there was a bee buzzing around in the cabin. They hadn't been able to keep the windows shut, what with the decrepit old van not even having air-conditioning.

'All done,' she said, coming back over. She put her camera back in the rear of the van and then went around to the driver's side. 'I thought *you* were in a hurry?' She repeated his own words back to him, a teasing lilt in her voice.

'I am. But there's a bee in the cabin.'

'Oh, you're scared of them, huh?' Her tone was matter of fact; he didn't detect any judgement or laughter at his expense.

'Yes,' he found himself admitting. 'But only because if I get stung by it, I'll die.'

'Oh. So will the bee, though. They don't want to sting you, y'know? Once it's figured out that you're not a flower, it will fly off. You're very obviously not a flower. No scent of pollen and you look like a black-and-white photocopy.'

He frowned, glancing down at his admittedly mono-chrome clothes. And he knew that his skin was one shade above snow, his black hair starkly contrasted. None of that was the point, though. 'It might panic. If it's trapped. It's easier to just wait out here and let it fly off.'

'Is it?' She gave him a quizzical frown. 'You are aware you're a witch? You don't even have to touch it to get rid of it.'

'I don't want to kill it.'

'I wasn't suggesting that. Are those your only two settings? Remove yourself from the vicinity or murder?' He swore he could see the hint of a smirk pulling at her lips.

'No, but I prefer not to risk it . . . it's very small and I'm . . .' He broke off and shook his head. 'Look, do you have a better plan?'

'Well, *I'm* not allergic or scared of them, so I could just leave.' She gave a little shrug. Now she *was* laughing at him – he could see the mirth in her warm brown eyes.

'If you didn't want me accompanying you, you wouldn't have driven me this far.'

'I think "want" is a strong way to describe my accept-ance of the situation. Besides, maybe it would just be all the sweeter to abandon you here? Miles from home.'

Miles from *her* home maybe. It wasn't like it made much difference to him, other than him not having his car. 'And I suppose you planted the bee after somehow hacking into my medical file back at your house, when you were packing and kissing your cat goodbye?'

'Could be that I spotted the EpiPen in your luggage?' She grinned and then sobered a little. 'You really should tell someone you're travelling with that you have a life-threatening allergy.'

He never actually travelled with anyone, so it hadn't even crossed his mind. He raised an eyebrow at her. 'What? So they could help me out of potentially life-threatening situations?' He waved a hand at the interior of the van, where the bee was now crawling across the top of the steering wheel.

She laughed. 'Touché.' She glanced into the van to see where the bee was, and at that moment it flew out of the driver's window. 'Ah-ha. Problem solved. Let's get going, shall we?'

By the time they'd crossed from Devon into Cornwall, night had fallen and Becca was insisting on singing along to what she dubbed her 'angry woman' playlist to keep herself 'alert'.

'I can drive if you want to rest,' he offered. His headache and the dizziness from the effects of Biddicote and the possible concussion had receded to a dull throb in his temples, but her singing was tempting it back.

'That's kind, but like I said before, my gift doesn't exactly throw directions at me in a timely fashion. Easier not to have a middle-man.' She rebuffed him and then went back to hollering along with Alanis Morissette.

'Fine. But . . . could you not play something a little less . . .' He shifted in his seat, struggling to find a word that didn't sound insulting.

She turned the volume down a little. 'Sorry, but it's *so* cathartic. Alanis, Olivia and Taylor are like the Holy Trinity of break-up artists. It's mandatory when a man has screwed you over.'

'You've just been through a break-up?'

'A couple of months ago.'

'You seem pretty upbeat.'

She laughed. 'Why do you sound resentful of that fact?'

'I don't . . . do I?' He shifted, uncomfortably aware that he might have tried too hard to cover up his initial, confusing feeling of excitement when she confirmed she was single. He cleared his throat. 'Maybe it's my accent.'

'I doubt it. Your accent tends to make things more pleasant to the ear.' She threw him a sideways look as she changed gear. 'Do *you* like to sing? I know I only hit the notes about eighty per cent of the time, but I bet you can hold a tune.'

Why were his cheeks getting warm? 'Do you get any images coming to you of where the lost item is?' he asked, instead of answering her question.

'Change of subject noted.' She slowed the car, her eyes darting around the darkened road stretched before them. 'Erm . . . no. Sometimes I get an idea of what the object looks like, but it's really just a sense of following my nose to find it. Ah-ha.' She clicked the indicator on to turn left down an unmarked lane.

'So, we have no idea what we're walking into.'

'Yeah. Well, it's going to be quite late, so I guess we can, like, stake it out and figure out what to do from there? Find a hotel, hatch a plan and return tomorrow, bright and early.' The van growled as she accelerated up the narrow road. 'It'll be nice to have someone to figure it out with for a change, actually.'

Connor did a little side-eyeing of his own. Did she actually mean that? Less than an hour ago she'd been joking about abandoning him at the side of the road. Was she teasing him then, or now? Or was she just totally inconsistent in her feelings?

'Usually, the hardest bit about finding lost stuff is working out how to retrieve it without raising suspicion,' she continued. 'For big stuff, I mean – when people lose their keys or something, that's easy enough – I just pretend to look for a bit and then "discover them". But other things can be more complicated – like Kay's suitcase last year. I knew it was in Italy but how do you explain you know that to an airline?'

Why was she telling him all this? He knew he'd asked a question, but he'd thought the Ashworths were a closed-lipped bunch. 'What did you do?'

'Nothing. Waited.'

'How did that affect your gift? Does it stop bothering you once you know exactly where it is?'

'It's actually to do with the ownership of the person. When the person lets go of it emotionally. Kay accepted she was never going to see those shoes again. She got her insurance pay-out and bought some replacements. Not that she needs them,' she added, with a laugh. 'To be fair, her addiction pays off for me, because we have the same size feet and she's kind enough to lend me even her favourites.'

'I suppose she can rely upon the fact that you won't ever lose them.'

'True.' She sent a smile in his direction and he found himself internally curling up in suspicion of it. Why was she chatting away and smiling at him? How did they get from talking about their plans when they found the amplifier to her borrowing shoes from her cousin's girlfriend? What was her game? The Ashworths had definitely been playing one back at Ashworth Hall, with all their silent communication, which even the ghost had bought into in order to keep their secrets.

Maybe it was like she'd said back at her house to her friend – she thought she'd be better off befriending him than being prickly – enticing him with cheese rather than poison. It was all fake. Maybe she was trying to ingratiate herself so he didn't report her for the summoning? Too late for that.

Although, he was supposed to be doing the same thing . . . she was just better at it than him. It didn't make him any less of a hypocrite.

Goddess, he was catching her flitting attention span. This was the problem with chatter, it made his brain overload. He was used to quiet and being able to hear himself think properly.

'Why is this spell so important?' he found himself asking.

'Which spell?' she said lightly, but her hands tightened on the steering wheel.

'The one the amplifier is missing from. There are hundreds of protective charms all over Biddicote. What's the difference if one of them isn't working? Especially if it's having side effects on the person who cast it? Lots of old spells don't work as well now. Our language and understanding of magic has changed.'

'You know, I think that's the longest I've heard you speak.'

'Uh-huh. Your turn to avoid the question, is it so?'

'No.' She wriggled in her seat and pressed her lips together. If he'd wanted to see what lay beneath her sunny smile, he'd definitely achieved that. 'We just take our responsibility as custodians of the history of Biddicote and Ashworth Hall seriously. You're right about magic changing – not in its essence, but in the way we wield it using spells and charms. That's why rune magic is so tricky, isn't it? But it would be sad to let it crumble away, just because we couldn't be bothered to put in the time to figure out how our ancestors did it. You're Irish, you deal with that on a whole other level, right? With your language and culture.'

'You mean when people like *your* ancestors tried to wipe it all out?'

She frowned and threw an apologetic look his way. 'Yeah. I guess not *all* parts of the Ashworth history should be preserved. But if we don't try to understand it, how will we learn from it? Make the decisions about whether it's time to change things or not.' Her expression turned thoughtful.

They crested the hill and though the road was still narrow and crowded by the thick hedgerows, at their bushiest at the height of summer, the moon was bright above them, sending silvery light into the car.

'So it's all about your duty of care? Nothing to do with maintaining your family's illustrious position within the witching community?'

'How do you mean?'

'Being an Ashworth is a privileged position, isn't it? Witches and non-magical folk alike look up to you. You're like a celebrity when you walk through Biddicote, and that holds a lot of sway when there are magical referendums.'

'I can't deny there is truth to that.' She chewed on her lip. 'But why is that such an issue for the Witches Council? Everyone still gets their vote *if* there is one. We're not brainwashing people in the basement of Ashworth Hall and running a cult. For one thing, there'd be no room among all the pentacles for summonings.' Her expression was clearly deadpan.

'No. But you're maintaining power and keeping secrets at the same time. You can't say that everyone who respects the Ashworths would do so if they knew you were hiding things from them.'

She frowned. 'You said yourself earlier, secrecy is an occupational hazard as a witch.'

'Between us and non-magical people. Not between each other.'

'Really?' Her voice pitched higher – not shouting but incredulous. 'Everything about you is a secret. And I appreciate partly why that's done, but are you the only one allowed to keep secrets?'

He had not expected the tables to be turned on him. Nor for him to be unable to come up with an answer immediately as to why the Witches Council – and he – were allowed to keep secrets from the witching community, and yet the Ashworths weren't . . . 'So you *do* admit you have secrets?' he threw out, somewhat childishly.

She narrowed her eyes at him and then concentrated on the road again. Adele carried on power-housing about her rubbish ex-boyfriend in the background and Connor told himself he was pleased Becca had given up singing along. Finally, a bit of peace for his overloaded head.

'We're almost there,' she said quietly.

BECCA

The tugging in Becca's head kept making her look over to the right on the dark road, but she couldn't see anything, despite knowing that it was coming up soon. She crawled the van along slowly and still got the sensation that she'd overshot it when the sensation started to pull her back. Where was the amplifier? Buried in a field?

That might make life easier. She could load it in the van and drive them both back to Surrey that night. In fact, maybe she'd make *him* drive them back.

'Are you looking for somewhere to park?' the grumpy man in her passenger seat asked. He'd spent the entire journey with his shoulder pressed against the door, as though he couldn't put enough space between them. It wasn't like it was a tiny interior. There were three seats in the front; they weren't on top of each other . . .

Don't think about that, she told herself, as it made her remember what actually being on top of him had felt like when she'd fallen out of the tree earlier.

'I wasn't, but that might be a good idea,' she replied. 'If we can get to the other side of the fence, I can search the field. You reckon it's buried, like treasure?'

'Well, I'd assumed it was in the building, but if your sense is saying it's in the field we'll look there. We just might have to be careful in case anyone is living there and spots us skulking about.'

She blinked, trying to make sense of his words. 'Building? What building?'

'You can't see it?'

'I haven't seen a building for the length of this road. Where is it?'

Connor turned in his seat and pointed over her shoulder. The heat of his arm was like a brand across her neck. Then she concentrated on where he was pointing and saw that the direction lined up perfectly with where her gift was guiding her to. 'I still can't see it. What is it? An enchanted house?'

He sighed. 'Looks like it.'

'So you can just . . . *see through* enchantments?'

He didn't bother to respond, and she searched along the road slowly, looking for somewhere to park now, trying not to think about what else he could do. She'd figured that as well as removing magic from witches, he must be able to remove hexes – because that was how Kay said she'd met him at work. But could he just see *through* magic, too? She hadn't been too worried about being in close quarters with such a formidable witch, because, honestly, he was awkward and closed off. Scared of bees and conversation. It was a timely reminder, before they embarked on this next step of the journey, that he was with her for a reason. And maybe he truly was an exception to every witching rule.

She found a wider section of road next to a long, metal farm gate, with enough room for her to park the van and not get in the way of traffic. They climbed out into the moonlit night, the air balmy, with barely any movement. She squinted back in the direction he'd seen the house, or whatever it was, still struggling to make it out. Most illusions could be broken, once you knew there was an illusion there, but this one was holding fast. For her.

Unless he was lying. Odd how she'd not been worried until this moment, when stepping outside of the van and realising what an isolated place she'd led them to. If he did want to strangle her and throw her in a ditch, there was no one around to help – except a potential magical artefact thief – and her magic wouldn't work against him, because he could just drain her of her powers.

She cast a wary glance at him.

Nah.

He was a number of things – aloof, arrogant, rude, ridiculously hot – but he didn't come across as a serial killer. Not that they always looked the same – sometimes Zeynep forced her to watch those true-crime documentaries – but she trusted her gut instincts and she felt surprisingly relaxed around him. The actual Abrogator.

'Are you going to stare at me all night, or are we going to figure out what this place is and if the amplifier is there?'

Impatient. He was super-impatient, too.

'Lead the way.' She made an exaggerated bow and flourished her arm to indicate that he should precede her. She followed, the shadows deep indigo in the light of the moon. 'What does it look like?' she whispered as they walked along the hedgerow.

'The building?' He cast a distracted glance back at her and looked forward again quickly. His hand was outstretched, hovering over the hedge, as though he were warming his fingers over a fire. 'Old. Maybe a few centuries. But well kept. Typical farmhouse style for down this way. Multiple chimneys but no smoke coming out – not that it's an indication of people being there or not, since it's summer.'

He was almost talking to himself now, cataloguing details like a detective, and as she looked over his shoulder she thought she might be able to see it. The edge of a roof, set well back from the road. Slate tiles, the colour of a storm cloud, winking in and out of her sight. She tripped on an unexpected dip in the road and he instantly reached out as though to steady her, but held back, his hand stopping a bare inch from her arm, when he saw she'd already regained her balance.

She met his eyes, surprised to see what looked like a glimmer of fear in them, but what could he be scared about? Her falling on her face? More likely she couldn't read his expression at all and she was imagining it. It was dark and so were his eyes, the pupil indistinguishable from the iris in the shadow of the hedgerow. Goosebumps spread across her lower back, but she wasn't cold, or scared, just . . . aware of him – his solemn scrutiny and the angles of his face as he looked down on her, exaggerated in the moonlight, the pair of them wrapped up together in the quiet warmth of the night.

She gave him a small smile, meant to silently reassure him that she was fine, and he turned back and started walking again. They'd driven further along than it had seemed in the van. Finally, he paused and crouched down. The hand which had hovered over the hedgerow – and her arm – now reached out so he could skim his fingertips over the leaves and woody vines, light as a teasing caress.

Calm down, Becca.

'There are powerful wards on this,' he murmured, and she crouched down next to him to hear better. 'No one is supposed to be able to enter unless they . . .' He paused as he brought his other hand up to the hedgerow, too. 'Unless they need a safe haven. And non-magical people can only come through if they're with a witch.'

'That's very specific. How do you know that?'

'In order to remove magic, I have to be able to read and understand it in the first place. Break it down into its component parts . . .' He trailed off and dropped his hands.

'Wow. Just by touching something that's been spelled?'

He nodded, and then added, 'Or some*one*. But that's not as clear or consistent—' He broke off again, as if he'd said too much.

'More secrets you and the Witches Council have been keeping, hmm,' she murmured. The minute she said it, it occurred to her that if that had been common knowledge, her family could have just asked him to read the tattoo spell on Harry's chest. No summoning of bigoted ancestors required. But . . . Connor would have taken that information straight back to the Witches Council. They would have made their judgement on whether the Ashworths could still use their unique magic to protect Biddicote and – most likely – forbidden it . . . because, like Connor admitted earlier, they were suspicious of one witching family being held in such esteem.

Connor hadn't exactly been wrong about the way the respect witches had for her family made their opinions carry more weight. But the last time Becca had any knowledge of it actually making a difference was a magical referendum the UK Witches Council held in the eighties. Despite having a strong line of influencers themselves, the Ashworths had supported the argument to prevent witches from selling their skills into corporations to sway business deals. It hadn't been popular with the witches who were making a living that way, for obvious reasons, but the support of a family like hers, with the ear of one of the largest populations of witches, had helped to tip the vote.

'What will happen if we try to enter the property when we're not in need of a safe haven?' she asked.

'You won't be able to enter at all. The hedge will be impassable. The building will never reveal itself to you.'

'So, you *have* to remove the magic— Hang on. You said for *me* to enter. But not you? You can walk through regardless?'

He paused for a beat, as though weighing up his answer, and then sighed. 'The magic doesn't work on me, no. Magic can't directly affect me. It can't read me or work upon me. I am the black hole of magic. Dark matter. The monstrous void.'

She blinked at him, realising that she'd relied upon the way that the Ashworth Hall wards warned them if people were coming to the property who meant harm to the family. It wasn't a fool-proof system, but the fact that he'd not sent the magical alarm bells ringing had subconsciously reassured her of his motives. And now he was admitting that he could have the worst of intentions towards her family and the wards wouldn't have even known he was there.

He was watching her face, his expression tight, and she remembered that the wards weren't the only things that warned her family about the Witches Council; her own instincts flared up, too. And they weren't flaring right now. In fact, they were telling her that he'd let her into another secret and that his tense body language, the rigid line of his shoulders and stiff neck, were betraying his own concern.

She gave a light laugh. 'You could do with working on your nicknames, Connor – they're a bit dramatic. Are you going to go in then, check it out?'

Again, he paused, looking back at something she couldn't quite see and pressing his hand to the hedge one more time. Then he shook his head. 'This place is definitely about protecting lost witches. Maybe that means it's an empty building – perhaps using the amplifier for the magic inside . . . though I can't sense a trace of it in the wards. But it could equally be full of people who have ended up here, and if I stumble in without you, I'll have to explain myself and you'll be stuck outside, which doesn't help us find the amplifier. Or, at least, makes the process a lot longer.'

The little burst of satisfaction that she felt at him comfortably acknowledging that they were better as a team was disturbing. 'So . . . I guess the only way we can get in is to put ourselves in a situation where we need a safe haven?'

'In theory.'

She let out her own little sigh of resignation. There was only one thing they could do, wasn't there? 'Come on, then. Let's get it over with.'

Chapter Nine

CONNOR

'It' turned out to be Becca sabotaging her own van.

Connor couldn't fault her logic, but the manner of sabotage was a little trickier to figure out. After all, if you were a witch, you could remedy a fair few simple problems that would put non-magical people deep in the shite.

They were back at the van and Becca was scooping her hair up into a messy bun, fixing it in place with a band she'd pulled out from her glove box.

'The problem is, anything we do to it, technically, you could just undo again, right?' she said, placing her hands on her hips to stare at her van.

He tamped down his immediate suspicion that she was trying to get more information from him about his magic. Warren had always counselled him to be circumspect about what he was capable of. If dangerous witches knew everything he could do, he would lose his advantage upon the approach. It had been very useful to be able to get onto a dangerous witch's property without alerting them to his presence more than once in the past. And if they knew magic wouldn't hold him at bay, they might be tempted to use other methods – like Dobermann dogs or barbed wire. Neither of which were too much of a problem for him, but they were definitely an inconvenience and required, extra time to get past which could allow the rogue witch to escape.

But it was too late to lament it now. He'd told Becca, and he'd just have to hope that she wasn't going to broadcast it to the entire witching world because she still felt like she needed him.

He cleared his throat. 'If the magic is continually working to cause a problem – like if we put a spell on the engine to . . . I dunno . . . continuously drain the battery – I could reverse that, just like any witch can reverse their own spell if it's not permanently changed the state of something.' It was, in fact, a lot easier for him than the average witch, since they needed to know the exact method and amount of magic that had been cast in order to reverse it, and that could be tricky to recall precisely. Most witches ended up in a bigger mess than they started in when they tried, and attempting to reverse someone else's spell was just asking for trouble. Whereas Connor had multiple options when it came to cancelling out magic, ranging from simply absorbing the magic to reversing it . . . 'But I can't *undo* literal damage. I can't turn back time. Just fix the problem, the same as you could.'

'I see, I see.' She squinted at the van and wrinkled her nose. 'I don't really want to cause irreparable damage to my van, though. It's special.'

Connor's eyebrow rose, looking at the rose-coloured van with white daisies stencilled on the bonnet and along the rear panels. 'It is that,' he said, drolly.

She gave him a look dry enough to suit the tenor of his words. 'It was my mum's,' she said simply, robbing him of all his sarcasm with the use of the past tense and the way her brown eyes grew a little warmer. She shook her head, as if she were shaking off her sentimentality. 'So, the parameters of the problem are that we have to *genuinely* be stranded. We can't use a spell because you could undo that.

We can't do something as simple as a puncture because we – and the magic of the wards – would know we can fix that ourselves. And we can't explode the engine or ram it into a tree because I'll cry. What options does that leave us with?'

Once again Connor was struck with the bizarre fancy that she wasn't quite of this world. Like when he'd thought of her as a faerie queen earlier. What strange species of witch, or even human, was she, that she could be so openly vulnerable, while simultaneously being pragmatic and keeping her humour?

Or maybe lots of people were like this, and he just hadn't made the acquaintance of many. Maybe he kept thinking she was special because if he looked at her too long, he began to feel hot in ways that didn't have anything to do with the heatwave. He cleared his throat. 'We could just crack the battery.'

'But I could fix a crack with my magic,' she said, with rueful certainty.

'Sure, but you couldn't replace the fluids that had leaked out.'

'Ooh, you're right. Good thinking. Let's crack it then.' She opened the driver's door and leaned in to press the button to pop the hood. He propped it up and she used her phone to light up the interior, because regardless of their being witches, clicking their fingers to generate an open flame when they were within inches of a combustion engine was not the greatest idea. 'How big?' she asked.

'It can be small. Probably best near the base or one of the other components so it could plausibly be inflicted by an impact.' He reached in, sneaking his hand into the tight space to find a spot to crack the industrial plastic. She caught his forearm and the sudden, intense warmth of her palm on his skin had him straightening as if she'd electrocuted him, and smacking the already tender back of his head on the bonnet.

'Fecking hell,' he growled, rubbing his head.

'Sorry, sorry.' She tiptoed up to look at the back of his head, raising her hand as if she were going to touch him again, and he flinched away. 'Holy grimoire, you're as jumpy as a cat on fireworks night.' She lowered her hand. 'I was just going to say, be careful. There's acid in batteries, right? You don't want to get it on your skin.'

'Yeah, thanks. So glad I've got you looking out for my well-being,' he said, sarcastically.

She flushed and he felt guilty for being so harsh. Because it was actually nice that she cared, on a basic level, seeing him as human just like her – and also because the bump to his head wasn't her fault, really. This time. He took a deep breath to make sure his tone didn't betray any lingering irritation. 'Did you want to do it? It's your van.'

'No, that's OK. I trust you.'

The ease with which she said it almost hurt. She *trusted* him? Him, the biggest threat to a witch on the planet? Not to mention the member of the Witches Council sent to investigate her family. That couldn't be true. She had to be lying – unless she just meant she trusted him to manage a touch of destruction, because it was his forte, after all.

Putting his hand back into the engine, he squeezed his finger and thumb together as though he were picking at a thread, harnessing the air, compacting it tightly and then forcing it like a scalpel between the atoms of plastic in the corner of the battery and prising them apart millimetre by millimetre. There. That should do it.

'Very precise,' she said, giving a little nod as he took his hand back out of the van and gestured for her to step back so he could close the hood. She disappeared inside the van again, reappearing with a wipe.

'I didn't touch anything.'

'Just in case.'

He plucked the wipe from her outstretched hands and cleaned his hands, enjoying the feeling of freshening his sweaty hands, despite not having got any grease or battery fluid on them. The heat of the night was still enough to make him clammy. As was the way she kept getting close to him. Or him to her. Incidentally.

'We just wait now then, I guess.' She leaned back against the driver's door, looking back in the direction of the building.

'Yep. You'll have to tell me if it appears to you.'

'It's like one of those Magic Eye pictures.' She exaggerated squinting and laughed. 'D'you ever do those as a kid?'

'No.' He shoved the wipe in his pocket rather than put it away in the van, wanting to keep a bit of distance, even if that meant the lining of his trousers becoming damp.

She let the silence grow between them this time. Occasionally an owl screeched into the night, or the dart of a bat made a soft flutter overhead.

'Oh, here we go, I think.' She pushed up off the van and went up onto her tiptoes. 'I see it. I see it! Oh, it looks cute.'

He looked over at the building, which he would never in a million years have called 'cute', and noticed that there were now three or four glowing lanterns on the outside of it. Like beacons, lighting the way for them.

'We cracked the code,' she said, grinning as she locked the van. 'Go us. Are you ready?'

Since she was already marching away along the hedgerow, he supposed he was going to have to be.

Chapter Ten

BECCA

When they reached the part of the hedge where Connor had stopped before, there was a faint rustle and, as she blinked, the branches pulled back, slithering and creaking their way into the shape of an archway just big enough for them to pass through side by side.

Despite there being the space, they didn't *actually* walk through side by side. Connor went first, and she followed, and she wasn't sure whether that was because he wanted space from her or was putting himself in whatever firing line there might be – she suspected a combination of both.

The moment she was through, the hedge knitted itself back together. That was some serious magic.

Between that and the enchantment placed over what she could now see was a significant building, there had to be at least one or two powerful witches living here. Or a witch using her family's amplifier. As her eyes tracked over the horseshoe shape of building, the tug in her mind grew stronger, making her look slightly to the right of the old front door that was set in a porch made up of black stained wooden sleepers. There was writing above the door but in the flickering light of the torches, it was too hard to make it out.

What she could make out were the sounds of voices, the gentle glow of candlelight from inside. It felt very much like standing outside the pub in the village when it got late, near to closing time.

Connor's back was stiff, his hands held a little out from his sides, as though he was a gunslinger in a western, waiting to see if he needed to draw his sharp-shooters at any moment. As they approached the door, she kind of appreciated it. She'd barely seen him wield his magic, but the way he'd sliced into the battery had been impressive. Most witches would have gone for an impact spell to crack something. It was far easier. But not as precise. If they were walking into a room of hostile witches, she definitely felt better having him at her side. Or in front of her, as it were.

The spell on the building might have been for witches in need, but that didn't mean the witches who created the place *wanted* to help. Vulnerable people were, of course, easier to exploit. Just because Becca's nature tended towards optimism didn't meant she was naive or gullible.

As they reached the door, she took a second to read the sign. The Meili Inn. That was the Norse god of travel, wasn't it? It was proclaiming itself an inn for travellers.

They didn't even need to knock on the door – it swung open for them, all by itself.

Connor went first again, having to duck under the low frame of the old door, and Becca had to have such a stern word with her reproductive organs that she almost missed the way the burble of conversation had died. On either side of her were heavy wooden tables lacquered with black varnish, on thick rugs covering the red tiled floor. The tables each had glass sconces with floating tea lights inside, and most were occupied. Small groups of two to four witches at each. And they were all looking in their direction.

Before she could catch anyone's eye or make any kind of assessment of the make-up of the crowd, the door swung shut behind her and she jumped forward a little, knocking into Connor. He glanced back at her briefly, his gaze darting around her, perhaps looking for possible threats, and then started forwards again.

She stuck close behind him, fighting the impulse to clutch a handful of his shirt and noticing the long bar now, stretching across the left-hand wall. At the furthest end were two barmaids. One, short with dark red hair, waving her arms around, long draping purple sleeves flapping as she spoke to the taller, blonde barmaid who had her back turned to them. When they got to the bar, Becca looked back around behind them at the witches at the tables. She could see why action heroes in movies stood back-to-back to fight off the surrounding enemy – it covered all the bases.

But the people in the bar were not a bunch of henchmen. They were a mix of all ages, races and genders, and their expressions ranged from suspicious, to nervous, to curious. An elderly woman with a pint of Guinness and a puzzle laid over the table gave Becca a smile, while a young trio – none of whom could have been older than their early twenties – with plates loaded with chips, narrowed their eyes and bent their heads together to whisper.

It definitely looked like a pub, rather than a gathering of nefarious witches hatching plans to steal family heirlooms. But you never could tell, she supposed.

A flash of movement brought her attention back towards the bar – the red-haired woman hurrying off through the gap in the counter to disappear into a door off to the right, almost but not quite lined up with that persistent tugging in Becca's mind.

Connor clipped his head on one of the numerous pewter mugs hanging from the ceiling. He ducked and swore, and Becca resisted patting him on the shoulder since he didn't seem to like it when she touched him. His head was really going through it today.

'Should you not have a health-and-safety sign for those?' he said, grumpily, addressing the barmaid, while Becca went back to examining the darkness of the doorway the red-haired woman had disappeared into.

'Maybe. But I can't say it's been too much of a problem,' the barmaid's voice replied, full of good nature. 'The door frames will do you more of an injury, but I suppose you're used to looking out for those.' Maybe it was just the faint rasp in her voice, but that sounded almost appreciative. Well, Becca could hardly blame the woman – another victim of the patriarchy, and Connor was a sight to behold.

Becca glanced along the wall to the side of the door. That was definitely the direction to head in. The tension in her forehead was tightening.

'Tankards hanging from the ceiling are admittedly a bit rarer, though,' the barmaid continued in a teasing tone. 'Do you want me to lodge an official complaint to my boss? Have you suffered an injury? Do I need to call in a healer?'

'I should survive,' Connor said, and Becca felt her attention drawn back by the way his voice sounded almost . . . friendly. She supposed he'd realised grumpiness wasn't the way to go. Must have been a trial for him. Although . . . was that the beginnings of a smile at the corner of his mouth? An actual smile. He hadn't cracked so much as *one* in her presence in six or seven hours, and within thirty seconds this woman was getting to see it? *Rude.*

'So, is this a hotel, then?' he asked, and she could have sworn he was exaggerating his sexy Irish accent. Did that mean he was *flirting*? They really should have discussed their plan on how to deal with different scenarios before they came in here. She supposed they'd both just been preoccupied with the idea of being attacked or ambushed or something, but the most sinister-looking thing in this building was a painting of smugglers hanging on the wall.

What *was* their new situation? The patrons here seemed to have an investment in finding out who they were, if the prickly feeling of many eyes still staring at them was anything to go by. This place was clearly not like a normal hotel where you were all just strangers passing by. These were witches openly using their magic, who – presumably – had only been given entry because they were in need. They were going to want a fuller explanation of who she and Connor were, over and above a couple of witches with a knackered van. They needed a back story.

'It is. We offer shelter to witches in a bind,' the young woman behind the bar said. 'Do you need a bed for the night?'

There was *definitely* a sultry emphasis on the word 'bed' there. Becca's heart clenched, an uncomfortable feeling crawling up from her stomach.

She was probably just worried about whether that narrative was going to work for them. People were going to assume she and Connor were a couple, arriving together as they had late at night. Connor flirting with someone wasn't going to endear them, no matter how charming he could pretend to be. They needed as many of these patrons kindly disposed to them as possible.

She cleared her throat and stepped out from behind Connor, sliding her arm around his waist but being mindful not to really press against him. Her arm rested along the line of his belt, a good inch from where he'd be able to feel it, and she hooked her thumb into the belt loop on his opposite hip. 'That would be amazing,' she said, filling her voice with relief. 'This is such a stroke of luck, isn't it, darling? If you have a free room that would be so helpful.'

The barmaid's eyes grew almost comically huge and she took a sudden step back. She would've knocked a glass off the shelf behind her if Becca hadn't caught it with a quick spell. The barmaid stared at it, suspended in the air, and then took it in her hand and fumbled it onto the bar.

Her reaction seemed a bit strong, but Becca supposed that it was not only disappointing that the handsome man you'd just been flirting with was already attached, but also embarrassing to be caught out so blatantly.

'W-we do. You just need the *one* room?' The barmaid was tall, with an hourglass figure, and now, up close, Becca could see that the fair hair she had pulled up into a high ponytail leaned towards strawberry blonde. Her eyes were a bright, striking blue. She was like the opposite of Becca. Maybe more Connor's type? And she definitely looked mortified.

Connor was looking at Becca as though she'd lost her mind, his back stiff as a board at her proximity. But, in for a penny. She'd apologise for cock-blocking him later. Honestly, this barmaid was so gorgeous even Becca felt the need to stare.

'Yes, just one. We're newlyweds.' She leaned her head against Connor's arm. 'Had to elope because my family didn't approve of me marrying someone non-magical. But now my van's broken down, which has kind of scuppered our honeymoon plans.'

She could almost *feel* Connor's glare boring a hole in her head. Maybe that was the reason her skull was aching with increasing ferocity. Maybe he'd found a way to magically transfer the pain of his own head injuries onto her?

'Oh, that's . . . erm . . .' The barmaid trailed off, her hand going to her mouth. Becca sent her a smile, trying to reassure her that she wasn't going to drag her over the bar by her ponytail because she'd had the temerity to be attracted to the same man Becca was attracted to. That had always seemed such a dumb thing to get angry about.

The woman dropped her hand and took a deep breath, looking away from Becca. 'I just need to talk with Rhiannon – she's the owner – but can I get you a drink while you're waiting?'

'That would be grand. Lemonade, please,' Connor answered, unclenching his jaw and again managing to sound pleasant to the pretty woman behind the bar. 'Rebecca?' he asked, the word loaded with sugar, playing along with the scenario in the most passive-aggressive way possible. She guessed she had backed him into a corner – he couldn't be seen to be ignoring his newly acquired bride.

'I'm fine, thank you, honey bunny.' She thought he might have actually suppressed a shudder at the pet name and she bit down on a smile.

The barmaid fetched him a tall glass of lemonade, fitting a wedge of lemon on the side and placing it in front of him.

'How much?' He dislodged Becca's arm as he reached into his pocket for his wallet.

'What can you afford?'

'Excuse me?'

'People come here for all kinds of different reasons. We only take what people can afford to give.'

'That's really kind of you,' Becca remarked.

'People are here because they need help.' The woman lifted one shoulder in an uneasy shrug, still not meeting Becca's eye. Connor told her to charge whatever the going rate was for anything they used while they were there, and they'd settle the bill when they left. The barmaid then backed away, as fast as possible it seemed. 'Excuse me, I'll be right back.'

As she left the bar, going off in the same direction as the red-haired woman, Connor leaned his elbows on the bar, burying his face in his palms. 'What did you go and say that for?' His muffled voice just about made it out to Becca.

She moved in closer to him. 'Which bit?'

'Any of it,' he growled.

She glanced around and noted that the nearest patron, a middle-aged woman who was reading a book, was frowning at Connor. And the group of young witches were watching them closely again.

Becca put her mouth next to his ear. 'Not here, pumpkin. We'll talk when we get to our room.'

Five minutes of uncomfortable silence passed – which Becca took as reluctant acceptance on Connor's part as he literally sucked on the slice of lemon from his drink – before the barmaid was back, but so was the owner, Rhiannon. She introduced herself and led them through to a door on a different side of the bar, unfortunately taking them in the opposite direction to that of the tugging of Becca's gift.

No matter. They'd get to it. A bit of midnight creeping around, maybe? She might not have packed a balaclava, but she was sure they could figure out some kind of spell between them to aid their sneaking once they'd got the lay of the land.

They moved into the small, square stairwell and followed Rhiannon up the narrow set of wooden stairs as Becca explained to the Welsh witch how the van had spluttered to a stop as they were on their way to Newquay. How they didn't have a hotel booking anywhere, and had actually driven all the way up to and then down again from Gretna Green in defiance of her father, which Rhiannon responded to as though she happened to be a fan of costume dramas. Either she wasn't with the times, or she was swept up in the romance, because Becca was pretty sure you couldn't actually get married, even at Gretna Green, at the drop of a hat.

'Well, I have the perfect thing for you two lovebirds. We don't use this room much, but it's very romantic.'

Becca turned to give a wide, guileless smile to Connor, who was following with his shoulders hunched, hands shoved deep in his pockets and a scowl etched across his forehead.

They switched back on themselves two times before reaching the first-floor landing. The smell of wood and cool stone always made Becca feel settled, having grown up in old buildings, with their history and strange mix of solidity and fragility as time wore away at them. Even magical buildings couldn't last forever without bricks and mortar crumbling, without wood weakening.

'Here's the key.' Rhiannon held out a brass key, which looked like the kind that would be on a big ring as a prop in a film for a dog to hold in its mouth. As Becca put her palm up to receive it, the cool metal tingled against her skin and then seemingly melted and crawled up over her fingertips, before vaporising and floating off in a cloud of pale silver sparkles that whipped up in a stream and funnelled through the hole in the door.

The locks clicked and the door swung open a few inches.

'That's a neat trick.' Becca smiled at the other witch, who looked rather pleased with herself.

'Isn't it? You won't need a key now. Just place your hand on the handle and the room will let you, and only you, in. We don't do housekeeping, because there are enough charms to see you through your stay, and if you have any issues, you can just let us in. The room technically belongs to you now and won't return to us until your stay here is over.'

'Such clever magic.'

'We like our guests to feel as safe and comfortable as possible. People come to us seeking refuge for all kinds of reasons, so please, take care not to pry into others' business if you get talking to anyone. And likewise, don't feel you have to share anything personal. You can stay as long as you need – the magic of the inn has invited you in.'

Becca forced another smile, trying not to feel guilty about all the lying when they were being so respectful and welcoming. Well, Rhiannon was – the other guests had definitely looked suspicious, but she supposed that, if they were all witches who'd come here seeking refuge, they might be especially anxious about strangers. 'Erm . . . what about my husband? He's not a witch; will the magical key work for him, too?'

Rhiannon nodded, her gaze, when it moved to Connor, slightly more assessing. 'Of course.' She handed Connor another identical key, and it repeated the same process. 'The inn will recognise you, too, now. You won't need to be with your wife to come and go.'

'Thank you.' Connor closed his hand into a fist. 'I'll go and fetch our bags in, shall I?'

Before Becca could even say yes, he'd turned tail and was hurrying back down the corridor, the way they'd come.

Becca bit her lip and caught Rhiannon's concerned look. 'It's been a long day,' she said, and had a strange flashback to the way her mother had always seemed to be issuing embarrassed apologies for her father's rude behaviour.

Rhiannon nodded and patted Becca's hand gently. 'If you need anything, you come and talk to me. There's a bell on the bar that I'll hear no matter where I am. *Anything* at all, at *any* time.' She gave Becca a long look that seemed to be trying to communicate something extra to her, though

Becca wasn't quite sure she knew what it was, and patted her hand once more before she left.

Becca stood on her own in the hallway, suddenly not as keen to go into the 'romantic' honeymoon suite. The long drive, the ups and downs of her worrying about Harry and the situation they'd found themselves in, not to mention following her gift for hours, all rushed in on her. She needed a cup of Zeynep's tea, and to message her and Harry to let them know she was safe and sound.

She pushed the door open fully and soft lamps flickered on. In the centre of the room was an enormous four-poster bed, with pretty lace voiles surrounding it and twinkly lights attached to the canopy. It was gorgeous – and she was pretty sure Connor was going to have an embolism when he saw it.

She closed the door behind her, noticing there was also a clawfooted bathtub over in the corner room. Not in a *bathroom* – in the bedroom, because obviously the occupants of the honeymoon suite would be more than happy to share bubble-bath time. Maybe with champagne.

Becca had never had a night in a hotel like this with an *actual* boyfriend. Now she was supposed to share this beautiful space with the Witches Council's professional thundercloud? Unless he decided to sleep in the van. She realised she didn't even have his mobile number to give him a call and find out where he was. There was a high probability he was walking back to Surrey.

She'd really pissed him off this time, springing the fake relationship on him, which, in hindsight, they possibly hadn't needed to do, given the inn's apparent policy on privacy.

Well, it was done now. He'd just have to get over it. It wasn't *that* big of a deal. It was only a matter of acting slightly more civil towards her than he would to a complete stranger. Why had he been willing to smile and flirt with the barmaid, but he couldn't bear acting like he didn't despise Becca in order to convince people they were newlyweds? They were meant to be a team and they'd come this far.

Fine. He probably did have the hots for the barmaid. And that didn't bother Becca in the slightest.

Of course it didn't.

She had much bigger things to worry about, like finding that amplifier and returning it to her family, where it was needed.

Chapter Eleven

CONNOR

It was nearly eleven o'clock at night and Connor was processing the fact that this probably wasn't even going to be the end of this very long fever dream of a day.

He was used to being asked to go places at short notice. It was the nature of his job. He was *not* used to having a sidekick waiting for him back at the hotel who he was going to have to communicate with, when all he felt like doing was burying his head under a pillow.

There was too much magic at this inn, and there was too much Rebecca Ashworth, full stop. With her 'bright' ideas, and bubbly humour, and her fecking *insanely* pretty brown eyes, and the way she always seemed to be within touching distance. And now they had to share a bedroom and pretend to be a *couple* because of one of those bright ideas. Was she trying to kill him?

He took a deep breath, leaning against the cold metal of the rear doors to her pink van. She'd said it was her mum's and she hadn't wanted to damage it. But she'd still done it. Either it wasn't as sentimental to her as it seemed, or the stakes regarding this spell the Ashworths were trying to figure out were higher than they were letting on. A secret she was not willing to relinquish, even though she was collecting his without even trying.

He needed to speak to Warren, to find out what they were going to do about it. Even if they got the Ashworths to agree to the anonymity charm, it didn't cover what the Abrogator could do. Just what he was. It was late, though, so he settled for simply texting Warren his location and the supposed set-up of the inn, and that he'd speak to him tomorrow.

He grabbed his and Becca's bags from the back of the van but he hesitated, regarding her camera and laptop. They were both expensive items to leave out in the van. He ran his hand over the doors of the van and found she hadn't placed any kind of theft-deterrent magic on it. Best to take them in, just in case.

Looping the extra straps around his neck, he locked the van back up with his magic, adding a quick ward, and went back down the road to the entrance to the property. Surprisingly, he didn't need to bypass the wards; they did recognise him, just as Rhiannon had said. The magic must have been reading him as an ordinary non-magical person, just like the key had. It wasn't trying to work upon him – it was just recognising his biological make-up.

The key, the hedge and just walking around the building had all given him enough of a sense that the place was riddled with old, old magic – the threads of which were more complicated to read than modern spells, like learning to decipher Shakespeare. It was very similar to Ashworth Hall in that way. Which could be a coincidence . . . or not.

Maybe the Ashworths had been the ones to steal the amplifier from this inn, once upon a time, when the family thought they were entitled to everything, and women and the Irish and any other minority who weren't male, blue-blooded aristocrats were all inferior? Just because a toffee-nosed ghost said it belonged to them, didn't mean it was necessarily true.

And regardless of any of that, Connor knew one thing for certain – the inn was going to make him feel on edge, the same way Ashworth Hall had. His skin wired, his head aching. The sooner they got this amplifier, and some answers, the better.

He cracked his neck as he headed for the front door. The first answer he wanted was what the hell Becca had been thinking when she'd announced they were newlyweds.

'I was thinking,' Becca said as she sat on the bed, propped up by a multitude of pillows, sipping blackcurrant tea like the lady of the manor preparing for a busy day of carriage rides and gossiping, 'that we needed to have a plausible back story for travelling around in the middle of Cornwall, at the dead of night.'

Connor dumped all the bags on the floor and held up his hand to stall her explanation for a moment. The thick wooden door was shut behind him, but he hadn't investigated the room for magical means of being overheard – or even figured out whether an ear to the door would suffice to eavesdrop on them. It was his own fault for asking her as soon as he walked through the door – but in his defence, the sight of the disgustingly romantic room with the enormous focal point of the bed had tipped his irritation over into despair.

'If you're worried about acoustics, I spelled the boundaries of the room to distort and muffle sound.' She took a sip of tea, and then frowned. 'Hang on – will that work on your voice? What with your "exception to every magical rule" status?'

He glanced around the room, sensing the fresh magic with Becca's vibrant signature, placing them in the equivalent of a sound bubble. 'Depends on the spell.'

'Can we tell by you doing your spell reading,' she wiggled her fingers at the air, 'or shall I go outside the door and you holler and we'll see what happens?'

'Going outside would probably be the most accurate test, but you don't think it will look a mite strange if someone sees you hanging around outside the door trying to eavesdrop on your "husband"?'

'Maybe.' She placed her teacup on the cabinet next to the bed and jumped down from its considerable height. He could have sworn the movement prompted a sprinkle of glitter to swirl in the air surrounding her. 'But trust me to think on my feet.'

'I do trust you to do that – what I don't trust are the actions that follow the thoughts,' he grumbled and went to sit on one of the armchairs by the door.

'You know what they say. Act in haste, repent at leisure.'

'That's meant to be a cautionary saying, not an aspirational quote.' He squeezed the bridge of his nose but heard her soft laugh in response.

He dropped his hand, and she was already at the door. He wanted to toe off his shoes, but it felt so intimate. Too intimate. Too much Rebecca Ashworth. Too much magic. He was so over this day. Even this armchair cushioned him with a net of well-meaning magic, trying to force the tension from his muscles. *Ha. Good luck with that.*

Becca slipped outside, closing the door behind her, without bothering to put her shoes back on. She had no such qualms about making herself at home. She seemed to feel entirely at home no matter where she was.

Now he had to think about something to say that would not incriminate them if someone else happened by and the spell wasn't working on him. What was a plausible thing for someone to overhear?

Pitching his voice at a slightly louder-than-conversational volume, he began to sing 'I Will Survive' by Gloria Gaynor. He only realised he'd closed his eyes and tipped his head back against the armchair, and was tapping his hands and feet to create his own beat, making it all the way to a musical interlude, when he heard the sound of the door closing again.

'A classic,' Becca said, standing over him, now holding a wicker basket and wearing a big grin. 'I need to add that one to my "angry woman" playlist.'

'So you could hear me from outside?'

'Not the words, just the melody of your dulcet tones, which is how the spell is supposed to work. And you did progressively get louder, so it was a thorough test.'

His cheeks warmed and he cleared his throat, sitting up. 'Well, you're right, it is cathartic.' Her smile widened and she put the basket on the coffee table in front of him. 'Where did that come from?'

'The barmaid came upstairs, of course. Typical timing. I had to say that I thought I'd lost something in the hall. Lucky she doesn't know what my gift is, eh?' She started poking about in the basket. 'Oooh, look, they've put scones and jam in here. Apparently, it's a welcome basket they usually have ready in the room for people. Which I thought was odd. How do they know people are coming?'

'Maybe one of them is a seer?'

'Maybe . . . but my dad has a clairvoyant gift and it's vague. All seer magic is notoriously so, isn't it?'

'You think the amplifier could be helping to make it more specific?'

She gave a one-shouldered shrug, looking more troubled than he had seen her in hours – and that included when they'd been walking through a magical hedge with no idea what kind of reception awaited them on the other side.

'It could also be that the magic on the property tells them somehow,' he volunteered, not wanting to examine why he felt the need to try to make her feel better. 'The enchantments on this place are deep and complex.'

She nodded slowly, and then another smile pulled at the corner of her mouth. 'Of course, it might just have been that she wanted to apologise for flirting with my "husband".' She winked at him and opened a packet of biscuits.

'That's . . . *what*?' He watched her pull a shortbread finger out of the plastic tray and bite into it. 'What are you talking about?'

'Downstairs. The barmaid. You two definitely had a *frisson* of some kind and I cannot blame you – she's stunning. But I didn't think it would do our back story any favours.' She took another bite of her biscuit, leaving tiny crystals of sugar glinting on her lips.

Connor blinked and rubbed at his forehead. There was so much about that which made no sense to him, not least because he'd been staring at her mouth. 'I . . . we didn't . . . we didn't have a back story at that point. Is that why you made it up, because you thought I was flirting?'

'No,' she said a little too quickly, and she turned away, heading back to the bed and her tea. Her cheeks were pink when she lifted her cup and sipped at the fruity liquid.

Connor swallowed hard and let the silence spool out between them, not daring to let himself even think about what the possible hint of embarrassment was suggesting.

'I just figured that most people seeing us travel together this late at night would assume we are a couple,' she finally explained. 'And that it wouldn't reflect kindly on you if they thought you were flirting with someone with your partner standing right next to you. We don't know who we're going to have to endear ourselves to in order to get access to the amplifier, do we? Best to keep our options open.'

'A member of staff will probably have the most opportunity with regard to access. Maybe it would have been more prudent to just say we were friends or work colleagues and let me flirt with her.'

Her brown eyes flicked up. 'So you *were* flirting with her?'

'I didn't say that.'

'It really seemed like you were. You *smiled* at her. That's practically a declaration of love for someone like you.'

'What d'you mean, someone like me?'

'Well . . . someone who doesn't smile very easily.'

'You've barely known me for a day and managed to cause me injury twice in that time. Maybe I smile all the time when I'm not around *you*.'

'Ouch.' She flinched, as if he'd assaulted her with a physical blow. 'Is your head still hurting? Would you like one of Zeynep's teas? It's working wonders for me.'

He stared at her for a moment, feeling like he was having a moment of clarity within a night of drunkenness. Just realising what a dick he'd been. And she had just taken it, as if he were being *fair*, and then offered to try to make amends. She *was* trying to kill him . . . with kindness. An apology stuck in his throat, the same way it had when he'd realised he'd hurt her elbow. Remembering that just made him feel worse.

He sighed, defeated in the face of her compassion and his utter ineptitude at human interaction. 'Is that the magic tea?'

'Yes. She is amazing. This one helps me when I can't get to a lost object quickly and it's like a little woodpecker, peck-peck-pecking at my brain. But she does all sorts of others, too, and tailors them to whatever your specific ailments are . . . Oh, that won't work on you, will it?'

He shook his head.

'That's rough.' She bit her lip and then drained the last of her tea, jumping down to pick up her handbag and pull out the tin her friend had given her. 'But . . . even if the magic won't work, some of them just have natural remedies in them. This one is for a normal headache. Want to try it?'

'It depends. Is it gonna taste of nettles and dirt?'

'No. But I can go out and dig some up for you if that's your preferred flavour.'

He looked at her; a dimple appeared in her cheek as she tried to hide a smile. Something warm poked him right in the chest and a wheezy sound came out of his throat that he realised was his laugh, resurrected from its tomb. 'That won't be necessary, but I appreciate the offer.'

Her smile, usually so quick to appear, spread slowly across her face as she looked at him. She went over to the kettle again. 'Right, so. One non-dirt tea coming up. Then, I guess, we'd better make a plan of action and address the elephant in the room. Sleeping arrangements.'

Chapter Twelve

BECCA

After weighing up the fact that they had no clue of the layout of the inn, with the exception of the bar and the room they were in, the plan for the amplifier hunt was to wait until daytime and figure out the movements of the staff and guests and whether they could easily access the place Becca's gift was telling her to go.

They were both tired and didn't want to act any more suspiciously than they might already have done, between turning up so abruptly and Becca being caught loitering in the hallway. The beautiful barmaid had looked very concerned when Becca had said she'd lost something, but that might have been because she could hear Connor warbling his seventies disco hit in the background, even if she couldn't make out the words.

Becca had been so right – he could totally carry a tune.

Finding him in the armchair, relaxed, eyes shut and mid-song, had been a thrill akin to finding him naked. Between that and having him actually laugh at her teasing joke about the tea – which must mean they really were as good as married, using her grump-o-meter – she was beginning to realise that she was more than a little attracted to him.

By now his personality should have been outweighing her biological and sociological programming. Particularly his rather prickly attitude. Instead, the attraction was settling in – like a cat curled up on her lap, stubbornly content regardless of your other priorities.

It was a little inconvenient, now they were having to share a room . . . and potentially a bed . . . but as she'd said to Connor when they'd started the sleeping-arrangement argument, they were both adults. They could share a bed – especially a bed that size – without it needing to be weird.

Connor had proceeded to say that he could push the two armchairs so they were opposite each other and stretch across them to sleep. Becca refuted the stability of the proposed engineering of that. He countered with offering to sleep in the bath, which admittedly he wouldn't fall off of, but Becca didn't want to deal with a Connor who had a cricked neck, aching back and sore knees from folding his six-foot-four frame into a hard ceramic tub. He didn't need new, legitimate reasons to be grumpy.

'We could top and tail if you'd prefer,' she offered as she pulled some pyjamas out of her bag, along with her toiletries.

'And have your feet in my face?'

'I would be the one with feet in the face – you would have almost a foot of clear space for your head.'

'And somehow I bet I would still end up kicked and kneed in the back. You have the look of a fidgeter.'

'I'm sorry if a small woman in your romantic history has traumatised you, but apparently I sleep like the dead. My ex would splash water on my face because I was so hard to wake up.'

Connor looked affronted to a level that was almost frightening. 'No wonder you like singing songs about what a dickhead he was if he water-boarded you first thing in the morning. He's lucky you didn't blast him across the bedroom . . . or is that why you broke up?'

'No, he dumped me for a whole raft of other reasons.' She waved a hand. 'But let's stay focused. I'm tired and I'm going to get into this dreamy cream puff of a bed. I will roll up the duvet – because it's too hot for a duvet anyway – and place it, with added magical fixatives, down the centre of the bed. To all intents and purposes, it will therefore work like two single beds pushed together and you can sleep safe and sound on the other side.'

Connor didn't appear to have any further arguments, so she sent him off to the en-suite, which luckily *was* in a separate room because the builders of the inn had wisely decided that using the toilet in front of each other wouldn't add to the romantic ambiance. Meanwhile, she quickly got changed herself and stowed her bags around her side of the bed – or the side of the bed she was claiming – but she didn't bother unpacking. Hopefully, they'd be leaving again tomorrow.

He'd brought her camera and laptop in, which had been thoughtful of him. If she woke up early, before they planned to go down to breakfast and do some more staking out, she'd try to get some of the photos of the Year 6 leavers processed. There were only sixty, so she should be able to get those uploaded fairly quickly and the email links sent off.

Levitating the mammoth selection of cushions from the bed and storing them in the bath, she rolled the duvet down, making it into a long sausage, as she'd described to Connor. It was probably no more than a ten tog, so it wasn't going to be that big a barrier, now she looked at it, but there were more than enough cushions to bolster it if he felt he needed more security.

She turned it so it ran down the length of the mattress, over the top of the fitted cotton sheet beneath. Then she clambered onto the bed and used a little spell her mother had once taught her to fix holes in her tights at school. She touched both the underside of the rolled-up duvet and the sheet with each index finger, sending out her magic to lift the tiny fibres, and then brought her fingers together, murmuring the spell, so they adhered to each other like Velcro, working her way down the rolled-up duvet at intervals of a few inches.

Such a practical little spell. Her mum had been creative – as well as also being a medium, she'd had a flair for alchemy, which now would have been acknowledged as a secondary gift – but she'd insisted that you didn't always need to change the fabric of something to make it work. Sometimes it was just a case of taking a closer look and adding a helping hand. Or changing the way you were using the thing in the first place.

Becca sat back and stroked her hand down the rolled-up duvet, smoothing out some of the creases and wondering what her mother would have made of the situation Becca currently found herself in. It wasn't like she'd even had much of a chance to talk to her mum about boyfriends and romantic relationships, let alone how to deal with sleeping next to your faux-husband who you'd only know for a day, since he came to investigate and undermine your family, but who you were still, definitely, attracted to.

'Listen to your heart,' she whispered to herself, because that's what her mother always said. *You've got a good brain; it'll figure out what your heart is trying to tell you – but only if you listen to it.*

'What'd you say?'

Connor's voice made her jump. He was back in the bedroom, now wearing only his boxers and a faded T-shirt, which hung off the sharp angles of his shoulders. His thighs were more muscular than she would have expected, because he had a lean frame overall, but the hem of his boxers caught at them and . . . Goddess, she was staring. Her eyes darted away in a panic and ended up roaming all over his body as she fought an internal battle between her hormonal compulsion and the unwritten etiquette of *not* ogling another human being. The battle left her a little dizzy as her brain greedily filed away the snapshots she hadn't resisted in time, and noted how she could fit snuggly on top of him like the next size down of a babushka doll. Maybe two sizes down. If they got lost at sea she could use him like a raft.

Becca swallowed and reminded herself that her heart had nothing to do with those weird thoughts – it was just attraction. And gender stereotyping. She didn't need a man to be large to make her feel feminine. She. Did. Not.

'Oh, just chatting to myself,' she said, after what she hoped was not too long a pause, and not too obvious an example of her checking him out. She turned and jumped down from the bed. 'I'll go brush my teeth. The sleeping barrier is in place. You can get comfy.'

'Grand,' he replied, in the kind of tone she would have expected someone to use when they'd been invited to tuck down next to a crocodile.

Grabbing her wash bag, she went into the bathroom, leaving him staring at the bed. She almost thought he'd still be standing there when she came back but he had turned off the lights and slipped under the top sheet, his back turned to the central reservation of the bed, his head buried in one of the big, puffy pillows.

Becca walked carefully around to her side, in case he'd already fallen asleep, and climbed into bed too, the cotton sheet settling coolly over her. She could barely see him over the bulk of the duvet between their pillows, and the distance between them in this super-sasquatch-sized four-poster was greater than when they'd been sitting next to each other in the van for hours . . . and yet she had to admit there was something so strangely intimate about settling down next to him. It was probably just the quiet and the dark – she could hear his soft breathing – and the vulnerability of trying to fall asleep in the presence of a stranger, in these private hours that were usually only shared with the people you loved or at least trusted.

And she *must* trust Connor on some level. She'd have felt confident in her ability to protect herself against any man because she knew the magical power she was packing. Connor hadn't been wrong to assume she could blast someone across a room if she thought she was under attack. But Connor himself was a different kettle of tea. *He* could roll over while she was sleeping and drain her of every ounce of magic with the touch of his hand – if that was how he did it. He could render her completely helpless. Perhaps she should have considered that before putting them in a position where they were sharing a bed. Maybe Drew was right when he said that she was always too self-assured and one day it was going to get her into trouble.

But nothing about Connor was giving her any red flags. *He* was the one who should have been running from her since she'd got them into this one-room situation and he did tend to have a jump scare anytime she touched him.

He moved onto his back, slowly, as though he was trying to move quietly, so as not to disturb her. He raised his arm and pressed it over his eyes.

'Did the tea help your head at all?' she whispered.

There was a pause and she figured he was trying to decide whether to pretend he was sleeping or not. 'Yeah. It did a wee bit, thanks.'

'Good . . . I am sorry for causing you injuries today.'

He sighed. 'It's OK, they weren't really your fault. And . . . I'm sorry, too.'

'For what?'

'Your elbow.' He was still talking with his arm pressed over his eyes, but his feet shifted down at the bottom of the bed, making the sheets rustle. 'I shouldn't have pushed you off me like that. So roughly. I was—'

'Winded? Surprised? Angry? All very valid and understandable.'

'No. There is no excuse.'

'Well, you're forgiven anyway. I know you didn't mean to hurt me. I'm not even sure it *was* you. It more likely happened as I fell out of the tree.'

He lifted his arm a fraction, turning his head ever so slightly in her direction, and the moonlight caught at the longer inky curls of his hair, but she still couldn't see his face over the duvet or the shadow of his forearm, and he didn't answer, other than to make a soft grunt. It vibrated through the mattress, and it shouldn't have turned her on, but her brain automatically leapt to other inarticulate noises that occurred in bed.

'This is kind of like having a sleepover when you're a kid, isn't it?' she said out loud, because it was not *at all* like any sleepover she'd had as a child, but she needed to get control of her rampant imagination.

'Not even slightly.' He echoed her secret internal thoughts, and she wondered if he was experiencing similar intrusive fantasies. Based on his allergy to her touch, probably not. 'It is a bit like boarding school, though.'

She lifted herself up on her elbows to look over the duvet. 'You went to one of the magical boarding schools?'

'Yes. Why? Is that hard to believe?'

'No. I was just fascinated by them. When I was a kid and I slept over at Ashworth Hall, me and Harry and—' She flinched as a pain tightened across her skull – she must have trapped a nerve by hunching her tired shoulders. She dropped her head forward again and rubbed the back of her neck as she continued: 'We'd pretend we were away at boarding school.'

'You didn't get sent to one?'

'No.'

'Huh. I thought all the oldest witching families packed their kids off there as soon as they could.'

'Not the Ashworths. It's important to the family that we grow up as part of the Biddicote community.'

'So the decision's still dictated by legacy, then?'

'I suppose . . .' She chewed her lip, thinking about some of the expectations her dad had of her, and Harry's parents had of him . . . although since Harry had gone off to Edinburgh to university and then returned home when Uncle Adrian got sick, there had been a shift. An acknowledgement that probably they'd been asking too much by expecting them to follow every precedent set by their ancestors, to centre every aspect of their lives around being an Ashworth . . . that their bond as a family was just as important as their duty to Biddicote. At least from Uncle Adrian and Aunt Elenor. Her dad was as disapproving of everything and everyone as always. 'My mum would never have let me go away to school though, even if that *had* been an Ashworth tradition,' she thought out loud and then gasped. 'Sorry, I didn't mean to imply that it was wrong of your parents to send you.'

Connor waved his hand, dismissing her comment, and finally dropping his arm from his face. 'My mum wasn't around and my dad is non-magical. When it became obvious I was a witch, sending me to Dentwood was the most logical thing to do.'

Becca was tempted to prop her head on the duvet barrier to see his expression. Because he sounded all matter-of-fact about it. But when Becca considered how that would have felt to *her* as a child, she didn't see how he could be so unaffected.

'Did you or your dad know if your mum was a witch?' It was rare for a witch to be born to two non-magical parents, but it did happen due to dormant genes. And Connor was an extremely rare specimen already.

'No. I don't really remember her, and if she was a witch, she must've hidden it from him. My dad was blindsided when my magic came in properly and the Witches Council turned up on our doorstep.'

Becca's eyes widened and she was glad he couldn't see *her* expression. OK, so that sounded dreadful. Having his magic arrive and no parent to tell him what was going on. Then being sent away.

'Being at Dentwood must have been a relief, getting to be around other kids like you—'

'The kids *weren't* like me,' he cut her off. 'They were from old English witching families who have known everything about the magical world since they could comprehend speech, and think they are entitled to run it just because they can trace their magic back through umpteen generations.'

Becca swallowed. 'That doesn't sound like the experience I imagined. No midnight feasts, laughing until you were sick and had to hide the evidence from the teachers?'

'Dentwood is an institution, not a holiday camp. Although *your* experience there probably would have been a bit more fun.'

Because you're one of them, were the unsaid words implied by his bitter tone.

'That sucks,' she murmured to herself. Mostly for him, but honestly a little bit for herself, too, because it sounded like he had some deep-rooted and not entirely unfounded prejudice against old witching families. But . . . 'I wouldn't have treated you like that.'

'I didn't say how I was treated.'

'You didn't really have to.'

'Well, either way, you wouldn't have been in my dormitory because you're a girl, and you wouldn't have been in any of my classes either because you're older than me.'

'Am I?' She smiled a little at the surprising tidbit, because he couldn't be that much younger – he'd been the Abrogator for nearly ten years. 'Find that out from my file, too, hmm?'

'Yes.' He wasn't even bothering to pretend he didn't have a dossier on her now. 'Nearly three years.'

'So you're closer to Harry's age. He definitely would have been kind to you.'

'Would he now?'

'Yes.' She couldn't help the defensiveness in her tone.

He made that grunt again, but this time it didn't make her go warm; she was too busy watching him roll over onto his shoulder, turning his back to her again. She waited to see if he would say anything else, and when it became apparent he would not, she laid her own head down on the pillow and tried to sleep.

It was a warm night, but that wasn't the reason that she couldn't get off to sleep. Despite the tea, her gift was tugging at her, making her head tight with tension, and every noise Connor made left her hyper-aware of him. Over there. Being attractive and not liking her. Or her family.

Sometimes her desire to make the best of every situation came up against truly shitty circumstances and she just had to let the desire go. This seemed like it was going to be one of those times, in more ways than one.

Then there was the way she was thinking about Harry now. She knew that the hypothetical scenarios she was talking about when it came to boarding school weren't as clear cut as she'd just made out. If their parents had wanted to send them to boarding school, they would have had different priorities than the sense of community which was the backbone of her family. But she was certain that Harry's kindness and generosity was not solely a product of his mum and dad's teachings about the Ashworth duty to Biddicote. It was his nature, and she hated the thought that the way he was always prepared to put other people's needs before his own was going to make him ill.

She couldn't bear the thought of losing him.

And she was in the same building as the amplifier that should fix it all – yet she was lying in bed, having to wait. She'd thought Connor was impatient earlier, but she wasn't exactly great at twiddling her thumbs either when things needed to be done.

She didn't know how long it had been that they were both trying to get off to sleep. The inn was quiet – there had been some soft footsteps in the distance, closed doors and wishes of goodnight between guests, but it had long since gone silent. Apart from the increasing noises of Connor moving around. Kicking his feet out from under the covers. Turning his pillow over. Going from his back to side to front to side again – but never facing her.

Eventually, she cracked. 'Holy grimoire, and you accused *me* of being a fidgeter.'

'It's hot,' he muttered.

'So take off your T-shirt and open the window. We can use magic to get the breeze swirling. I'm surprised you didn't think of it – you obviously don't like the heat.'

'I do usually do that spell, but . . .'

'What?'

'I didn't want to make you cold.'

She turned her face into the pillow to stop herself from groaning out loud. Oh, Goddess, why was he so unexpectedly sweet? It wasn't fair that he hated her, and she wasn't supposed to like him either, but he kept sneaking these little moments in to throw her decision to detach herself completely out of balance.

She emerged from the pillow, keeping her voice level. 'That's OK, I can add more layers. When you're too hot you can't take off your skin.' *Way to make it gross there, Becca.* Maybe gross was for the best, though. She shouldn't be indulging in a crush on the Abrogator, poster boy of the Witches Council's authority.

He got up and went to the window, opening it a crack and then casting a quick spell to keep the air moving gently through the room, like a fan. He didn't take his T-shirt off until he got back to the bed, sitting on the edge, his back to her.

She tried to shut her eyes. She really did. But there was something that refused to let them close those extra couple of millimetres. Instead, she looked through her lashes as he pulled the T-shirt over his head, caught the quick reveal of shadowy skin before he lay back down on the other side of the duvet barrier.

They needed to get this amplifier sorted *tomorrow*. She

needed to make sure Harry was going to be well. And she needed her and Connor to go their separate ways. Another night in this hotel room with him was going to have her drumming her foot like a cartoon rabbit. And the worst part was, this was all her fault. She was the one who had volunteered that they were newlyweds.

'Better now?' she asked.

'Yeah. Thanks. You're not sleeping either. Is your gift bothering you?'

'Only a little.'

'You want me to make you another tea?

'No, thanks.' She sighed, feeling the sleepiness creeping up on her now. Maybe half the tension had been because she'd been trying to go to sleep while she thought he was upset with her. Or, at least, had reminded himself why he didn't like her. Now he was being all sweet again. 'You know what might help?'

'What?'

'You could sing me a lullaby.'

He paused before he said, 'Feck off,' but there was that strangled little laugh in his throat again, and her mood lightened a bit more.

She smothered her own giggles in the pillow. As they tailed off, she heard him say, 'Go to sleep now, Becca,' soft but firm, and another thrill went down her spine.

Chapter Thirteen

CONNOR

A strange scraping noise woke Connor.

He could tell it was light without opening his eyes, but that didn't mean it was a reasonable hour. In the summer the sun was up and assaulting his eyelids at stupid-o'clock until the blessed release of autumn.

At first, he had no recollection of where he was. None of his senses were giving him references that he recognised. He was used to staying in budget hotels in town centres – they were the most convenient and the least likely to be riddled with magic. He was *not* used to perfectly comfortable and generous mattresses, adorned with Egyptian cotton sheets, deliciously plump pillows and a gentle breeze cooling his skin, even while it hummed with awareness of the magic surrounding him. He wasn't used to some sort of fruity scent – maybe peaches? – delicately threaded in the air he was breathing. Nor the steady sound of someone *else's* breathing in the same room as him.

The same bed as him.

His eyes flew open despite the rude glare of sun and everything was fluttering white fabrics and pale morning light and Becca.

She was still asleep, but they were as close as they could possibly get without one of them breaching the world's least sturdy barricade.

Or without breaching it *completely*, he should say. Because they were both hugging it. Becca's head was snuggled up

147

to the side of it, utterly ignoring her pillows, and she had one arm and leg propped over it.

His leg was also hooked over it, and yet somehow they had managed not to touch.

His chest eased at the realisation. He hadn't touched her. They were just close. Her knee was up so high she was almost in the foetal position, whereas his was beneath hers . . . they were like the zig-zag of a broken mirror, pieces lined up but not glued back together.

Her dark auburn hair had fallen out of its bun in messy clumps, one of which trailed across her face and partially over her chin. Her lips were slightly parted and her eyelashes fanned her cheeks beneath the almost straight lines of her eyebrows. She wasn't frowning; her face was completely at rest, making her look younger in the way that everyone did when they were sleeping, and it made him wonder what she *had* been like as a teenager. How she would have been if she'd gone to Dentwood. He didn't know her well enough to figure it out, but something he did know was that he would have been completely infatuated with her.

Maybe that was part of the reason that he couldn't bear the conversation they'd been having in the dark last night. She'd been so convinced that she and her cousin wouldn't have treated him badly, but he'd felt that cliquishness even in the short time he'd been in their company at Ashworth Hall. They were of a different world to him.

The scratching noise came again.

He rolled away as quietly as he possibly could and pushed himself upright, looking around the room for a clue as to where the noise was coming from, and encountering more visual reminders of what trouble this woman was as he looked around the *honeymoon* suite. Holy fecking grimoire.

Scritch, scritch, scritch.

It could have been birds picking at the shingle around the window, but it wasn't coming from that direction. Swinging his legs out of the bed, he levered himself up and narrowly missed smacking his forehead on a wooden beam across the ceiling dormer. The likelihood of him having another day without multiple head injuries in this old inn, built for pint-sized people, was not looking great.

Keeping his swearing under his breath, he realised the scratching and scrabbling was coming from the other side of the door to the hall. He swung it open quickly, hoping to shock whoever might be attempting to break in on the other side, one hand raised and ready to react with magic if necessary.

A streak of black immediately zipped around his legs and jumped up onto the foot of the bed. Connor rubbed his eyes and looked out into the hall to check there wasn't anything or anyone else out there, and then turned to regard the . . . cat?

It was large and black and busy licking its paws and cleaning its face. Connor tilted his head and the light seemed to go straight through it.

Right, so, a ghost cat.

'Why didn't you just walk through the damn door, instead of waking me up?' he grumbled, pushing the door shut again since he didn't have to worry about trapping it inside.

As he came closer, the cat stopped cleaning and regarded him with yellowy-green eyes. It came to the corner of the bed and bumped its head against Connor's hand.

Weird – he could feel it. Had he imagined that it was a ghost? He rubbed its head, feeling heat and the tickle of hair, but nothing like a real cat. His gift tingled and he very, very carefully directed some of his power to see if he could read the magic involved. He'd never tried it with a ghost before.

It came to him in a wispy impression. Someone had loved this animal so much that their magic had kept it alive longer than it should have been. They'd healed it when it was sick – or taken it to a healer. Perhaps all that extra magical energy had given it a more corporeal form than the average ghost. He pulled his hand away, mindful that he didn't want to start drawing magic from the phantom creature accidentally, and then his phone rang.

The cat scarpered off the bed, racing through the closed door. 'So you *could* have come in without scratching,' Connor muttered, shaking his head and diving for his phone to silence it.

'What was that?' Becca mumbled, still snuggled beneath the sheets. Her relaxed tone didn't suggest she was experiencing any of the disorientation *he'd* had when he'd woken up.

An echoing flash of the anger he'd felt last night when she'd mentioned her ex-boyfriend splashing water on her face to wake her up went through him. She didn't sleep *that* heavily. It was such an aggressive thing to do to someone. He remembered the way his heart had pounded when boys in his dorm would levitate glasses of water over him and tip them out while he was sleeping. The drenching cold shocking him out of the one bit of peace he got during his days there.

'Ghost cat,' he said.

She pushed herself upright in a second, thick hair bouncing around her face and neck as she straightened the strap of her vest, which had slipped down her shoulder. His heart did a little shimmy in his chest.

What was *that* all about?

Probably reflux. He needed some food.

'Where? Has he gone?'

'Yep. No doubt he'll be back, though.' Now he thought about it, perhaps some of the phantom cat's solidity had been because of its proximity to her, with her gift as a medium.

She made a little keen of disappointment, the sound cracking slightly as her voice was still foggy with sleep. She was squinting a little too as she looked in his direction, the focus of her eyes bouncing around like they had last night when he'd come out of the bathroom, ready for bed, and he realised his state of undress might be making her uncomfortable. He snatched up his T-shirt from the floor by the bed and yanked it over his head as she asked: 'What kind of cat was he?'

'Dead.'

She laughed and started to tug the loose band free from her hair and pull it back into some kind of order again. 'Yes, but was he big, small, long-haired, short-haired, ginger—?'

'Black,' he interrupted, thinking that would put a stop to the endless questions. Wrong.

'All black or did he have a bib and booties? A little tuxedo?'

'All black. Maybe you should just get dressed and go find him.'

'Might be a good excuse to wander off into other parts of the inn.' She rubbed her arms and, without even thinking about it, Connor reached out a hand, feeling for the thread of the spell he'd cast the night before to create a breeze, and snuffed it out.

Her eyes widened and he dropped his arm and went to grab his clothes. 'Maybe so. You could certainly convince anyone you're obsessed enough with felines to be hunting one down.'

She laughed again. 'I'm not obsessed . . . OK, I'm a little obsessed. It's Michael's fault. He introduced me to the wonder of cats.' She gave a little sigh. 'If I was at home, he would have woken me up this morning with increasingly aggressive chin bumps until I got up to feed him.'

'Sounds grand.'

'It is,' she said, so earnestly, despite his sarcasm, that he had to bite the inside of his lip against the sensation it was causing in his chest. He couldn't keep blaming acid reflux. 'I hope he's not fretting.'

'You've only been away from him a day.'

'The bond between a cat and its human is something very special.'

He grunted. A weak part of him was unable to resist asking: 'Why *is* he called Michael?'

She raised her eyebrows at him, as though surprised he was interested. *He* was surprised he was interested. 'Well, he only has a bit of white around his eyes. The rest of his coat is black, so it made me think of Batman.'

'Batman? Batman's name is Bruce.'

'Yeah, but he didn't look like a Bruce.'

'Still doesn't explain how you got from Batman to Michael.' He shook his head.

'Michael *Kitten* is his full name.'

He narrowed his eyes at her, because she was focused on him with an adorable look of anticipation and patience on her face, as if she knew it'd come to him and was just waiting for the penny to drop. As if he could think of anything other than highly inappropriate things when staring at one of the most gorgeous women he'd ever met, surrounded by rumpled sheets in a four-poster bed. The strap of her vest had slipped down her shoulder again and he wrestled his mind into thinking of the conversation before the fact that he was only wearing his boxers became incriminating.

'Oh . . . I get it. Like Michael *Keaton*.'

'Exactly.' She lifted her hands in an expansive gesture. 'Is he your favourite Batman?'

'No. I mean, they all have their strengths and weaknesses, but his was the only name that fitted with a cat pun.'

Connor found himself running through all the actors who had played Batman and shaking his head. 'You could have called him Robert. Like, Robert *Catt*inson.'

Becca's brown eyes widened. 'Goddess, you're *right*. How did I not think of that?' Then she shook her head, too. 'Nope. Actually, it wouldn't have worked. I went out with someone called Rob once; it would have reminded me of him all the time. I must have subconsciously eliminated him from the running on that basis.'

The 'once' indicated that this was further back in time than the ex-boyfriend she was talking about last night, but probably just as crappy by the sounds of it. The reasoning behind her 'angry woman' songs was getting more and more understandable . . . not that he should care even slightly about her dating history.

'Who's your favourite Batman?' she asked, getting out of bed.

He turned away to check his phone, which had spooked the ghost cat in the first place. Missed call from Warren. He was right not to answer it. He couldn't have a frank conversation with him while Becca was in the same room. He'd have to find a time to call him back in private.

'Connor?'

'Hmm?' He looked up, simultaneously sending a quick message to Warren that he'd call him back as soon as he could.

'Who's your favourite Batman?'

Connor dared to glance at her and saw that she was sending that same guileless smile at him. But he knew she had plenty of guile. He'd witnessed it yesterday both at Ashworth Hall and when they arrived here – coming up with plans to get into the place and a 'back story' for them.

'A sad-boy billionaire? Goes around beating up henchmen and bad guys, rather than rehabilitating the deprived areas of the city and giving the people living there better choices than a life a crime? No. I don't have a favourite Batman, they're all rubbish.'

Becca's eyebrows climbed. 'Whoa. I mean, good point about the rehabilitation, but purely from a sense of *fun,* you must have a favourite.'

He rolled his eyes. Why did his grumpiness never seem to shut her down. She was so . . . resilient, in this infuriating way, because she acknowledged his complaints, rather than shooting them down. 'Fine. In that case . . . Adam West.'

'Oooh, good answer. The OG.'

'Glad you approve,' he replied, sarcastically. 'Think we can get on with the day now?'

'Of course.' She straightened up from rummaging in her bag and shook out some flowery material. 'You want to use the bathroom first, or shall I?'

Chapter Fourteen

BECCA

If Becca had harboured any illusions that Connor would be more cheerful after a good night's sleep, she would have been disappointed. By the time she'd made the bed, he'd cleaned up the mugs of tea from last night, and they'd both dressed – her in a suitably cool and comfortable jumpsuit, and him in another monochrome combination of shirt and trousers guaranteed to encourage heat stroke. They were ready to go downstairs to get breakfast. The tugging in her mind was a distraction, but she was used to it to a certain degree.

Before they left, she stopped by the door, blocking his progress. 'Listen, I'm not suggesting we go for any showy PDA or anything, as part of this ruse – I'm not trying to force myself on you and make you uncomfortable – *but* it might prevent any suspicion about us if you do, just occasionally, act as if you *like* me. Throw me the odd smile, maybe?'

One of his eyebrows lifted slowly as he considered her words and then he gestured towards the door. 'Noted. Let's go.'

The downstairs looked even prettier in the daytime, though Becca would have bet that it's best time of year was evenings in the autumn and winter when the two fireplaces – one in the centre bisecting the room and the other at the exterior wall to the right – were lit. The bar was empty, with sunlight illuminating the room, making all the brickwork warm and the deeply varnished woodwork gleam, the bottles behind the bar a rainbow of colours like a Rembrandt painting. There were pictures all around, as well as the tankards hanging from the beams, and she wanted to go around and have a look at all the details, but they had an agenda.

Voices came from the doorway Becca had been trying to see through last night and which she could now make out was actually a dining area. Calling it a restaurant would have been a stretch, but there were smaller tables with ordinary wooden chairs, rather than the armchairs and padded benches in the bar. They stepped down onto large pale-beige flagstones and a few of the other guests looked up from their coffees, but it wasn't quite as aggressively curious as it had been last night.

It was an odd sensation, entering the room and knowing they were being assessed as a couple. Did they look like a strange match? How much of the first impression these other people had of them was based on what they looked like and how they acted together, rather than independently?

The blonde barmaid was there again, serving a middle-aged woman a plate of something steaming gently, and the whole room was full of the scents of bacon, toast and coffee.

'Oh, yes, proper coffee,' Becca murmured. She loved tea, but this morning definitely warranted a harder hit to get herself firing on all cylinders.

'Sit anywhere you like,' the barmaid called over to them. She looked pale this morning, with dark smudges under her eyes, and it was no wonder if she'd been working until nearly midnight and was up again this morning to serve breakfast. 'Oh, apart from that one,' she added, pointing to a small table closer to the kitchen, which had a clutch of wildflowers in a little white jug at the centre.

That was no trouble as far as Becca was concerned, since she wanted the table nearest the door at the back, where her gift was pointing her. Connor took her lead and they settled into the chairs, warmed by the sunshine coming in through the small leaded windows behind them. Becca scooted her chair closer to his and tried not to take offence at the way he stiffened. At least he didn't lean away.

'Through that door,' she murmured.

'The blue "Staff Only" one?' he replied, in an equally low tone that seemed to sneak in and tickle some aphrodisiac switch in her brain.

Ignoring the goosebumps, she replied: 'Yes. Can you see if it's warded?'

'No. I can sense that there's magic everywhere, but unless I touch something that holds the magic, I can't read the details of the spell.'

'But you did the thing this morning, to turn off the magical air-conditioning?' She waved her hand in a similar fashion to how he'd seemed to affect the magic without touching anything. Even when it appeared that magic was being done in thin air, it usually had some kind of catalyst – a touch of friction, a natural breeze or moisture, and even if you were reversing your own spell, it took more concentration and time than a casual click of your fingers. For other witches anyway.

'That was something else—' He shook his head and dropped his voice even lower. 'This probably isn't the place to get into it, since we're in public and I'm not meant to be a witch at all.'

'True.' Becca glanced around the room. There was no way of slipping through that 'Staff Only' door without it being witnessed by someone. 'Should we just cut our losses and speak to the manager? Come clean?'

Connor blew out a slow, measured breath and folded his arms on the edge of the table, leaning in closer to her. The solemnity of his expression probably stopped it from looking romantic to anyone watching. 'We could, but what do we know about her? I could try to get some information, but until we have a better idea of who these people are and what their game is, I'm reluctant to confront someone with the power of this amplifier behind them. There are a lot of people here if it gets ugly. I can't protect them all.'

Becca tilted her head, looking at him. Soft curls and cheekbones. She never would have imagined the infamous Abrogator was a twenty-seven-year-old who concerned himself with protecting people.

'OK. I hear you,' she said slowly. 'So we need to find out about the staff, figure out if we can get back there undetected, or when the place might be empty?'

He nodded but didn't speak again, and Becca realised it was because he had noticed the barmaid – or waitress now? – coming over. He leaned back in his seat again, so far away she was concerned he might tip the chair. Was he feeling self-conscious because he *wanted* to flirt and couldn't any more because of Becca's back story, or because she had pointed out that the *woman* had been flirting with him?

'Morning.' The lady in question tucked her hands in the pockets of the apron she was wearing – the white ties of it accentuating her nipped-in waist and generous hips and bust.

'Hi.' Becca smiled up at her, finding her brain repeatedly catching on the lovely features of the barmaid's face, as if she had a hangnail and was trying to pull on a pair of tights. So weird. It wasn't like she was attracted to her. The man sitting by her side was a very loud reminder of her preferences. 'Working again?'

She shrugged. 'There are only a few of us here to run the inn with Rhiannon, but the magic does a lot of the heavy lifting.'

'The basket last night was lovely. Thank you for that. It's like we were meant to break down here, right, Connor?'

He made a noise that sounded like an agreement and the barmaid/waitress glanced at him quickly and then away again. Her strawberry-blonde hair was in another high ponytail with a cute blue bow fastened on it, ends swinging.

'I'm sorry, I never asked your name before?' Becca said, figuring that if Connor was going to do background checks, they should start with the basics.

'Oh, right.' The barmaid glanced back towards the kitchen, as though she was distracted by something, although Becca couldn't see or hear anything coming from that direction. 'It's Samantha.'

Becca smiled, about to introduce herself and Connor properly, but she was hit with the oddest sensation – like when she would dunk her head underwater and her ears would become all echoey, with the need to drain or pop. She shook her head slightly, and a faint ache started up, making the tug of her gift all the more apparent.

'I'm Becca and this is Connor,' she said, with a split-second delay.

Samantha gave them a thin smile. 'Did you sleep well?'

Becca sent a side-eyed glance to Connor. He was looking at her with another scowl on his face. This one was slightly different to the last one he'd been wearing, which she thought had been more about concentration. He had a whole repertoire of scowls, she was finding, and she had a hunch that this one was more about concern. Perhaps he was worried about what she was going to say about their bedroom antics to perpetuate the idea that they were newlyweds. She allowed herself a sly grin and said with affected innocence, 'Oh, yes, we slept very well, thank you.'

Connor blushed and glared down at the table, and it was all Becca could do not to laugh out loud – because how silly was it for him to be annoyed about her implying that their fake sex life was satisfactory? There were worse things to have to deal with.

Samantha cleared her throat. 'Well, breakfast is a combination affair. You can help yourself to the buffet over there—'

'Great.' Connor shot up from his chair and strode over to the long table in the opposite corner of the room that Samantha had pointed to for a millisecond.

'Or . . . we can cook you something hot. Pancakes, waffles, porridge, full English . . . so, can I get you anything?'

'No, thanks, I'll grab some cereal probably. I'm not much of a one for big breakfasts.'

Becca had no idea why that should make Samantha look like she was going to cry for a split second . . . maybe no one wanted to try her pancakes and she'd got up at 5 a.m. to make the batter? Maybe she was here because she'd needed refuge from something, too, and Becca had just triggered her. Whatever it was, she got herself under control and continued as though the expression had never crossed her face.

'Well, we do lunch at half past twelve and dinner at six. And if you're hungry at any other point, there is usually someone in and around the kitchen all day – just knock.'

So, there was someone here almost all day. The exception probably being the evening, when everyone was in the bar and would notice them coming out into the eating area, when there was literally no excuse to be in it. *Excellent.*

As Samantha left the table, Connor was already coming back with a bowl of fruit salad, some yoghurt and a coffee.

'Ooh, that looks good,' Becca said, standing up as she eyed the melons and strawberries in the silver-and-cream dish he placed on the table. As he sat down, she caught the eye of two of the young people she'd noticed the night before, eating chips in the bar. One leaned closer to the other, whispering, still watching Becca and Connor.

'I brought you coffee because you mentioned it, but . . . I should have asked about what you wanted to eat,' Connor said, his sharp cheekbones still pink.

She blinked, wondering if this was what he thought a husband should behave like. And, of course, every marriage was different, but *she* never would have expected her husband to deliver food to her when she hadn't seen the options. She liked picking for herself. She wasn't going to point that out, though, because they were meant to know each other's quirks and preferences, weren't they?

'Thank you, lovebug, that was really thoughtful.' She pretended to brush a kiss over his hair but didn't actually touch him. It probably just looked like it. She blinked as she noticed him shiver. Was that because of revulsion . . . or something else?

She grabbed herself some fruit, too, going heavier on the blueberries and kiwi, and then a slice of wholemeal toast from one of those conveyor-belt machines, which actually worked because of magic.

When she went back over and tucked in, one of the young men from the next table who'd been watching them came over, holding his coffee, and pulled up a chair without waiting for an invitation.

'Hello,' he said, in a thick Italian accent. 'I'm Frankie.' The friend he'd left back on his own table was now scrolling on his phone, looking about as socially inclined as Connor. 'You're Becca and Connor. You don't need to tell me that.'

'Because you were eavesdropping.' She speared a piece of kiwi and smiled to stop it from sounding like a scold. 'What else do you know about us already?'

'That you're a witch and a non-magical pair of star-crossed newlyweds whose van broke down . . . though you don't look particularly lovey-dovey.'

Connor's eyes narrowed and he stirred his yoghurt aggressively. The somewhat cocky look abated a little from Frankie's face. Before Becca could gently inform the boy that not everyone felt the need to make out in public, Rhiannon breezed into the room and started setting up the reserved table with three place settings and a huge chocolate cake that Samantha brought out from the kitchen.

'Is it someone's birthday?' Becca asked Frankie, since he seemed the type to make things his business.

'No. New guests arriving—' Frankie cut himself off as Rhiannon walked over.

'Good morning, how are you settling in, my lovelies?' She gave them a big smile, pausing between Becca and Connor, inadvertently pointing out the gulf of space Connor seemed to have reinstated between their chairs. But couples didn't have to be glued to each other when they were eating, did they? Becca was grateful for some elbow room.

'Wonderfully, thanks,' she said. 'I was just asking Frankie if it's someone's birthday, but he said more guests are arriving? Is it Bruce Bogtrotter by any chance?'

Rhiannon blinked at her.

'From *Matilda*,' Connor explained, and pointed his spoon towards the reserved table. 'The kid who's forced to eat the enormous chocolate cake.'

'Ohhhh,' Rhiannon laughed. 'No. Not Bruce. A mum and twins, around eight or nine years old. They've had a tough morning already, and the chocolate cake is the kids' favourite. Thankfully, I received the vision just in time to ask Karl to rustle it up this morning. They'll be here in . . .' she checked her watch . . . 'thirteen minutes, so I must get ready to greet them. But you let Sam know if there is anything you need. And young Francesco, no nosing in people's business – you know the rules.' She tapped Frankie playfully on the head and left again in a swirl of her maxi-dress.

Becca couldn't have cared less that Frankie was a bit nosy. In fact, it was great. If she got him on side and he'd been here a while, he could be a valuable fount of information about all the guests and how things worked at the inn.

'Are her visions always so precise?' Connor asked, clearly thinking along the same lines as Becca. 'I thought the, err – seer designation, is it? – was fairly woolly.'

Frankie sipped his coffee. 'I have to admit, I probably have about as much of a clue as you. My mamma is non-magical and left my father when he told her he was a witch, raised me on her own away from his "unnatural ways". She was hoping the magic wouldn't manifest in me, but . . .' He gave a big shrug. 'So, I'm not sure about other seers, but Rhiannon always knows in good time when someone is arriving, and how best to help them settle in.' He tilted his head, his honesty segueing quickly into the nosiness Rhiannon had called him out for. 'Apart from you two. It was a shock, how you suddenly appeared last night. She'd barely had the vision and you were walking through the door.'

'It was a shock to us, too.' Becca injected some wryness into her tone. 'One minute my van was working, the next

163

we'd broken down and there was a whole big building by the roadside that had appeared out of nowhere. Thank the Goddess for it, though.'

Frankie smiled. 'What's wrong with your van?'

'It seemed like an electrical problem.'

'Oh, maybe it just needs a jump start? I could help with that. I have a car.'

'That would be great, thanks.' Becca beamed at him, knowing that it wouldn't work, and would therefore buy them more time and credibility. Although they *were* going to have to figure out how to get it genuinely fixed. That was something they hadn't thought about when they were hatching their plan last night. How they were going to leave when they got hold of the amplifier. Quite the oversight, but they had both been tired.

'After breakfast?' Frankie suggested.

'I'll do it,' Connor offered gruffly. 'You can chill out, Becca, and have a . . . er . . . bath or something.'

Becca smiled. Was that him trying to look like a doting husband again?

'Thank you,' she told him quietly, her voice warm with genuine gratitude. 'I can get that work finished and out of the way, then.'

'Why are you working on your honeymoon?' Frankie asked, his disgust evident.

'Well, it was an impromptu wedding, wasn't it?' She smiled at Connor and looked back at Frankie. 'You probably heard that bit, too.'

'About your dad disapproving? *Si*, like I said, "star-crossed lovers" – very Romeo and Juliet.'

'I fecking hope not,' Connor muttered.

'Right?' She nudged his shoulder. 'Why do people *ever* use that as an example of romance? Even without the multiple murders and double suicide at the end, Romeo is blatantly just thinking with the contents of his trousers.'

Connor gave a faint smirk and she felt like cheering because he'd smiled at her. 'Exactly.' His dark eyes met hers; the light spearing in through the window showed their colour more clearly than she'd ever seen it before – a smoky grey that made her breath catch in her throat. 'He was all "Rosaline, Rosaline" two seconds before. If they'd lived, he would have been having it away left and right, guaranteed.'

'What? He literally killed himself because he thought she was dead. He loved her that much,' Frankie objected.

Becca managed to drag her attention away from Connor. 'Please. He was the ultimate drama queen. And Juliet was just happy to find an attractive alternative to Paris.'

Frankie gave a bemused laughed, assessing them both. 'Maybe I *can* see it with you two.'

'Glad we meet with your approval.' Connor's voice was so dry it could have leached all the coffee from her cup. She pressed her lips down to hold in a laugh.

Frankie held up his hands. 'Sorry, sorry. I think the way my mamma kept the magic secret from me for my entire childhood has left me with the opposite problem. I share my opinions far too easily. And finally being somewhere I can be myself . . .' He gave another expressive shrug.

Becca found herself giving him a sympathetic smile. He couldn't have been much older than eighteen. 'How long have you been staying here?' Becca took a sip of her drink. Connor had even added her one sachet of sugar and the milk to it. He must have noticed when they stopped at the services the night before for a comfort/beverage break.

'Nearly three months.' Frankie leaned forward, lacing his hands around his cup. 'I came to England to find my father, but he wasn't very interested in me and my meagre gift for magic, so I didn't feel welcome there either. My cousin offered for me to stay at his house. But he's on an archaeological dig somewhere in Scotland. He'd left the key in a flowerpot by the door for me, but I couldn't even get to the door, because he'd warded it against trespassers. I thought I was going to have to go back to Italy – though I couldn't afford it and my mamma said not to come back if I was going to go over to the "dark side". Three more months he's going to be away digging up bits of old pot.' Frankie sighed.

'Cernunnos's balls, that's rough.' Becca patted Frankie's arm. 'And I'm really sorry about your dad's crappy attitude. I can't imagine why it should matter how much magic you're capable of, or what you choose to do with it.' She sighed. 'My dad and yours have got some messed-up prejudices in common, unfortunately.'

She glanced at Connor. One of his scowls was back in place as he dumped his leftover strawberries in his yoghurt, mashing them in with his spoon so the thick, creamy substance began to bleed. 'Has no one here mentioned that you could get the Witches Council on the case?' he asked, in a surprisingly even tone, considering the food massacre. 'Could they not lift the magic from his cousin's place?' he asked Becca, as though he wasn't 100 per cent certain they could, and also 100 per cent capable of doing it himself.

Before Becca could join in with the charade, Frankie answered. 'I suppose I could. But I wouldn't want to get my cousin in trouble.'

'He's not going to get in trouble for a warding spell on his house,' Becca said.

Frankie shifted awkwardly. 'When I called him, he admitted there might be a couple of hexes, too. He has a lot of old, valuable things in his house.'

'Oh . . .' she winced. 'That is a bit naughty.'

Frankie snorted. 'Exactly. I do not want to – how d'you say? – burn bridges with the one relative who's been kind to me, by drawing the evil eye of the Abrogator down on him.' He gave a theatrical shudder and Becca's heart stuttered in her chest. 'No. I can stay here in this lovely place and keep safe and sound for a little while longer.'

'This place is a gift,' Becca said, wanting to fill the silence that had threatened to fall over the table. She didn't even dare look at Connor to see his reaction to being referred to as . . . as some kind of terrifying monster. How often did he hear himself talked about like that? That must hurt, when he was the one trying to make people safe. No witch liked the idea of losing their magic permanently, but where had this idea come from that the Abrogator would prey on innocent people? They all knew there was a legal system, but even she used to think of him like that before she met him. Now it seemed grossly unfair.

If it bothered Connor, though, he never showed it. He just finished his breakfast and agreed to meet Frankie out the front of the inn in about half an hour. Frankie went back to his friend and Connor fetched himself some orange juice, while Becca finished her breakfast, did her best to track how many staff were working in and around the kitchen, and to ignore the questions bubbling at the back of her head about what life was like for her temporary ally.

Chapter Fifteen

CONNOR

'Are you OK?' Becca asked when they got back to their room. The honeymoon suite. Which his grumpiness was doing *nothing* to convince anyone that they belonged in together.

Connor hadn't been in any long-term relationships – nor grown up with one in his home. Surely not every couple constantly smiled and threw adoring looks at each other and couldn't keep their hands off each other, like they did on TV or in films?

Becca's relationships probably were like that, though. She never seemed to do anything without being fully invested. She'd said they didn't need to do PDA in their charade, but then she'd brushed that kiss against his hair just because he'd brought her a coffee, and his insides had fair liquefied. He was already feeling paranoid that the other guests thought he was a feckless husband, and then she had to act so sweet and affectionate, as if it were as easy for her as breathing, and make him look even *worse*, because he didn't think he'd even managed to smile at her once like she'd asked.

Why did this even matter? He didn't know these people. And they certainly didn't know who he was. He wasn't even a real person to most witches – he was just 'the Abrogator'. But he did care about the fact he didn't seem to know enough about healthy, loving relationships to fake one.

'Why wouldn't I be?' he replied, pushing the door shut behind him with an unnecessarily strong kinetic spell that made it slam, which left him annoyed at himself for releasing his tension through his magic and demonstrating that he wasn't OK at all.

Maybe it wasn't just about his pride being dented. Maybe it was the magic making him twitchy again. The effect here wasn't as intense as in Biddicote, but it was still all around him.

'Frankie, I guess.' Once again, she took his bad mood in her stride and just carried on talking to him as if he were a reasonable human being, rather than a cranky old goat. He was getting a little sick of *himself* at this point. 'Oh, wait—' She tilted her head as though she were listening to something.

There. A soft, intermittent buzzing.

She picked up a saucer off the coffee table and went over to the window by the bath, where a bee was bashing its head repeatedly against the glass. She used a touch of gentle magic to blow the bee onto the saucer and tipped it out of the window so it could fly off, back into the world.

'Now. Where were we? Err . . . yeah, Frankie, acting like you're the big bad wolf. I'm sorry about that.'

Connor swallowed, watching her put the saucer down on the windowsill, as if that would be a good place to have it, because she fully intended to quietly deal with all the bees while they were here.

It was such a stupidly small thing to do for him. She'd held on to that knowledge and reacted, without comment, in the interest of his welfare. It was another reminder of how alone he'd been for so long. And if he didn't want that to hurt, to eat him up inside, he had to remind himself that there was a very good reason for him being alone.

'You don't need to feel sorry for me. I *am* a monster when it comes to witches.'

She raised her eyebrows a bit, but then shook her head. 'But . . . his cousin wouldn't really be in *serious* trouble, would he? He wouldn't end up on your, like, hit list or something, would he?'

'A witch putting dangerous curses on their property without caring how it might hurt others? Especially someone young and naive to magic like Frankie?' At best it was ignorantly disregarding the fact that Frankie hadn't grown up around magic, and at worst it was malicious magic. 'I should be finding out his cousin's name and reporting it.'

'Oh.' She nodded, but the disappointment on her face was clear. Best he made sure she realised here and now – he wasn't some poor misunderstood witch. He was exactly what the others thought – the black hole of magic that stood between everyone and dangerous witches. And to do that, he had to accept being just as dangerous.

Holy grimoire. Did he subconsciously think *he* was Batman?

No. He wasn't rich and he didn't have a playboy alter ego. Plus, he was part of the law enforcement. Not some rogue vigilante.

'If you *do* want to say sorry for something, it could be apologising for telling everyone I'm not a witch – so now I can't use my magic at all.' He crossed his arms. 'It's fecking hard remembering that I'm not supposed to know all the ins and outs of magic, not to mention that I could have taken him to that house and lifted the curses for him.' Although, by the sounds of it, this inn was offering Frankie more than his so-called family.

'Right. Sorry.' She winced. 'It was an on-the-spot decision and I suppose I subconsciously assumed you were more used to the secrecy than I am. Obviously, I have to hide my magic around non-magical people, but I live in Biddicote. You . . .' She trailed off.

'I have to hide my magic even around witches,' he concluded for her.

'Yeah . . .' She frowned. 'But why is that, again?'

'What?'

'Well, I get why your identity as the Abrogator is confidential. Some witches are anti permanent nullification of magic no matter the charges. And it could put you at risk of retaliation. But . . . your other skills are really useful, and the Witches Council do ask you to use them. So, why haven't they told the witching community there's more to you than nullification?'

'It'd lose me an advantage when I'm trying to get to a dangerous witch. If they think they have a ward that can keep me out, I can take them by surprise.'

'You mean the kind of witches where it's nullify first, ask questions later?'

'The ones hurting people. Yes.'

She nodded slowly, running the tip of her index finger over her bottom lip, as though deep in thought. He wished she'd stop that; it was making him think about how soft her mouth looked. Then she did stop, and that was worse because *he* wanted to touch her lip now it was available.

'It's more of an open secret within the Witches Council upper echelons, though, right?' she asked, and he struggled to remember what they were talking about.

'Err, no. Not really. Very few people know and you're going to have to agree to the anonymity charm when we get back.'

'Of course,' she agreed, easily. 'And Kay and Harry. And whoever it was who told Kay.'

'About that. Did she mention to you how she found out?'

'Someone in the folklore department? I'll get their name for you.' She tilted her head. 'The question is, how did *they* know? The simplicity of anonymity charms is what makes them so watertight. The intention of telling reinforces the spell.'

He shook his head, his mind scrambling over too many thoughts at once. Edward was in the folklore department. But he'd agreed to the anonymity charm at eighteen when he came to work in his job at the Council that Warren had gifted him. Becca was right, they were watertight.

And was she really as bothered about it on his behalf as she seemed?

'It's being looked into,' he said, because Warren would definitely be making sure there were no leaks when it came to Connor's position. 'Can I have the key to your van? Since I can't open it how I did last night, what with Frankie thinking I'm non-magical.'

'Sure. It's in my handbag – help yourself.'

He went over to her side of the bed and found her bag, feeling slightly weird that she was willing to just let him go through it. 'How long is your work going to take, d'you think?'

'Oh, maybe a couple of hours, but I don't have to do it all at once. I can finish up later – whether we're here or high-tailing it back to Biddicote.'

'What is it you do?' *Other than drive me to distraction.*

'That little detail not in the dossier?' she teased, and he found himself vaguely annoyed that *she* wasn't annoyed about the file he'd had to leave back in his car. Didn't *anything* ruffle her feathers?

It wasn't that he wanted her to hate him, but he was starting to worry that her perpetual good humour could mean her being treated pretty badly and just letting people get away with it. Like ex-boyfriends who threw water on her face. Or himself being a moody arse with her.

'No. Or, if it was, I didn't read that bit.'

'Not your prime candidate at the time, eh? You were more focused on Kay? Little did you know you'd be stuck with me. Bwa-ha-ha.' She did an impression of an evil laugh, and the contradiction of it coming out of her, with her heart-shaped face limned in sunlight, and a flowery jumpsuit flowing around her, as she'd just shepherded a bee gently out of the window, made his lips drag into an irrepressible smile.

She was too much. He *did* still think that. But with the way his chest kept heating up around her, he was beginning to wonder if it was 'too much' in the same way that looking at the world from the top of a mountain was, or when the winter sun rose over a blanket of snow.

Her impression of a Bond villain had stopped a few seconds ago and she was watching him, her smile slowly easing from her lips, but her brown eyes still wide. And he knew it was because he'd been staring at her, but he couldn't seem to stop himself straight away. There was something frightening and thrilling about holding her gaze – she was a freight train hurtling towards him and all he could do was watch, transfixed.

He cleared his throat and finally looked away, settling her bag back down by the bed. 'Are you going to tell me what you do for a living?'

She fiddled with the strap on her jumpsuit as if she'd never really taken any notice of it before. 'I've already told you. I'm a photographer.'

'Oh, I thought it was a hobby.'

'Well, some might think of it like that. I only really do family and local community events.'

'Why d'you say it like that?'

'Like what?' She dropped her hand from the strap.

'Like . . . apologetic or something.' He quirked an eyebrow. 'Isn't like you to sound humble.'

She gasped and laughed. 'How rude. And entirely accurate.' She came over and sat on his side of the bed. Seeing her there, where he'd slept, made something dark and wanting curl in his gut. 'You're right. I would never usually be so self-effacing.' She smoothed the wrinkles in the white sheet and Connor attempted not to shiver at the thought of her palm gliding over *him*.

'Drew just made me feel a bit embarrassed about it, I guess,' she continued. 'Like it was just a hobby, rather than work. The little rich girl playing at grown-ups. I'd told him how much I'd loved taking the class pictures and how next year would be the first time I'd have taken them for every year the leavers would have been at school – from Reception to Year 6; their whole primary-school journey – and he'd said it was a bit sad to think of all that change happening for *them* and nothing changing for *me*.' She crossed the fingers on both her hands and pulled a face as she deepened her voice: '"Fingers crossed you won't be stuck here in another seven years. I know I won't be."'

'Do you feel stuck?'

'No. I'm proud of what I do. Getting to capture these big moments in people's lives is a privilege – and I love it. Getting paid for it is even better.'

'Drew sounds like he didn't understand what makes you tick,' Connor said. And then, because he couldn't help it: 'He also sounds like a massive dick.'

She laughed again. 'Well, only figuratively.'

And that was Connor's cue to leave. Hearing anything mildly suggestive – even if it was derogatory towards another man – and seeing her sitting there, on his side of the bed they'd shared, was *not* helping him keep his thoughts in order.

He shoved her van key in his pocket. 'When the jump start doesn't work, I'll use the opportunity to look for a member of staff downstairs to get a number for a local mechanic.'

'Thank you. Bet Sam will be willing to help you.' She winked at him.

He shook his head as he left the room, making an effort not to slam the door again in his irritation. Because he couldn't care less about Sam. The only woman occupying his thoughts was Becca. And that was entirely inconvenient and inappropriate.

One benefit of Connor running away from his increasingly awkward attraction to Becca was that he finally got to contact Warren, although again, he could only manage a quick volley of text messaging, as he was waiting outside the inn for Frankie.

Connor: So, Rhiannon, the manager/owner I messaged you about last night, is also a seer. A powerful one. And the barmaid is Samantha. The chef is Karl. For the background checks.

Warren: This is all very vague and not particularly helpful though.

Connor: It's hard to get full names without attracting suspicion.

Warren: Have you considered just getting Rebecca Ashworth to lead you to the amplifier and taking custody of it? I'm not sure why you are delaying.

Connor rubbed a finger along his hairline, unsticking some strands of his hair. Taking custody of it? He thought he was here to see if a dangerous witch had stolen it and make sure things didn't erupt into a volatile confrontation. Maybe he'd misunderstood. There had been a lot going on in the last twenty-four hours. Regardless of what Warren expected him to do once they found it . . .

Connor: There are at least a dozen guests here. If you want to send the enforcers down with warrants we can clear out the inn? But that will mean unravelling all of the warding spells, too, so they can get access. And this place is old. Not to mention it would tip off the thief and they could make a run for it.

Warren: True. You don't want to be on a wild goose chase. Plus, the heritage department would be at my throat. Have you at least managed to get any more clues from Rebecca about what her family are up to?

Connor: Not really. But she did tell me that the person who leaked my identity to Kay was in the folklore division. Do you think it could have been Edward?

Warren: Of course not! How would that even be possible? Far more likely that when Kay was rummaging in our restricted files she discovered it. Don't let Rebecca take you in. She's an Ashworth. They are canny. Keep me up to date.

Becca *was* canny. Connor couldn't deny that. But what reason would Kay have had to give away that she knew who Connor was? It would only have implicated her when he arrived at Ashworth Hall yesterday. He hadn't said why he was there yet, just that he wanted to talk to her. Unless she was *that* frightened when Becca had been arguing with him that he was going to lose his temper and hurt her. *Pleasant thought.*

When Frankie brought his car around to where Becca's van was, Connor popped the hood up. For the same reason they hadn't used magical light to see in the engine when they were considering their methods of destruction the previous evening, it wasn't the best idea to use a magical burst of energy to revitalise a dead battery. Sometimes the non-magical methods were better suited, since the elements involved – like car engines – had been designed without magic.

So they attached the jump leads between the two vehicles and attempted to start the van. For a moment the van heaved itself back to life, but as soon as they removed the jump leads the engine died again.

At least one benefit of coming across as a quiet, grim, grumpy sort was that he wasn't required to act too much – no great hopes to be dashed. Just getting on with a job and watching as it inevitably failed.

Things got a little trickier however, as they tidied up and Frankie plied Connor with questions, in the manner of a three-year-old who'd eaten a whole packet of cookies to themselves. A level of interaction Connor was in no way prepared for.

'How did you two meet? You're Scottish, aren't you?'

'Irish.'

'Ah, close.'

Not really. But to someone whose first language was not English, excusable, he supposed. He made a neutral noise.

'So, how did you meet?' Frankie asked again.

'Through work.'

'Hers or yours?'

'Both,' he said, suppressing his exasperation and opting for the shortest answers he could get away with. This kid didn't know when to give up. Maybe it was concern for this tight-knit community, or maybe it was a renewed fascination for the magical world and all its inhabitants, now he'd had the veil lifted. Connor recalled feeling that way . . . for the couple of weeks between discovering he was a witch and arriving at Dentwood. It was good Frankie had finally found a soft place to land. Connor wondered how many witches out there were blindsided because of the circumstances of their childhood – divorced parents, orphans, recessive genes.

'What does Becca do?'

'She's a photographer.' Thank the Goddess he'd asked before he came down.

'Oh, right, so you hired her?'

'Err, no,' Connor answered, because at that precise moment he couldn't think of a reason why he would have hired a photographer which didn't lend itself to the narrative of him being a shit husband. Why *would* a grown man hire a photographer other than an engagement party or a wedding or a christening?

He could say he was a teacher – but who the hell would believe that he was good with kids? And also, why wouldn't he be working now when it was still the school term? This hypothetical back-story stuff was harder than it seemed.

'So, you were working where she was?' Frankie leaned on the bonnet of his tiny pea-green European car. 'You are really making this difficult. I'm looking for the romantic details here.'

Romance. Right. 'It was a wedding. I was . . .' He couldn't say a guest – which was of course what he should have gone with in the first place – because he'd said he'd been working, too. So what jobs were there at a wedding at the point when the photographer would be free to mingle? 'Err . . . singing, in the band.'

'No way! It's making even more sense now. You are both artists.' Frankie nodded, as though satisfied. 'You know, there's this lovely woman, Aveline, staying here, too, and it's her birthday party on Monday night. She wants an eighties karaoke. You could sing for us.'

'Oh, I don't know.'

'We'd love to hear how you serenaded your beautiful bride.'

'Well, maybe.' He tried to look willing and excited at the prospect, because that was two days away and they should be long gone by then. Shouldn't they? His life would get a lot easier again. And, he could reluctantly admit to himself, boring.

Chapter Sixteen

BECCA

There was a pretty little vanity table in the honeymoon suite, painted pale grey and adorned with white enamel handles. Becca settled herself down at it to do some work. Her gift was nagging at her, as well as her general sense of impatience. It was annoying her that when they'd damaged the battery in her mum's van they had overlooked the fact they'd need to get it fixed before they could leave again – and that it wouldn't be wise to approach the thief until they were sure they could get away, given that they didn't know how the confrontation would play out. It would be sensible to wait until they either knew it was safe to retrieve the amplifier or had their getaway vehicle fully functioning. Not that she imagined Connor would be the type to run.

Regardless, in the meantime, she needed to get these files processed so the parents and carers could order their children's commemorative photos. There was something reassuring about the inevitability of these events, just like the seasons and the sunrise. Her mother always used to say: *No matter how dark the night, the sun will always rise – you can rely upon that.* And as a teen, Becca might have argued that eventually the earth would actually be subsumed by the sun but as an adult she understood what her mum had been getting at. Life goes on and you can take comfort in that.

The inn was peaceful; she'd opened the windows and her muffling spell only worked one way, so she could hear birds singing and the occasional snatch of conversation from guests or staff walking around the building. It seemed like there were gardens and, depending on what Connor had been able to discover, she thought maybe she'd suggest their going for a walk around them to see if there was a back entrance to get to the area her gift was directing her to.

After half an hour, she made herself a cup of tea and called Harry. She gave him some further reassurances to her texts from the night before that she was safe and things were on track, if going to take slightly longer than antici-pated, and then she asked – with not a little guilt – about how Horatio was behaving himself.

'I imagine it's a lot like having a toddler with no sleep schedule,' Harry mused. 'He kept walking into our bedroom last night asking questions . . . and that was after we'd had a *long* discussion about why it is now totally normal and acceptable for unmarried couples to share a bedroom.'

'Holy grimoire. I'm sorry. If it's untenable, I guess I'll have to figure out how to exorcise him.' Becca winced as she stirred her tea. 'It just felt so mean to use him and then send him back.'

'What are you apologising for, Becs? Your idea *worked*. With any luck we've got our answer and if putting up with an awkward relative for a little while is the price we have to pay, it's more than worth it.' Harry laughed. 'Kay might have a different opinion, though. She volunteered to walk him through the last couple of centuries of historical events and they've been down in the library since breakfast.'

'Let's be real, Kay's probably enjoying it. Oh, that reminds me – could you ask her to text me the name of the person who told her Connor is the Abrogator?'

'Sure,' Harry said softly, and paused for a moment. 'How are you managing with him? If I'm honest, I might not have been able to sleep last night for worrying about you, even if Horatio hadn't been popping in and out.'

'You don't have to worry about me,' she said, even though she knew he still would. 'He's not as scary as people make him out to be.' *Or as he tries to make himself out to be.* 'Although, I suppose we're working to the same goal at the moment.'

'Do you think he has an ulterior motive?'

'For helping us get the amplifier?' Harry made a noise of agreement and Becca tapped her fingers on the lid of her closed laptop. She thought of how Connor had assessed the risk to the guests earlier. How he believed strongly that no witches should be setting curses on their properties in case anyone got hurt and how he'd described having to confront witches who were a threat to others. The idea of that had left a queasy feeling in her stomach. 'No. I think he's genuinely here to make sure it's safe for everyone. I just don't know how far he'd go to uphold what he believes is right as far as keeping everyone safe is concerned, if that makes sense?'

'I think so.' Harry gave a little embarrassed laugh. 'I'd really pictured him quite differently, y'know? Like Anthony Hopkins or Willem Dafoe.'

'Tell me about it.' Becca squeezed her eyes shut, doing her best not to picture Connor how he'd been that morning, only in his boxers in the warm morning light. A study of angles and lean muscles—

'Another example of Ashworths overreacting about the Witches Council?' Harry interrupted her before she could start drooling.

'I don't think that idea is unique to the Ashworths,' she said dryly, recalling Frankie – who had barely entered the witching world and still knew the Abrogator was the definition of the bogeyman for witches. 'And you're literally shacked up with someone from the Witches Council.'

'I know. Who would have thought my dad would happily have a member of the Witches Council living at Ashworth Hall?'

Becca played with a strand of her hair, brushing it over her cheek and thinking about how her Uncle Adrian had always been so adamant the Council weren't to be trusted. And not just for the reasons they all knew – it had bordered on the edge of paranoia, and he'd put it down to a touch of seer instinct. Which Becca's dad scoffed at, of course, since Uncle Adrian's gift was to influence with his voice. 'Times change.'

'Goddess, having Horatio running around the place judging everyone is a reminder of that,' Harry agreed. 'Just wait until he finds out I've openly had boyfriends as well as girlfriends.'

Becca laughed. 'Maybe he'll exorcise himself in shock? But I hear what you're saying. You think maybe the Witches Council's suspicion of us is a direct result of our suspicion of them, y'know? A vicious cycle?'

'Could be. Unless someone takes a risk to change things, how will we ever know if we could make it work? Living alongside the Witches Council without all this secrecy and suspicion would be good for everyone, wouldn't it?'

'They keep a lot of secrets themselves, too, though . . .' Even though she knew she could trust Harry with anything, she still deliberated a moment before she continued. 'This is just between us, but Connor can read magic – it's not just that he can remove it. He can pick it apart to understand it. He could have just put his hand on your chest and read all the components that make up the tattoo.'

'No way. Really?' The groan in Harry's voice mirrored the chagrin Becca felt about it, too.

'Really. If we'd known, we could have just asked him to help, rather than spent months researching and sneaking around the archives and summoning ghosts.' Years when Uncle Adrian could have been well. 'But we didn't know, because the Witches Council have hidden that information from people. And I can't think why. He says the less that's known about him, the better, when it comes to catching rogue witches but . . .' She scratched her head. 'I can't help but feel it's a power thing, too. Like the way they just hate that we have all this history and information they can't get their hands on. Kay's told us how much they're storing that doesn't belong to them. Grimoires and artefacts from all over the world. And then there's what they'll do if they find out about the tattoo.'

'I know.' He sighed. 'Just because I *want* things to be different, doesn't mean that they are. I can't risk a whole village of witches because I find politics distasteful, and I wish everyone could be kind to each other.'

Becca made a sympathetic noise. This conversation was making her think of the one she'd had with Connor on the drive down to Cornwall. 'What d'you think would happen if the village knew?'

'About the tattoo?'

'Yeah. Say – hypothetically speaking – that they all knew, and yet somehow the Witches Council didn't get wind of it. Do you think they'd feel differently towards us?'

'Erm . . . maybe? But not in a good way. If they knew we could simply choose not to have the anchor tattoo put on a new heir, and all the protective magic would fall apart, wouldn't they feel beholden to us to keep us happy? It would be an axe to wield over them. Keeping it secret is, for want of a less cringeworthy word, the nobler thing to do, isn't it?'

Something she hadn't realised was bothering her eased. Connor hadn't been wrong to question people in a position of power having secrets, but he didn't know what *their* secret was or why they were keeping it. 'Yeah. I think you're right.'

After they said their goodbyes, Becca wishing Harry luck with the phone call he was hoping to have with his parents later that day about the amplifier and Horatio, she sipped at her tea, considering that secrets were very much like magic. The ethics of keeping them depended entirely on the intention.

Chapter Seventeen

CONNOR

The last thing Connor wanted to do was go for a stroll when the merciless summer sun was at its height. But he couldn't deny that Becca's suggestion to explore the grounds was a good idea.

He'd returned to their room just before lunchtime and updated her about the car jump-start pantomime with Frankie, the invite to the party, that he'd arranged for a local mechanic to come out and look at the van on Sunday, and when he'd gone to ask for the number, he'd seen there were at least four members of staff hanging around the kitchen and spending a lot of their time either in the bar or through the doorway her gift was telling her they needed access to.

He'd also updated her on his new fake career as a wedding singer, in case anyone talked to her about it. She'd only laughed about it for a full two minutes, which, according to his estimation of her sense of humour, was probably restrained.

After he'd stoically waited for her to recover, they went downstairs for lunch and took their sandwiches outside for a 'walk' around the grounds to follow the call of her gift.

'Do you usually have to do stuff like this?' she asked him as they headed left from the front door, crossing the gravel driveway to a small gate between the inn and another building that looked like it would have once been the stables.

'No. I do my best to avoid long walks during a heatwave, whenever possible,' he said, frowning at the sandwich he had wrapped in greaseproof paper. The bread was beginning to curl already. Not that he was especially hungry. His skin was prickling from heat and magic . . . and the way Becca's bare arm was close enough to brush against his as they walked side by side.

She laughed as though he'd made a joke. 'I meant casing joints. Doing surveillance. It's like being a spy.'

He made a non-committal noise. Judging from Warren's frustration earlier, he wasn't doing a great job of it. And Warren wasn't even aware that Becca was the one gathering most of the information – including about him – and coming up with all the plans.

'Are you amenable to us holding hands?' she asked after they'd been following the path through the grass for a minute or two in silence.

'Err . . .' His heart leapt into this throat with a touch of fear and excitement, as though she'd suggested them stopping to have a quickie against a tree. 'I'm not much of a hand-holder.'

'OK, linking arms, then?' She leaned in closer to him, pressing her shoulder into his arm as she lowered her voice. 'There's someone over there on a bench reading, so it'll let me nudge you in the direction my gift is calling without us looking like I'm leading you on a march.'

Case in point – she was aware of their surroundings and thinking about their cover story. There was a woman sitting over in the shade, on a bench surrounded by heather. She glanced up from her book every so often, and with the wide expanse of grass between them, it looked like he and Becca would be in her field of vision for a while.

He stuck out his elbow awkwardly, wishing he hadn't rolled up his sleeves but knowing it would only look odder if he pulled them down when all Becca was doing was slipping her arm through his.

Her skin was warm and smooth against his as the underside of her forearm pressed against the top of his and she tugged subtly to lead him off the path. Why wasn't she worried about touching him? Almost every witch he'd been around who actually knew he was the Abrogator was one flinch away from leaping two metres back from him if he so much as looked in their direction. But not Becca. He didn't know what to make of it.

He didn't like the way it made him imagine that giving in to his urge to touch her would be OK.

A minute or so later, her arm still laced through his, they turned around the corner of the inn and came up against a massive, old exposed-brick wall. Like a lot of old walls, it looked like layers of slate stone just piled together, but *unlike* most of them, this one reached up over his head.

'Wow, that looks like a hazard,' Becca said, tipping her head back, the sunlight making her brown eyes glow with a rich warmth.

He unwound his arm from hers and pressed his palm to the sharp edges of rock. 'It's bound together with magic. Not about to collapse anytime soon.'

'What about wards?' she murmured.

'Yeah. Those, too.' Magic threaded along the top like invisible barbed wire to stop anyone climbing over it.

She caught his arm with her hand this time, to lead him onwards. Not holding his hand, but as good as, with the press of her palm and fingers making a gentle cuff. His lungs felt like they were being crushed.

He did his best to concentrate on where they were going, following the wall along, wading through increasingly longer grass, wildflowers splashing colour around them in russets, and pinks, and yellows. With any luck, she wouldn't notice that he was on the verge of a panic attack.

They turned the next corner and found that the wall continued for another expanse, with no rear gate of any kind. The grass stretched away from the property until it reached a tree line, but they continued around the last corner, finding themselves facing back towards the rear of the inn, with the uninterrupted enchanted wall on their left as well as the bit of the inn where their room was.

'It must be a private garden for the staff,' Becca sighed. 'No way in other than scaling the wall. Which only you could do without tripping the wards.'

'That would be no less conspicuous than trying to sneak through inside anyway.'

'Some might even say it would draw more attention,' she deadpanned.

He bit the inside of his cheek on a smile, but she seemed to notice anyway, her eyes dancing as she looked up at him. 'Shall we go back?' he asked.

'In a minute. Why don't we stop and eat. This sun is baking, and you look like you're going to combust if we don't get into the shade.'

For a change, it *wasn't* the sun making him hot and flustered, but he wasn't about to admit that to her. She was still holding on to his arm. He half expected to find a red burn in the shape of her hand when she finally removed it.

She commandeered him to the nearest tree – there were no benches on this side – and finally let go as they sat down in the grass, leaning against the wide trunk. Connor was absolutely not thinking about the last image he'd had in his head of Becca up against a tree. He took a huge bite out of his sandwich and immediately wished he'd brought a drink of some kind, as the turkey and lettuce leached all the moisture out of his mouth.

Becca was nibbling quietly on a ham and cucumber roll, her brow furrowed as she looked back at the building. From this distance, they could see the top floor of where the staff accommodation must be.

'You said there were four members of staff when you went through to the kitchen earlier, right?' she said after a while.

'Yes. Rhiannon, Samantha and then there were two men: the chef, Karl, and a kitchen skivvy, whose name I didn't catch.'

'How old were the men?'

'Karl is late thirties maybe. The skivvy was only a lad. Eighteen perhaps.'

'Well, it can't be him, then. If Harry and I have never had any knowledge of the amplifier, it couldn't have been stolen by someone younger than us.'

'By that logic it would rule out Karl, too. And Samantha – she's about our age, would you say?'

'*Our* age?' She turned to him with an amused expression. 'I'm nearly thirty. Isn't that an old woman to a young whippersnapper like you?'

He rolled his eyes and finished off his sandwich. 'That only leaves Rhiannon as someone old enough to have stolen it – and that's not taking into account the assumption you made back at the Hall that your dad and Harry's parents couldn't have known about the amplifier either. How old are they? Late fifties?'

'True. So the thief isn't here? Just the amplifier.'

'Unless there is someone older living in the staff area who we haven't seen yet. One of Rhiannon's parents, maybe?'

'I'm starting to think they won't be that frightening a prospect if we're looking at someone who is pushing eighty.'

Connor grunted. 'Older witches are powerful, Becca. They've had their whole life to hone their craft – that's a lot of experience to come up against. And that's without an amplifier of this kind. Don't underestimate them.'

'Have *you* ever come up against dangerous older witches?'

He looked up at the solemness of her tone. It wasn't the usual light curiosity she adopted when probing him about his favourite Batman. This was a serious question, and it was such a novelty to be having a conversation about what he did that it gave him pause. When had anyone who knew his role ever *asked* him about what he did? He supposed they wouldn't because they either knew his orders – because they'd issued them – or they didn't want to think about it.

'A few times,' he found himself answering. 'Honestly, with the older ones it's more often than not dementia, and they've lost control of their powers and grown frustrated.' He swallowed, because it was hard to take away their magic – not just because of them lashing out at him, but because of how they seemed so lost once he'd done it. What choice did he have, though? The last old witch he'd had to nullify had hurt her grandchild without meaning to in an episode of confusion, thinking she was still a child playing with her sibling, unaware of her own strength. The loss of control would only get worse, and she would have ended up having to isolate from her family. At least without the magic, the family could spend more time together.

'I never thought about that. Witches with dementia being a risk, I mean. That's heart-breaking.' She placed the paper her roll had been wrapped in down on her lap and began folding it. 'What about the times when it's not something like that?'

He let out a breath and looked back at the inn. The sky was blue with wisps of white cloud over it, the sunlight picking out touches of purple in the grey slate. It looked like a painting, and every witch inside whom they'd met had seemed harmless, if not extraordinarily kind. But appearances could be deceptive.

'*Those* times are even worse,' he said, almost under his breath, the thought of Becca facing off against a witch like that made him feel cold to the bone, despite the heat of the day.

He blinked as a white paper dove flapped in front of his face, and he tipped his head back to watch her origami creation work its way up into the tree branches above them. He raised an eyebrow as he looked at her. 'I thought you cared about the environment?'

'I'll call it back when we leave. What do you want? Another dove? An owl?' She held out her hand for his paper wrapper and he handed it over to her, his fingers grazing her palm. He blinked when he realised he hadn't gone out of his way to avoid touching her. And she hadn't flinched even slightly. In fact, she was smiling.

'Maybe you should do a ghost,' he said dryly. 'I seem to remember they like hanging out in trees.'

'Only the irritating kind.' She groaned. She folded another corner and then flipped it over, pausing with the head tilt he was coming to recognise as one of her thinking mannerisms. 'Is that something we should try here? Maybe there's a spirit who could tell us if the amplifier is being hidden or used by someone, or if it's just under a floorboard somewhere because a smuggler stashed it here a hundred years ago and forgot about it.'

'The dead aren't just sitting around in a waiting room for you to call upon with your questions, y'know? They aren't at your beck and call just because you're a medium. Let them rest in peace.'

He'd meant it as a joke, but she flushed. 'Goddess, I know that,' she almost whispered. 'I know you're suspicious about me summoning Horatio, but that really was the first time I've done it and it was an absolute last resort. I never would have if it wasn't—' She cleared her throat. 'I know it's not something to be done lightly. My mum . . . she was a medium, but she died before we even realised that I was, too.' Her head bent further over her paper, and her nail scored along the fold, hard and steady. 'Even so, she'd spoken to me about the responsibility of the gift. It is not for casual conversation or to appease the grieving, no matter how hard they are finding it . . . because it would only hurt more in the long run—' She broke off, her breath catching in her throat, her hand coming up to flick a droplet of moisture from her cheek before she carried on with her crafting.

There was a whole world of yearning and pain in what she'd just said to him. He felt it in the same way he felt magic pressing against his skin. Only it sank into him, too, making him ache. She'd lost her mum, and then found out she was a medium, and hadn't ever summoned her back to see her? He wasn't sure what it spoke of to him more: her respect for her mother's wishes, her willpower or her good sense.

'I'm sorry,' he said quietly. 'I was being flippant, and it isn't something to joke about. I'm not . . . great with talking to people. You might have noticed.'

She gave a little surprised laugh and looked up at him. 'Yeah, I might have noticed.' She nudged him with her shoulder, the way she had that morning when she'd agreed with him about Romeo and Juliet. 'But I like talking to you.'

He stared at her, knowing he was frowning because he didn't know what to do with that. Could that actually be true? This witch who was all laughter and ideas and paper doves, whose moods swept in and out like summer storms but always seemed to settle back to sunshine. She actually *liked* talking to him . . . when he was everything she was not?

'Did your dad ever ask you to use your gift to summon her?' he asked, wondering if that could be the reason she'd hinted at that her dad was disappointed in her. For a split second he tried to tell himself he was asking because Warren wanted him to get more information about the Ashworths, but he couldn't even entertain it because the idea felt so wrong when she was doing nothing to hide her grief from him.

'My mum? Only when he was very drunk, and very sad.' Her smile turned lopsided. Connor could see moisture clinging to the bottom lashes of her eyes, despite her smile, and he wanted to brush his thumb along it, wipe it away.

'Must have been hard to say no.'

'Well, doing what's for the best isn't always easy, is it?' Her gaze moved slowly over his face, making his mouth go even drier. He knew she was talking generally – or maybe even referring to when he had to nullify witches with dementia – but all he could think was, *No, no, it's not easy.* Because he wanted to kiss her. To press her back into the grass and tangle his fingers in her hair and be responsible for her lightning-quick mood change. Take her from sadness to desire. Make her gasp and sigh.

Which was *not* for the best. And probably not even slightly what she wanted. Just because she didn't flinch at his touch didn't mean she wanted to kiss him.

And yet her eyes were lingering on his mouth, and he was holding his breath. Her gaze moved back to his and it was like the moment they'd had in the bedroom that morning. But more so, because there was so little space between them this time and he could feel the charge in the air. As if she'd cast an attraction spell and hers was the only magic he couldn't seem to resist.

But then she shook her head, her shoulders going back and her head lifting again. 'And it's not like I'm not used to falling short of his expectations. Anyway, I only suggested the summoning because you seem so worried about the possible fall-out. This seems like an exceptional circumstance. To prevent anyone getting hurt.'

He tried to pull in a lungful of air without her noticing before he answered.

'Look, it's not a bad idea, but maybe as a last resort.' He echoed her words before, and he knew now for sure that there was something bigger, more serious, that the Ashworths had avoided telling him about the spell they needed the amplifier back for. If, as a teenager, she could withstand the desire to see her mother again, and the pressure of a grief-stricken parent to do it, what *had* pushed her to summon Horatio?

'Back to plan A, then.' She nodded and looked back down at the paper in her lap. A few folds later and another winged paper creature was darting back and forth above their heads.

'Is that meant to be a bat?'

The little dimple that appeared when she was teasing him flashed in her cheek. 'What else, for a man who describes himself as "the void", "the black hole of magic"?' She imitated his deeper voice and Irish accent, and he huffed a quiet laugh, looking up at it.

If it was a bat, she had infused it with all its lighter characteristics. It's playfulness, grace and skill.

His attention was drawn to her again, her upturned face bathed in the dappled green light from the sunshine slicing through the leaves above, the occasional grey shadow crossing over her smile. That sensation that she wasn't truly real hit him again, but this time it was coupled with him not feeling real either. As if he'd stepped outside of his life for a moment and was playing a part. And the clock was ticking on it.

Chapter Eighteen

BECCA

Being mad at the friendly guests and charming staff at the inn for making Becca and Connor feel at home during the evening meal, and then in the bar afterwards, was like being mad when your cat brought you a live bird. You were grateful they cared enough to include you, but also frustrated because now you needed to chase the bird around your living room when you had places you needed to be or Netflix shows to watch.

Neither she nor Connor could get anywhere near the staff door, first because the dining room was full and then because the staff were still in there clearing up, and obviously waiting for them to stop nursing their dessert – the leftovers of the kids' chocolate cake, which was so gooey and delicious it was frankly a crime to be picking at it slowly . . . but needs must when you were looking for an opening to trespass.

They eventually took the hint, finished their cake and went into the bar, where Frankie called over to them as they waited to order their drinks.

'Hey, Becca. We're playing Four Towers and we need another player. Will you join us?'

OK, so he wasn't really calling over to both of them. Four Towers was a magical game, which meant, once again, that Becca's impromptu back story for Connor was leaving him stifled. She knew the guilt was all over her face as she looked up at him, but he just frowned down at her: quizzical edition. 'What? You don't need my permission.'

'I know, but . . .' She chewed her lip and looked around them to see who was paying attention to their conversation. For the millionth time that night, she caught Sam watching them. All throughout the dinner service it had been the same, but whenever Becca caught her or she came over to bring their drinks or food, she couldn't seem to get away quickly enough. She must have it bad for Connor.

Becca shook her head and looked back at him, stepping into the space between his body and where he had his arm on the bar, so it looked like they were cosying up, but she wasn't actually touching him. She wasn't doing it to declare him her territory to Sam, even if that might have been normal kind of behaviour for a new bride who knew someone was persistently checking out her husband. Becca couldn't use that as an excuse to get close to Connor when he didn't want that.

Although sometimes she thought he *might* be attracted to her, like when they were in the gardens earlier and he'd been looking at her as if . . . well, frankly, as if he wanted to kiss her. But then other times having her close clearly stressed him out. Or it was a confusing combination of both. Like now. His hand was white-knuckled on the bar and yet, when her eyes met his, his pupils were dilated, his gaze intent on her, eyelids hooded.

Maybe it wasn't *quite* so confusing, actually, because even if he *was* attracted to her, the situation was complicated. At any given moment, they were trying to talk tactics, under scrutiny, hiding secrets from each other and – for Becca at least – battling an inconvenient attraction. It was a lot.

'But what?' he prompted.

'But . . . you'll be left out.'

His dark brows drew even down further: confused edition. He studied her for a moment, before he let out a soft snort. 'Don't be an eejit,' he said, his accent prominent and warmth evident in his scold. 'It's a good opportunity to get them talking. And besides, I don't even know the rules.'

Becca dropped her head, because that only made it worse. He'd never played Four Towers? That was like a non-magical person saying they'd never played Monopoly. She wanted to get a list of every kid in his year at Dentwood, drive to their houses and set stink-bomb hexes under their doormats so they had to go about their whole day reeking and being avoided. And that was just for starters.

But she swallowed all that down because she remembered how he'd told her not to feel sorry for him. How he'd refused to acknowledge the treatment he'd received.

'All right.' She nodded decisively.

When they got to the table, Frankie, Archie – the unsociable young man from breakfast – and Danika, the young woman the pair had been sitting with last night, were divvying up the enchanted blocks. They'd left a pile of blue ones on the table before the bench seat, so Becca and Connor could sit next to each other.

'Mum, Mum, look – they're playing Four Towers. Can we join in?' The dark-haired twin who'd arrived that morning appeared between Frankie's and Danika's chairs. The other twin appeared next to Connor and his leg pressed into Becca's for a moment as he flinched in surprise.

'Yeah, we can do teams,' the little blonde girl said.

'Girls, let them be.' Their mum looked over from the table by the window that they'd escaped from. 'Maybe we can play after.'

'Oh, but it's more fun when you have four or more. You'll let us play, won't you?' the brunette twin addressed the adults around the table without a hint of doubt in her expression.

Frankie, Danika and Archie were exchanging awkward looks, obviously unsure of the etiquette here. Did their mum want them to let them play or not? Would they end up babysitting? All of it played out in painfully obvious expressions across their young faces.

'Sweethearts, come back over and stop pestering, please.'

'But, Mum—'

'Chrissy, we don't play it the same way grown-ups do.'

'What? Since when?' The outrage on the fair-haired twin, Chrissy's, face was a sight to behold.

Her mum's eyes widened for a second, as though realising she'd made a misstep. 'You're both still young in your magic.'

'Goddess, Mother,' the other twin said, with a level of grave disappointment a fifty-year-old would have been proud of. 'You've been making us play the *baby* version all this time?'

The poor woman was clearly exhausted and needed a break. Becca leaned forward, catching the eyes of both girls. 'I remember feeling that way when I was a kid. So, in my family, we'd pair adults and children in teams, and then the kids got to be the *spell-masters*.'

The twin sisters looked at each other and asked, simultaneously: 'What's a spell-master?'

'Spell-masters get to decide the moves – attack, defend, build or enchant. *And* the spells to use.'

'Ooh, yes, let's do *that*,' Not-Chrissy said, gripping the backs of Frankie's and Danika's chairs and bouncing herself off the ground.

'Erm . . . how . . . what?' Frankie blinked at Becca and she grinned.

'Chrissy, you can be Archie's spell-master. And what's your name, honey?' Becca asked the swinging twin, and received 'Jemima' as an answer. 'Jemima, you can be Danika's spell-master.'

'So, you two get to . . . play on your own?' Archie said, disgruntled, but at least trying to cover it up.

'No. Connor's going to be my spell-master.'

'What?' Frankie laughed. 'But he's got no magic.'

'I reckon that makes it fair, right?' Becca said. 'Did you get to play this much as a kid?'

'Not at all,' Frankie admitted. 'But I've been practising since I got here.'

'Right. So. I'm the most experienced witch here, but Connor will advise me. That evens it all up, right?'

'It's going to be a bloodbath,' Danika said, her Eastern European accent lending a gravitas to the pronouncement.

'Don't be so sure,' Connor said. 'I've been taking notes since I met Becca.'

Becca looked over at him and he gave her a half-smile, a teasing glint in his eye. Was that an 'in-joke' just for them? Her stomach gave a little flip, and then he rested his arm along the back of their bench seat.

'Now, is someone going to explain the rules?'

It was the best–worst game of Four Towers Becca could ever remember playing. The progress of the towers seemed to be forever stalled at two rows high, because the twins were aggressive and chose, nine times out of ten, to attack another player's tower rather than shore up their own. Kinetic spells flew across the table, sending bricks flying and sometimes ricocheting back when they hit enchanted bricks. A random number of the pieces in each colour were pre-charmed so that when players were trying to build, they might begin shaking and take the whole tower down, or bring along three bricks with them and give an advantage. Even if Connor had been able to play with his magic, his spell-reading wouldn't have given him an advantage because witches weren't permitted to physically touch any of their blocks.

Throughout the course of the game, they learned via Frankie's inability to respect anyone's privacy that Archie had dropped out of university and was worried about going home to explain himself to his parents. Danika was an asylum seeker who'd left the non-magical family who'd taken her in two years ago to go back-packing but had underestimated the cost-of-living rise and run out of money. And the twin girls had told the dramatic story of how their house had flooded that morning. If Becca hadn't known better, she would have thought that Frankie's gift was the ability to get people to talk, but since he wasn't extracting any truths from her, thankfully, that couldn't be the case. He'd also mentioned an elemental gift for finding water – which wasn't exactly sought-after these days and was probably the reason his snooty dad had been unimpressed. Becca would have been grateful for it during a drought, though . . . or if she was a plumber. Some people were so short-sighted.

For an eight-year-old, Chrissy was calm and calculated, and it was hilarious to watch alongside Archie's ultra-competitiveness, as he pouted and cheered. Frankie was clearly happy to be holding his own, having not had any experience of the game growing up, and Danika was blatantly encouraging the aggressive tendencies of Jemima, who was revelling in being allowed to instruct an adult to try to blow something up and them actually doing it.

Connor stuck to simple defensive spells – nothing showy or special that would give away his impressive understanding of magic, to a degree Becca suspected not many witches were capable of. She supposed it was his ability to read magic that gave him an almost encyclopaedic knowledge of it, but he still only concentrated on shoring up their tower and ensuring that anything a little overambitious fizzled out before someone got hurt.

Becca and Connor got to spend a lot of time leaning their heads close to each other and whispering, which she couldn't help enjoying, the faint scent of oakmoss and rosemary from his faded aftershave imprinting itself on her, the hint of lemon from his drink as his breath touched her cheek. In actual fact, it was only Connor whispering in *her* ear, because if they appeared to be conferring, rather than Becca just being instructed, Archie accused them of cheating. Then he *still* accused them of cheating, because he couldn't hear what spells Connor was suggesting. And despite everyone ganging up on them, they were still winning.

Eventually, the lack of progress bored the kids, though, and they wandered off to explore the room. As the others debated restarting the game from scratch, Becca watched the girls examining the pictures on the wall, which ranged from pets, to former guests, to landscapes and old paintings of witches and mythological creatures. Sometimes Chrissy would pick up Jemima so she could see better. Sometimes they'd squeal at a particularly creepy image from folklore and chase each other around pretending to be it.

Becca rubbed at her forehead, the nagging of her gift beginning to wear on her, aggravated by the noise and the persistent use of her magic, so much so that it had become a generalised headache.

Connor nudged her gently with his elbow and she turned her head towards him, finding that he'd leaned in again as though to whisper to her, even though the game was over. Their cheeks brushed, the heat of his skin and the barely there graze of his stubble making her dizzy for a moment. She sensed the sudden tension in him, but if he recoiled in that way he sometimes did, it would look really weird. He didn't. He eased back just a fraction and pitched his voice low.

'Do you need to go up and rest?' he asked.

'Maybe. But we haven't got very far, have we?'

He gave a small shrug. 'I can stay down here if you want some peace.' He cleared his throat. 'Try to talk to people.'

She laughed a little at the hint of dread in his voice – though he'd been fine during the game. 'No,' she said slowly. 'I mean, I think we should go up together. For appearances' sake.'

He studied her eyes and then looked around, no doubt catching his stalker, Sam, watching them. When he looked back to Becca he nodded. 'Good point.'

'I'm just going to grab a bag of peanuts – sometimes the salt helps with the headache. No idea why.'

He nodded again and she reluctantly moved out of the bubble they'd been in, heading for the bar. It was only Sam behind it; Rhiannon hadn't been around that evening. She looked up from a dress-making magazine – Becca was pretty sure she'd been reading the same page for the last half an hour – and gave Becca a small smile.

Becca requested her snack and as Sam brought over the bag of peanuts, she tipped her head towards the table. 'All done with the game?'

'Yeah – nobody won.'

'You were close, though,' Sam said, giving away the fact that she had been watching. 'He's picked up a lot about magic from you?'

Great, *now* she wanted to talk, when it felt like there was a labourer with a pneumatic drill doing roadworks on the inside of Becca's skull. 'Oh, yeah. It fascinates him.'

'How long have you been together?'

'Oh, about, err, one –' *day* – 'year.' She glanced back over to Connor, to find that the twins were standing in the space she'd left on the bench seat – probably to look at one of the pictures on the wall – and were actually chatting to Connor, who'd pressed himself further into the corner to give them room but was smiling at them.

'Really?'

Becca looked back to see that Sam's lips, a vision in vivid red, were parted.

'Why so surprised?' Becca picked up the peanuts from the bar and massaged the back of her neck with her other hand.

'I guess I just . . .' Sam cleared her throat and started refolding a tea towel. 'That's not long to know someone to get married, is it?'

Becca lifted her eyebrows. Was it not? That sounded fairly average.

'Or maybe it's OK for some,' Sam backtracked, 'but . . . you mentioned your dad disapproving and sometimes that can make things seem a lot more . . .' Sam obviously caught the growing outrage that Becca was feeling. 'I'm sorry. I'm overstepping. I just . . . we see so many different types of relationships come through, and sometimes—' She paused to swallow and put her hand across the bar, as though she was going to place it over Becca's, but then she stopped short. 'Well, we know we might have to initially take in a couple *together*, but really the inn is only offering sanctuary to *one* person in the couple, and we have to politely ask the other person to leave. We're prepared to do that if the need arises.'

A swirl of emotion swept through Becca. Gratitude and sorrow for how the inn needed to offer that, had seen situations like that – but also a pain in her heart that Connor was being perceived that way. She guessed she had it wrong that Sam liked Connor. At all. But she didn't know what he'd done to deserve so much suspicion. She took a deep breath and met Sam's blue gaze, so bright it hurt her head the same way switching on the big light would. 'I appreciate the concern. But if Connor leaves, I leave. He's my husband.'

Sam's eyes held hers, and there was a sadness in them so deep, it cut at Becca, too. Is that what had brought the beautiful barmaid here? Then Sam blinked and offered a weak smile. 'That's good. No problem.'

Becca nodded, and when she got back to the table, the twins were now sitting in her spot, Chrissy resting her head on Jemima's shoulder and listening as Connor told them a story about the giants in the illustrations on the wall. She hovered, not wanting to interrupt, enraptured by his gorgeous voice describing battles and land masses being formed from the fall-out. When he was done, the twins were virtually asleep, and Becca wanted him to tell her a bedtime story every night.

They said goodnight to everyone and started up the stairs, Becca munching on her peanuts, only in small part to try to keep her hands to herself. She'd finished them by the time they got to their suite and was feeling marginally better. Kicking off her shoes, she clambered onto the bed with a groan. Aside from the frustration of them not getting any closer to the amplifier, it had been a nice evening. A nice day, in fact.

'Does it seem to you like there's something sinister going on here?' she asked, trying to keep the frustration out of her voice. Because it was niggling at her, as though she were missing something obvious. But maybe it was just the insistence of her gift, because, honestly, there was nothing she could put her finger on.

He leaned against the post at the end of the bed, the dim light making it hard to read his eyes. 'Not so far as I can tell, at the minute.'

'No . . . me neither. They all seem so genuine. And they really love it here.' She laughed, pushing away the disgruntlement she heard in her voice. Because, of course, it was a good thing that the inn was offering witches a safe haven and asking for nothing in return. 'Like, those girls – they were gutted this morning, and by this evening they were utterly comfortable and having fun.'

Connor nodded slowly. 'It looks like being here's done a power of good for Frankie, too. The first time he's been properly welcomed into a magical community . . . that's a valuable thing.'

Becca's chest tightened as she felt the hesitancy of his words and the thing he left unsaid – the thing he might not even admit – that Connor had *never* been welcomed into a magical community. She bit her lip. He deserved better than that, when he was out there risking his life to make other people safe. Was that really just the way it had to be for some people? Their lives a sacrifice to the greater good? Like her uncle and Harry? Except she wasn't going to let that happen, because they *could* fix it. 'This place reminds me of home,' she finally admitted.

'The inn itself, or . . .?'

'Just the whole thing – the ethos of it, I guess.'

Connor frowned, but the shadows playing over his face meant she couldn't decipher this one. 'The magic is similar.'

'I thought you hadn't pulled out any specific spells?'

'No, but it's old. It feels different. And that's similar to Biddicote and Ashworth Hall. The magic is entwined beneath it, like the roots of an ancient tree . . .'

She blinked. So, the ethos was similar and the way the land and building were enchanted were similar . . . could that mean that the amplifier was being used here, for good? What was she supposed to do if that was the case?

But there was still the possibility that Rhiannon was using it for her own gift. She hadn't been in the bar all evening. Perhaps she'd been back in the staff area with an elderly relative. Maybe that elderly relative had told her that the amplifier was a family heirloom and shown her how to use it? Or maybe she had just purchased it from someone? Was there a black market of stolen magical artefacts? There had to be, didn't there?

'Have you asked your sources for the background intel on Rhiannon yet?'

He laughed. 'You really need to stop talking like we're special agents.'

Becca smiled up at the canopy with the twinkly lights at the pleasurable rasp of his laugh over her nerve endings. 'Why? It's fun. *Have* you asked . . . whoever it is you work with?' She leaned up on her elbows to watch him as he pushed away from the bedpost, taking off his own shoes and tucking them neatly away as he took a seat in the armchair he'd been singing in last night. 'Who *do* you work with?'

'No one. You could say I'm a lone wolf,' he added with a fake American accent.

'You don't play by the rules,' she joined in, with a terrible impression of a New Yorker. 'They told you to hand in your badge, but the job was your life, see, so now you take private cases and sleep at the office because your wife is going to cut you loose.'

'Don't worry, the femme fatale I've just taken a case for will end up making out with me, even though I'm twenty-five years older than her and do nothing but chain smoke cigarettes and drink whisky.'

Becca exaggerated gagging and then put on a fake pout. 'Only then she'll break your heart because she was out to trick you the whole time. She changed her mind at the last minute because your hard-bitten ways were just too seductive, but it was too late, and the bad guys killed her and dumped her in the river. You'll be haunted by visions of her perfect breasts forever.'

'Tragic.' He laughed again, and suddenly Becca didn't feel tired any more. She felt like every cell in her body was lighting up. 'And the real answer to your question is yes, I have asked for background checks but not received any information back.'

She sighed as her brain threatened to start spinning theories again.

'We should watch a film.' She sat up. 'I feel the need to decompress. This undercover stuff is hard. Especially when it doesn't seem to be working – the staff are still suspicious of us, I think, because of the way we turned up.'

'I think they're suspicious of *me*,' he corrected her, undoing two buttons at the top of his shirt and exposing the base of his throat and collarbones. Becca blinked and dragged her gaze back up to his face.

'It's both of us, surely,' she said. 'Sam was probing me about our story – how long we'd been together, that sort of thing.'

He shook his head and turned on the kettle. 'It's my vibe. Witches find my presence about as reassuring as the Grim Reaper turning up at Christmas dinner.'

There was a lot of conflicting evidence about that as far as Becca was concerned. The kids hadn't been nervous of him. Whereas Sam had definitely been checking to see if Becca had got herself shackled to someone she might appreciate unshackling from. But that was probably more about Sam and the things she'd experienced herself and at the inn than about Connor.

'You sure you're not projecting that? The nervousness could be due to the fact that you're six foot four and scowl constantly.'

His scowled deepened, but this was a little bit of a pouty one as he corrected her moodily: 'Six foot three.'

Lies – she was an expert on male height. For her sins. 'I never even knew you were a *witch* when I first met you. Let alone picking up whatever "forbidding" vibes you think you emanate.' *That* was totally true.

'Having you straddling me may have distracted us both.'

Becca's stomach flipped and then executed a swan dive into her lower abdomen. The loaded imagery sat between them, their eyes locked, until the kettle clicked to say it was done and he pulled his gaze away.

'What film do you fancy, then?' he asked, his voice lower and a little rougher as he concentrated on making tea.

'Something funny, I think . . . Oh, I know just the thing.'

The look Connor gave her after they'd both got ready for bed and settled themselves either side of the duvet buffer, propped up by pillows and facing her laptop where it was sitting on the breakfast tray, made her warm, fuzzy feelings zip from her stomach down to her toes. His eyebrow rose while the line of his mouth twisted in wry amusement.

'*The Wedding Singer*,' he said. 'Very clever. Is wind-up merchant your second profession after photography?'

She crossed her legs at the ankle and sipped her blackcurrant tea, all innocence. 'Look, it just made me remember that I was recommended it once. It's meant to be good.'

He wrinkled his nose, which, on his sharp features was frankly adorable. But he didn't offer any more objections.

They started the film and the way they fell quiet, other than laughing and groaning at certain moments, along with the magic of Zeynep's special tea easing her headache, made the tiredness creep up on Becca. When she looked over at Connor, he'd slumped back, too, one arm bent back behind his head, his biceps tugging at the arm of his T-shirt. There was a crinkle in his forehead, as if he were making a concerted effort to stay awake and keep up with the film.

The next time she checked, the crinkle was gone and his eyes were shut. She turned out the lamps and turned down the volume on the film so as not to disturb him. His bottom lip had gone slack, some of his black curls falling forward from his hairline to lie against his forehead. She wanted to slide her finger beneath them, continue down to the pronounced edge of his cheekbone . . .

She drew in a shaky breath and reached quietly for her phone to text Zeynep.

Becca: Zee, I have a code red alert. I repeat, a code red alert. Just to make you aware.

Zeynep: What? Who? How has this happened?

Becca: Connor. Who I came to Cornwall with. And I will tell you how . . . HE'S SO PRETTY I THINK I'M

GOING TO DIE

Zeynep: I'll make sure the freezer is stocked with ice-cream for when you get back.

Becca: Thank you.

Zeynep: Is anything going to happen? If it's a code red, it doesn't matter either way. You're doomed. You might as well get something out of it, right?

Becca: I don't know. It's complicated.

Zeynep: All the best things are.

Chapter Nineteen

CONNOR

The phantom cat arrived again the following morning, but this time Connor knew exactly where he was and who was with him. That smell of peaches infiltrated his senses, mouth-wateringly light and sweet, which was no surprise as, when he opened his eyes, he found that his cheek was pressed to the top of Becca's head.

She was in the same position as yesterday, hugging the duvet barrier between them, but he seemed to have fallen asleep during the film and slumped sideways, gradually collapsing through the night, as if he'd been shot. His head was half on his propped-up pillows, half on the rolled-up duvet, which meant that not only was his cheek on her head, but *her* cheek was pressed partially to his shoulder.

Thankfully, he was still wearing his T-shirt tonight. The air was cool in the same way it had been the first night when he'd used the spell to create a breeze – but this magic must have been hers. For him. Because she had the white cotton sheet tightly wrapped up around her curled-up body, as if she were cold in the middle of a heatwave, and thank the Goddess for that, too.

He was aware of every single centimetre of his body in relation to hers. It was torture.

No. That was ridiculous. Torture was a terrible, awful thing and *this* wasn't *that*. But it was overwhelming him with desires that he didn't know how to handle.

His experience with women was on a par with his experience with people as a whole. In that it was sporadic, awkward and unfulfilling generally. Aside from his soul-numbing experience with Selena, who'd known him from Dentwood and had dated him for the 'thrill' of it, he'd attempted seeing some non-magical women for a while, but that had been difficult with how often he moved around. Any attempt at a love life had dwindled to hook-ups. And then dwindled even further to involuntary celibacy.

Or maybe it *was* voluntary. He couldn't be bothered to put in the effort any more, to only satisfy a fleeting sexual urge with a stranger, so it *was* his choice.

But his body was telling him that – on a fundamental level – it was perfectly willing to put in the effort now, with Becca. It was just his mind objecting on the grounds that no witch wanted him to touch them, and that probably went triple for a witch whose family he was supposed to be investigating. She wasn't naive – she knew the Witches Council had a file on them. She might joke about it, act like it wasn't a big deal, but it was an undeniable truth that lay between them, and it would be a damn sight harder to get over that than the flimsy duvet barrier she was breaching every night. And cosying up to him at night was just because she was used to sleeping next to someone, her subconscious casting him in the role of dickhead Drew. Any proximity to him she *consciously* chose was because of the act they had to put on. It had to be, surely?

Frustration mounting in his blood, when the *scritch, scritch, scritch* noise came at the door again, he couldn't help letting out a groan and muttering, 'Just come in, cat. You're dead, you can walk through fecking doors.'

Which, of course, woke Becca up. And for some reason, he hadn't yet moved his head from the top of hers, which meant they were still partially snuggled up together.

But rather than her snapping into consciousness and separating herself quickly from him, she *nuzzled further* into his shoulder. Her nose was in his throat and she was making a soft little humming noise, like it was a pleasurable place to be, turning his skin to fire and ice.

Then she froze, as though she'd realised where she was and with whom. She drew her head back gradually, looking up at him through her fall of thick, dark hair. 'I . . . err . . . sorry.' She pushed herself up so she could move back properly, and he was too boneless to move, so he ended up with a direct view of her cleavage, all the heat in his body rushing south.

He squeezed his eyes shut. 'Sorry,' he said, too.

'You don't need to be sorry.' Obviously, she hadn't noticed him staring straight down her vest. 'I'm clearly encroaching on your space, not the other way around.' Her voice became more distant as she moved away. 'Is our feline friend calling?'

When he heard the snick of her opening the door, he deemed it safe to open his eyes and sat up, bunching the sheet in his lap and hoping it was not too obvious why he was doing that.

The phantom cat came in and jumped on the foot of the bed the same way it had yesterday, this time with Becca following, crooning to it and sitting down close by, offering her hand to it to sniff and decide whether or not it wanted to be petted.

The cat brushed its head against her hand, and she gave a giggle and a little shiver, hunching her shoulders. 'That feels weird.'

He concentrated on the cat strutting around on the bed, rather than the movement of her shoulder blades, the way the curve of her breasts made the cotton of her

vest cling, and how her shorts had ridden up her thigh . . .
Cat. Dead cat.

By the time it climbed into his lap, the sheet was no longer in danger of incriminating him by being tented. He held out his hand in offer, the same way she had, and the cat brushed against him, flexing and purring. The strange almost-there-ness kind of willing him to keep stroking until it became properly solid again.

'Ah, I see.' Becca went around to her side of the bed and started to organise her clothes and toiletries. 'You're one of those people who *acts* like you don't like animals, but they naturally flock to you.'

'I don't dislike animals. I've just not had them before.' He tried to drop his hand and the cat nudged at him again.

'No pets? Not even as a kid?'

'No.'

'Cats are a good place to start then. They are independent enough that you can still travel when you need to. They'll just think your home belongs more to them than to you . . . which, to be fair, is the case regardless of whether you travel for work or not.' She took a brush out and began running it through her hair, the strands growing smooth and shiny. He wanted to gather it in his hands, silk against his skin.

He made himself look at the cat. 'I think I draw the line at getting a house just for a cat to live in. Aren't landlords anti-pet, anyway?'

'Not always these days. What's your landlord like?'

'I don't have a landlord.'

'So, if you own your own place, what's the—' She broke off, her brushing paused as she saw him shaking his head. 'Connor. Are you saying . . . you don't you have a permanent home?'

'Not technically. There's no point. I travel too much.'

'Of course there's a point. Even if you travel a lot.'

He shrugged. 'Why do all the extra back and forth-ing when I can just stay where I'm working until I'm needed somewhere else?'

'Well, for one thing, because you could have a cat.' She pointed at his lap with her brush and the phantom cat promptly jumped off and ran out through the door. 'You could get to know your neighbours. Have staycations where you can just sit at home in your pants watching Netflix surrounded by all your creature comforts. Plant a garden. Decorate it with furnishings you enjoy. Own more clothes than just those that fit inside a suitcase.' Her voice was rising. 'I can't believe I'm trying to sell the ideal of having a *home*. What the hell, Connor? Even if you don't like those ideas, it'd save you a lot of money, surely, rather than staying in hotels all the time?'

He got up, feeling strangely cold now the cat had scarpered, even though it couldn't possibly have been sharing body heat with him. He set about grabbing his own clothes. The ones that he carried around in his suitcase. 'I don't have to pay for the hotels.'

'The Witches Council cover it?'

He nodded. 'Bottomless credit card. Or I assume it is. I've never been asked to cap my expenses.'

She frowned, as though she were thinking hard. 'But they do pay you a separate wage, right?'

'What for? They pay for me to live.'

'Connor . . .' She dropped her brush and held on to the sides of her face as she shook her head. 'That's not right.'

'Why are you freaking out?'

'Because . . . it's like . . . it's like they *own* you. What about your personal life? Your own autonomy? What if you don't want to work for them any more? You don't have anything to call your own. You have no savings to fall back on. What would you do?'

He opened his mouth to say that he had his dad. His cousin. He could go back to Ireland. But could he, really? He'd barely seen them recently – and shamefully, his sporadic visits had been at their worst at a time when he should have been there for his cousin. He'd spent more time with the twins last night than with his cousin's daughters over the last two years. He could probably have made an educated guess about what to buy Chrissy and Jemima for their birthday.

But there wasn't anything he could do about that, because it was a stupid hypothetical question. 'I'm not going to leave the Witches Council. It's not a desk job. I'm the Abrogator. This *is* my life.'

Quiet fell between them until she said, in a devastatingly serious tone, 'And you're happy with it?'

'It's my duty. If I don't do this job, who will?' At the sight of her stricken face, his stomach began to churn. 'You should understand this. You're an Ashworth. Your family's whole reputation is based on the continuing protection you offer to the community of witches in Biddicote. It's the same thing.'

She paused, as if to think about it, then shook her head slowly. 'No. It's not. There *are* things we do to continue to protect the community there and responsibilities we take on . . . but we still get to be ourselves. I have a job that I love, Harry has a job that he loves. We have relationships, friends, lovers, *homes*. Biddicote is important. The history of our family is important. But we're not just tools.'

His hands clenched in his clothes. 'I am *not* just a tool.'

Her expression softened and somehow that was even worse. 'You must have been doing this since you left school. Did they come to you and ask you before you left? Did you ever have a choice?'

He frowned. As soon as they'd known what his gift was, the Witches Council had been there because he'd needed help. They'd known he needed special mentoring. Warren had brought him the grimoires from the last Abrogator, a witch who'd died fifty years before Connor was born and who had operated during the Second World War. Warren had helped him decipher them, to understand how his gift worked, and seeing it there – how an Abrogator had to deal with dangerous witches, not to mention the mistakes that were sometimes made – he'd realised what a responsibility it was, because he *had* to. Immediately. Or he risked hurting the witches around him.

'I got a choice about which Witches Council I would report in to.'

She took a short breath in and pressed her lips together tightly. 'And you chose the UK Witches Council – why?'

'Because it made sense. I was in England already, I already knew them and they had the grimoires from the last Abrogator to help me—'

'Why does the UK Witches Council have the grimoires of the last Abrogator. Wasn't he a Swedish witch? That's what the history books say.'

'I don't know. I never really thought about it.'

'Well, maybe you should have.'

'As though everything your family owns has always rightfully belonged to them. You think your ancestors were above taking whatever they wanted? Has it ever occurred to you that the amplifier might not have been your family's to begin with? Just because Horatio *thinks* it belongs to you doesn't mean that's the truth of the matter, does it?'

Her cheeks flushed. 'OK, fine. You're right. There probably are artefacts that we have, which, if we look into it, should be returned. Maybe even this amplifier. And I'm *not* trying to minimise that. I agree, my family should put that right if it's the case . . . but those are *things*. Not a living, breathing person. They had no right to make you think the only option was between either letting a Witches Council you knew or one you didn't run your life.'

'So, I should have just said "no, thanks" and wandered off to let hundreds of Tenet Enforcers across the world be harmed as they tried to detain powerful witches bent on hurting innocent people? Because my being able to own a *cat* is more important? I'm the only Abrogator that witches know of alive today. It's not some overprivileged family dynasty where I can break whatever rules I like and people will still fawn over me. This is it. It's what I'm needed for, and you'll be glad of it, if the witch who stole your precious family heirloom tries to hex you and the people you love with the power of a dozen dragon-eye stones behind them.'

Her face paled and he saw her throat ripple with a swallow. It was only at that moment that he realised he'd raised his voice. The hot, sickly feeling crashed through his stomach. He'd probably scared her. He might as well have yelled at her that he was death and destruction incarnate and set fire to the room. The last thing he wanted was for her to start fearing him the way everyone else did. 'I'm s—'

'No. No. Don't apologise.' She cut him off. 'You're right. I *am* glad of having you here, but that doesn't mean I'm glad they've made you think and feel like *this*.'

And what was the 'this' she was referring to? Him being a puppet, a tool, a loser, in her eyes? That stung. So much, he couldn't help lashing out again. 'What about how your dad makes you feel? Like a disappointment.'

'That's family. It's complicated.'

'It's fucked up.'

'Well, it takes one to know one.' She crossed her arms over her chest.

'Very mature.' He gritted his teeth and yanked on his trousers, grabbing his shoes, a pair of socks, his toothpaste and mobile phone. He could use magic to clean his clothes and teeth without a bathroom. He just needed to get out of this room. 'I'm going out to meet the mechanic.'

He stomped out of the door, slamming it behind him, and found himself in the hallway with a very shell-shocked-looking woman, who'd been halfway out of her own door. He pressed his lips together, remembering that even if the words weren't audible from inside their room the general tenor and volume of the 'conversation' were. Another black mark against his fake husbandry.

The door behind him opened up and he spun around to see Becca, his heart giving a strange little leap even in among the mess of sickening feelings overwhelming his chest. But she wasn't calling him back in, or shrugging off his behaviour this time.

She pushed something small and hard at his chest, and he automatically lifted his hand to trap it before it fell, her hand sliding out from underneath his as her brown eyes blazed. 'You'll need that,' she said, and then slammed the door closed in his face.

He looked down and saw the key to her van. Of course. He couldn't open it for the mechanic magically.

Turning on his bare heel, the woman in the other room flinched when she caught his eye and hurried back inside her room, slamming her own door closed.

And Connor was on his own, once again.

BECCA

Becca had not survived her teenage years living with an argumentative, grouchy dad without developing some survival strategies.

First, reminding herself – extremely firmly – that very often the anger and bitterness that had just been directed her way was *his* problem, *not* hers, and she could choose to let it go. She didn't need to try to atone for it or fix whatever had prompted it.

Second came the process of actually letting it go. Today she was opting for a nice cool shower and washing her hair with an extra-long head massage.

When she was about to rinse off the shampoo lather, though, she realised that she was too angry herself to wash the residual bad vibes down the plug hole. And despite Connor shouting at her and reminding her of all the prejudices he held against her family, it wasn't even *him* she was angry at.

Of *course* he had lost his shit when she'd basically been pointing out that the only people who appeared to value him had, and were still, exploiting him. She'd seen the confusion on his face when she'd asked why he didn't have the basic levels of comfort and security that any adult should expect from their life. It sounded like, from the moment they caught a whiff of Connor's magical gifts, the UK Witches Council had swooped in and made it clear to him what was expected. From a teenage boy.

Whatever tiny softening she might have been experiencing towards the Witches Council had been burned to ashes by how they'd taken advantage of him. And something deep in her gut told her that it hadn't been accidental. He was isolated, the witching community left to believe he was some kind of magical high executioner, and it had gone on for so long that he thought it was all he could expect of his life.

She let out a little scream in the bathroom. She'd only known him two days, but even if she'd only known him two hours, his situation would have upset her just on a basic decency and humanitarian level. The fact that she knew him to be such a . . . a . . . beautiful pineapple made it so much worse. He was all prickly on the outside to protect his sweetness inside.

But what could she do about it? Try to open his eyes? It wasn't her job to convince him that he was being mistreated. All she could do was show him that she knew he was worth more. It was up to him whether he then took the blinkers from his eyes.

Chapter Twenty

CONNOR

In hindsight, storming off with the intention of spending the day outside, beneath the blazing, relentless sun, was only a punishment for himself.

He'd used the gents toilets off from the bar area to finish getting himself ready, using the water and toothpaste to fuel spells to clean his clothes and his teeth – only remembering when he came out that if anyone had walked in on him and caught him sprinkling water and magical words at the sink, he would've given the game away about being a witch. But there were only a couple of members of staff moving around the kitchen and dining area and, despite looking over at him, they didn't seem to want to approach or talk to him.

Maybe Becca was right last night and the reason people didn't warm to him was nothing to do with him being the Abrogator. Maybe they just picked up on how much of a moody arse he was and could not be bothered with him. Becca was just an exception to the rules because she forgave everyone too easily, and he hated the thought that she accepted people treating her badly, but he wasn't above hoping she would forgive him for yelling at her.

He'd had no right to do that. Getting mad at her because she couldn't understand why he had to live this way was like getting mad at someone for not speaking the same language as you. Her life was so fundamentally different from his, how could it make sense to her? She spent her days taking photos of people enjoying their best moments with family and friends all around them. She was a celebrity in her own village, who couldn't walk past the pub without half a dozen people wanting to talk to her. She went home to her princess castle to snuggle with her cat, had a best friend she adored and visited her cousin, whom she thought the world of, in his magical manor house. If their lives were films, hers was a musical with an ensemble cast that would break the box office, and his was a black-and-white art-house picture with one actor, which no one ever saw. But both had their reasons for being made that way.

He left the inn and went to sit by her van, waiting for the mechanic who wasn't due to turn up for a couple of hours. The heat rose along with the sun and so he opened the back doors to sit on the edge of the van and get a little bit of shade; as much as part of him was convinced that he deserved to suffer for yelling at Becca, he couldn't actually stand the heat and he needed not to be passed out when the mechanic arrived. He'd get the van sorted out and attempt to gather himself into some form of reasonable human being before he faced her. Easier said than done when the thought of her being mad at him – or worse, *pitying* him – genuinely made him want to vomit.

Half an hour into his boredom vigil, staring back at the inn and feeling only slightly relieved about being outside of its incessant magical atmosphere, he received a text from Warren.

He didn't look at it straight away. And he couldn't say why, other than the way a heavy weight already seemed to be sitting on his chest, and it felt like seeing what his boss wanted from him would only add to it. Warren would either want to know what was happening or have another assignment for him. And it was only the latter possibility – that he was urgently needed – which got him to pull his phone free and check the message.

Warren: Any progress?

Connor's relief was sharp, and he knew it was only partly because another day without a dangerous witch he had to confront was a blessing. The other part was because he wouldn't have to leave Becca. Here. Alone.

He took a deep breath. Now to answer the question. 'Any progress?' When had he last checked in with Warren? After breakfast yesterday. And what had Connor achieved in the last twenty-four hours? Nothing, apart from learning how to play Four Towers, watching half of an Adam Sandler film, and developing a very confusing crush.

Connor: Not much. It's harder than we expected to get into the part of the building where we think the amplifier is and we still haven't worked out who has it. Or if it's being used for the magic of the inn.

There was no response for so long Connor put his phone down again, figuring that Warren had accepted that as his progress update. But then another message came through.

Warren: Do you think there is a possibility this has all been a ruse to remove you from Biddicote? Take the spotlight off Ashworth Hall?

Connor blinked, turning over the events of Friday in his head. *Was* there any chance of that?

Connor: No. It was the ghost who brought up the existence of the amplifier. And he was definitely not willing to talk initially.

Warren: He couldn't have been part of it?

Connor: They didn't know I was coming so how could they have planned for it?

Warren: They have a seer in the family, don't they?

Connor: Yes, but his gift isn't very strong.

Warren: According to who? Rebecca Ashworth?

Connor rubbed his chest as heat prickled through it. Had she told him that? Yes, but he'd already known it from the dossier. He recalled each profile, complete with details about their gifts and family connections . . . and how none of it gave him a clue about what kind of people they truly were.

Connor: What are you getting at? You don't think the amplifier exists?!!

Warren: I just want to make sure you're considering all the possibilities. Not being sucked into an Ashworth web of lies.

Connor: If she's lying about it, it's a plan that won't go anywhere, since I'll find out soon enough.

Warren: Will you? She's managed to detain you for an entire weekend so far.

Connor: For reasons we've both agreed are valid.

Warren: I appreciate this is a new experience for you. I probably should have prepped you more thoroughly for these challenges. But I need you to understand that your time is too valuable to waste in this way. And this amplifier cannot be left unregulated.

The amplifier that, thirty seconds ago, Warren was questioning the existence of. Maybe the heat was addling Connor's brain?

Connor: Are you saying you're going to pull me out, or send the Tenet Enforcers down?

Warren: Not yet. To either. But this can't go on much longer. This inn and the amplifier seem to have flown under the radar for a long time, and witches keeping secrets is always a red flag.

Connor: I don't think the people at the inn are actively keeping secrets from the Council. It's just the nature of the place. It's designed to keep them safe.

Warren: In their small picture. We work to the bigger picture. And sometimes to protect everyone we have to make tough choices.

Connor understood that. Of course he did. But these witches needed the inn. They were vulnerable people who had been gifted an opportunity to rest and repair in a place of security. He wasn't going to be responsible for taking their last port in a storm away from them.

Connor: Don't worry. I'll get this wrapped up asap.

Warren: I know you will.

He put his phone away and blew into his hands, casting a spell so the movement of air curled back on him, cooling his face. Taking a moment to sort out yet more confusing theories and puzzling through the situation.

He knew Warren was suspicious of Becca and the Ashworth family, but Connor couldn't settle those suspicions comfortably in his own mind. He'd spent too much time with her. She couldn't be putting on an act *all* the time. A devious act where she included eight-year-olds in magical board games to give their mother a break. Where she worried about leaving people out, or them getting too hot in the night or . . . What was he thinking about again?

This spell her family were trying to fix might be a secret, but Connor had recognised the similarities between the inn and Biddicote before she mentioned it. The tenor of the magic was the same . . . safety and protection. And what had her family ever done that was so bad?

He wished he'd had time to read the whole file, or that he'd brought it with him, because it felt like he was missing something that was going on here. He understood Warren's feelings about old witching families – Goddess knows he did. But was it possible that Warren's desire to overturn the old guards of the witching community had made him paranoid? His overthinking of the events, imagining this whole thing was an elaborate plan involving a seer's visions and deceitful ghosts seemed to point towards that.

The growl of a van coming up the hill interrupted Connor's thoughts. The mechanic was here. He'd get the van fixed and then they'd be in a position to figure out getting hold of the amplifier. They'd get a plan together. He and Becca. Because they had made a good team so far – despite the seeming lack of progress . . . OK, so maybe an adequate team. Their hearts were in the right place, at least.

And if his beat a little faster whenever he was near her, he'd just have to learn to ignore it.

Chapter Twenty-one

BECCA

Becca ran through so many emotions that day, she actually thought she might transcend to a different plane of existence. Initially, she'd been resolved. Angry on Connor's behalf but understanding of his resistance and resolved to give him whatever space he needed.

When she went downstairs for breakfast, Frankie had reported seeing Connor outside with the mechanic, and she was grateful. Touched that he'd continued to deal with the van for her. Even if she knew it was mainly an excuse for him to get out of the inn for a little bit.

She'd hung around in the bar area, appearing to read a book on an app on her phone, but actually taking notes of the movements of the staff and trying to ignore the way that Rhiannon and Sam in particular seemed to be whispering about her.

Finally, Rhiannon had come over to check in with her around lunchtime about the argument that had been overheard, and to give her a more heavy-handed version of Sam's speech last night. Impressing on her that they were there to help her, and dropping in a story of a partner they'd had to ask to leave because of the way he had been mistreating his wife. It landed like a sledgehammer to Becca's chest. She appreciated that they were looking out for her – it was coming from a good place – but what was it about her or him that screamed that this was their relationship dynamic? So what if he wasn't very chatty? It wasn't a crime. And so what if they'd had an argument – that was normal, surely?

Or did she just think that because she was used to seeing a similar dynamic play out between her mother and father? Her reticent, unsociable father, and her mother, always making excuses on his behalf. It made the explanation she gave to Rhiannon, about this morning's argument just being a lovers' tiff after all the stress of the elopement and her father's disapproval, taste sour in her mouth. But that was stupid because she and Connor were not really a couple.

And, of course, the longer Connor was gone, the more she looked like she was deluding herself. It started to get a little humiliating. Frankie kept coming over and asking if she wanted ice cream – which the twins then got wind of, and they all ended up eating multiple ice creams supplied by the kitchenhand, Yusuf. So she found herself sticky, full and a bit annoyed at Connor again for leaving her in this situation.

But then even *more* time passed and she started to get concerned.

She went out to where the van was parked and he wasn't there. Presumably, he'd gone for a walk. He wouldn't have just called an Uber and left . . . would he?

No. He believed – to a point which had caused the argument that morning – that it was his duty to protect her and all the innocent witches at the inn, when it was time to retrieve the amplifier. He would be back.

She returned to the room to wait for dinner and spoke to Harry about how her aunt and uncle had taken the news about having Horatio as their new house guest. (Apparently, surprisingly well). And Kay had messaged her about the person who'd told her about Connor's status as Abrogator, and she couldn't even forward the information on to him, because she didn't have his phone number.

Then dinner rolled around and he *still* wasn't back. Could something have happened to him? Why hadn't they exchanged telephone numbers? She couldn't bear sitting in the bar with everyone giving her sympathetic looks, but she braved it for an hour or two, just so she could take some more notes about the movement of the staff. His absence and the rumours about their 'relationship' were clearly putting the other guests on edge, which she then started to feel guilty about. They were probably scared there was going to be another confrontation when he got back. She hated the fact that despite everything they were doing not to rock the boat, they'd still inadvertently managed to make the guests feel unsafe.

Finally, she headed up to the room, deciding that if he hadn't come back by morning, she would have to organise a search party. She took another shower before she put on her pyjamas, purely to kill some more time, and when she came out . . . *there he was.*

He looked up at her after he'd finished putting something down beside the bed, his slate-grey eyes meeting hers, and a lightness that made her dizzy swept through her.

She launched herself at him, only restraining herself from wrapping him in a bear hug when she caught his reflexive flinch. Landing awkwardly in front of him, she couldn't help but grab his upper arms, partly to feel the solid heat of him, to reassure herself he was real, but also to stop herself from landing on him and toppling him onto the bed.

'You're back.' The words expelled out of her in a gust of relief. 'Finally. Thank the Goddess – I thought something had happened to you.'

'I . . .' He seemed at a loss for how to respond, looking down at her, and her heart beat in her throat as his dark eyebrows drew together, tightening every angle in his face. 'What could have happened to me?' he finally managed.

'I don't know. A bee could have stung you. Emergency call to deal with an evil sorcerer. Alien abduction.'

That raspy laugh escaped his chest and made every muscle tighten in her own.

'Not sure how likely the last one would have been,' he said, the corners of his eyes crinkling. He looked tired, and a little pink across the bridge of his nose and cheekbones, which she supposed made sense if he'd spent almost all day outside. She couldn't even offer him her magical after-sun – it wouldn't work on him.

'You never know.' She raised one shoulder in half a shrug and let out another relieved sigh. 'I was worried.'

He blinked a few times, his eyebrows drawing even closer together. 'You were . . .? I'm—' He stopped and swallowed. 'I'm sorry I worried you.' His tongue swiped across his lower lip, and she made herself remember that it was probably because he was thirsty. *She* was thirsty, too, but in an entirely different way. 'And I'm sorry for yelling at you and walking out earlier.'

'It's OK,' she said quietly, her eyes sneakily dipping down to the column of his throat and the open neck of his shirt, which her head was only just level with. Holy hormones, she either needed to put a lot more space between them, or a lot *less*, immediately. 'I'm sorry for upsetting you, too.' She squeezed his arms, throwing a bone to her poor, deprived libido, and then forced herself to let go of him and step back.

And for a split second, his hands rose as hers fell, as if he wanted to catch them. To retain them. Butterflies swarmed in her stomach.

But then he turned away and sat down on the edge of the bed to take off his shoes. 'The mechanic got the van sorted. We can get cracking with a plan now to get this amplifier.'

'Thank you.' She backed away further, sitting on the edge of the bath, which was still full of cushions – like a tiny ball pit for adults. 'Frankie said he saw you out there.'

He made a little amused huff. 'Ahh . . . yeah, I think Frankie might be worried. Or his curiosity is killing him.'

She tilted her head in question, and he nodded towards the door, lining up his shoes under the chair.

'He followed me up after I came into the bar. I dropped the van key on the stairs as I was walking up and when I bent to get it, I could see him hiding around the corner. I reckon he's still out there now trying to hear what's going on between us.'

Becca didn't dispute it, knowing how disquieted everyone had been at the rift between her and Connor.

'Luckily, he can't hear anything we're saying or doing,' Connor added as he got up and went to the table to pour himself a glass of water from the jug that was enchanted to stay cool permanently.

'Is it lucky, though?' A smile pulled at Becca's mouth, an idea occurring to her about how to fix some of the guests concerns and . . . OK, maybe how to get a little bit of revenge on Frankie for being irrepressibly nosy. 'Maybe we should take the muffling spell off – give him some . . . audible reassurance.'

'That door is still thick even with the spell off. Resolving an argument at a volume he'd be able to hear wouldn't give the impression of peace and harmony, would it?' He tipped the glass up to his mouth.

'If you're purely thinking of resolution equalling amicable conversation, I'd agree. But we're supposed to be newlyweds, Connor . . . have you never heard of make-up sex?'

The water he'd just started drinking threatened to come back out of his mouth in a flurry of spluttering and coughing. 'Wh-what are you talking about?' he croaked, thumping himself on the chest with his free hand.

She hopped off the edge of the bath and went to the door, her skin prickling as his shocked gaze followed her. Crouching down, she made a small circle by curling her index finger and thumb tightly and whispering a spell that gave her a magical periscope of sorts, then held it up before the keyhole. Sure enough, Frankie *was* out there, hiding really terribly in a doorway nearby, blatantly trying to listen in.

Bless his heart. But it was still such an invasion of their privacy. Rhiannon would not approve – or at least, she would *say* she didn't approve, but Becca betted she'd still want to hear about what he'd overheard.

She sniggered and stood up. 'We should give him something to report back to the others with. Convince them we've reconciled. Think of that scene from *When Harry Met Sally* . . . At the diner. Where she proves how convincing a fake orgasm can be.'

'You want us to make *fake sex noises* for him to listen in on?' Connor still sounded like he was choking, even though his airway was clear of liquid now.

She nodded. 'Come on, it'll be fun. Everyone has been looking at me like I'm such a sad, lovesick woman, married to a man who doesn't treat me well. Let's change the narrative and convince them that you know how to treat me *extremely* well. It will set their minds at rest.'

He was quiet for a moment. But it was a different kind of quiet. She could feel it filling the space between them. His focus steady on her. He drank down the rest of his water and wiped his long fingers over his mouth and chin, skin rasping over the stubble on his chin.

'OK,' he said, slowly, and put the glass down with a decisive clink. 'If that's what you want.'

Becca's thighs trembled at the low tone of his voice. Suddenly it felt like she'd drawn his attention to a big red button with a sign that said 'Do Not Press' next to it, and his agreement was making it light up. Maybe this *wasn't* such a good idea, and yet she found herself nodding – figuratively jamming her hand down against that button.

His eyes fastened on hers and she couldn't look away from their dark intensity. She touched the door behind her, recounted the steps she'd taken to create the muffling spell she'd placed on the room and concentrated hard to reverse it.

'You should come closer.' Something about this felt like a dare now, a game of chicken, and her pulse was making itself known, fast and strong, at various points in her body. 'Can't have make-up sex from all the way over there.'

He started towards her, and she thought she might pass out at the sight of him walking over to her. She didn't think he meant it to be predatory – he was just that much taller than her, he couldn't help looming in that way – but then, when he reached her, he slapped his palms onto the door behind her shoulders, the noise of the impact conspicuous.

'Is this better?' he asked. The scent of him – oakmoss and rosemary, mint and citrus – rolling over her; it took everything she had to resist licking or biting her lips as she looked up at him.

'I missed you all day, darling,' she said, injecting her voice with breathlessness but making sure she kept the volume up.

'I missed you, too,' he countered, with a growling tone that had the fine hairs on the back of her neck rising. 'I'm so sorry.'

'Me, too.' She took in the curve of his bottom lip and imagined what would happen next, if it were real. The gasp she let out was only half fake as she pictured him trapping her between his body and the door, pressing his mouth to hers and then lifting her to wrap her legs around his hips as they got lost in a long, hot kiss.

Less fantasising, more acting, she instructed herself. She tilted her hips forward and then bumped her butt firmly against the door and let out a soft moan.

'Becca,' he said, half like a prayer and half like a warning as he closed his eyes for a moment, and the danger of the game they were playing skated across her skin like static.

'Connor,' she volleyed back at him, raising her voice slightly as if she were surprised and pleased, and his eyes opened again, fastening on hers. She held his gaze, raising her hips and dropping them again, so her butt banged against the door once more.

Frankie should be getting the gist now.

But when Connor's gaze dipped down her body and back up to her mouth, she honestly couldn't have cared less. She couldn't hide the way she was breathing faster now, but maybe he'd think it was all part of the act.

'How would my wife best like me to show my remorse?' he asked, in that same growly voice, and she pressed her legs together involuntarily.

This was getting too much now. It was self-sabotage, and she knew it.

'You know how I like it, baby. Hard . . . and fast,' she managed to get out, repeating to herself that this was an act, only an act. 'That's right. Oh, Goddess, right there.' And then she moaned even louder.

He swore, loudly, and then backed away a few steps, letting out the order: 'On the bed. Now.'

She couldn't help it. She shivered. Luckily – or unluckily – he'd turned his back and was running his hands through his hair. Maybe this was going too far for him as well?

If she wasn't careful, it was going to be really obvious that she was getting aroused by this and not only would it be embarrassing, but if *he* wasn't getting aroused, that would be wrong.

She had to get them out of this. Walking as though she were drunk, she staggered into the chair and the table, doing her best to make it sound like they were bumping into furniture as they made their way to the bed. Connor turned his head, whatever look she'd been unable to decipher before giving way to confusion.

She winked at him and threw herself onto the bed, so it made an audible squeak. 'Oh, Goddess, yes. Give it to me, *big boy*.'

His eyebrows climbed and he pressed his lips together hard, so she knew he was trying to hold in a laugh. 'Yes, yes!' She couldn't help grinning back at him, scooching into a sitting position so she could start bouncing up and down on the bed, creating a steady, rhythmic squeaking. 'So good. Faster.' She waved a hand to get him participating again. 'Give me more. I can take it.'

'I know you can, you . . .' His exaggerated growly voice was a little undermined by the way he trailed off, raising his palms, his brow scrunched up as he struggled to find the right words.

She mouthed 'Good girl?' as a suggestion and fluttered her eyelashes at him.

'*Bad girl*,' he said firmly, his eyes lit with amusement. 'Very. Bad. Girl.'

She bit her lip on a laugh. It was working. Oh, she was still buzzing with desire, but the edges of it had softened with the simpler pleasure of shared silliness.

He went over to his side of the bed, kneeling on the mattress and putting his hands on the headboard, starting to bang it into the wall at a counterpoint to her bounces. They increased the tempo, looking at each other, as though they were playing tennis, waiting for the other's next move. Their hair fell all over their faces, cheeks growing pink with the sheer physical effort of abusing the bed.

Becca started to do her Meg Ryan impression, groaning at increasing volume, and then poking Connor in the ribs to get him to join in. He shook his head; he was biting his free fist, his eyes crinkled at the corners. Fine. Anyone who'd met him would probably assume he was the silent type, but oh, Goddess, did she want to find out if she could make him moan.

She'd settle for seeing if she could make him break into laughter, though. Even if that wasn't the point of . . . whatever this was. She escalated her noises, turning them squeaky and earning a pained look from him, until she let out a howl and he let go of the headboard entirely and buried his face in the pillow, shoulders shaking.

Utterly satisfied, she decided to bring the show to a crescendo and gave an enormous guttural shriek, rattling the headboard in a frenzy and then stopping suddenly. Knowing that she was going to crack and start laughing, too, she quickly leaned off the bed to press her hand to the wall and gasped out the sound-muffling spell again. As soon as it was in place, a soft pop of her ears confirming it, she collapsed, her stomach cramping from laughter.

'By all the gods, Becca.' Connor's voice was dampened by the pillow he was still burrowing his head into. 'If he stayed to listen to all of that . . . I don't even know what he's going to think.'

'Mission accomplished, I'd say.' Becca couldn't stop grinning. She propped herself up on her elbows and looked over the duvet barrier, which she had flattened a fair bit in her exuberance. His broad shoulders were hunched from his position, making his T-shirt tighten in certain places and drop loose in others. It had ridden up enough to expose a good few inches of his waist. The line of his hip bone. She wanted to bite it.

She tipped her head back to stop herself from ogling him more. Her chest felt emptied out – honestly a laughing fit was as good as sex sometimes.

It didn't stop her *wanting* the sex, though.

'Aren't you going to be embarrassed facing him tomorrow?' Connor finally lifted his head.

'Maybe. A tiny bit. But it was too much fun, and *he* should be the one who's embarrassed really. *You* don't have anything to worry about, though.' She wiggled her eyebrows and shifted her weight onto one of her elbows, rolling onto her side. 'You can strut your stuff, *big boy.*' She winked at him again. 'You're welcome.'

He shook his head, laughter soft this time, his eyes meeting hers, alight with humour. The moment stretched, like it had a few times before – here in the bedroom, under the tree. And each time it happened, they seemed to be getting closer to each other.

His gaze broke away from her eyes and she *felt* it skating down to her lips, further to her chest, and she belatedly realised she was giving him quite the view from this angle, with her pyjama vest somewhat askew from their antics. Her heart rate ramped up again. She held her breath as his eyes moved back up to meet hers again. Hot and intense now. There was no misreading that look. And if she could have wished for anything at that moment, it was for him to lean across the barrier and kiss her.

Instead, he clamped his jaw tight and swallowed. Took

a deep breath and pushed himself up, off the bed. 'I'm going for a shower.'

She nodded. Yes, that was for the best. Hormones should *not* be put in charge of wishes. If she really had just one wish, she could do something a lot more useful with it. Because *she* could do something about this thing that kept happening between them – the wanting, the notion that he wanted it, too – off her own back. She could just *ask* him.

But not now. Emotions were running high, and he'd chosen space. She didn't want to make it awkward for him when they had to share a room and a bed, if she was reading him wrong. She didn't think she was, but just because he might feel a physical attraction to her, didn't mean he wanted anything to happen. Maybe, once this whole thing was done and they were leaving the inn, she could talk to him about it.

Until then, in lieu of being able to take another – ice-cold – shower herself, she grabbed herself a glass of water and checked out the keyhole again. Frankie was gone. She brushed her hair, trying to calm the jangling feeling through her body at the thought of getting into bed for another night with Connor beside her. Just being near him.

This was worse than a code red, if that was possible.

Turning off the main lights, she tucked herself in, attempting to do some meditative breathing. With any luck she'd fall unconscious soon. Before Connor returned. She wished Michael Kitten was here to distract her. Cat therapy was real and invaluable.

Eventually, Connor came back. She kept her eyes tightly shut as he climbed into bed next to her, the fresh scent of his shower gel wafting over towards her, the movements of his big body making the mattress dip and her muscles clench in response.

Don't start, body, she growled internally.

It all went quiet, and she figured he thought she was asleep already so wasn't bothering to make conversation. Like he'd said earlier, they could get on with their plan now they had the getaway van back in action. But they could talk about it in the morning. There was no sneaking into the staff rooms in the middle of the night, when the occupants would be in there asleep.

'Oh, shit.' Connor's quiet mumble interrupted her thoughts, and she opened her eyes to see the shadowy shape of him rustling around beside the bed. 'Becca, Becca, are you awake?' he said softly, as he twisted back around, something in his hands.

'I'm awake,' she said slowly, trying not to sound too alert.

'I . . . er . . . I almost forgot, but I went into town with the mechanic, when he was getting the new battery for the van. And I got these. D'you want one? They're a wee bit crushed now.'

Paper tore and when she sat up, he was ripping one side of a large square white bag to reveal something that must have once resembled intact food. 'What are these?'

'Iced buns. But they're pink.'

She looked up at him. He was sitting opposite her, staring at the buns as though waiting for them to do something. 'Connor . . . is this a midnight feast?'

'Technically, it's an eleven-eighteen feast. And it's not much of a feast.' He picked up one of the buns, sticky icing trying to bring the second bun with it. 'But I wanted to say sorry.'

Becca's heart swelled. 'You didn't need to do this. But I'm glad you did. Thank you.' She pulled her bun away from his and they ate them quietly, licking their sticky fingers and exclaiming about how delicious the raspberry-flavoured icing was.

Tomorrow they were going to try to get the amplifier, and then they were going to leave and go their separate ways. Unless . . . there was a slim possibility he wanted to spend more time with her. These past couple of days had been like having back-to-back dates with him and she wanted it to carry on. She wanted to continue watching silly films with him, going for walks in the sunshine with him, having picnics under trees with him, surprising *him* with midnight feasts. And she wanted to kiss him and kiss him and kiss him.

But even once they left the inn, it wasn't the end of the complications between them, so she had to warn herself that this might be all she got: these precious moments. She'd learned at a young age not to take those for granted.

When they'd finished their buns, she lay down on her side of the bed, her stomach full of sweetness and her heart even more full, and faced in his direction, taking in the slither of his face she could see over the duvet barrier and committing it to her memory.

Chapter Twenty-two

CONNOR

Connor couldn't remember the last party he'd gone to. He'd been on the peripheries of teenage parties at Dentwood, just existing in the general vicinity because he literally couldn't go anywhere else, but since leaving school it wasn't like he had progressed to getting invited to witching festivities, or office parties. He'd had an invite to Warren's fiftieth birthday, but at the time he'd been recovering from a minor stab wound to the leg, caused by an ambitious witch in Canada who'd decided he'd quite like his own army of the dead and his recruits the fresher the better. Being impaled by a discarded femur bone actually came second in his top ten worst memories of that job.

All of which was to say, Connor wasn't entirely sure what to *do* with himself at a party. Or whether he even liked parties. Not that it mattered. Aveline – whose birthday it was – hadn't invited him herself, and he and Becca were only there because they had agreed that this might be the best opportunity to get into the staff area, according to their notes on the staff routines.

The party was in the gardens. Outdoor furniture had been moved to surround a large area of lawn and some temporarily placed stones for a bar and the grill. The sun was still up, making the floating tea lights unnecessary except to repel bugs, and because dinner had been a barbecue rather than a sit-down meal inside, he and Becca had predicted that Karl and Yusuf would be able to join them outside sooner than they would usually come into the bar on an ordinary evening.

So no one would actually be in the building.

They'd all be outside enjoying the party and, maybe bolstered by the shenanigans last night, no one would really think it was odd if Connor and Becca sloped off at some point.

Despite everyone at the inn potentially thinking that she howled during sex, Becca had got up that morning, petted the ghost cat, showered, dressed and headed down to breakfast as though she had zero fucks to give. If he hadn't admired her before, there was no avoiding it now.

He was feeling significantly more self-conscious about his fake bedroom performance. Every time he thought about how he'd growled at her to get on the bed he died a little bit more inside, mainly because he'd only partially been acting. Thank the Goddess she'd played up the absurdity of it, otherwise he would have been struggling to hide his arousal at her breathy moans and the way she'd moved her hips right there, next to him, at the door.

And when the act was over, and she'd been lying next to him on the bed, pink-cheeked and prettily dishevelled, with laughter on her lips, he'd almost tried to kiss her. He was in serious danger of blurring the lines between acting and his growing obsession with her.

Tonight, she was wearing a bright-yellow summer dress imprinted with dark flowers – the first time he'd seen her in a skirt – and it floated just above her knees, with an elasticated top and sleeves that were off the shoulder. And none of that was relevant to the job they needed to do tonight. But he was still letting himself watch as she talked to the other guests, as though he were an infatuated husband – instead of just an infatuated . . . what? Fellow spy?

He took a seat on a wooden garden chair away from any bushes that might attract bees and tried not to spiral into a depression that she wasn't his and could never be. Previously, he'd thought the way people gravitated towards her was because she was an Ashworth and it was Biddicote, but the same thing had happened here. It was just because she was Becca. Helping to find the right cable for the speakers, chatting with the quiet woman whose birthday it was, and being drawn into the dance the twins were doing in the centre of the lawn with Sam and Danika. It involved a lot of pre-co-ordinated hand moves and jumping back and forth in a line and seemed to go on forever.

Jemima broke away for a minute and ran over to him. 'Come join in, Connor.'

'I'm not much of a dancer.'

'That's all right—' She went to grab his hands and he quickly held them up and leaned back so she couldn't get hold of him.

'I've got two left feet. I'll crush everyone.'

She pouted at him, but Chrissy shouted at her to come back, so she skipped back over. His eyes automatically flicked back to Becca and a thrill went down his spine when he saw she was already watching him, even as she kept up with the dance moves. The smile she gave him was only small, though, and he wondered if she was worried about finally trying to get hold of the amplifier.

Sam left the dancers when the song changed, going back inside for a while before reappearing with a big cake. Aveline was sitting opposite Connor, seemingly more comfortable observing despite it being her party, and she pressed her hands to her chest at the sight of it. The music dipped and Becca hurried over to him, grabbing his elbow to get him up from his chair and linking her arm through his to pull him over to the crowd gathering to sing Aveline 'Happy Birthday'.

They all clapped and the candles were blown out. Karl and Yusuf had come out, too, but Karl and Sam went back inside to cut up the cake. Perhaps once the cake was handed out would be the best time. Connor rolled his shoulders, knowing he needed to look relaxed, but the thought that they were going to discover who had the amplifier and possibly have to confront them, with all these innocent witches around them, concerned him. As did the thought that Becca would be by his side for the confrontation.

A large floating black box caught his attention, and he looked over to see that Frankie was levitating a karaoke machine out to the makeshift patio, leads trailing across the grass.

Becca gasped and bit her lip, sending Connor a look, her big brown eyes lit with mischief, which immediately put the fear of the Goddess into him.

'Becca . . .'

She cackled. 'I'm putting your name down,' she said before hurrying over to join Frankie and Rhiannon, who were now poring over the book of song choices.

'Don't you dare,' he called after her, but she poked her tongue out at him and continued. And he just laughed and dragged a hand down his face.

Frankie was in the middle of a rendition of 'I Wanna Dance With Somebody' when the first bang and fizzle sounded. The hairs on the back of Connor's neck immediately stood on end and he spun to see where it had come from.

'Are those fireworks?' Chrissy said from behind him, but another bang followed her innocent question, and this time he saw a flare like plasma above their heads and a red-hot stone or rock tumbling down from the protective hemisphere that the wards had thrown up over the inn and its land.

Someone – a witch – judging by the unnatural glow to the rock, was throwing things at the inn. Or in the direction of the inn, depending on whether or not they knew it was there. If they didn't know, the strange behaviour of the projectiles would soon tell them there was something magical being protected here.

'Aveline!' a man's voice yelled. 'I know you're there.'

Connor looked back at the middle-aged woman whose birthday it was they were all celebrating. She'd grown pale and Rhiannon rushed over to her.

'That's her *bastardo* husband,' Frankie's voice came over the top of the soundtrack as though he'd been explaining it to someone and forgotten he was holding a microphone in front of his face. It squealed as he fumbled it, and it swung down by the speaker and then the music clicked off.

Three more projectiles hit the warding in quick succession, making the little girls cry out and run over to their mother.

'I just wanted to celebrate your birthday with you,' the man yelled again, and Connor shook his head. Because throwing magically fuelled rocks was the best way to wish someone you loved many happy returns. Becca had explained to him about Rhiannon removing the invite from someone who had been staying here because he mistreated his wife, and it wasn't a leap to guess that this was the guy. 'Come out here.'

Connor strode over to Aveline and Rhiannon, who were sitting back down. 'Do you want me to go tell him to jog on?' he offered.

'That's kind of you, Connor, but he's a witch. It would be safer for someone with magic to go—' Rhiannon started.

'Just leave it, he'll go eventually,' Aveline said quietly.

'I don't want you having to go through this, my lovely,' Rhiannon told her firmly. 'Yusuf, go grab Sam and Karl from the kitchen, would you?' she called out to the kitchenhand, and then she squeezed Aveline's shoulders again. 'We'll deal with him.'

Connor glanced around at the crowd. These witches were all either too young or too old, or had dependants to care about. He knew they didn't think he had any powers, but he couldn't leave this when there was a witch out there causing harm.

A large rock hit the warding again, this time exploding into little pieces, and some of the guests gasped and cried out in shock.

The warding was strong and it would protect them, but it wasn't stopping this fecker from scaring everyone – or creating a public scene, which could not be explained if a non-magical person happened by.

'I'll deal with him,' Connor muttered and headed for the gate.

BECCA

Becca knew Connor was going to go out there before he even started walking towards the gate. She pushed her drink into Danika's hand and hurried across the lawn to intercept him.

'Where do you think you're going?' she asked breathlessly.

'Out there to get rid of this great tool.' He nodded towards the gate and the driveway that lay behind it, still walking briskly.

She caught his elbow. 'You don't have to do that.'

'Don't worry.' He dipped his head closer to hers and lowered his voice, even though there was no one anywhere near them. 'I won't give the game away.'

She recoiled, her mouth falling open. 'Goddess, Connor, that's *not* what I'm worried about.' Did he really think it was so inconceivable that she would care about him getting hurt? 'They've dealt with this guy before, OK, before we were here. And this place will keep everyone safe. You don't need to put yourself in the firing line.'

His eyebrows drew together but he didn't say anything until another rock hit the warding. He glanced up at it and then back to the guests in the garden. 'You can't expect me to stand here and let him terrorise them all.'

Becca sighed. 'No. I suppose I can't.' She didn't like the idea of the kids being frightened, and of poor, traumatised Aveline having her birthday under siege, either. 'But I'm coming with you.'

'Becca.' He frowned.

'Two is better than one – and this way you can still avoid using your magic.' She crossed her arms and raised one eyebrow, daring him to object, to give her his lone-wolf spiel, and see how far it got him. Just because the Witches Council always sent him off on his own to face Goddess-knew-what, didn't mean *she'd* let him stand alone.

Obviously picking up on her stubbornness, he gave his head a small shake but said: 'All right. Fine.'

'Let me lead, OK?' she said to him as they crossed the gravel. 'We want to de-escalate, right?' she continued before he could object. 'I'm used to dealing with drunk, belligerent people at weddings.'

They crossed the gap in the hedgerow as soon as it was big enough to fit them, side-stepping through. It immediately knitted together behind them, the magic shoring up its defences again. A couple of metres away, in the centre of the single-track road, was a stocky man of average height and thinning hair, large rocks in each hand, one raised and ready to throw.

'And who are you two supposed to be? Security?' He sneered. 'Where's Aveline? I'm not leaving until she comes out here. I bought her a present. I made her dinner and she never turned up – ungrateful bitch.'

Connor stiffened and Becca felt the tension in his arms rippling down to his hands, as if he were readying them, the way he'd done when they walked into the inn the first night, not knowing what they might find. But he didn't say or do anything. He left it to her, as she'd asked.

'Sounds like you went to a lot of trouble,' Becca said slowly and softly.

'More than she deserves. I did everything for that woman. Everything. And this is how she repays me – kicking me out. Ignoring me.' The raised rock in his hand started to glow red. So, he had some elemental gift with fire. That made for a charming combination with his obviously stellar personality.

'Break-ups are hard. I went through one not so long ago. It really hurt.'

'I'm not hurt. I'm fucking livid,' he spat, but he lowered the glowing rock.

'I know it might not feel like it's possible now,' she said, shifting, and Connor's fingers gripped the back of her dress suddenly, as though he'd thought she was going to approach the man. She paused and glanced back at him for a second.

It was the most contact he'd instigated with her. And it made sense – because he was protective to his core, but something about it just clicked in line with what she'd noticed when Jemima tried to take his hands earlier. He avoided skin-to-skin contact. And yet, he still had the impulse to reach out and touch her . . . he still sometimes looked at her like he wanted to kiss her . . . so what was that about?

Now wasn't the time to puzzle it out. He wasn't even looking at her, his dark eyes were trained on the aggressive witch. She touched his chest for a second to reassure him and then turned her attention back to the man. 'But I've found someone I'm really happy with now,' she continued. 'He listens to me and looks after me. You could have that—'

'I don't want to find anyone else,' Aveline's ex shouted. 'I want *her*. Marriage is until death do us part. She belongs to me.'

A chill went down Becca's spine and she grew a little unsure about her methods.

'You're going to open up that hedge for me and let me in,' the man said, and suddenly he was approaching, glowing hot rock brandished at her like he was threatening her with a knife.

Connor pulled her behind him in a second, and then grabbed the man by the front of his shirt, his arm extended, elbow locked to hold him at a distance. Becca barely regained her balance in time to catch the man swinging the burning rock at Connor's head, but the difference in their reach left him unable to make contact while he was still holding it. The man shouted a projection spell to throw it, but without the natural momentum needed to fulfil the spell, it didn't launch with the strength of his other projectiles. It was still enough to make it glance across Connor's cheekbone as he ducked his head, though.

The man started to swing his other arm with the second rock, closer to Connor's dipped head now and Becca leapt forward, shouting, 'No!' She threw her weight onto the man's arm and pushed her magic into it, making it as heavy as possible. He grunted and staggered a little, trying to rebalance and cursing at her. Once he had his feet beneath him, he reared his head back, and jutted it forwards as though trying to headbutt her, but Connor ripped him away from her, spinning him away. He took the man's jaw in his free hand and, in the space of two heartbeats, the witch's eyes rolled back in his head and Connor was easing him, unconscious, to the ground.

Becca swore on a trembling exhale. It had escalated so fast and now it was over. Just like that. Two seconds and Connor had incapacitated him.

She dragged her eyes away from the unconscious witch and caught Connor's gaze, his expression strangely wary. It reminded her of when he'd walked into Ashworth Hall. He had all that power in his hands, but in spite of it . . . or maybe because of it . . . she could still see he was vulnerable. Adrift in a world that either didn't know who he was or feared him.

'It's only temporary,' he told her quickly. 'Are you OK?'

She nodded, but *he* wasn't – his cheek was bleeding. She made to step forward and the hedgerow opened again, this time Karl and Sam coming out in a rush.

'What happened?' Karl walked up to Connor, staring at the man at his feet.

'Glass jaw,' Connor said. 'Becca tried to calm him down, but he got violent.'

'So you laid him out?'

'Well, I wasn't going to let him hurt her,' Connor snapped.

'I'm not blaming you, mate.' Karl patted him on the shoulder. 'I'm impressed. Sam and I can take it from here.'

Sam approached Becca, her blue eyes wide. 'Are you sure you're OK?'

'Yeah . . .' Becca snapped out of her shock at Sam's tentative touch on her arm. Unfortunately, it seemed to make all the tension rush through her body and hit her head, in a sharp throb. She rubbed the back of her neck and took a deep breath, letting it out slowly. 'I'm fine, thanks. You don't need any help?'

'No, we've got this. We know where he's staying. We'll take him back there.'

Becca nodded and Karl caught her eye. 'Your hubby took a hit. We've got a first-aid kit in the kitchen – Yusuf will show you where it is if you can't find it, but I'm guessing he'll prefer your tender ministrations.'

Becca nodded again and went over to Connor, putting her arm around his waist, steering him back towards the inn. 'C'mon, Rocky Balboa – let's get you sorted out.'

'*Rocky?* Really?' he muttered as he let himself be led.

She laughed. 'I'm ashamed I didn't even think of that pun.' And then she dropped her head against his arm, cheek pressed to his shirtsleeve, unable to help herself, needing to feel closer to him. Reassuring herself he was all right.

Chapter Twenty-three

CONNOR

Every witch's magic felt slightly different. It was all energy, but depending on the person, their gift and designation, and how much he removed from them, it left Connor with a different physical response. He hadn't completely nullified Aveline's husband, though he had dearly wanted to when he threatened Becca – *twice*. But even the temporary amount Connor had taken had left him feeling like he'd swallowed an electric eel, and it was threatening to crawl its way up his oesophagus, burning and slimy.

Still, that was nothing compared to his roiling confusion about Becca's reaction. It was a sucker punch to see the same deep shock on her face as when she'd found out he was the Abrogator . . . but he could make sense of that. What he didn't understand was why she was now pressed close to his arm, leading him across the driveway, footsteps swift on the gravel.

Frankie and Danika came out of the side gate in a rush, as though they'd heard their approach.

'Oh, poor baby.' Danika bit her lip, staring at what Connor assumed was the sight of blood on his face. It was only stinging. And throbbing a bit. Next to the other sensations, he was barely aware of it. 'Are you OK?'

'He's going to be fine,' Becca answered, because Connor was too thrown by the weird breathiness in Danika's tone. They hadn't been running that fast, though maybe it was partly worry. Frankie's eyes were wide, and he kept looking over to the hedge and overhead.

'Karl and Sam are escorting Aveline's husband home,' Becca continued. 'There shouldn't be any more trouble. But . . . maybe don't mention the . . . er . . . fisticuffs?'

'Right, for sure.' Frankie nodded and then paused. 'You did win, right?'

'Oh, yeah, don't you worry about that,' Becca said, and Connor's heart fractured at the grimness in her tone. Maybe this was all just an act, to cover up the fact that he'd used his magic, and she *was* horrified deep down but knew she couldn't show it. 'Like I said, Sam and Karl are just dropping him off at home – he is out for the count.'

Frankie and Danika nodded, but in very different ways: Frankie's a frenzied bobbing of released tension and Danika's slow, her eyes roving over Connor in a way that made him want to cover his private parts, even though they were already covered.

'We're just going to clean up and cool down.' Becca tugged gently on Connor's arm, and both groups headed off, but Danika let Frankie go ahead slightly, catching Connor's eye and holding up seven fingers while mouthing, 'My room,' at him. When he almost tripped, Becca turned to see what was keeping him and Danika hurried off.

'Looks like you've recruited another fan, there,' Becca commented dryly, obviously having caught what Connor was slowly realising might have been a proposition. And a ballsy one at that, with his 'wife' right there.

'It'll only be because of your propaganda last night.' His cheeks warmed again at the memory. And then a horrifying thought occurred to him . . . if he *had* tried to kiss Becca, would she have let him – because of the power he had over her? Or her dedication to getting this amplifier back for

256

her family? She was too brave for her own good. 'None of them would tolerate me if they knew what I really am.'

Becca's arm, looped through his, stiffened. 'Who.'

'The witches here—'

'No, that's not what I meant.' She shook her head as they went through the door, muttering: 'Propaganda *does* have a lot to answer for.'

It was warm and dark inside; only a couple of the sconces on the tables flickering on as they passed through the dining area towards the kitchen. They pushed through the swinging doors and found a typical farmhouse layout, but on the larger side of average, with industrial-sized appliances.

'Now, where is that first-aid kit?' She finally let go of Connor's arm, leaving him feeling cold on the outside, in stark contrast to the fiery energy still buffeting his digestive system. Goddess, that man's magic had been foul.

He leaned back against the counter, swallowing back the burn. 'Your gift can't help you?'

'It's not lost,' she said ruefully as she slowly scanned cupboards, before picking one and opening it up to find the kit right there. 'But . . . years of finding things for other people has given me a better sense of where things are likely to be, nonetheless.'

She came back over, holding the green zip-up bag, and then looked up at him, her eyes scanning his and resting on his cheek. 'This will be a lot easier if you sit down on a chair, then I won't have to go on my tippy-toes.'

So, she was still determined to act like she wasn't scared of him. No one wanted to come near him, let alone tend to his wounds. Even if he hadn't been immune to magical healing, he would have ended up at non-magical hospitals because witches didn't like touching him.

257

He reached out for the bag, placing his hands top and bottom, while hers were on either side. He tugged it towards him, trying to get her to let go. 'I can do it myself.'

'It'll be easier for me. I can see the wound.' She tugged it back towards herself.

'I can use a mirror.' Tug.

'But we're right here now, and you need to stem the blood flow.' Tug.

'It's a graze, not a gushing artery.' Harder tug. 'You don't have to do this.'

'Connor, please, just *let* me help you. I *want* to.' Tug back *and* downwards.

'What's wrong with y—' he exclaimed, and cut himself off, letting go of the kit a little suddenly, so she rocked back on her heels.

Her eyes narrowed on him and then she pointed to the chair by the small table in the corner. 'Sit. There. Now.'

He obeyed immediately, knowing better than to put up a fight when she was this determined. Maybe she was trying to prove something to herself. She unzipped the kit somewhat aggressively and rummaged through it, getting out two alcohol wipes. She cleaned her hands with one and then tore open the packet of the second and put her thumb to his chin, guiding his face to the side so that he could only see her leaning close from the corner of his eye.

'This is going to sting,' she said, her breath fanning against his cheek, and then the wipe was sliding against him, cleaning blood away and making the cuts throb. He hadn't realised the rock had made more than one. 'It didn't burn you?'

'If it had been held against my skin, it would have. It was just a glancing blow.'

'So you aren't immune to elemental magic?'

'Only if it's worked directly on me. But if the magic has been used to change the state of something already – like heat generated to boil a kettle – it's still boiling water. It won't feel cold to me.'

She nodded. 'OK, I think I'm getting it.' She wiped once more and straightened up, the skirt of her dress brushing against his knee. 'So . . . why do you think something is wrong with me?'

His mouth went dry. 'I don't . . . I'm sorry—'

'Don't lie.' She folded her arms. 'Is it because I'm not scared of you? Is it because I'm not frightened to touch you?'

'Becca. You don't have to pretend.' He shook his head.

'I'm *not* pretending.' Her voice was low and fierce.

'I saw your face after I drained him. You looked pretty freaked out then.'

She huffed out a breath. 'Well, sure. Your power is . . . whoa. And I never expected it to work so quickly either—'

'I was just incapacitating him. It's not permanent.'

She nodded. 'You already said. I believe you. And I'm *not* scared of you.'

'You're not scared that I could take away all your magic, your identity as a witch, with the touch of my finger?' He scoffed.

She gave him a gently withering look. 'Should I be? Are you planning to nullify me because I put your name down to sing "You Spin Me Round"?'

'Of course not.' His heart pounded against his ribcage and he rubbed his chest, trying to ease the sensation of pressure that was only partly from the magic he'd pulled from Aveline's husband.

'Exactly.' She pulled some plasters out of the bag, looking at them critically to find the right-sized one. 'You're not going to take my magic unless I start lobbing homemade cannonballs at people and become an abusive bully. And since I have no intention of doing that, why should I be worried?' She delivered all of this speech matter-of-factly and then tore the paper from around the plaster she'd selected. She pressed it over the cuts, smoothing it into place, his cheek tender and aching beneath the gentle touch, which she removed from him quickly. Then she bent down, holding on to the armrests of his chair, so he was forced to shift back.

'You're *not* a black hole *or* the big bad wolf *or* a monster, and I'm *not* scared of you hurting me, or what will happen if I touch you.' Her eyes were big and serious as they held his from barely thirty centimetres away. 'But I understand if you're not used to that; if you've spent years thinking that's a reasonable way for people to react to you, and you're not comfortable with having me close.'

No, he wasn't comfortable with having her close. He was coming *out of his skin* because of her words and the implications of them. The way she was waiting there, in his space, her hair swinging forwards, glimpses of her bare shoulders beneath, her lips pink and there – right there – where he could lean forward and kiss her . . . How did this feel simultaneously like he was dying, but also like one of the most thrilling moments of his life?

He moved forward as if he weren't in control of his own body. As if she were drawing him in with some magical string, which wouldn't have even worked on him. Her eyes fluttered closed and—

The door to the kitchen swung open and Yusuf walked in. 'Oh, Goddess, sorry, guys, I, err . . . didn't mean to interrupt.'

Becca's eyes flew open again and she snapped up straight to standing. 'That's OK, I was just seeing to Connor's cut.

How is everyone doing?' She sent a bright smile Yusuf's way, but there was a wobble to her voice.

Shit, maybe she *hadn't* been interested in him kissing her. Maybe she'd just been making a point about not minding being close to him? It didn't mean she wanted him *that way*, did it?

Connor sat back heavily in the chair, concentrating on his breathing, clearing the disorientating feeling of almost kissing her – again – and letting his body assimilate the foreign magic in his system. He needed to get himself back on some kind of even keel.

'Not too bad. Aveline's gone back up to her bedroom, but Rhiannon went with her for company.' Yusuf carried on into the room, reassured that he wasn't walking in on them doing what everyone expected newlyweds to do at every possible opportunity, and went over to a big silver platter. 'I thought I'd bring the cake out, though, give everyone a bit of a comfort-food boost and a nightcap before we pack up.' He lifted the platter, showing the individual slices of cake tucked into napkins.

'That's a good idea.'

'You coming?' he asked, heading to the door, turning his back to it so he could push it open.

Becca glanced at Connor, too quickly for him to read any more of her expression, but then she shook her head at Yusuf. 'No, I think we're going to call it an early night. I'll just tidy these bits up.' She gestured to the first-aid kit.

'No worries. Night, then. And thanks for helping out with it.'

'No problem.'

Yusuf disappeared out again and Becca gathered the packets and bandages, shoving them briskly back in the green kit bag. She grabbed it and took it back to the cupboard, using her magic to put it back on the shelf.

'I think this might be our opportunity,' she said, turning back to Connor, one hand on the counter, and for a traitorous moment he thought she was referring to them, but then she added: 'Everyone is occupied elsewhere. Are you ready to go get the amplifier?'

Chapter Twenty-four

BECCA

Becca may not have been about to start creating homemade cannonballs, but she had been very close to screaming like a banshee when Yusuf had strolled into the kitchen, on his generous quest to bring cake to the traumatised. He did not deserve to feel the brunt of four days' worth of sexual frustration, so she kept it to herself.

It was a very sad state of affairs when she was jealous of her fake sex life. And other people were trying to get a piece of it.

She couldn't even be mad at Danika about it. She was still so young and had been through a lot – the idea of there being a man as gorgeous as Connor, who was actually good in bed, within touching distance, was probably enough temptation to have her disregard Becca's feelings. It was enough to have Becca disregarding her *own* feelings, if she was honest, and she knew nothing about his level of sexual prowess above the way that he could turn her on just by saying her name.

But she had to place that in a cauldron and put the lid on it for now, because it was time to focus on the reason why she was actually there. Getting the amplifier back.

Connor followed her out into the empty dining room, and she tried to ignore how in tune her body was to his every movement. The lights that had turned on automatically in the bar showed there was no one there either, and voices from the garden were just barely audible through the thick stone walls.

Thinking of the guests out there, about all the staff rallying to comfort and assist in the aftermath of the incident, Becca faltered.

'Everything all right?' Connor asked her softly.

'I just . . . what if the inn needs it?' she found herself whispering. What if the amplifier had been responsible for protecting the inn and these people? Boosting the magic so that Aveline's husband couldn't get in? So the rocks he'd turned into weapons hadn't hit someone?

He frowned at her, in that way he had that said he was trying to figure out what was going on in her mind. 'We'll only know that once we've found it and I can read the magic. At the moment anything is possible. I won't remove any spell until I know what it's being used for.'

'Right.' She nodded. And what if he then argued that they couldn't remove it from the inn until it had been proven that it rightfully belonged to her family? Would she have to tell him about the anchor spell in Biddicote? Make him understand that her uncle and cousin's health was at stake?

She pushed her hair behind her ears. This was pointless hypothesising. Like Connor said, they needed to find it and then he'd be able to read and assess the magic tied to it. They'd approached this slowly and carefully for a good reason. There was still a possibility it was being used for something nefarious and they had to make the most of this opportunity to figure out what was going on without risking an ugly confrontation. These people had had enough of that for one evening. And, in some cases, probably for their lifetimes.

She led him over to the door to the staff area and reached for door handle. He stopped her with a soft touch to her wrist.

He'd *touched* her. Voluntarily. A flicker of hope rose that he really had heard her earlier in the kitchen and wanted to give in to this pull between them. Even if the touch was fleeting, so he could wrap his own hand around the doorknob instead, it was progress.

'It's not locked and there are no wards,' he whispered.

That was a good sign, then. Maybe? It was a tiny bit more likely that it was buried in a wall somewhere, like she'd suggested the other day, hidden by a smuggler, and no one at the inn had any clue about it. That would be *ideal*.

'I should go first. I have to lead the way,' she reminded him.

He moved back, though she could tell by the stiffness of his shoulders that he wasn't keen on the idea; he was so indoctrinated by the idea that it was his life's purpose to throw himself on magical hand grenades. If she ever found the people responsible . . .

Beyond the door was a cool, narrow hallway. There was one door off to the right and then a step down into a second, carpeted hallway. To the left an archway revealed a communal room, and there were two more doors and the bottom of a staircase just visible in the shadows. So far, so very normal and cosy-looking. The inn looked after its staff as well as its guests.

She paused by one of the doors, but the tug in her mind was coming from above. She pointed towards the staircase, and they moved quietly down the hall.

'I feel like Bluebeard's wife,' she murmured.

'Blue-who?' Connor muttered, close behind her as they went up the stairs slowly, slowly, using a slight lightening spell on their feet to cushion their footfalls, because the wood was well worn into its creaks and groans.

'What are they teaching you kids at school these days?' she teased under her breath as they came out onto a small landing. He gave a soft snort behind her.

She paused. There was a window looking out onto the garden and she could see the flickering tea lights set out in a circle, like a floating faerie ring around the party. Scanning the interior again, she tried orientating herself along with the magical guidance tapping against her skull. It didn't seem to correlate between the door and the entrance to another hallway, but she decided to go for the hallway, to see if it would come back around. Sure enough, it had a switchback.

Her gaze immediately went to the second door along on the left. Heart beating in her ears, she led Connor to it and stopped.

'This one?' he all but breathed, and she nodded. It was a normal door, typical of all the other ones in the inn.

He rounded his fist against the wood, whispered a spell and leaned his ear against it, as though he were using a glass to better amplify any sound coming from inside. Then he did a similar trick to the one Becca had used to see if Frankie was out in the hallway last night to look through the keyhole. Possibly the staff should replace these old door handles with something more modern and less convenient for spying.

Or maybe they liked it that way.

She gave a little shiver and Connor glanced up at her, eyebrows lifting in question. She shook her head to dismiss his concern, telling herself that his noticing her tiny movement while he wasn't even looking at her didn't mean he was as hyper-aware of her body as she was of his. He was probably just on high alert in case someone was coming.

He stood up again, leaning close to her. 'It's dark and quiet inside, so unless someone is sleeping, no one is in there.'

That was a little relief. No scary witch lurking so far.

He touched the handle to the door, his brow furrowed as though he were listening to someone speaking to him that no one else could see. She wanted to ask what it was like to read the magic of the world the way he did. Was all the spell work laid out in a blueprint? But now wasn't exactly the time.

'There's a very powerful ward on this door,' he said quietly, and the whispered tone in his gorgeous accent made another little shiver work its way up her spine for a different reason. It wasn't the time for that either.

'Different to an ordinary ward?'

'I'd say so. If you try to go through without me unravelling it, I doubt it will be pretty.'

'Well, that makes sense. It's definitely in there.' She tapped her forehead. The sensation in her head was almost burning now, they were so close. 'Can you unravel it, so we can go in?'

'I could, but if there are other hexes and wards inside, I might not be able to remove them all in time. It might be better for me to go in first and read the magic that's in the room and on the amplifier.'

She didn't like the idea of him going into this alone but could understand the logic. It was quicker and safer this way.

'I suppose you're used to dealing with these things by yourself,' she commented softly, and his matter-of-fact nod confirmed what she had suspected. The Witches Council didn't care one tiny bit about his welfare. Whether they thought him invincible or were just happy to let him be cannon fodder, it made her angrier than ever at them. She took a deep breath, forcing her anger back. 'OK, you go in and I'll guide you from here.'

He nodded and turned back to the door. This time, when he put his hand on the doorknob, he grasped it firmly and made a sharp beckoning motion with his other hand. He might be able to walk through the ward, unhindered, but he still had to unlock the door. There was a click as the bolt slid back easily and he pushed the door open, stepping inside without wasting any time.

It was dark inside and Becca drew as close as she could without encroaching on the threshold of the door. Connor conjured a small ball of light and turned around the room slowly, illuminating a generous space, with a double bed, a dressing table and wardrobe, as well as a desk. They were all in white painted wood, with pastel-coloured soft furnishings. Connor stopped his turn about the room and looked back to Becca, eyebrows raised.

No. It didn't look like the lair of a cat burglar or evil sorcerer, but . . . it did look strangely familiar to Becca. Which was odd, because how could it be? She'd never been to this inn before in her life . . . The pressure in her head increased and, beneath it, an insistent tug towards the bed.

'Try under the bed.' She inched closer to the doorway; the pull to walk inside and look around herself was intense. Being this close to finding the lost thing was the most unsettling stage. The anticipation could feel unbearable sometimes, like a sneeze building.

Connor went over to the bed and got down on the floor in a swift move that left him in a pose reminiscent of someone doing push-ups, or something else that involved upper-body strength and being horizontal that she didn't really want to let her imagination run away with.

'Whoever it is, they look like they're helping out the local shoe store with surplus stock.' His dry comment soothed something inside her. It meant he'd relaxed a little, too.

'Do you recognise any of the shoes?'

'From *where*?'

'From people's *feet.*'

'I don't pay any attention to people's feet,' he said, like it was the weirdest thing anyone had ever suggested. 'Besides, it's mostly the boxes. All lined up. Are you able to give me any pointers about whether it's likely to be the head or foot of the bed before I start looking through them?'

'Give me a sec to concentrate.' She closed her eyes, narrowing in on the insistent pull in her head. 'Nearer the head end.'

He made a soft grunt as he reached underneath the bed and an irrational fear that a hex was going to attack him gripped her. No hexes could hurt him, could they? Unless they made the edges of the box turn sharp or red hot . . . She forced herself to look away, trying to see if there was anything that could help identify the owner of the room. The decor seemed to suggest a female occupant, but that was just an assumption. There were no other clothes out on display. It was so neat. No photos that she could see either . . . her gaze snagged on the bookshelf by the door, which was partially lit from the light in the hallway. There was a collection of thin, colourful books that looked very familiar . . .

A sharp pain travelled across her head again and she winced. Maybe there *was* some kind of hex on the amplifier, or she'd got too close to the wards.

'You OK?' Connor was looking back at her.

'Yeah,' she said, rubbing her temples. 'I'll be fine, you—' She broke off in the middle of encouraging him to get back to his search. Footsteps on the stairs. 'Abort, abort,' she whispered. 'Someone's coming.'

In a few swift moves, Connor extinguished his light, pushed all the boxes back under the bed with a wave of magic, and jumped up to his feet, eating the distance between the bed and the door in a couple of long strides and slipping through.

She barely had time to back away before he was easing the bedroom door shut. Her heart pounded as the footsteps continued up the stairs and then grew quieter as they reached the carpeted hallway around the corner. The lock clicked into place and Connor turned, bringing them chest to chest, so she had to tip her head back to look at him.

'What now?' she mouthed. The corridor was a dead end. The only way they could go was back the way they had come, which was exactly the direction whoever was on their way was coming from, too.

Connor scanned their surroundings, nodded at something over her shoulder and made a yanking gesture with his hand. A door swung open behind her. She turned her head, confused, because how would going into another one of the bedrooms be any better than staying in the one they'd just been in? Whoever it was could be heading to that very room. But Connor wasn't asking her opinion.

'C'mon,' he breathed, and that was all the warning she got before he lifted her bodily and deposited her in the small, dark space, crowding in after her and closing the door softly behind them.

Oh, it was a closet of some kind. Full of cleaning stuff and bedding. How had he known . . .?

'Can you see through walls, too?' she whispered, trying not to squeak.

'No. Hinges,' he explained.

He could see through *hinges*? Then she figured out what he meant. The hinges had given away that the door opened outwards, rather than inwards. 'Oh—'

'Shhh.' He raised his finger, as though to press it to her lips, but jerked to a stop, as if reins were pulling him in.

Her heart squeezed. He was still fighting it, as if he'd hard-wired it into himself not to touch people. She wanted to lean forward and lick his finger, just to show him how OK she was with direct contact. *If* he wanted it. She'd grab him and rub herself against him like a cat to prove it to him. *If* he wanted it.

But he hadn't said that downstairs. He'd leaned closer . . . but he hadn't said, 'Yes, I want you close.'

Did this proximity panic him now? The heat of his body was all along her front, the thin material of her summer dress hardly any barrier and the exposed skin of her upper chest tingling with the nearness of him. She swallowed and raised her eyes to meet his in the darkness. They were barely a glimmer, but he *was* looking down at her, too, and when he took a deep breath his chest just barely brushed against the curve of her breasts, sending thick heat to coil in her stomach.

He let out that breath, which wasn't quite steady. It stirred the strands of hair around her face, and although she didn't feel steady either, he could have been feeling that way for entirely different reasons.

She blinked and cocked her head, trying to make herself focus on the more important issue – the footsteps in the hallway. There was no point casting the muffling charm; it only masked the definition of noise, rather than covering it up entirely. Whoever it was would still wonder why there were noises coming from the cupboard.

A door opened and closed, but through the thick wood, she couldn't tell what room they'd gone into. What did they do now? Make a break for it? Whoever it was might hear them walking down the hallway, or just happen to come out when they were going past. They might have only popped back for a moment.

She lifted onto her tiptoes to try to whisper in Connor's ear, to discuss their next move, but because she was resisting the impulse to put her hand on his chest for balance, she ended up swaying towards him. He leaned backwards to compensate and hit something behind him. He wobbled and dropped back, his butt landing on whatever it was behind him with a dull *thwump* and she almost fell against him; only his hands landing on her hips stopped her.

Becca's shoulders rose to her ears, cringing at the noise, and she couldn't help but automatically put her hands on his shoulders. Holding her breath, she listened again. There had been no other door opening or footsteps – it hadn't given them away.

Her heart thumped at triple speed, blood rushing around her body, but as they continued to wait, frozen in the darkness together, the position they were in took more and more of her attention. His hands on her hips. Large and warm and firm. His thighs bracketing hers, the material of his trousers causing hot friction against her skin where her skirt had been pushed up above her knees. The top of his head level with her eyes, now he was propped on whatever was behind him. She could make out the shine of the individual curls of his hair and the muted smell of his aftershave beneath the sharpness of the antiseptic she'd cleaned his cuts with earlier.

She bit down on her lip as she thought about that moment in the kitchen. His shoulders shifted and she realised his eyes must be level with her mouth. Was he staring, the way he had been earlier?

She released her bottom lip slowly, her mouth tingling, and it felt natural to leave her lips parted. His fingers spasmed on her hips, digging in first, tugging her towards him before releasing suddenly, as if he'd been burned. She reached for his wrists, grabbing them without thinking. 'It's OK,' she whispered, dropping her head to the side of his so she was speaking directly into his ear. 'I want you to. If you want to.' If he told her he wasn't attracted to her, at least she could move on. A couple of days of awkwardness was not going to kill her. This tension, this desire, was what was killing her.

He reached for her hips again. Hands landing softly this time, but his thumbs smoothing the material of her skirt, tracing crescents between the edge of her navel and the upper crease of her thighs. Her breath gusted unsteadily over the shell of his ear, her hands coasting over his bare forearms, caressing the tense muscles there.

He tilted his head back, and her lips drifted across to his forehead. She could feel the crinkle in his brow beneath her mouth and moved back enough to look at his beautiful face – another iteration in his repertoire of scowls, but the gleam of his stormy grey eyes in the darkness was unguarded.

She lifted one hand and pushed a curl of black hair off his forehead, trailing her fingertip down his temple, over the sharp dip of his cheekbone on the side without the cut, the deep hollow beneath and along the angle of his jaw, skating over bristling stubble until she reached his chin, where she tipped it up a couple of centimetres higher, as she leaned down towards him. Slowly, slowly, to make sure he had plenty of time to say no or push back or push her away.

He closed his eyes and his hands slid higher, tightening on her waist, drawing her just that bit closer. A purposeful grip, solid and committed. It anchored her. Sent goosebumps over her skin. His lips were within tasting distance, parting beneath hers.

And then they were kissing.

Gentle warmth as he moved his mouth, soft and slow, against hers. He kissed like he spoke, that beautiful melody of his voice belying the abruptness of his words sometimes. His lips might look unyielding, but they gave in to her. And more than that, they beguiled her, twisting up her insides with each tender exploration, forming knots of anticipation as she felt the slightest edge of his hesitancy still, the way he was careful, so careful, to let enough control spool out between them . . . but then tugging the threads taut as he betrayed his efforts at restraint by grazing his teeth over her bottom lip or tilting his head in search of more. She had this idea – in equal parts terrifying and seductive – that it would be impossible to unpick the tangles they were creating between them with this kiss.

It was all a spinning fury of need inside her, and calm and constraint on the outside. She wasn't sure she could keep it up, no matter how delicious it was. She wanted more of him. She wanted him to know he could let go with her.

But the only way to do that, without pushing him further than he might be ready for, was to communicate how much *she* was revelling in his touch, and the moans and sighs struggling for release were not for here and now. They were meant to be hiding. Being quiet. Even as the thought popped briefly into her mind, she couldn't bring herself to listen. It disappeared in the whirlwind inside her, a snatch of cautionary voice, whipped away in the hurricane.

Her hands fluttered up to cup his jaw, then stroked down his throat, because holding his face felt too domineering, especially with her leaning over him, and she was worried about his sore cheek. A different pulse of tenderness moving through her at the memory of him being hurt, putting himself between her and danger. She moved her palms down to his shoulders, fingers gripping and greedy against the firm breadth of them, restless, as she tried to hold herself back, waiting for him. Holding herself back from wrapping her arms around him, pressing herself tight, tight to him like she wanted.

His kisses grew in decisiveness, mouth coaxing hers wider, and when his tongue dipped in to touch hers, she could have sobbed with the relief. He tasted of lemon, sweet and sharp like everything about him, and it was a hook digging into her abdomen, dragging down with a heavy, pleasurable ache. His hands *finally* moved from her waist – not that she didn't love them there – but her whole body was jealous for their attention. He scooped her hair back from her shoulders, gathering it in handfuls, and broke away from their kiss to trail his lips down her throat and across her collarbone. She arched her back and this time she had no hope of repressing her moan. She tried and it came out soft, then cut off as she drew a sharp breath in to try to stop herself.

He surged to his feet, looming over her, burying his fingers in her hair to cradle her head as he found her mouth again in a deep, devouring kiss. She clung to him for dear life as her knees threatened to give out. His shirt gave under her clutching grip, one of his buttons losing its own battle to keep the garment together.

And then, just as suddenly, he pulled away. She nearly collapsed at the shock to her system, going from all heat, all Connor, to space and cool air, nothing but her own weak limbs and swollen mouth to reassure her brain that she hadn't imagined it all.

'Wh— what is it? Is someone out there?' she managed to whisper.

'No.' He eased himself back down to his leaning position, putting more space in between them. 'I just . . .' He dropped his head, scrubbing his hands back through his hair and over his face roughly. 'We need to stop. We need to get out of here.'

'OK.' She smoothed her dress with shaking fingers. She didn't think that was entirely the reason why, but they could talk about it later. When he'd collected himself again. When she wasn't a human-shaped puddle of lust. He was right, they did need to get out of this cupboard.

Chapter Twenty-five

CONNOR

Becca took his undignified retreat with all her usual grace – as if he could have expected anything else. She wasn't an angel – there was too much playful mischief in her for that – but he was beginning to wonder if she might be his angel.

And the last thing he wanted to do was hurt her.

He'd been so lost in the euphoria of kissing her, he'd almost missed the tingle of magic touching his palms as he cradled her head. The sheer desire he had to take everything she was offering . . . had it been drawing her magic to the surface? Or was she just so powerful a witch that it sat on her skin?

He didn't know. And if he didn't know, he couldn't risk it. As much as it felt like tearing one of his own limbs off to detach himself from her.

They listened out again, having to wait until their own heavy breathing had calmed enough so that they could hear above themselves. There was no more movement in the hallway, but if someone had come out of one of the rooms when they were kissing – even if they'd been doing the can-can in the hallway – there was no way he would have noticed. The building could have fallen down around them and he wouldn't have noticed. Which didn't speak well of him protecting anybody.

Becca smoothed her dress and hair, and pushed the door open slowly, peeking out into the hallway. After a moment or two, she carried on the whole way and he followed. It was darker now, the last of the sun having well and truly set. She pointed to the wrong end of the corridor, even though it came to a dead end, with nothing there except for a dormer window with a short, flowery curtain tied back and a potted fern beside it.

He followed her again, because he was beginning to realise that there was always a plan brewing in her mind and, whether it was through her sheer determination or actual strategic instinct, it usually worked out. And even if there was a chance that it wouldn't, he'd still want to be with her.

Running her finger carefully along the seals of the window, whispering a spell, she unlatched it and swung it open. Outside was a flat bit of roof between two slopes of tiles, and, perpendicular to the roof, was the part of the inn their room was situated in. They never would have known about this window from being inside their bedroom, or even from the gardens outside the staff's secret garden, with the way it was tucked behind the other bits of roof. It felt out of place, but then old buildings like this were often higgledy-piggledy in their layouts, extensions being added throughout the years.

With the window open, the sound of voices carried around from the gardens on the other side of the building. There was no time for him to object because within a second of him absorbing all that information, she was climbing out of the window. On the plus side, the thought of either of them falling to their deaths should cool his ardour. He climbed out after her, contorting his spine to fit through the small window and then using magic to close the curtain and refasten the window behind them.

'Are you sure about this?' he asked quietly, as they stood on the flat bit of roof.

She nodded and leaned around the corner, and he couldn't help but reach out and grab her waist again, despite the sensations it sent racing up his arms and then cascading over his body like the fallout from a firework display. She placed one of her hands over the top of his, patting him reassuringly. Such casual trust in him.

And so much for the prospect of plummeting off the roof killing his ardour. Why would it? He already felt like he was in free-fall.

'Well, actually – before we plan our escape, perhaps we should decide whether or not to go back.' She stepped away from the edge so he had no excuse to keep hold of her. She wrapped her arms around herself as she looked up at him, her lips reddened from their kisses.

He dragged his mind away from her mouth and made himself focus on what she was saying. 'We've got no idea who came upstairs or what room they're in. We could be found out before I've even checked to see if they're in the room the amplifier is in.'

She sighed. 'I know. We were just so close. And . . . I don't know . . . hiding it beneath a bed in a shoe box doesn't seem the logical place to keep something vital for the magical infrastructure of the inn, *or* like master-criminal behaviour.'

'You'd be surprised how blasé criminals can be. But there was a really strong ward on that room. Either they don't trust the people they live with, or they know they have something valuable that needs protection.'

'Or they had a bad experience, and it just helps them feel secure.' She frowned.

'Could be,' he agreed softly. 'Or any combination of the three. It's not always black and white. What I *do* know for definite is, they're no slouch when it comes to wielding magic. At least I have a reference for their magical signature now. I should be able to narrow down who it is if I can get my hands on other spells the staff have cast.'

'Right, so no paying attention to people's shoes, but you can tell their *magic* apart?' Her eyes were wide as she looked up at him with what seemed to be a mixture of amusement and wonder. She cocked her head to the side. 'What's *my* magical signature like?'

It's like drinking espresso on a piazza under a perfect blue sky. It's like a summer thunderstorm, sweeping in to lift the oppression of the heat and make it bearable. It's like sunlight sparkling on the sea.

He swallowed, unable to say any of those things, because none of it really came close, and it was so painfully precious, it just made the idea that he could take it from her hurt more. 'We should go back to our room,' he said quietly. 'We can figure out what to do next there.'

'True,' she muttered, rubbing at her forehead, and it made his heart stutter. Was her head hurting? Had *he* done that to her?

'Are you OK?'

'Just a headache. I haven't had such a prolonged delay when I've been in the immediate vicinity of a lost object before. I don't think my brain likes it. It keeps jabbing me like it's trying to remind me there is something I should be dealing with.' She took a deep breath and lowered her hand. 'It eases off quite quickly.'

'I'll try not to drag this out too long.'

'Connor, I'm not trying to rush us for that. If it wasn't for the fact that my family need the amplifier and I have work to get back to, I'd be happy to stay here with you for as long as you wanted.' She bit her lip and looked away, as if she hadn't just rearranged his brain chemistry. 'So, what do you think would work better: a spell to help us float down to the ground or some kind of tether to climb across?'

He leaned out a little further from the sloped roof to look, in the same way she had earlier. Her hands found his waist, too, but he didn't dare touch them.

'If we go down from here, we'll still have to climb over the wall of the garden and I'll have to remove the wards for you,' he pointed out, easing back. 'I know a spell for increased grip, though.'

She nodded, and that's how they found themselves traversing across the roof of the inn, keeping low, trying not to dislodge tiles, with their fingertips and shoes adhering to the surfaces. When they got level with the first window to their room, he lowered himself down to the ledge and pushed it open further. Sticky fingers of one hand clinging to the wall, he held his other arm out like a safety rope as Becca attempted to lower herself down, too. When her feet wouldn't quite reach the windowsill, he wrapped his arm around her waist and she let go, utterly confident that he would hold on to her. And probably in her own ability to react and save herself with a levitation spell if necessary.

She ducked through the window and there was a muffled thump as she jumped to the floor, and then he followed, pulling the window to but not quite closed behind them. He had a feeling he could do with the cool air.

One light was on; the room bathed in pale-grey shadows, and she was standing next to her side of the bed, slipping off her shoes and testing the stickiness of her fingers against each other as if they were covered in glue she was trying to shake off.

'That's an awesome spell,' she said, when she caught him watching her. 'Do you often need to scale buildings like Spiderman?'

'Not often, no.'

She sat back on the bed and immediately her hands caught on the sheet. She shook her hands ineffectually as the light cotton clung to her. 'Crap – how long does it stick around?'

He raised his eyebrows, a smile tugging at his mouth even as he felt the weight of their being alone in the bedroom, facing the prospect of sleeping in the same bed. They were going to have to talk about the kiss. '"*Stick* around"?'

Her dimple appeared. 'You're the one who keeps noticing the puns. It's purely accidental on my part.' She separated her hand from the sheet, only to get it caught in her hair. 'Can you help a girl out?'

'What do you want me to do about it?' He shoved his hands into his pockets.

'Can you unravel the spell, so I don't have to collect all the soft furnishings like a piece of flypaper for the next hour?'

'Becca.' He breathed out her name in a rough exhale. 'You don't have to do this. I get it. You're not worried about me taking your magic.' He shut his eyes, forcing himself to say it. 'But *I* am.'

The room went quiet for a while, and he didn't want to open his eyes again.

'Would you sit down next to me, please?' she asked gently.

He opened his eyes and she was still untangling her hair from her sticky fingers. The spell worked with dense, heavy objects, such as bricks and tiles, because they had so much weight to them and were already fixed in place; it was a pain for lighter things.

He sat down next to her, wanting to take over and help, but too worried about consciously trying to unpick a spell connected to her, when he'd felt the magic on her skin without even trying before.

'Is that why you stopped?' she asked, finally getting her hands free and curling them in her lap as she twisted around to face him.

'Yes. I could feel magic on you.' He'd reacted quickly enough that he hadn't felt her magical signature, but she almost glowed with power and energy. His gaze coasted over her face, heart-shaped and achingly pretty.

'Is that normal? When you're not actively using your gift, I mean.'

'I've not had it happen before, but then I've not touched a witch for any prolonged amount of time in years without the *intention* of removing their magic.' He looked down at his hands, flexing his fingers, knowing the power was just resting, ready and waiting in his bones. 'My gift is usually already reaching. You've seen how quickly it works.'

'It was in the blink of an eye with Aveline's ex,' she agreed, but it was in that matter-of-fact way she had. No awe, no disgust. Just an observation.

'Well, I didn't nullify him permanently. It was just enough to deplete him. Knock him out and keep him from using his powers for a day or two. I wouldn't nullify anyone permanently without there being a trial or assessment of health.'

'I doubt anyone would have blamed you if you did.'

He gave a humourless laugh. 'Plenty of people would blame me if I took the law into my own hands.'

'OK, fair point. So, you can control it to many varying degrees. How did you learn that?'

'Trial and error. Some of it's instinctive, but . . . the other witch's magic flows *into* me, and when I first started I couldn't always . . . deal with it. It would take a couple of tries.'

'Does it hurt you?' Her voice was low and full of concern he wasn't sure how to deal with either.

'No. But it's not always comfortable.' The gross feeling of the magic he'd taken on earlier had long since dissipated. She'd thoroughly distracted him.

'When did you start learning how to do this?'

'When I was at Dentwood. My mentor got me access to the last Abrogator's grimoires and started off with bringing me objects . . . then I went out with him to deal with witches.'

'They brought hexed objects to a *school*?' Her eyebrows climbed her forehead. 'He took a *teenager* on field trips to confront powerful, grown witches?'

'How else would I learn?' Even as he said it, he realised the hypocrisy in the argument when it came to mediums – they were just told not to use their gifts. But it *was* different. 'My gift is too dangerous for me not to know how to control it.'

She pushed her hair back with both hands and then swore when she realised her fingers were going to get all tangled up again. She growled and yanked and finally got free again. Taking a steadying breath, as if praying for patience, she levelled a look at him that warned him not to prevaricate. 'So, you're worried that when we were kissing, your control was slipping?'

He nodded.

'Has that ever happened with other witches when you were being intimate?'

'Becca.' He turned his head away, rubbing his hand – free of the sticky spell with a simple thought – over the back of his head. 'I don't really want to talk about it.'

'I appreciate that. I do,' she said, her tone softening but still firm. 'I'm asking you to try, though. Just a little bit. Because you're telling me that you're worried you could have drained my magic while we were kissing, and I would appreciate knowing if that's happened with someone else before. Not so I can judge you, but because if you want to kiss me again, I'm going to need a really, *really* concrete reason not to kiss you back.' Her eyes were wide and fixed on his. 'You are so sexy, and sweet, and funny, and kind, and I'm up for doing *a lot* more than kissing. But no matter how horny and impulsive I get, I'm not completely self-destructive, so please, just be honest with me – and yourself – about this. Have you ever nullified someone when you were getting hot and heavy?'

He blinked. Why was it that absorbing gross magic from an abusive dickhead was so much easier than processing compliments from this beautiful woman? And knowing she wanted him was the best form of agony he'd ever experienced.

'No, it's never happened before,' he told her, finally finding his tongue. 'But I've only ever had one girlfriend who was a witch before.' He could have left it there, but since they were doing this, and she was talking about self-destructive tendencies and asking for honesty, it was the perfect time to find out if there was any part of her that had only wanted him because of a sense of danger – the same way Selena had. 'I never . . . never got so caught up with her as I did just then with you. She always told me how much she liked the danger of being with me, which . . . made me too self-conscious, I guess.'

'She *got off* on the idea of you removing her magic?'

'She said it made her feel alive, the way that at any moment I might snap and drain her.' *I don't mind that you're a monster, it's exciting.*

Becca sighed and looked up at the canopy on the bed, muttering to herself. 'It is *so* hard not to kink-shame sometimes.' Then she shook her head. 'No, fuck it, it isn't kink-shaming. What a bitch. She was putting that label on you. *Real* you. That wasn't role-playing. She was treating you like . . . like the last thing you wanted to be treated as, just to get her own rocks off?'

'We were young. I—' He broke off before he said that he was just grateful anyone had wanted to have sex with him, because there was a limit to how honest he could be and still hope this gorgeous woman would respect him.

She didn't press him on what he was about to say, just nodded slowly. 'OK, we might have to shelve that. Has it ever happened with *any* witch accidentally, whether you were kissing them or not?'

'Only one, when my gift came in. I didn't know what was happening.'

'Were they OK?'

'Guess it depends on what you mean by OK,' he said ruefully. Her concern didn't feel like judgement, so he somehow found himself telling her how it had been a kid from Dentwood. They'd got into a fight. He'd been pushing him away, his hand to the other boy's face, not unlike how he'd drained Aveline's ex earlier, and then the kid's magic had been flowing into him. The small group who'd been there, egging them on – including Edward – were stunned and then terrified at what he'd done. The boy's magic had come back, but everyone said he was never as powerful as it had been predicted he would be.

Becca sighed again and plopped back onto her pillows, stretching her legs out into his lap. 'Most witches accidentally hurt someone when their magic comes in. Drop things on their heads when we're trying to levitate something, push them over in anger . . . You'd have known that if you grew up around them,' she said almost to herself. 'If anyone had taken a moment to tell you about the common experiences witches share. Welcome you properly. Not just dump you in Dentwood with a lot of magical snobs. I mean, forget about the kids, what about the teachers? I'm starting to think there needs to be some kind of systemic overhaul of these institutions.'

He wouldn't disagree with that. Witches who didn't come from magical backgrounds were so obviously overlooked.

She pushed herself up on her elbows. 'You've had a really rough deal, Connor. You know that, don't you?'

Did he? Maybe on some level – but thinking about it didn't exactly help. It didn't change anything.

She flopped back down. 'It doesn't sound to me like you're going to accidentally take my magic in the throes of passion. It sounds like you do everything you can, and *have* been doing everything you can for years, to keep other people safe.'

His hand hovered over her shin, tempted to stroke along it but still battling his concerns. 'It felt different with you, though.'

'Where and when did you feel the magic? It has to be skin to skin, doesn't it?'

'Yes.'

'Using your hands?'

'No, but that's the easiest conduit.' He leaned back at the reminder, pressing his palms into the cotton sheet behind him.

'Interesting. Did you feel it on my lips . . .?' Her voice lowered. 'On my tongue?'

'Becca . . . what are you doing?'

'I'm just trying to understand,' she said with an innocence that wasn't fooling anyone. 'We could do some trial and error ourselves. I *guarantee* it would be more fun than when you were at Dentwood.'

287

He closed his eyes and groaned. Was he fighting this unnecessarily? Was she right and they could figure it out together? He opened his eyes and turned to stretch over her, planting his hands just above her shoulders. She slid her right leg to one side of him so he was kneeling between her thighs, her dress ruffling up.

'You are a menace, Rebecca Ashworth. Don't tempt me.'

'I'm sorry.' He wasn't sure that she was; the heat in her eyes was lighting them up too much. 'I am genuinely trying to figure this out. If the kissing was OK, the only other time you touched my skin was down here . . .' she traced the back of her fingers down her throat, tipping her chin up – 'across here . . .' she moved across her upper chest – 'and when you put your hands in my hair.' She slid her fingers deep into her auburn locks, the position pulling her breasts up high. He couldn't stop himself from dragging a look down from her head, along her body and back again. 'Maybe we could do things over the top of clothes? I could even put *more* clothes on, if that would make it better.'

'I don't want you to put any more clothes on,' he admitted.

'No?' She grinned at him, full of mischief, and put her feet flat on the bed, her knees pressing into his hips, and her skirt fell all the way up to her waist, putting the narrow strip of her underwear on display.

'Goddess, help me,' he muttered. 'It was your head; I felt the magic in it beneath my hands.' When they were running through her thick hair, finally getting to relish it as he kissed her, as if he were suffocating and she were oxygen.

'That could make sense – it's the centre of my magic. But maybe you were just reading the way my gift was working? It's constantly there, telling me where the amplifier is.'

'Maybe.' That *could* have explained it.

'Want to test the theory?' She wiggled her eyebrows.

'And how would we do that?'

'Kiss me, touch me – everywhere but here.' She ruffled her hair, making it a mess around her head, and when she laughed, his heart flipped. 'You'd have a job, anyway, considering my hands are stuck again.'

'All the better to keep you out of mischief,' he murmured and sank down onto his elbows slowly, just enough to press his body along hers, without flattening her. The heat and softness of her was exquisite. She pressed her lips together and made a quiet hum, her hips shifting beneath his and causing her to brush against his groin. Burning-hot pleasure crackled up from the base of his spine.

'Are you trying to get me back for crushing you the first time we met?' she said, her voice drowsy with desire, her eyes heavy-lidded. 'Because I warn you, this is no punishment.'

He didn't answer. He couldn't. Even without their skin touching, he was utterly undone. And it frightened him. This intimacy – not just the wanting and desire being met physically, but the way she listened and laughed and was gentle and funny and *enjoyed* being with him – it was over-whelming. His whole body was vibrating on a molecular level. He hadn't been lying earlier. He'd *never* felt this way before, and he was worried about how easy it would be to forget himself. To imagine he was someone different and the damage he could do if he did.

'Becca . . .' he said slowly, as though the word were being prised out of him, because he couldn't believe what he was about to say to this beautiful woman who was offering herself to him, in any way that made him feel comfortable. 'I—' His voice cracked.

'It's OK,' she said when he didn't fill the silence with the words he needed to say. 'If you don't want to. I'm not trying to pressure you into anything you're not ready for.'

'It's not because I don't want *you*. Please don't think that.'

She smiled and shifted her hips a tiny bit again. 'Don't worry, I figured that out, *big boy*.' He laughed with her, and the shaking of their bodies together made the laughter fade into groans. 'We should move, though. Get some sleep.'

He nodded and began lifting himself up reluctantly. But he couldn't help pausing, dipping his head and brushing the lightest of kisses against her sweet, sassy mouth. And then he put the space back between them.

Only it didn't feel aching and empty any more. It was full of warmth and acceptance. A connection.

Chapter Twenty-six

BECCA

Becca woke up when it was still early, which wasn't like her. The tears threatening her eyes weren't like her either. Sometimes she would dream of her mum and wake up hurting . . . but it wasn't that. She recognised that grief now. It was a familiar pain. A reminder, which she never *wanted* to be entirely free of.

This was different. Aggressive and inexplicable. The weight of it pressed on her, made her head hurt and her throat ache. She rubbed the heel of her hand over her eyes roughly, belatedly pleased when she realised the sticky spell had finally worn off. She quite liked having eyelashes.

She had curled herself into a tight little ball, snuggled up against the duvet barrier, and Connor was sleeping, face down, right up against the other side, so it was like they were both trying to burrow beneath it to each other. His arm had made it across to her, though, his hand on her hip, and the contact made it a little easier to breathe under the strange emotional weight. The pain in her head ebbed, but it was still bad enough that she felt the need to slide out from beneath Connor's hand and get her phone. She needed to know her family were all right, and this wasn't some kind of magical intuition warning her that something was seriously wrong back home.

Becca: Sorry for the early-morning text but is everything OK with my Uncle Adrian and Harry?

As she waited for a reply text from Kay, she went over to the cold-water jug, poured some out into a cup and fetched one of the last of Zeynep's teabags. She'd heat the water magically so as not to wake Connor. She really had been flying through those teabags – her friend had not been wrong with her intuition. Becca pinched the bridge of her nose as it burned with unshed tears. What was wrong with her?

Sure, she was frustrated. They'd been so close to getting the amplifier yesterday. And she was worried about what would happen when they did get hold of it. Would one of the kind people, Rhiannon or Sam, reveal themselves to be using the inn as a cover for something bad? Or was it as simple as them needing to protect the inn with it? And what was she supposed to do if she found out that was the case? Her family needed it. Biddicote needed it. When she added all of that to the highs and lows of her growing feelings for Connor, it would have been weird if she wasn't feeling exhausted and overwhelmed . . . but this was so visceral, it was like someone had planted the emotions in her chest. As though she was being influenced, but there was nothing she'd eaten or heard or seen through the night that would account for that. And Connor would have felt it if there was anything in the room or around the bed that had been enchanted. It made no sense. What would even be the purpose of someone sneaking into their room to plant magic like that?

No. She had to accept it – if everything *was* fine at home: she was just in need of some sleep, some Connor and some success with this treasure hunt, in whatever order the Goddess deemed fit to bestow them.

She was just removing the teabag when her phone vibrated with a reply from Kay.

Kay: No worries. I'm getting ready for work. Harry is fine. He's been a bit tired but that might be down to Horatio! I'll go check on Adrian. Give me a minute.

Kay: All good. Elenor said he's planning to go into the village today.

Becca let out a shaky breath. Sleep, Connor and getting her hands on the amplifier it was.

Becca: Thank you. Was everything OK when you went back to work yesterday?

Kay: They haven't said a word to me about the files. I don't know what to make of it.

It *was* odd. First, they send Connor to speak to Kay about it, rather than just disciplining her at work, and then they forget about it entirely? Were they just waiting for him to get back and do a full report or was it off the record? What *had* been his purpose when he'd arrived at Ashworth Hall, what felt like a million years ago?

She could ask him about it. The complication of him representing the Witches Council and her being an Ashworth hadn't been at the forefront of her mind when he was kissing her boneless last night, but it *was* still there and ignoring it wasn't going to make it go away. But they could figure it out . . . couldn't they?

He only wanted to keep other people safe, and if she explained to him the reasons why she and Kay had broken the rules, that there was more at stake than her family simply wishing to understand an old spell . . . what? He'd go easy on them in his report? Or turn around and tell the Witches Council everything her family had sought to keep hidden for centuries because his loyalties – rightly or wrongly – lay with the Council?

What other choice would she have if it turned out that Rhiannon or Sam were using the amplifier to help protect everyone at the inn? Explaining that Harry's and Uncle Adrian's lives were literally at risk would be the only way to make him see why she wanted to remove the amplifier from the inn without her looking heartless.

But did that mean that she was risking everything her family had sought to protect since Biddi founded the village, just so she didn't lose the opportunity of a relationship with Connor? It wasn't just her secret to tell. Harry had told Kay without the agreement of the family – but he was the heir, his dad had been unable to speak at the time, and Harry and Kay had been in love with each other since they were teenagers. This situation was a smidge different.

She didn't know what to do. It was a rare and uncomfortable experience for her. Maybe that was the root cause of the crushing sensation in her skull and on her chest.

Kay: Are things OK with you?

Becca debated sending a laughing emoji, followed by a crying emoji, but knew that would have Kay waking up Harry and phone calls ensuing. She settled with a criminal thumbs-up and hoped Kay wouldn't hold it against her. She winced and rubbed at a sharp pain in her head as she set her phone down.

'Becca?' Connor rolled over and sat up so fast, it was like he thought she'd been abducted.

'Relax, I'm here.' The sadness in her chest eased a little bit at the way he'd been worried about her. And at how gorgeous he looked, dark curls mussed, long fingers rubbing at the stubble on his jaw.

'What are you doing up?'

'Just getting a cup of tea. Go back to sleep. It's still early.'

He made a dubious-sounding grunt but lay back down. One of his legs was barely inside the covers and she entertained herself for a short while tracing the shape of it with her eyes, the ridiculous length of it stretched all the way down the mattress and off the edge of the bed, despite the furniture itself being huge. She didn't even tell herself off for finding his height attractive. It was just one part of the whole package she was enraptured by.

'Are you going to get back into bed, or just keep staring at it?'

Busted. Although he thought she was just randomly staring at the bed? Goddess bless him, he truly had no idea how obsessed she was becoming. Every time she glanced at him, she caught a new angle to his jaw or cheekbones, a new expression in his eye or fall of his curls that made her want to get out her camera and take as many photographs as she could and then study them, as if she could figure out why his particular combination of features was making her so ridiculously horny.

And that didn't even cover how she felt about every small smile, huff of laughter or new iteration of scowl he gifted her. Every time he let her in on something she knew he held close – the secret layers of his gift, his fears and vulnerabilities. It made her want to wrap herself around him like a koala, and cling on tight, tight, tight.

But that was not what he needed from her. He needed patience and space. Sometimes the hardest thing about caring for someone was doing it the way they needed you to, rather than the way you wanted to.

She strained the teabag and took over her cup, climbing back onto the bed beside him. He sat up beside her, tugging his twisted T-shirt back into position, to her disappointment.

'I think we should get out of here this morning. Get a change of scenery – so we can think straight. Decide on the best course of action,' he said, leaning his head back against the headboard, his grey eyes dancing over her face.

'Oh, so early in the day for this kind of decisiveness,' she teased and took a sip of her drink. 'But OK. Where do you have in mind?'

CONNOR

Polperro was a tiny village on the coast of Cornwall, about a twenty-minute drive from the inn. Having been there already with the mechanic, Connor was familiar with the way it sloped down to the sea, the narrow alleyways shooting off from the main road, and that the only place for people not living or working there to park was right at the top of the hill in the public car park.

Being there with Becca still made him feel as though he hadn't seen it before.

She brought her camera and stopped every few minutes, taking photographs of the stream that ran down to the fishing harbour. Of small gates outside cottages. Of seagulls perched on low, white-painted walls. Of the shadow of the occasional tourist as they approached an alleyway entrance, and the house on the cliffside, hidden among the trees. He steadied her when she stepped up onto a bollard to get a better viewpoint, hands around her waist, and it was another brushstroke on the portrait of her that now had permanent residency in his chest.

Seeing her in her element also made him think of what she'd said the day they'd argued about how her life was not just an obligation to her family legacy. What might he have done if he hadn't discovered he was the Abrogator at fifteen? His only real personal interest was consuming media, because it could be done easily wherever he was. It fitted around his lifestyle. What other avenues might he have explored if things had been different? He tried to tell himself it didn't matter, but the thought didn't subside as easily as it had a couple of days ago.

'Wow, this is . . . decadent,' Becca said, when he handed her the breakfast he'd gone to fetch while she was taking photos of a green tugboat from the harbour wall. He'd doubled back to the tiny bakery where he'd bought the iced fingers for their midnight feast, this time choosing freshly baked bacon-and-cheese twists.

'Good?' he asked, still unwrapping his while she was already tucking in.

'Savoury heaven.' She finished chewing her mouthful, swallowed and narrowed her eyes at him. 'Any chance you picked this for the high salt content?'

'You said it sometimes helps your headaches.' He gave a small shrug.

'Thank you.' She reached out with her free hand, stroking it down the centre of his chest and then curling her fingers into the material of his shirt for a moment, tugging him a step closer. His stomach muscles clenched at the press of her fist against his stomach, her heat seeping through his shirt into his skin. And then she gave him a small smile and let go.

'Did you just wipe your greasy fingers down my shirt?' he forced himself to say when he could draw a breath again.

'It's just so pristine, it's begging to be messed up.' Her smile widened. But despite her reassuring him earlier that she was feeling better, he could see shadows under her eyes and a tightness across her face, which gave away that her gift was weighing on her. He'd hoped the distance from the inn would help as well, working on the assumption that it tended to help him – although strangely he wasn't noticing the effects of the heavy magical atmosphere as strongly any more, as though spending prolonged time at the inn had helped him acclimatise to it.

Becca was recovered enough, though, that her busy brain was getting creative, thinking of all the different things they could do to get more information, before they attempted either to access the amplifier again or approach the thief/owner of it.

They talked about ways to get hold of the surnames of the staff at the inn to help with the background checks – like striking up conversations about whether she should change her surname to his, in order to get people talking about their own surnames – the possibility of them holding another party, so Connor could find a moment to sneak off to the room again; things they could ask each member of staff to do magically so he could feel their magical signature.

It didn't stop Connor being annoyed at himself for taking so long to do this, though.

He'd been a box or two away from having the amplifier in his hand and figuring out if it was being used in any active spells. There had definitely been a field of magic around the boxes under the bed that matched the magic of the wards on the room. It had a metallic signature, but flexible – like beaten copper. If he'd just moved more quickly, Becca wouldn't be suffering right now.

'I'm sorry I've held this up.' He crumpled up the greasy

paper from their pastries, putting them in a nearby bin, before turning to lean his elbows on the wall, looking out at the deep navy blue of the sea.

Becca pushed herself up to sit on the wall beside where he was leaning. She was wearing some kind of summery top that tied up behind her neck and sunlight painted the line of her bare shoulder and arm, made the crown of her hair glow red. She nudged his ribs gently with her bare knee, her shorts putting a distracting amount of her thigh on show, a few scant inches away from his head. 'You don't have to be sorry. We've been right to be cautious. Look how frightened everyone was because of Aveline's husband, and he didn't even get access. Nor did he have the juice of an amplifier behind him for his little meteor strike.'

'I know. But if I were better at the . . . subterfuge stuff . . .' he looked up at her with a raised eyebrow, daring her to make a comment on his surrender to her idea that they were undercover agents, 'we could have moved this along quicker.'

She chewed on her bottom lip, trying to hold back a smile. 'You don't normally have to do this kind of thing?'

I don't normally do this *kind of thing*, he thought to himself, cautiously putting his arm around her waist to anchor her to him. She immediately settled her hands on his arms and released the full force of her smile on him.

'I go in either for emergencies, or once the verdict has been passed and the enforcers have narrowed down a location for me to extract the witch from. Or I'm visiting the elderly in their homes or going to council offices after hours to deal with artefacts.'

'What kind of schedule is that?'

'Typically, I spend two to three days in a given location. A day either side travelling.'

'Constantly? Do you get holidays? Or a chance to do things like this? Pop out and be a tourist.'

'It's pretty busy. There are a lot of countries.' It was hard to fathom, though, as he stood there, the cool breeze from the sea easing the heat of the sun, the scent of salt and peaches all around him, and Becca in his arms. He might have believed there was nothing else to the world than this.

'And they all rely on you?'

He gave a one-shouldered shrug.

'Look, I'm not trying to minimise what you do.' She touched her fingertips to his hair, sifting through the ends lightly so she didn't touch his scalp, and he wanted to lay his head in her lap. 'But – for example – something like investigating the amplifier would usually be dealt with by a Tenet Enforcer right? Or the heritage department?'

'I suppose so.'

'So, why can't they do that for everything bar the emergencies when you want to take a holiday? Witches had to cope in the fifty-odd years before you came into your gift. I know the population has grown, but why is it so relentless?'

'I'm the most efficient way to deal with these things. Usually,' he added darkly.

'Right . . .' She took a deep breath in, and he thought he sensed a hesitation in her. He lifted his eyes to her face from where – he was embarrassed to admit – they'd been resting on the curve of her chest. 'So what's made this the exception to the rule of only using you efficiently?'

Ah, that explained the hesitation. They were skating closer to a topic they hadn't touched on in a couple of days. 'I . . . I suppose because it involves you. Your family.'

She removed her hand from his hair and rested it on his shoulder. 'My family aren't doing anything terrible, you know. I promise you,' she said, her voice low and earnest.

'Then why keep everything a secret?' he asked, softly. 'Most people would let your family get away with murder, it's so old and respected. So Warren sent me—'

Becca leaned back. 'Warren? As in Warren Barraclough? He's your boss?'

Connor nodded. It wasn't that strange that she'd heard of him, but the change in her demeanour was odd.

'Since when—' She took a deep breath, cutting herself off from whatever she was about to say. 'He's the PR Council Member, though.'

'What's a bigger PR emergency than rogue witches misusing their magic?' He removed his arms from her waist and straightened so he could study her face better. 'Plus, he was my mentor at Dentwood, so when I chose the UK Witches Council, it made sense to stay under his umbrella.'

She nodded slowly, her brown eyes fastened on his, a million thoughts seeming to dart around in her head that she wouldn't let out, until she looked down. 'Right.' She fiddled with the lens cap on her camera, where it hung around her neck. 'And it's him that sent you to us? To talk to Kay about the restricted records – while she was at home, at Ashworth Hall, instead of at work? When you don't normally deal with anything like that but handily have the ability to read magic?'

His mouth dried out. She was speaking evenly, but there was no denying that she'd retreated. He couldn't help the facts that had led them to this point, though. He was the Abrogator – she had known that from within fifteen minutes of meeting him. And she was too smart not to have figured out that Warren had wanted Connor to find out more than why Kay was looking stuff up that she shouldn't. The irony of it was, he knew as much about the

Ashworths' magic as he had when he'd arrived at the Hall on Friday . . . and yet Becca knew almost every nuance of his gift, which he'd kept hidden for years.

'That's about the size of it,' he agreed, waiting to see if she was going to probe him more. Find out what he'd reported to Warren − if he had read any of the magic when he was at Ashworth Hall.

But she just gave a quick nod and jumped down from the wall. 'OK, well, we should get back, shouldn't we? That intelligence won't gather itself.'

The sun was higher in the sky by the time they walked, silently, up the steep hill, the back of Connor's neck burning under its heat. As they passed by one of the houses where a stream ran down along their front gardens and tiny bridges connected them to the street, a stocky man stepped out from a gate and almost collided with them.

'Sorry,' Connor apologised before he had a chance to register the man's face.

It was Aveline's husband.

But he just looked between Connor and Becca, muttering, 'Watch where you're going,' before walking off down the hill towards the shops.

Without conferring, both Connor and Becca stayed stock still on the pavement, watching Aveline's husband walk away.

'He didn't recognise us,' Becca said, but it was almost a question.

'No. He didn't.'

'That's . . . weird.' She crossed her arms over her chest, frowning at the man's back.

Connor's stomach churned queasily, as though recalling the sickly burn of the magic he'd removed. 'Very weird.'

'I guess it was getting dark last night.'

'Not *that* dark.' Connor rubbed his chest. 'You'd think he would've recognised *one* of us. You'd think he'd remember what I did, even if it did just seem to him like I'd knocked him out.'

Becca tugged on a lock of her hair, turning to start walking again. 'When you . . . y'know . . .' she glanced around in case there were any non-magical people around, but the road was empty, 'use your gift, does it cause any type of generalised amnesia?'

'No. If it's quick, they might not realise what happened, but the actual magic doesn't affect their recall,' he said grimly, thinking of the witches he'd had to take multiple tries at when he was learning to absorb the magic fully. The hate and fear in their expressions.

Becca was quiet again as they walked the rest of the way to the van, but it wasn't the awkwardness they'd experienced earlier – she was preoccupied. As they got in, she paused in the driver's seat, hands on the steering wheel, her face pale.

'What if . . . what if he had a memory charm put on him?'

'You know they're not that good. He would have had a flicker of recognition, at least. Influencing memories doesn't hold up against reality, literally coming face to face with you in that way.'

'No. Not usually, but . . .' She spoke almost to herself. 'But what if . . . what if someone with that kind of gift had the amplifier?'

'An influencer with a specific gift for making people forget things? Has that ever happened before?'

'There was someone in the Ashworth family, in the late 1800s, who could do it. I don't . . . I don't know why we didn't consider that as something that could have led

303

to us forgetting about the amplifier . . .' She massaged her temples and then shook her head, muttering. 'But that wouldn't make sense, because everyone was fine until Uncle Adrian.'

Connor lifted his eyebrows. 'And you think either Karl or Sam might have that gift? That they used it when they brought him back home last night?'

She nodded slowly. 'It would make sense, wouldn't it? If you stole it, why wouldn't you then *use* the amplifier to cover up the crime? Have everyone forget about its existence.'

'It's a possibility, I suppose.'

She lifted a shaking hand to the key in the ignition and he reached over to touch her wrist for a second. 'Are you OK? Should I drive?'

She blinked as she looked over at him and then nodded, offering him a small smile. 'Yes. Yeah, I actually think that would be a good idea. I'm feeling a bit off again.'

They got out of the van to swap sides, and as they were settling in, him moving the seat back, her buckling up, he knew they were going to have to deal with this amplifier fast, because – no matter whether the Witches Council and Ashworth tensions would get in the way of their attraction to each other – he couldn't watch her suffer any longer.

Chapter Twenty-seven

BECCA

The weight of sadness had returned to Becca's chest. The severity of it was still surprising, but she could at least pinpoint a catalyst for it.

Connor worked for Warren Barraclough. And now suddenly that gulf of understanding between her and Connor – which had felt surmountable first thing that morning – was looking too deep and wide for them to breach.

Becca had only met Warren once, maybe twice, when she was eighteen. But it had been enough to know that she didn't like him and didn't trust him, and that the feelings were completely mutual. He must have been around forty then, and a handsome man, full of arrogance. Eager to come into Ashworth Hall and try to play the superior witch, with his position on the Council, even though he'd been subordinate to someone else.

Perhaps he'd already known he had his clutches in Connor at that time? Connor had said his gift came in at fifteen, and the Witches Council immediately moved in to 'help' him learn about it. Warren. Warren had moved in on him. So maybe Warren had been feeling confident that he could throw his weight around with her family, given that he was mentoring the new Abrogator. Or maybe he was just that up himself? What Becca *did* know was that the wards had gone off around the Hall to warn them when he arrived. Not at full strength, but to make them aware he didn't mean well towards her family. And he'd tried to muscle in on fixing a small problem with a rune or charm in the village. Made noises about the Witches Council taking over, before Uncle Adrian and Beckett Kirby from the Council had put him back in his box.

No, it wasn't much to condemn the man. And she might have believed what Connor said about Warren being suspicious of the Ashworths and being frustrated that so many witches respected them, worried that it would have reflected badly on *him* to be seen to come down heavy on them. But she knew it went deeper than that. Warren's family had been affected by the referendum Uncle Adrian had been vocal about – the one which prohibited witches selling their services into non-magical corporations to sway business deals – and the Barracloughs held a grudge about it.

Warren would have been poisoning Connor's mind against her family for over a decade – and Becca knew Connor was too good a person to do anything to harm her family directly. But she also knew she wouldn't be able to trust him with the secret of the anchor tattoo. It felt like she'd just discovered that this flower of a relationship between them had no roots. It wouldn't grow and blossom – it's stem had been cut and it would wither away.

It wasn't like her to feel this defeatist about something she hadn't even taken a good run at to make work. And yet, this sense of loss was permeating her.

Sunlight flashed through the leaves on the trees outside, lancing into her head as she sat in the passenger seat. The painful headache was returning, and she didn't think it was just because they were heading back towards the inn. Fragments of thoughts were swirling in her mind, and she closed her eyes against the bright lights.

She knew Connor was driving her mother's van, and yet she was experiencing déjà vu about someone else doing it, but when Becca was older . . . but that couldn't have been her mother. Because her mother was gone. All she had were memories.

She leaned forward and held her head between her hands, trying to contain the pain as it pushed and pushed at her brain.

'Becca?' Connor's voice was sharp. 'Becca, what is it?'

'I—' she tried to reassure him but couldn't. 'It hurts,' she whispered.

'OK, we'll be back at the inn soon. Just hold tight. They're bound to have something that will help. Or shall I take you to a hospital?'

She tried to shake her head but even that was too much.

The rest of the drive was to a soundtrack of soft swearing in an Irish accent. Occasionally she felt the heat of Connor's hand hovering near her, but there wasn't anywhere he could touch her that wouldn't be skin to skin, so it would disappear again, to be followed by more swearing.

'We're here.' Gravel crunched loudly under the wheels and then Connor's door slammed. Footsteps. Connor opened her door. She leaned back, letting the fresh air get to her face and managing to open her eyes enough to see him start to lean in towards her, before high-pitched squeals of, 'Giant, giant, get him!' erupted.

'What the—' Connor stood back up in time for Jemima and Chrissy to arrive and promptly wrap themselves around each of his legs.

'Let's tie him down,' Chrissy said.

'Cut out his heart,' a characteristically blood-thirsty Jemima added.

If Becca had been capable, she would have taken photographs. The fearsome Abrogator, letting two eight-year-olds attack him. As much as the sound of the girls laughing together lifted her spirits, she grew woozy, too. Her mind was a merry-go-round – like one of those zoetropes – only images seemed to be missing. She thought of the playground of Biddicote Primary School and playing horsey. Underneath the blossom of a tree. Confetti and snow.

'OK, you got me, you got me,' Connor laughed, but it was strained. 'I'm not a giant, though, I'm a knight, and I have a princess to rescue.'

'Who, me?' Chrissy let go of his leg.

'No, y'wee messers, you're both fierce knights, are you not? It's this beautiful maiden here.'

'Will you come and play with us after?' Jemima asked, letting go, too.

'I'll do my best.'

A second later, Becca was up in Connor's arms, and he was carrying her across the drive. She pressed her face against his chest, listening to the rapid beat of his heart.

'I think they're going to try to make a baby,' Chrissy whispered loudly to her twin sister as they followed behind.

'Oh, good. I heard Mum saying men are quick at that. He'll be out to play giants with us in about one minute.'

Becca wanted to laugh but it ended up sending shooting needles across her scalp and down her neck. The girls were running off again, towards the garden. One fair, one dark . . . More fiery pain. She whimpered and Connor squeezed her closer, ducking through the open door into the bar, then passing straight through, into the kitchen, calling for Rhiannon.

Her eyes must have shut again because all she heard was the middle-aged witch's voice. 'What's happened? What's wrong?'

'I don't know,' Connor's words were clipped. 'Are there any healers staying here? It's her head. She's been complaining of a headache, and she's been using magical tea, but it's just getting worse.'

'Take her through to our staff lounge. I'll send Sam in with our strongest remedy, while I see if I can get in contact with the nearest healer.'

'Good plan,' Becca mumbled into his shirt as he took her through the door into the staffing area. Her mind flickered through the events of last night. Shoe boxes organised underneath her bed. A flash of board games and tubs with colouring pencils in. Slim, colourful books in a grown-up's bedroom. Children's stories. Pastel decor, in a bedroom. Here, and at the Hall. Empty patches on the wall where photos should have been.

Ashworth Hall. She had to get back to Ashworth Hall. With the amplifier. The person who took it could take away memories.

Connor put her down on a sofa. She clutched at his arm. She wanted to keep him while she could.

Someone else was in the room. Connor was talking to her while he knelt beside Becca. A young woman. Becca forced her eyes open, squinting in the bright golden light.

Golden hair, red highlights.

The kaleidoscope whirled in Becca's head again. Thoughts and images, and voices and laughter, spinning, spinning, pressing on her, joy from her childhood, sadness and confusion, spinning, spinning.

Until it broke – the pain finally shattered, and she woke up in Connor's arms again.

'Becca? Becca? Are you awake? Can you hear me?' Connor's voice shook as he wiped at a trickle of warmth beneath her nose with a tissue.

Her heart was thundering, but not with fear. 'Is she here? Is she still here?' All she could see were Connor's grey eyes, dark brows crinkled. *He* was scared.

'Who?'

'My cousin.'

'I don't understand. You mean Harry? We're not at Ashworth Hall.' Connor dabbed the tissue under her nose again.

She shook her head and pushed his hand away gently, struggling to sit up. To look around Connor to see the other person in the room. 'No. Not Harry.' Connor put his arm behind her back, helping Becca up . . . and there she was. Wide blue eyes meeting hers. 'Sam. Samantha Ashworth. My cousin.'

Chapter Twenty-eight

CONNOR

Connor had just about been getting used to how unpredictable life was around Becca. And that was saying something for a man who regularly had to confront witches with megalomania. But the last half an hour had thrown him completely for a loop. Becca had gone from collapse to sitting bolt upright; she was pale but her bright brown eyes were as sharp as ever. And she was staring at Sam. Saying she was her *cousin*?

'Ashworth?' he repeated, still crouching beside the sofa, his hand pressed between Becca's shoulder blades in case her strength left her again. 'Samantha Ashworth – *this* Samantha – is your cousin?'

Becca nodded but didn't move her gaze from the other woman, who had frozen, a small tincture bottle clutched tightly in her fist.

'And you're just remembering this now?' He sounded like a moron, he knew he did, but in his defence there was very little information coming his way.

Becca flinched and took a shaky breath. 'It was her gift. *Is* her gift. When we saw Aveline's husband and I remembered about the Ashworth ancestor who had such a rare gift for influencing people to forget specific memories, it must have been the last piece of the puzzle. My headaches . . . they haven't just been about my gift. My mind's been fighting to remember her since Friday.'

Connor forced himself to pay more attention to Sam as the implications of what Becca was saying finally became clearer. The strawberry-blonde woman hugged herself, blue eyes wide like a hunted animal. 'You're saying, she managed to influence you to forget her?'

This time, when Becca nodded, tears shone in her eyes. 'It's a powerful gift. When it manifested we thought that it might even skirt a healing designation, as well as influencer, because of how it affects the brain. But still, it wouldn't have worked on all of us, for this long without that amplifier.' Her breath hitched and she whispered as she looked at Sam, 'Eleven years. Eleven years you've been gone.'

Sam put her hand over her mouth. She looked like she was the one who was going to pass out now. 'I'm sorry,' she mumbled into her hand.

Connor stood but Sam didn't pay him any attention. And that was mostly how it had been the whole time they'd stayed at the inn. Samantha watching *Becca*. Not Connor. Waiting for the axe to fall. To see if the prolonged exposure to her presence would finally break through the amplified influence of her spell. She'd stood by as a war waged within Becca's mind, violently enough he'd nearly rushed her to the hospital.

'You should sit down,' he told Sam, aware that his tone barely skated civil. 'And explain yourself.' He crooked his finger, pulling the armchair behind her forward so it nudged the back of her legs and she folded into it, as if she'd only just been managing to stay upright.

She blinked and looked at Connor. 'You *are* a witch.'

'I think the accusatory tone is a bit rich, don't you?'

Sam's cheeks flushed and she fumbled the tincture bottle onto the coffee table.

'Connor,' Becca said in weak censure.

'What?' He turned to Becca, his hackles immediately lowering when he saw the pain in her eyes. Not the pain she'd been experiencing in the car. This was a deep, deep hurt, and it made his bones ache. But it didn't make him feel sympathy for Sam, because she was the one responsible. 'She has the amplifier. She's used it on *you*.'

'I know that.' Becca swiped the heel of her hand across her cheeks and sat up straighter, turning her attention to Sam. 'You took it—' she started and then shook her head. 'Goddess, I can't believe I didn't realise straight away. How could I not see it the moment I looked at you, even with such a powerful spell—' She buried her face in her hands.

Sam rose as though to go to her, but Connor snapped his head in her direction, pointing at her in a clear communication to stay put. She sat back slowly, and Connor took a seat beside Becca, putting his arm around her. She was shaking, but when she lifted her head, there were no more tears.

'Sorry, I needed a moment.' She cleared her throat again. 'You took the amplifier. You hid it, and yourself, from us. *Why?*'

Sam slumped back in the armchair. 'It was a mistake. One I couldn't undo once I realised. I was young and I panicked. I thought what I was doing was for the best – and part of it still *is* – but it . . . it's so complicated.'

Becca took a deep breath. 'Maybe you should start at the beginning. In fact, maybe you should tell us as we drive back to Biddicote with the amplifier. We can get the spell removed—'

'I can't go back.' Samantha shook her head. 'And you can't remove the spell.'

'Sam, we have to. We *need* it.' Becca scooted forward, coming out from beneath Connor's arm and he couldn't help but notice how quickly Becca co-opted Sam back into her 'we'. The inclusion of a rogue family member, seemingly so swift and instinctive – as with the ghost. 'Your dad and Harry . . . they're getting ill. We almost lost your dad last year. This is serious.'

'What? What do you mean? Because of the anchor? Harry has had the tattoo now, too?'

Becca's shoulders stiffened.

Right, Sam had just let the cat out of the bag, presumably thinking Connor was a member of the family and in on the secret. The big secret. That the Ashworths were using an anchor spell . . . for what? Connor assumed it was the lynch pin for all the overlapping protective magic surrounding the community in Biddicote. Anchors were rare, and he'd never heard of one being used in such a way that it needed an amplifier, too. But even so, it wasn't that part they were trying to hide, was it? It was the tattoo.

Harnessing a spell – making it dependent on a living person – was illegal. It harked back to the days of sacrifices and innocent people being used by witches in experiments, draining them of their own magic or simple life source – or making them permanently obey. No wonder the Ashworths hid it.

'Might as well carry on,' he said after the quiet spooled out for a minute. Sam seemed to have cottoned on that she'd made a misstep. 'I know now.'

'Shit.' Sam looked up at the ceiling. 'He didn't know before, because he's not your husband. I *knew* it didn't add up. You were with that smarmy-looking guy on Facebook until a couple of months ago. And people can't elope to Gretna Green any more. And even if your dad did disapprove of you being with non-magical people – Connor does have magic. None of it made sense.'

Connor almost flinched. Of course he and Becca didn't

make sense.

Becca heaved a sigh and shook her head. But then she reached out and put her hand on his knee, squeezed it once, hard, before drawing her hand back and wrapping her arms around herself.

'No. Connor isn't my husband,' she explained, her voice calm but detached. 'He's from the Witches Council. He came down here to help me retrieve the amplifier. We – Harry and I – summoned an old ancestor to try to find out what we'd done wrong with the spell, why it was draining your dad and Harry. The ghost told us the amplifier was missing, so my gift kicked in. But obviously we had no idea *how* it could have disappeared from Ashworth Hall. And given the power of the artefact, we were worried that it might have been stolen by a witch with bad intentions. Connor came to ensure no one got hurt.'

'So . . . the family is working with the Witches Council now? Amicably?'

Becca snorted. 'You could say that Harry and I have been developing some strong one-to-one relationships. But . . . on the whole . . .' She shook her head. 'Wait.' She stood up and moved over to the space in front of the fireplace, so she could start pacing. 'When you left school, *you* went to work with the Witches Council. *You* wanted to improve relations between our family and them. Show we could co-operate by helping to smooth over serious magical reveals. You were . . . you were working for Warren Barraclough.'

Connor's heart gave a strange lurch before he realised that Warren couldn't remember that, because Sam had clearly wiped herself out of existence with her amplifier-powered memory spell.

Sam gathered her apron in her hands and started twisting

it slowly. 'Yes. And to start with it seemed to be going well. But he started pushing me to tell him more about the family. He . . . he got me to tell him about the magic at Ashworth Hall, the anchor, the amplifier. Told me that there would never be any hope of fixing the relationship between the Ashworths and the Witches Council if we weren't completely honest with each other. That my parents were stuck in their ways and it was us, the younger generation, who had to be brave. That he believed in me. That he'd help me.' She tightened the knotted material in her lap until her hands were white and then let go suddenly, fingers shaking as she smoothed them over the wrinkled apron. 'And I *wanted* it to work. So badly. Because if I failed . . .'

'My dad would have said he was right all along.' Becca pressed her hands to her face, shaking her head, similar to the way she had when Connor was telling her about how his role within the Witches Council worked. 'He was being his usual bitter self. Saying that you weren't worthy of being heir, and that you were being overambitious. Full of yourself.'

Sam just nodded miserably. 'And then, when I'd spilled every secret, Warren convinced me it was dangerous – the amplifier – and that he needed to examine it. He said he didn't want to embarrass the family by putting in an official warrant or causing issues between me and my parents, and that's why . . .' she shut her eyes as though bracing herself to say the next bit, 'I helped him take it.'

'And then what? He checked to see if it was dangerous?' Connor asked.

'He took it away somewhere. Said the Witches Council would take custody of it, and that way the family wouldn't be in trouble if anything ever came to light about it. And nothing changed in the village. Dad was fine. The magic was still working. I had no reason to think it had done any damage. I promise you, Becca, I didn't know. I . . . I believed him. All the things he told me. It all seemed to make so much sense . . . until it didn't.' She shook her head hard. 'He started asking more of me . . . things . . . again, that seemed OK in the moment, but when I looked back on them I realised he'd been using me. Lying to me—'

'About what?'

Sam's brow wrinkled as she looked at Connor. 'All sorts of things. Everything, really. People he'd taken me to use my gift on . . .' She swallowed. 'And I couldn't *tell* anyone – because *I* was the one who'd taken people's memories.' She bit her lip. 'I found the amplifier at his home. It wasn't in the Witches Council archives like he told me. So I stole it back. But the anchor spell had already been removed – I don't know how – and I . . . I knew how badly I'd fucked up. The only way I could think of getting myself out of the situation without bringing the family into it – and yes, admitting to everyone how much I'd messed up – was to remove the amplifier and myself from the equation. I worked a spell to remove any memories of myself and the amplifier from people's minds, harnessed it to the amplifier . . . and then the box it's kept in sealed against me and . . . I've been carrying it ever since.'

'Holy fucking grimoire.' Becca went over to Sam, kneeling down by her chair. And even though there was still a smear of blood beneath her nose, evidence of Becca breaking free of Sam's powerful spell, she reached out and hugged her cousin. 'Why didn't you tell *me*? I understand that you were worried about getting into trouble, but we told each other everything. Or I thought we did.'

Sam started crying and buried her face in Becca's shoulder,

her arms coming around the smaller woman so suddenly that Connor tensed. 'I know. We did. But . . . I'm so sorry. Warren dropped these little comments. Like poison in my ear. And they seemed kind. As if he were concerned for you or for me. How busy you must be with your degree. How it must be hard for you to be put in between me and your dad. And I started to think that you were better off in the dark. I was stupid and I should have known better. But you'd been through so much, losing Aunt Erin, and—'

'It's not your fault. It's OK.'

Connor had to get up because he didn't want to watch Becca comforting the woman who'd lied to her face for nearly a week, who'd put her through so much pain that Connor had thought she was having a stroke or an aneurysm . . . but he also couldn't look away, because he wanted to keep an eye on Sam. Becca might believe her, but Connor wasn't ready to accept everything she said at face value. It was an elaborate story, based on some small pieces of information that Becca could remember, but that didn't mean it was all true. Sam had a formidable gift, which she'd harnessed to an amplifier and used against her own family in order to abscond with a powerful artefact. That was a fact.

'No. It was stupid. But it just snowballed. I panicked,' Sam repeated. 'I'm sorry.'

'It's OK. We can fix this.' Becca sat back on her heels, her hands on Sam's shoulders. 'Together. As a family.'

'No, Becca, we can't. I told you, the box sealed. I can't remove the memory spell. I can't get to the amplifier. The wards won't let me touch it.'

Connor could feel how hard Becca was consciously choosing not to look at him. Because he knew she had an answer to that problem right on the tip of her tongue. The question was, was she holding it back because she wasn't sure whether he'd agree to do it, or because she was respecting that it was a secret that he could penetrate wards?

'We'll figure something out. Even if we can't get into the box, you can come back to Ashworth Hall. We can tell the family, and they could break the memory spell like I have, just seeing you and explaining it will surely prompt their minds to break free, the way mine has. And then we'll have you back.'

'But what about the anchor? You said my dad and Harry are ill because it needs the amplifier. How bad is it?'

'Don't . . . don't worry about that for the minute. At the moment, they're managing because they're sharing the burden.' She paused to take a deep breath, and Connor could read how she was trying to keep her worry from her face. Trying not to worry this woman who had caused all the anguish in Becca's family.

Becca forced a smile as she continued: 'And you never know, maybe the box will let one of them open it because they're the heirs. You never got the tattoo, so maybe that's why it locked you out?'

'Or because she chose to do something harmful with the amplifier,' Connor pointed out, and both women looked over at him.

'Maybe,' Sam agreed. 'The wards did seem to be connected to the amplifier once it was spelled. They seemed dormant when the amplifier wasn't in use.'

Again, there was an opportunity for Becca to point out that Connor could give them definitive answers; he only needed to hold the box. But she held back. Standing up, she took Sam's hands in hers and pulled her up to standing, too.

'We'll figure it all out,' she repeated. 'But, please, go get the amplifier, pack a bag and *come home*.'

Perhaps it was the mix of reassurance, plea and authority in Becca's voice, but it worked like a potion blended to perfection. Sam nodded and headed out of the door, hugging herself tightly. The sudden quiet in the sitting room was heavy.

Becca finally looked at Connor: it felt like it had been days since she'd met his eye, and even now it didn't feel right. There was an unfamiliar wariness about her.

'You don't think she'll make a run for it?' he asked, unable to stop himself from thinking through the ways Sam might try to escape and how he would apprehend her with minimum disruption. He should follow her—

'No.' Again, Becca's voice was full of reassurance. 'She won't do that.'

'You sound very sure.'

She straightened her spine. 'I *am* sure.'

'You don't know her any more, Becca. You've been apart for – what – ten years?'

'Eleven,' she said, like it was just an immaterial fact. And maybe it was – Sam was blood; to the Ashworths that seemed to trump everything. He'd heard the word 'family' so many times in the last twenty minutes he was starting to feel like a secondary character in a gangster movie. One who ended up at the bottom of a canal once he'd served his purpose in the plot.

She shoved her hands in the pockets of her shorts. 'What's going to happen now? Are you going to let me take the amplifier home to my family, and try to reintegrate it into the anchor spell? Or has Warren asked you to take it straight to him?'

'I won't take it *straight* to him.' Connor realised he'd discarded the bloody tissue from her nosebleed on the coffee table, so he levitated it up, set a tiny friction fire on it and sent the ash over to the fireplace. 'You need it returned to Horatio to stop your gift from troubling you.'

She caught her breath and then nodded. 'But after that?'

'He wants me to take it into custody,' he confirmed.

'Right. Were you ever going to mention that?' She moved her gaze to a spot somewhere above his head and answered herself: 'Probably not. Guess I wouldn't have been so keen to show you where it was if I'd known you weren't going to let me take it home and stop my family from getting ill,' she said, sardonically.

Connor reared back. 'I guess *I* was focused on making sure the amplifier wasn't being used for something bad. And it's not like I knew how serious the situation was, because *you* never told me.'

'How could I tell you?' She dropped her gaze to his again. 'It's not solely my secret. And I knew if I did, you'd end up reporting me. Us. Kay and I are already in trouble, aren't we?'

'I honestly don't know. Nothing is official yet.'

'But Warren Barraclough knows what we did?'

He nodded reluctantly.

'And he's the one suggesting you keep this off the record?' She narrowed her eyes at him. 'And he made out it was because we'd be able to corrupt the Tenet Enforcers, right? Use our name to "get away with murder".' She quoted the words he'd used in Polperro back at him. 'All the while, he's skirting warrants and sending you to snoop through our magic.'

'Which, as it turns out, *is* being channelled into something highly illegal.'

Becca's cheeks flushed red. 'We're not hurting anyone.'

'Sam made you bleed by misusing that amplifier.' He raised his hand to indicate to her face. 'You want to reinstate the same amplifier in conjunction with an illegal magical tattoo.'

'It's only ever gone on heirs to Ashworth Hall. Who have a choice.'

'How do you know that? You said yourself, back at Ashworth Hall, that you had to summon Horatio because you only knew about it through oral history. You don't think it's possible your ancestors left out a few key details about putting the anchor tattoo on servants? Subordinates who couldn't say no? Why drain your own magic when you have minions to take the risk?'

'No. It wouldn't work on anyone else. The runes—'

He shook his head. 'Don't tell me you understand all the runes. If you did, you'd have known about an external amplifier.'

'Fine.' Her chin tilted and her eyes flashed. 'But *you* can read them. When we get back to Ashworth Hall, you can put your hands on the tattoo and tell us. And then we'll *all* know. And *you* can decide.'

'Decide what?'

'Our fate. Whether you're going to tell your boss. Whether you're going to take the amplifier. Remove the spells on it or the tattoo on my uncle and my cousin. All of it. It's in your hands, Connor.'

Chapter Twenty-nine

BECCA

If there had ever been a more awkward car journey, Becca wanted to know about it. Three witches and an amplifier. It sounded like a cheesy eighties movie.

Rhiannon had walked in just after Becca had – rather dramatically – declared that her fate was in Connor's hands, and they hadn't had another chance to talk in private since. It was, perhaps, a blessing in disguise. Because she'd wanted to point out all the ways in which Sam's story mirrored his own with Warren. A young witch with a powerful gift, thinking they'd found an ally, gradually being isolated from other people. It seemed so clear to her, but in some ways, it was like Connor was under a spell himself – unable to consider the possibility that his mentor and boss had impure motives. Becca would only push Connor away the more she attacked the one adult Connor had seemingly been able to rely on in his life.

Instead of more emotional turmoil, Sam had come down, explained to Rhiannon that she had a family emergency, and that Becca and Connor were going to give her a lift back to Surrey. They'd packed their bags and paid the bill; Becca had petted the ghost cat goodbye, and they'd been seen off by the lovely people they'd been able to spend a few days with. Smiles and a touch of confusion in the rear-view mirror. Becca supposed, despite Rhiannon most likely being aware of Sam's gift to influence memories, she hadn't been clued in on the whole 'erasing herself from existence' extravaganza.

When her cousin decided to do something, she didn't do it by halves.

Thoughts like that kept making Becca experience a mental lurch. The notion coming so easily, until she caught herself. Like one of those dreams where you thought you were falling out of a tree. Her thoughts and emotions catching up with her physical body. *Yes, this is real, you're not sleeping.*

OK, so maybe there was a smidge more emotional turmoil.

And now they were sitting in a neat little row of trauma. Connor was driving again because he thought Becca still looked pale, but he'd also insisted Sam should sit in the middle because he clearly didn't trust her and wanted to be next to her to react if she tried anything.

Sam was tense – probably because she was sitting next to a huge, brooding man who didn't trust her, as well as heading back to her childhood home to flip the script on her entire family. And Becca . . . well, apart from the nudging of the lost object in the back of her van, she found she was one big tender wound, so many conflicting emotions warring for precedence, she decided the best thing she could do was dissociate to some music and stare out of the window.

Fun times.

They got back to Ashworth Hall in the afternoon.

Becca asked Sam if she wouldn't mind staying in the van for a bit, and since her cousin was looking at the manor house as though it was the jaws of a kraken waiting to swallow her down, she got a very effusive nod of agreement in return. Handy, since Becca wasn't sure how in all the magical world she was going to co-ordinate this.

She had a rather unenviable to-do list:

1. Somehow engineer the breaking of the memory spell for Harry, Aunt Elenor and Uncle Adrian – oh, and she supposed her dad, too – without hurting them. It hadn't been gentle for her, and Harry and Uncle Adrian in particular weren't exactly in peak condition.
2. Explain to her family that the Witches Council were likely to be knocking on their door very soon, knowing absolutely all their secrets, and that the PR Council Member would be heading the charge.
3. Find a way to take down said PR Council Member, because he was responsible for tearing their family apart and probably a whole lot of other awful things, including exploiting young witches to suit his own personal agenda and desire for revenge.
4. Say goodbye to Connor for the foreseeable future because he was most likely going to be responsible for point two on her to-do list, and any possible relationship between them would be difficult given Becca's determination to fulfil point three on her to-do list.

In theory, saying goodbye to Connor would be the easiest thing to orchestrate . . . but if doing her first summoning had taught her anything, it was that theory and practice often worked out very differently.

She met him at the back doors to her van. It was strange to look at him now, back on the driveway where they'd first met. He'd seemed so cold and self-contained then. Now, when she looked at him, she could see the signs everywhere that he was anything but.

The cuts on his cheek – he'd lost the plaster at some point – from stepping in and dealing with Aveline's husband. Protecting Becca and everyone else. The blood on his shirt from her nosebleed, from being right there for her when she'd been in agony, even carrying her into the inn, like her own knight in shining armour. Only his armour was suit trousers and a dress shirt, long sleeves rolled up, because he was hot but for some reason only owned long-sleeved shirts. The scowl on his face, which she could now decode enough to know he was struggling with this whole situation as much as she was.

When she opened the doors to the van, all he took was his small bag, dumping it at his feet and then frowning at the remaining luggage.

'I'll remove the wards on the box the amplifier is in, if you want me to,' he offered, quietly.

'What? Why?'

'So the memory spell can be removed – by Sam. When you have your family gathered.' He shifted on his feet, shoulders hunched, and Becca felt that same tug she always did as she dared to believe what he was offering. That compulsion to close the distance between them. And the same disappointment as she remembered that she couldn't – though this time it was for a different reason. It pressed deeper and harder through her chest. This was not a fleeting hurt; this one was going to stick around.

'Are you saying . . .' She licked her lips. 'Are you saying, you're going to leave it with us for longer than it takes to show Horatio?'

He nodded slowly. 'For now. I can't lie to Warren when he asks me, but I won't volunteer the information that we're back. It'll give you the time to deal with your . . .' His eyes flickered higher to look in the direction of Sam in the front of the van, his eyebrow lifting. 'Your family reunion.' He lowered his head, his bag suddenly fascinating, and a black curl fell forward over his forehead. She remembered the feel of them as she stroked his hair just that morning, and imagined a time when they'd lie in bed together and she could soothe him off to sleep, because he wasn't worried about hurting her with his touch. 'It was frightening, seeing you break free of that spell,' he admitted, still focused on his bag. 'You said your uncle and cousin aren't well; this way, it shouldn't hurt them as much. Or you, having to see it.'

Becca was many things, but she wasn't an idiot and she didn't lie to herself. She had fallen for this man. She knew most people would say it was too fast to call it that, but the speed with which it hit you was the whole point. They didn't call it strolling into love. They called it falling for a reason. The sensation of your stomach losing anchor in your body, your heart in your mouth, beating hard and fast in panic. The suddenness – the way you weren't expecting it and then BAM, it hit you all over. Full body blow.

Some people might say it was just infatuation or lust, but Becca knew herself. She knew what Connor meant to her, and the only person whose opinion she cared about when it came to her falling in love with him was his.

Which was unfortunate, because if she told him how she felt, it would probably just freak him out. What with them only having known each other five days and being on opposite sides of a magical-politics power struggle. There was also the possibility that he'd think she was trying to manipulate him into helping her family get away with things. She'd hate for him to think it had been a lie. He deserved so much love, and she wished she was the person who could give it to him. But their romantic relationship was so fledgling it was still just a crack in an egg in a nest, and it couldn't take priority, for either of them. No matter how it ravaged her heart in this moment when he was giving her all he could.

'You are . . .' she said, giving in to take that step closer to him, and he lifted his head sharply, the bright sunlight a contrast to the stormy depths of his eyes. But then she couldn't think how to finish the sentence without giving herself away. She took a deep breath and all she could manage was a simple, 'Thank you.'

He nodded and pointed to the brown leather holdall in the back. 'This one?'

'Yeah.'

Connor pulled it towards him and unzipped it to reveal a wide shoe box inside, large enough for knee-high boots. He let out a soft snort and looked at her, and for a moment she felt that warm connection between them again. Her blood sang.

Goddess, this was not fair. She wanted him. Why couldn't she have him? She closed her eyes tightly and swallowed hard, gathering herself together. *Because he has to want you, too. Because sometimes life just doesn't work out that way.*

She opened her eyes again and he'd lifted the lid off the box. Another wooden one was tucked inside, covered in runes, just as Horatio had described. Connor stretched out his hand, long fingers splayed – hesitating just a moment before he pressed his hand to it. That look of concentration on his sharp features, as if he were listening to something only he could hear. She wanted to cup his face in her hands and kiss him on every inch of it. To thank him for doing this for her again, and to hold him close. Forever.

Stop. Stop, she tried to tell herself.

He pulled his hand away, an oddly queasy look on his face, and she wondered if it had left him feeling ill. He'd said that absorbing magic didn't hurt him, but she didn't entirely trust him to be a good judge of what caused him harm. 'There, it's done.' He stepped back, and before Becca could stop herself, before she could even register that she was doing a terrible job of listening to herself, she stepped up close to him, caught her fingers in his belt loops and started talking:

'Would you . . . if things work out . . . however they might work out . . . because life is mysterious . . . but if it ever becomes a possibility . . . I'd love it if you called me. Came to find me. I know that probably seems ridiculous . . . but you never know . . . maybe we could—'

'Becca.' He stopped her with his hands – not on her wrists, hovering just above. 'I don't know that I can.'

She bit down on her lip, nodded tightly and pulled her hands away. He stood there for a second, the space between them so small but deep, like an icy crevasse, no hand or footholds available, just an endless drop. Then he walked away, pausing for a moment to murmur something to Sam, and when she heard his car driving away, she looked up at the blue sky and couldn't even be sorry that she'd tried, no matter how much it hurt.

It also occurred to her that she and Zeynep needed to reconsider their relationship disaster rating system, because code red was not going to cover this.

CONNOR

It was perhaps a strange time to go shopping for a book on mythology, but if Connor was going to have a mental breakdown, he might as well be productive during it. He drove to the nearest town outside of Biddicote, bought a present – which he had no idea if he was going to even get a chance to give to his cousin's daughter – and went back to the car. To sit. Because he had no idea what direction to drive in.

He was still suspicious of Samantha Ashworth; he didn't want to go far from Biddicote, in case Becca needed him . . . but all those hours driving back from Cornwall had given him too much time to think. To turn over everything in the story Sam had told, about Warren, about how he was with her, and Connor couldn't deny that some of it also sounded . . . like the way Warren was with him.

Despite how quickly Becca had embraced her cousin again, Connor couldn't accuse them of colluding. He'd watched the reunion happen before his eyes. Felt a ricochet snap of magic when the spell broke. There had been no way Sam knew that accusing Warren of exploiting her in that way would have this effect on Connor – she still didn't know who he was aside from someone from the Witches Council.

Becca had kept his secrets and protected his identity without the anonymity charm. He wouldn't have expected anything else from her. She knew how to keep secrets – but she did it to protect people.

Connor had believed that of Warren before. Could he say that now?

Taking the amplifier from the Ashworths, when Warren knew the anchor spell was reliant on it and it would leave Adrian Ashworth at risk of death, and then subsequently the village of Biddicote without the network of protection it had relied on for centuries . . . it was hard to see how that was a 'bigger picture' decision for protecting anyone.

Maybe if Connor spoke to him – after Sam's memory spell was removed – Warren would tell him that he hadn't known the consequences of his actions. But . . . even if Sam had lied about telling Warren what the spell on the amplifier was being used for, even if there was some scenario in which Sam had taken the amplifier for her own reasons and talked Warren into getting the spells removed for her, Warren had *chosen* to do it without asking Connor to confirm that it was safe.

Connor knew for a fact that had been an option, because he remembered having that amplifier in his hands, back in the empty classroom where Warren had visited him at Dentwood.

As soon as Connor had lifted the lid from the box in the back of Becca's van, the runic pattern on it had struck him as familiar. And then he'd removed the wards and the signature of the magic – warm and old, sturdy as standing stones, resonant like a ley line, with the strength and flexibility of far-reaching roots – brought it all back to him.

Warren had asked him to remove the spell on what (he'd been told) was a piece of stone-age art imbued with a dangerous spell. But so that the wards remained, because the *box* was apparently the special thing, designed to protect the magical item inside while it was active, like the lock on a washing machine so you couldn't open the door when it was full of water. Connor had thought it was a test of his control. He'd obediently unlooped the spell from the amplifier, so the call of the anchor tattoo would have experienced it like a slipped stitch.

Warren had *known* Connor could read the spell prior to removing the anchor from it, but he hadn't asked him to, because he'd either already known the consequences of what would happen . . . or hadn't cared.

If Connor hadn't removed the spell from the anchor in that particular way – if he'd simply torn the whole spell apart – the biggest witching community in the country would have been instantly exposed. As it was, the strain it had placed on Adrian Ashworth had nearly resulted in his death. All because Connor hadn't thought to question Warren.

Still, Connor's mind struggled against it. Tried to throw up explanations, like Warren being young and inexperienced . . . but he *hadn't* been young. He'd been forty years old. *Sam* had been young. *Connor* had been young. And so naive when it came to magic, he hadn't even recognised that the artefact was fused dragon-eye stones.

Warren hadn't logged any details about the amplifier back then. He couldn't have because when Connor had been messaging him about the inn and the amplifier, he'd said they'd both flown under the radar. He'd even questioned the existence of the amplifier. So there was no paper trail. Which backed up Sam's answer to Connor's question as he left Ashworth Hall: had she removed all evidence of the amplifier manually as well as memories of it magically? She'd admitted she did that for herself – any records, photos she could find – but not for the amplifier, because she hadn't needed to.

But maybe Warren just hadn't got around to it yet. Or the systems had been different. Connor didn't know. He *wanted* to believe that there was a reasonable explanation. Every argument Warren had raised against the Ashworths had *some* value. They *were* respected in a way that held sway. They *did* have secrets and *had* broken tenets.

But if they were not above the law, neither was Warren.

Connor's phone rang, and his heart sank further. The man in question, with immaculate timing.

He wasn't ready for this. Connor hadn't been able to pick over every unearthed question. The inside of his mind was like a beach after a storm, covered in detritus, and the waves were threatening to consume it all if he didn't give himself a chance to grab it first.

'You're back from deepest, darkest Cornwall.' Warren's voice was bright.

'How d'you know that?'

'I have my ways.' Warren chuckled.

Well, they weren't magical ways. But all of Connor's trackable data was contracted to Warren at the Witches Council. They owned his car and his phone. Warren could check what purchase Connor had just made in the bookshop on the high street.

That was . . . unsettling.

'Connor, are you there?'

'Yes.'

'Are you on your way to the office? Because I'm not there. I had a day off for a golf tournament. You could meet me at my house. Bring the amplifier there and give me a debrief over dinner.'

Warren sounded so pleased. And yet all Connor could feel was a creeping dread. Warren's house. That was where Sam had said Warren had kept the amplifier last time. Instead of in the vaults at the Witches Council with the other dangerous artefacts.

Connor licked his lips, trying to get some moisture back in his mouth. 'I can't.'

'What's wrong? Why not?' The light humour Connor was used to hearing in Warren's voice was giving way to confusion. 'You do *have* the amplifier, don't you?'

The silence was long and profound enough for Connor to hear the whack of golf balls in the background. If Connor's doubts were unfounded, then it wouldn't matter; Warren wouldn't care that he had to follow the proper protocol. He'd said he wanted to go 'softly, softly' with the Ashworths to get to the heart of the bigger secrets they had. And Connor had done that – more by accident than by design – so now, regardless of what Connor believed or didn't believe about people's motivations, it was time to investigate it all properly.

'No. I don't have it,' Connor admitted.

'Was it not there after all? Were you being led a merry dance by Rebecca Ashworth?'

Connor breathed in, sharp and deep, at the accusation towards Becca, and had to give himself a second before he responded. 'No. We found it. But it's back with the Ashworths.'

Silence, stretching out between them again.

'I beg your pardon?' Warren finally spoke, low and cool. 'You were under explicit instructions to bring the amplifier to me, once you recovered it.'

'But I had no warrant to do that.' Connor swallowed, hoping, hoping, hoping that Warren would do the right thing. Say the thing, whatever it could be, that would alleviate his worries.

'You are the Abrogator. You do not need warrants.'

That was not the thing to reassure him. And even worse was the fact that Connor had said something similar to Becca when he'd arrived at Ashworth House on Friday. What had he almost been complicit in . . . again? 'Of course I do. The rules are meaningless if I don't follow them, too.'

Warren gave a small laugh and then someone called his name in the background. Connor recognised the voice: Edward Cochrane. 'Yes, on my way,' Warren answered the young man whom he'd always made out to Connor he only tolerated at work for the sake of Connor's anonymity. And yet, they were golfing together? At the course Edward's "insufferable and over-privileged" family owned? 'Sorry. I need to go. I can expect your report when? You know, actually, don't worry too much. Perhaps take a couple of weeks holiday? You sound out of sorts. Go back to Ireland, like you've been meaning to. I can deal with everything from here.'

Connor hated that he immediately felt grateful to be given his first holiday in nearly two years.

I'm sure he'll get in touch if he wants to talk.

Grief is a strange time; he might not want to have you fussing around him – especially while he has kids to look after.

I know, it's a shame you can't tell them how important what you do is. I'm sure he'd understand then. Being born the Abrogator unfortunately means a level of sacrifice few other people, non-magical or witches, will ever understand.

All things Warren had said to him as Connor had tried again and again to arrange a time to return home to Ireland and visit his family, his grieving cousin. But there had always been something that came up, and an apologetic rebuff from Warren. A new assignment halfway across the world that . . . maybe could have waited or been handled by someone else.

They hung up without saying goodbye. Warren hadn't even asked how the retrieval had gone. Whether the witch who'd had the amplifier was dangerous. Whether anyone had been hurt. All he'd cared about was whether the amplifier was coming to him.

Becca had cared about the people at the inn, even though her family needed the amplifier back. She cared about everyone even when they didn't necessarily deserve it.

He'd been a fecking eejit to react the way he had when he'd recognised the amplifier, scared in that moment about how she'd feel if she found out he was the one who had removed the anchor spell and endangered the lives of her loved ones – threatened the community she adored. In his heart, though, he knew she wouldn't blame him for that.

He was confused about a lot of things, but not about her.

And he couldn't leave Becca thinking that he didn't want the same thing as her. Some kind of dream where they got time in hotel rooms and by the beach, singing to songs in the car, and it was just theirs . . . whether or not it would ever be possible. He needed her to know the truth.

Chapter Thirty

BECCA

'Becs! You're back.' Harry came out of Ashworth Hall as Becca was grabbing her handbag from the van, the holdall containing the amplifier already over her shoulder. Sam looked up at her with terrified, shining eyes at the sound of her brother's voice. Becca remembered the books she'd seen in Sam's room at the inn, which had looked so out of place, because they'd been children's books. All the ones Harry had illustrated.

It had always been the three of them as kids. Running around the Hall, playing at primary school – before Becca's dad had insisted she went to a different secondary – sleepovers and festivals; related by blood but bonded by the fun they had together. The things they could share that no one else could quite understand about being Ashworths, with all that expectation and privilege as a backdrop to their childhoods.

Or at least, that was the way Becca remembered it. Maybe it hadn't been the same for Sam – as the oldest and the heir, maybe there was more obligation and pressure on her than Becca could have appreciated as a child . . . but she knew the love had been there. Was *still* there, despite all the years they'd lost.

'I'll come out to get you when we're ready,' she whispered to Sam, squeezing her arm quickly, before she closed the door and met Harry halfway across the drive by the rowan tree. He threw his arms around her, and she hugged him back as tightly as all the bags she was carrying would allow. Had it really only been that morning when she'd woken and was scared something bad had happened to him?

'Why didn't you call to say you were coming back? Is everything OK?' Harry pulled back, his crooked smile fading slightly as he examined her. 'You look exhausted. What's been going on?'

She already felt like she'd gone through two weeks' worth of emotions today, but she had to dig deep and carry on. This couldn't be delayed. Connor had said he wouldn't volunteer anything to Warren, but his boss could have called him within seconds of him leaving Ashworth Hall, asking for an update. Connor wouldn't lie − she couldn't expect him to. And that meant there was a ticking clock on how long they had before the Witches Council were back again.

'I'll explain everything, I promise.' She found enough motivation for a smile. 'I have it, though, that's the main thing.'

'The amplifier?' Harry's eyebrows climbed. 'Holy grimoire. You are amazing, Becs. Thank you. Let's get you in and make some tea. Where's Connor? Can he join us? We need to thank him, too.'

Her smile froze in place. Trust her cousin to have listened when they had their conversation the other day. To accept her judgement and speak genuinely about Connor like the person he was, rather than the Abrogator. She wished he could have been there to feel some of the welcome of her family . . . but, no − she'd used up all her wishes when it came to Connor and they hadn't come true. 'He . . . had to go. There's a lot for us to talk about.'

He nodded and reached for her bags, and, for her sins, she did pass him one so they could share the burden together. 'Mum and Dad are at home.'

They started walking. 'Excellent. I should probably call my dad, too. See if he'll join us.'

'Of course.'

'I'm busy,' was her dad's response when she called him, repeatedly, trying to get him to pick up. Harry, Uncle Adrian and Aunt Elenor were sitting in the study in the oldest part of the house. Horatio had popped in, too, to receive *his* thanks for pointing her in the right direction, alleviate the nagging of her gift . . . and then excused himself to go watch the History Channel.

'Please, Dad. This is really important,' she said, staring up at the painting of Biddi and the first members of their family to live in Ashworth Hall.

'They always think it's important,' he grumbled and hung up, which she took as his gracious acceptance of the invitation. They all had a cup of tea while they were waiting to see if he would turn up, and Becca was about to call him again when he came in.

'Well, this is a novelty. Being invited in to discuss family matters.' He sniffed and took a seat in the armchair by the fireplace, as though Becca hadn't just had to beg him to come.

Uncle Adrian was in his seat behind the desk, frowning at it and doing a great job of completely ignoring his older brother. She supposed he'd had years to harden himself to her dad's bitterness, but it still must hurt. Particularly the way he hadn't even tried to reconcile things as Uncle Adrian fought for his life last year. A familiar fatigue at her father's attitude stole through her – she couldn't believe she'd ever entertained the idea that there was a similarity between her mum and dad's relationship and hers and Connor's. Connor might be grumpy, but he was big enough

339

to apologise, humble enough to listen, and he hated the idea of hurting other people in any manner—

Don't think about Connor. You have other priorities.

Aunt Elenor and Harry had pulled over chairs from the table for the rest of them and Becca went to fetch another now, causing curious quirks of eyebrows. 'I need to go get someone I brought back with me from Cornwall before I can explain things any further.'

'What's to explain? You got the amplifier, didn't you? Just hook them back up to it and we can all go about our day again.' How Becca's dad could be the oldest person in the room and still act like a petulant child was one of life's great mysteries and Becca didn't even dignify it with a response. She went to fetch Sam.

Her cousin walked through the Hall as if she were on her way to the gallows. At the door to the study, she faltered and turned to Becca. 'I can't do this,' she whispered, tears spilling down her cheeks.

Becca took hold of her hands, and a million memories of running and skipping together through the gardens, spinning on the grass until they fell over, hand-clapping, dancing – it all came at her in a rush. She hoped the same was true for Sam, but then realised she hadn't forgotten anything. She'd had to live with all those memories, knowing that her family had no idea she existed.

'You can,' she told her. 'I'm right here with you.'

'If I take the memory spell off, he'll remember too, though: Warren.'

'It's going to happen sooner or later anyway,' Becca pointed out grimly. 'Connor has to report that the amplifier is back.'

'But if I leave the spell on, Warren could be told about the amplifier without becoming aware of me again.' A tear dripped off the bottom of Sam's chin.

340

'He could. But if you take the memory spell off, everyone will know—' At Sam's stricken expression, Becca shook her head. 'No – it's a *good* thing. They'll want to know why. And we can tell them. When this memory spell comes off, he'll remember you exist and, if he has any sense, *fear* it. You are just as powerful as him, Samantha Ashworth. And what's more, you'll have your family at your back. I promise you. We'll stop him.'

Sam took a shaky breath and squeezed Becca's hands. 'OK. OK. How, though?'

'Give a girl a minute, would you? It's been quite a day. But I'll have a plan in place by dinnertime, don't you worry.' She winked at Sam and her cousin laughed. 'Ready?'

Sam nodded and Becca led her into the study.

In hindsight, Becca should have made sure there was more than sweet tea and her uncle's disgusting whisky in the study. An industrial-sized box of tissues would have been useful. Maybe some smelling salts – Horatio could have told her what they looked like.

The moment Sam had walked into the study, a confused sense of expectation permeated the air. Aunt Elenor hadn't been able to take her eyes from her, similar to the way Becca had been drawn to her at the inn. Becca half suspected the memory spell was unravelling purely at the sight of her daughter.

They wasted no time. Becca put the box containing the amplifier on Uncle Adrian's desk and Sam went straight over, opening it and hefting the fused wreath of glossy dragon-eye stones out to hold in both hands. It took a while to reverse the complicated spell, and Becca found herself marvelling at how eighteen-year-old Sam had managed to pull off such a feat. A spell to make everyone who'd ever met her forget she ever existed: it was unprecedented . . . epic.

But then, even without the amplifier, Sam's gift had always been formidable. Becca was sure that was why Warren had gravitated towards her. If he could control the witch, he could control the power, and the ability to make people forget was a weapon. The ability to get away with anything.

At the first gasps and tears, it was clear the spell was broken. Sam put the amplifier back in the wooden box and looked across the desk at her dad. Uncle Adrian rose to his feet slowly and leaned across. He took his daughter's face in his hands and whispered through his tears: 'Samantha. Sweetheart. I dreamed of you. When I was ill. I saw you playing with Harry in my dreams, growing up, and I thought I was seeing the baby your mum and I lost before you were born. I didn't realise. I didn't realise.'

'I'm sorry. I'm so sorry,' Sam sobbed, and Uncle Adrian came around the other side of the desk to hold her tight. Harry and Aunt Elenor joined them. They held out their arms to Becca, gathering her in, too.

'Thank you so much for bringing her back to us.' Her aunt kissed Becca's head and, despite all the pain and all the trouble, something settled in Becca's soul. Her family was back together again.

They weren't the only people whose memories of Sam flooded back. All their phones were ringing and buzzing with messages; a reminder that they would have to weather the storm of explaining this. Becca supposed it was a scandal – the Ashworth heir running away – but she didn't care about that, and to her uncle and aunt's credit, it didn't appear to be a concern for them either.

Once upon a time, when Becca, Sam and Harry were kids, that might not have been true, but the ups and downs of the last few years had definitely reframed their focus. Biddicote mattered, the legacy of Ashworth Hall mattered, but the way her uncle hadn't even questioned looking into removing the anchor tattoo when they realised it was making his son – as well as him – ill, showed that his family's welfare came first. Becca knew he would be responsive when she explained that Connor knew about the anchor and that Warren would soon be recalling it, too. They had to face the reality that things were about to change and the family were going to be held accountable for the rules they had broken.

It might not be a bad thing entirely. They could defend their position; show the evidence that their intentions were good, and use their position to ensure that any case made against them was pushed through the proper channels, so that the right decision was taken to protect *everyone* – the people of Biddicote, *and* the people Warren had exploited.

The only call Harry stepped out to take was from Kay, who was heading back from work and had thought she'd accidentally sipped her colleague's 'special' tea when the memories came back to her.

When Harry returned to the study, he brought cake, and Becca went over to the table to help him plate up the enormous slices of carrot- and orange-flavoured sponge. He told her how Kay had mentioned seeing strange translucent bonds linking each of the Ashworths that she'd never been able to understand – it had reminded her of the grey of grief, but no one else's looked that way.

'How did you know, before the spell was reversed?' he asked Becca.

She gave a theatrical sigh. 'I can't help being a know-it-all.'

He laughed and shook his head. 'This is . . . I don't know . . . I think we all might benefit from some therapy.'

'Counselling vouchers all round for Christmas, then?'

He shook his head and put his arm around her in a quick hug, before scooping a big forkful of cake into his mouth. There was a time when his mother would have influenced it in some way to make it bring comfort, but this one only made you feel better because of all the sugar and fat.

Later, the conversation turned to the problem of Warren and ideas for how they might deal with the fall-out. Different plans according to each possible fall-out and the reaction of the Witches Council.

'I'm sorry. I'm so sorry, I failed you.' Uncle Adrian's teacup clattered as he set it back down in the saucer. 'I failed both my children. When you were gone, Samantha, I *felt* it. We all did, but I didn't react well. I put so much pressure on you, Harry, as though you weren't enough, and it was never your fault.'

'No. It was *my* fault—'

'Dad, it's OK—'

Both Harry and Sam spoke at the same time, and broke off, looking at each other, their eyes bright blue but slightly different shades.

'I wish you had felt you could tell us about what was happening,' Harry said. 'But I know it's not always that easy.'

'I saw you,' Sam confessed. 'A few times. You seemed . . . you seemed to be haunting me for a while. I went to Edinburgh first – tried to get as far away as possible from here, and then you turned up anyway.' She gave a small smile. 'It made me think of when we were kids and I hid in my room and you'd always end up outside in the hallway, running up and down, sketching, or bouncing a ball against the wall, waiting for me. I was so tempted to speak to you, to try to tell you. I wish I had, but I was too much of a coward. So I moved to London, and saw you *there*, too. When I ran that time, I ended up at the inn and I didn't see you anymore.'

'Do you think it was your secondary gift, Harry?' Becca asked. 'Telling you where you needed to be?'

'Maybe.' Harry rubbed a hand over his chest where – what Kay called his 'itchy magic compass' – would flare up to nudge him in a direction the seer magic felt he needed to go in. The reasons why very rarely came clear until after events had taken place and this seemed to fit as an explanation for Harry's desperation at the time to move so far away from the family to go to university in Edinburgh. Even if he hadn't remembered his sister, his magical gift seemed to have been trying to find her. Becca wondered why it had stopped. Perhaps the priorities changed; Harry was needed at home, and Sam needed some time to heal, which the inn was expert at providing?

'Will you stay?' Aunt Elenor asked Sam.

'Of course.' Sam took her mum's hand. 'I have a lot of making up to do.'

'We *all* do.' Elenor pressed Sam's hand tightly between hers, as though making sure she was there. Then she looked at her son and husband. 'The first thing we need to do is reinstate the amplifier, though.'

Becca jumped up. 'I'll go get the notes. I don't know how easy it will be to loop it back into the spell. Do you think the ritual will need to be done again?'

Harry got up, too. 'Becs, you're exhausted. We can look into it. You should rest.'

Becca took a deep breath and nodded, every bone in her body seeming to show their agreement in a wave of exhaustion. Maybe it was partly relief, too. 'You know. That's not actually such a bad idea. I would like to check on Michael Kitten. But let me know if you need me, OK?'

They all hugged again and when Becca's eyes caught her dad, still sitting, quiet in the corner, he stood up. 'I'll take my leave, too. It's not like you need me for anything.'

He followed her out, and for once Becca didn't try to fill the silence between them with chatter, in an effort to compensate for his bad mood. It occurred to her that she'd used that tactic when she and Connor were first thrown together – that it had been ingrained in her – but his response had quickly made the dynamic so different. Fun and rewarding. They had sparked off each other – there was a give and take, despite it seeming like he was negative and she was positive. Connor gave back to her in their exchanges with his thoughtfulness, his dry humour, the sweet reveals of his softness. He paid attention to her, cared about how she felt, looked after her.

She got nothing from all her effort with her dad except more of the same. Case in point:

'So . . . you spend a week sorting out their problems and when it comes to sharing the family secrets, they kick you out. Typical,' he said as they stepped out of the front door.

'It's not like that.' She glanced at her van and decided, despite her tiredness, that she was going to walk home. The peacefulness of the woods would soothe her.

'You're smarter and more powerful than all of them put together, Rebecca, but you let them walk all over you.'

'No, I'm not.' She shook her head, a tight ball of frustration gathering inside her. 'And even if I was, it's not a competition. We're a family. We help each other.'

'The way the prodigal daughter helped everyone out by screwing everything up? By telling our secrets to the Witches Council, and stealing, and wiping our memories?' He scoffed. 'And I thought *Harry* was a pathetic choice for heir to Ashworth Hall. Adrian's stubbornness about picking one of his own children has ruined this family.'

Becca paused on the grass and turned to face him. His sour expression, always accompanying his digs and criticisms. She'd had enough. 'Or maybe it all went wrong with *you*. So damn bitter. Trying to make your younger brother feel like a failure, instead of *supporting* him. Maybe if you'd been there for him, he wouldn't have felt he had to prove so much, and none of us would have felt that way either. If you hadn't resented Sam, she would have come to us with her problems, instead of feeling like it would be used against her. You're like poison in this family. We've all had to endure it, to love each other harder to compensate for it. If you hate us all so much, why don't you just pull your own vanishing act?'

'How dare you—'

'I tell you how "I dare". Because they've loved me. Because Mum loved me. I'm so lucky to have had that and still have it, because it means your approval – or disapproval – doesn't even touch me any more. I know what I'm worth. My life is not wasted because I'm not choosing to pursue whatever arbitrary goals *you* think are important. I love my life and the people in it, and it's up to you whether you want to be a part of that or not – but don't expect me to listen to your bitterness or compromise my happiness for you. I don't want that in my life any more. I hope you'll try to make things better between us, Dad, I really do. But it has to come from you.'

Her dad's eyes burned into hers, his mouth pinched at the corners, but he didn't say anything, and she supposed in some ways that was an improvement. No arguing. No passive-aggressive comment. She sighed and walked away, heart aching but lighter. She didn't even look back as she slipped into the cool shade of the trees.

She pulled out her phone, but not to respond to the messages about Sam. She could deal with that later. She just needed to message Zeynep. The closest person to her who had never met Sam.

Becca: I'm back from Cornwall. Thank you so much for looking after my precious baby.

Zeynep: He was an angel as usual. Are you OK? Is it still a code red?

Becca: No. It's worse than that. But we can talk about it when we meet up. Are you free tomorrow for dinner – my treat, as a thank-you for angel-sitting?

Zeynep: I can do dinner tomorrow. Fancy that Mexican place that opened up?

Becca: Yes! They will have tequila.

Zeynep: I'm not carrying you home. And you shouldn't resort to drink to deal with your problems.

Becca: OK, that's fair. The endorphins released from spicy food and ice cream will work just as well anyway.

Becca put her phone away, knowing that actually it wouldn't be any of those things that would help her feel better. She'd get through it because of all the wonderful people around her. Goddess, she was lucky to have so many.

And yet, with all those people, she still wanted one more.

So when Becca opened her gate and saw a tall, dark-haired man sitting on her doorstep, with a black cat curled up on his lap, she couldn't help but burst into tears.

348

Chapter Thirty-one

CONNOR

Connor had no idea how to react when Becca burst into tears. He appreciated that she probably hadn't expected to see him so soon – given the way he'd put his foot so far into his mouth that his stomach was figuring out how to digest shoe leather – but he'd figured she'd be more shocked than distraught. Which was the only way to describe her response.

These were not the small tears she'd shed occasionally in the short time he'd known her – a few rolling down her cheeks, which she flicked away, unembarrassed and accepting, as she continued talking. These were the kind that conquered your whole being. Face scrunched, breathing interrupted, and he wasn't in any way prepared to deal with that. Especially since her cat was sitting on his lap and his initial impulse had been to jump to his feet, which would have evicted the cat – who she loved and probably wouldn't want to see dumped unceremoniously on the ground.

Maybe *that* was a good plan. Pick up the cat carefully. Stand. Present her with the cat.

Nope. That was making her cry more.

But she still reached for the cat, giving the creature a hug until the little fecker wriggled its way out of her arms and ran off.

'That *was* your cat, wasn't it?' he asked, suddenly wondering if he'd been sitting there with some feral feline from a local farm. But it had the Batman thing with the eyes, which wasn't common in cats. He thought.

She nodded, her sobs closer to hiccups.

'Why'd he run off then? I thought they were supposed to be emotional support animals or something?'

She half hiccuped, half laughed and wiped her face. 'He's a cat. He doesn't want me blubbing over him. Plus, I left him – I'll be punished for that for a couple of days at least.' She smiled, and it was sunshine breaking through the clouds. 'Told you animals gravitate towards you.'

He let out a relieved huff of laughter and shoved his hands in his pockets. She wasn't crying because she hated him. Or, at least, it didn't sound like it. 'Are you OK? How did it go? If it went?'

'It went. And better than expected. Thanks to you.' She took a deep breath, pressing her hand to her stomach and breathing out again. Tears continued welling in the warm brown of her eyes and he hated seeing her like this. Valiantly pulling herself together. He understood that she could. He didn't think he'd ever known anyone like her, raw and honest and vulnerable, but strong and sure, too. 'What are you doing here, Connor? I thought . . .'

'I know.' He wiped a hand down his face. What *was* he doing here? He'd wanted her to know how he felt, but facing her – this amazing witch who could seemingly handle anything thrown at her – was only making him realise how much of a mess he was. But she deserved better than him chickening out again. She deserved his honesty. Whatever happened between them, he didn't want there to be any more secrets.

Now try saying that to her, Mr Socially Impaired.

'I'm sorry. For earlier. I didn't mean to make it sound like I didn't want anything to happen between us, at some point, when this is all a lot less . . .'

'Fucked up?' she supplied, making him laugh again.

Holy grimoire, just the thought of her actually returning his feelings made him tingle all over. His whole body was desperate for hers to be near.

'Yeah. But it is . . . even more than you realise . . .' He swallowed. 'I recognised your family's amplifier.'

She blinked, her eyelashes wet and spiky. 'You . . .?' She pressed her lips together and nodded, putting it all together. 'Warren got you to remove the anchor spell on it? When he took it from Sam.'

He pinched the bridge of his nose. 'I'm sorry. I didn't know. I *should* have known—'

'Don't.' She stepped forward suddenly but stopped short, within reach but holding back. 'Don't apologise for being taken advantage of when you were a *child*.' More tears spilled from her eyes and she wiped at them furiously. 'Ugh, it just makes me so angry.'

His heart lost a few beats, jump-starting in his chest, and it was unbearable not to be holding her. 'Can I hug you?' he asked.

'Goddess, yes, please.' She threw herself at his chest, wrapping her arms around his waist and pressing her wet face into his shirt. The only kind of overwhelming heat he wanted was her body flush to his. 'Why did you even ask? You know I told you I'm not scared of being close to you,' she scolded, while she continued to hiccup intermittently.

He folded his arms around her, slow and purposeful, his limbs filling with a rush of comfort, even though he was meant to be consoling her. 'How d'you know I wasn't asking 'cause I'm the one who's scared of you?' he joked.

'Well, I am small and mighty.' She lifted her head, the mischievous light back in her eyes, and it was all he could do not to gather more of her into him, hook her legs over his hips, get her arms around his neck and entwine them as closely as possible. Her breathing finally settled, her chest pressing against his stomach in a steady, intoxicating, rhythm. 'D'you want to come in?'

He nodded. He really did. But he was also revelling in this moment of intimacy and how right it felt. He didn't think physical touch with another person had ever felt this mind-altering combination of safe and exhilarating. Terrifying and perfect. One step at a time, though.

'Just a minute more hugging,' he said, his voice low, and he felt her shiver. He tightened his hold. She pressed her cheek to his chest again and he lowered his head to kiss her hair, breathing in her peach scent. Drawing it into his lungs because it was like pure oxygen to his soul.

And then he noticed what wasn't there. The magic. He sent out his gift tentatively, the one he used to read spells – he'd never dare touch her with his ability to draw magic – and felt nothing. He pulled away and slid his hands into her hair, tipping her face back. Her eyes widened, pupils dilating, as he smoothed his fingers through the thick strands of her hair, rested his hands against her scalp, and then let out a shaky breath and smiled.

'It's not there. I can't feel the magic,' he explained, when her eyebrows pulled together quizzically. 'Maybe it was the memory spell on you? Or your gift calling out like you said, but it's gone now. Nothing is projecting.'

Her hands fisted in his shirt at the back; the scrape of her fingernails on his lower back was dampened by the cotton, but sparks still shot up his spine.

Her tongue swept across her bottom lip. 'You think that would change if you kissed me?'

His heart kicked hard, as though warning him not to get the answer to this question wrong. 'I'm not sure, but I don't think so.'

The slow, mischievous, smile that made it difficult for him to breathe crept onto her impossibly pretty face. 'Sounds like we should do some trial and error to find out.'

He didn't wait for any further invitation. He lowered his mouth to hers and tasted the salt of her tears and her sweet sigh, as she eagerly parted her soft lips. And a moment later his wish from earlier came true as she threw her arms around his neck and hoisted herself up, wrapping her legs around his hips, and he had no choice but to grab her butt to support her.

OK, so he had a choice and, Goddess dammit, it felt like he was making the right one when she bit his bottom lip and tugged it, yanking him deeper into the kiss. He squeezed her tightly against his body, her curves colliding with his hardness, and she let out a moan and pulled back a fraction, her breath gusting over his mouth and chin as she said, 'Inside. Now. Please.'

He stumbled back towards her doorstep and before he could start groping blindly behind him, she slapped a palm to the wood and it swung open with a blast of unnecessarily intense magic . . . but that was the *only* magic he felt. 'Step up,' she warned him, before kissing him again, her fingers now deep in his hair, holding him fast. Not that he wanted to go anywhere.

Heart racing, he made it up the step, through the door – which swung shut again – and found a table or chest of drawers or some kind of furniture beside it, which lost most of its surface contents to the floor as he slid her onto it.

And now he could finally concentrate on kissing her. Over and over. On moving his hands up to her hips, the dip of her waist, the flare out to her ribcage. The way she arched beneath his palms, stretching into his exploration, her body warm and vital and responsive to him. She wanted this. She wanted him and he *wasn't* hurting her with his gift. He had no intention of hurting her. Quite the opposite. And with every brush of her tongue, every gasp and groan, the mental tether that used to tug him back and say, 'No, this is dangerous,' simply dissolved.

BECCA

Becca remembered how she'd felt like she was going to collapse when Connor kissed her the first time. When his control had slipped and he'd stood up in the dark heat of the cupboard at the inn, she'd been overcome with his body crowding hers and the renewed determination of his kiss.

This time there was no snap in his control. They had started hot and now they were blazing. Each press of his fingers and slide of his lips and tongue against hers, had her desire surging.

Despite him seating her on the side table by her door, she had kept her legs wrapped around his waist, but the height of the thing was not conducive to her pulling him in close enough. The solid shape of his arousal was a good few inches higher than she wanted it to be, and only brushed against her stomach incidentally. That would not do.

They needed a different spot. But she also needed to get underneath his clothes. And the latter was marginally easier to bring into effect. Her hands went to the buttons of his shirt, and she dragged her mouth away long enough to ask him if it was OK. He made affirmative noises as his lips teased hers, sweet for a moment before they both abandoned sweet for fervent.

Goddess, she wanted to swallow him down. He'd spoken of the way he absorbed other people's magic and she felt like she was on the cusp of willing herself into the role of Abrogator just by her sheer desperation to draw him into her.

Somehow, she made her fingers work on the buttons of his white shirt and – holy grimoire – why were there so many? His body was *so* long. Or had he been getting fashion tips from Horatio and this was actually a nightshirt? She almost gave up halfway because now a lot of his chest was on show – but no, she was *not* about to let the shirt win. She wanted that bit of clothing gone, for good. He was never allowed to wear a shirt again . . . except if he wanted to. Because it was his body. But, oh, sweet solstice, finally she was untucking it and undoing the last button, and they were wrestling a bit because he didn't seem to want to move his hands from her waist, and yet that was entirely vital to her getting the offending shirt far, far away from him.

They compromised between huffs of laughter around their kisses, him releasing her one hand at a time, and then his shirt was caught in an accidentally-on-purpose gust of magic. She didn't waste any time after that getting her hands on his chest. Goosebumps spread across his skin as she mapped out every inch of it as if trying to figure out what it was made of, because bones and muscle were surely too ordinary to make a body this glorious? He was like one of those sculptures of Lucifer made by artists who *completely* understood that the concept of a fallen angel was sexy as hell.

But then he let out a sound that was almost pained and dropped his head to her shoulder, nuzzling into her neck as though he needed to hide.

'Too much?' she asked, voice hoarse, pausing the traversing of her hands. He shook his head, still buried in her shoulder, but she moved her hands to his hair, smoothing it back. 'You need to go slower? To stop?'

He lifted his head to look her in the eyes, his pupils blown up like he was intoxicated. 'No, I just needed a second. I don't want to stop. Do you?'

'*No.*'

And then he nipped at her lips, trailed his mouth down her throat, across the skin exposed on her chest, down over her shirt between her breasts, to the waist of her shorts, and he was dragging it all down – shorts, underwear – her shoes popping off when he reached her ankles.

He dropped to his knees, and she was not quite so miffed about the height of the side table any more as his big hands ran up her thighs, pressing them wider apart, and his head came down between them.

Every bit of clawing, lust-filled heat inside her body rushed to meet the play of his lips as he lavished open-mouthed kisses along her sensitive skin, higher and higher. Her knees rose as his tongue swept through her, leaving euphoria in its wake, and he hooked her legs over his shoulders and pushed closer, deeper. Then he slowed down to drive her completely mad with his dedicated exploration, sucking higher, softly, stealing all her breath, every thought from her head. She was pure want being delivered increasing ecstasy.

She swore . . . swore again and guided his head back before she passed her peak, though her body did not thank her for it. 'Upstairs, or the sofa – I don't care which.'

He stood, lifted her, and the brush of her bared sex against his naked abdomen almost made her pass out. When they got to her room he put her on the bed, but rather than lie down she went up on her knees and got to work on his belt, pushing his trousers down. She couldn't help but smile up at him as she took hold of his length and dragged her hand firmly up and down, exulting in his silken shape. 'Goddess, I *love* it when I'm right.'

His cheekbones flushed pink, but his embarrassed laugh turned to a hiss as she bent to lick at a leaked bead of moisture. His hands found her head, but disappointingly it was to ease her away. 'I'm too close.'

Her disappointment didn't last long, though, as he removed her top and strapless bra. He dropped to his knees again, gathered her to the edge of the bed, cupping her breasts, pressing kisses and praising words into the curves of them, soft and abrasive at the same time, as his lips worshipped her and the stubble of his jaw awoke every nerve ending in her delicate skin. He tugged her nipples, layering the pleasure throbbing at her core with another sharp, delicious ache.

She made half-hearted attempts to get his attention, because she wanted to give more to *him* and this position made *her* the prize. She tried stroking along his cheekbones, cupping his jaw, reaching down between them, but his body was miles too long, and besides, she was too caught up in how good it felt, his breath warm on her chest, tongue wet and soft. One of his hands moved down between her legs, wide palm hot and firm where she was silky from his mouth and the consequences of his every touch. Her hips snapped of their own accord, dragging her against him, searching, and he pressed his forehead against her breastbone, a low moan escaping him, as his chest heaved. Now *she* was too close again.

'Enough,' she breathed, suddenly, as much to tell herself. He pulled back immediately, and she tugged him up to his feet again, manoeuvred him into sitting at the head of her bed. 'I need you now.'

She grabbed a condom from her bedside cabinet, taking her time to roll it onto him as his stomach tightened and his fingers trailed restlessly over her arms, shoulders, breasts, stomach and thighs, his hot gaze following their path, as if he needed to memorise her. And then she was lowering herself onto him, his broad tip breaching the soft heat of her body, and his hands cupped her rear, helping her control the slow descent as he parted her, filled her, and, Goddess, that was *full*. Her eyelids fluttered as her eyes threatened to roll back in her head in the wake of the bliss.

They stayed still for a long moment, gasping at the overwhelming satisfaction of the connection. He tilted his head back, looking up at her with half-closed eyes burning with all the things she was feeling, too. She grabbed her headboard behind him and leaned down to kiss him gently, and it might have seemed a waste to have all that generous manhood lodged inside her and yet not be riding it to its limits, but the sweet, sensuous grind they moved into was right for them now.

This man *was* going to rail her numerous times in the future if she had any say in it, but now was the time for this aggressive closeness, this building of deep, earnest pleasure, their kisses fraying at the edges as he tightened his hold on her, coaxing her hips with gentle authority in a way that made her weak with arousal. She let go of the headboard in favour of his flexing shoulders, widening the spread of her thighs, letting him move her faster, reaching an electrifying place deep inside and finding perfect friction outside that made all the luscious, decadent pressure build and build and build until she thought she might pass out.

It was the sound he made, low and ragged, humming through his chest and throat, into her, into their kiss, followed by her name, which catapulted her over the edge. She had to break away from his mouth to cry out as the violent shudders racked her body, and then he was pressing even deeper with a throbbing surge that prolonged her pleasure.

He gathered her close, wrapping his arms around her body, and she pressed her cheek to his head, damp curls adhering to her skin. She attempted to tighten her thighs around his hips but found her body entirely devoid of strength. But it didn't matter because he had her, safe and snug. And she had him.

They took a ridiculously squashed but in no way unpleasant shower together in her tiny bathroom, laughing wistfully about the waste of the massive bath in their honeymoon suite at the inn. When they finally made it out, in lieu of his exiled shirt, Becca presented Connor with one of her satiny dressing gowns to wear over his boxers. Covered in palm trees and parrots and cocktails, it barely reached his mid-thigh. The way he grimly put it on – a smile he was trying to repress tugging at his mouth when he saw the way she was grinning – filled her heart with joy. Who knew that the perfect thing to seduce her was a stoic man's affectionate indulgence at the odd things that amused her?

She sent him down to the kitchen to find something to eat in her freezer before she was tempted to leap at him and tumble them back into bed. They both needed to eat. When she got downstairs he was standing, arms crossed, staring out of the window, brows pulled together in a contemplative frown worthy of a Renaissance sculpture, as though he wasn't wearing a dressing gown with piña coladas emblazoned across it.

'Oh, sweet Mother Nature, pizza,' she exclaimed as the smell from the oven hit her olfactory senses. 'You *genius*. And bless you, Zeynep, for not eating them.'

He turned in towards her as she put her arms around his waist, but his expression remained preoccupied and distant.

'What is it?' She tucked her thumbs into the silky belt of the robe and gave it a gentle tug, trying her best not to panic that *he* was now panicking in the aftermath of the glorious sex. Oh, so very glorious.

He scooped up her wet hair, lifting it from where it was making a damp patch on the oversized T-shirt she had thrown on, and the action soothed her worry almost instantly. 'Not such a genius. I didn't know what else to do. All your homemade stuff. I had no clue what to do with it – did it need defrosting overnight or could it be heated straight away with magic or in your microwave?'

'And . . . that's made you pensive? Why?'

'What kind of grown man doesn't know what to do with frozen leftovers? All the hard bit of the cooking is done and yet I'm still clueless . . . because I don't ever cook for myself. I don't know my way around a kitchen. I'm twenty-seven and I don't have my *own* kitchen.'

'Ah.' She tiptoed up and pressed a kiss against his cheek, beneath the cuts on his cheek. 'Well, sadly, you would not be the first man who is utterly useless in the face of domesticity, and at least you have a genuine excuse.' She brushed her finger over the line of his stubble and went back down onto her heels with a smile. 'No point beating yourself up about it. You can always learn.' She chucked him on the chin. 'I can help.'

He caught her wrist and pressed his lips to her finger-tips. Then to her palm and wrist . . . the spot beneath her jaw . . . taking his time, lips warm and tender . . . finally working their way to her mouth. The kiss was long and lingering, and she was seriously debating whether or not it was *entirely* necessary to eat food when something tickled her calves, and then little pin pricks dug into her thigh. Not enough to draw blood but enough to make her gasp and pull away with a groaning laugh: 'Sweet solstice, Michael.'

'It's a good job I know that's your cat's name,' Connor commented dryly, catching her earlobe in his teeth as she turned her head to look down at her feet. She shivered, then smiled at her cat, who was staring at her with big, accusatory green eyes.

Connor let go of her so she could scoop up Michael Kitten.

'Now you want snuggles, hey?' she said, rubbing her head against her cat's, who bumped her back. 'Or . . . is it really food?' He confirmed it when he pushed away to be put down and sauntered over to the mat by the door where he had a bowl of dry biscuits, a water fountain and an insultingly empty bowl waiting for meat.

By the time she'd fed him, the oven timer had gone off and Connor had plated up the pizzas. They sat together at her small table, knees touching, as they refuelled themselves quietly.

It was hard not to imagine how wonderful it would be if this was them, regularly. But she knew the outpouring of their pent-up desire didn't make that a given. There was still a lot of that fucked-up stuff they were talking about earlier to overcome.

'Now you're the one looking sombre,' he commented, dropping a crust on his plate. No wonder he had thought they'd need two large pizzas between them if he didn't eat the crusts. Sacrilege.

She grabbed the crust off his plate and waved it dismissively. 'Just wondering . . .'

'About?'

'About what will happen next, now Sam's lifted her spell.'

'I wish I knew.' He picked at a piece of cheese that had dried on the plate and shifted in his seat, his thigh sliding against hers. 'I did tell Warren the amplifier was back with your family . . . and that I wouldn't be doing anything without any warrants.'

She placed her hand on his knee, forcing herself to consider how much Connor's life had been reframed with the revelations of the last day. 'Sam's preparing herself to tell everyone what he did.'

He pushed his plate away. 'Is that your family's plan? To fight the Council?'

'Not exactly.' She chewed her lip. Warren Barraclough wasn't the Witches Council, after all. Maybe that blurred line had been part of the problem over recent years. 'We just want to fight to make sure there is a fair judgement. If it comes down to that.' She sent him a sly smile and tore off a piece of his discarded crust with her teeth, crunching down on it. 'And sometimes the best defence is a good offence.'

His grey eyes skated over her face before he mirrored her smile. 'I think you've been taking strategy tips from Jemima.'

'She would give Sun Tzu a run for his money.' Her laugh cut off as her heart gave a sudden lurch of fear, and it must have shown on her face because Connor leaned forward and took her hand.

'What's wrong?'

An intrusive feeling – similar to the sadness she'd woken with that morning. It was separate from the moment she was in, skirting the edge of a panic attack and sending her magic rushing through her body at the same time.

'I don't know. Something.' Before she could explain further, her phone started ringing from the living room.

She got up and ran to it, seeing her cousin's name on the display. 'Harry?'

'Are you OK? The wards have just gone off . . .' He paused and she heard someone talking to him in the background in a high pitch. 'Right.' He came back on the phone. 'It's the Witches Council. They're here.'

Chapter Thirty-two

CONNOR

'Do the wards always go off when the Witches Council come to Ashworth Hall?' Connor asked as they hurriedly dressed themselves – Becca handily fetching every item of his clothing the minute it occurred to him that he didn't know where it was. Maybe it was because her gift was centred around being useful to people that she'd just the developed the habit in every other area of her life.

'No. Only when people are coming to the Hall who mean harm,' she said, wedging her feet into flat shoes. 'I've never felt it this strongly before though.'

'How do the wards call out to you? Is it only to those with Ashworth blood?'

She shook her head, tying her damp hair back. 'It's sparked by old runes that communicate to anyone who considers Ashworth Hall a home. In the old days the servants would have felt it, too. Whether that was so they could be prepared to help or because my ancestors were good enough to consider their welfare too is anyone's guess. Are you ready?'

He nodded and followed her out of the oast house, even though he was still buttoning and tucking in his shirt. He was trying very hard not to let the fear that their blissful oasis was coming to a premature end overwhelm him. It wasn't like they hadn't known trouble of some description would kick off – but he'd thought they might have more time. An interlude to revel in the privilege of their hard-won intimacy: the freedom of touching her and being touched by her, without guilt or fear.

'When was the last time it happened?' He forced himself to focus as they crossed the front garden.

She hesitated before answering, pausing with her hand on the gate. 'It was just after Sam left and Warren came to a summer event we were having. The only other time he visited was a Samhain party before that.'

'And it didn't alert you, then?'

She shook her head and yanked open the gate. 'I don't know why. Maybe he didn't have any particular bad intentions when he arrived, just general resentment? The wards aren't flagged by someone we're in a fight with, or that we've pissed off on a general, normal level. But anyway, that was when Sam met him the first time and he told her an internship was hers at the Witches Council if she wanted it when she left school.'

The last part she delivered mostly as a growl, and Connor's heart sank. It could have been innocent enough. Schools talked to you about career prospects at that age, and Warren had been Educational Liaison at Dentwood exactly for that reason. Could he have been trying to improve the relationship between the Council and the Ashworths? And when it didn't work out it turned him bitter against them?

But Sam's spell would have removed any of Warren's memories about those events – hypothetical or otherwise. So why his obsession with the Ashworths since she disappeared? Connor had looked through the file in his car again earlier, and there had been nothing truly incriminating against the Ashworths. Minor misdemeanours over the years, which were unavoidable when witches had to live secretly from the majority of the non-magical population.

If Warren had always harboured a grudge against the Ashworths for their status and privilege, why approach their daughter and offer her a job?

Connor followed Becca as she led him through the paths in the woods. The sun was setting now, the trees casting long shadows over the cool earth, and she flitted in and out of them. He would have thought of her like the faerie queen he imagined when they first met, but she was too determined, though she paused every minute or so to reach back and check he was there with her, and they would catch each other's hands for a moment until the terrain forced them to push something out of the way or go around a tree.

When they came out at the grounds of Ashworth Hall, the red bricks of the manor were ablaze with the golden light of the sinking sun. Beneath the rowan tree on the drive stood five witches, surrounded by a shimmering veil of magic which came up from the edge of the circle of grass. It was barely visible, almost like dust motes in the air, but Becca's gasp made him realise she could see it too.

'The tree is protecting my family,' she whispered, glancing at Connor as they hurried closer. 'I've never seen it do this. Only heard about it happening in the past.'

'What will happen to the people it's holding?'

'Nothing. It just detains them until their intentions are no longer a threat to us.'

As they drew nearer, Connor recognised two of the people by the tree as Enforcers who had carried out the role, before he came along, of making and administering the nullifying objects or potions to rogue witches. Another two, younger witches, were no more than university age and he didn't recognise them. And then there was Warren.

Connor supposed this was what his boss had meant by dealing with everything. But that conversation must have taken place before Sam removed her memory spell from the amplifier. Surely it would have gone very differently if he'd remembered her then; Warren would have told Connor his side of the story. Wouldn't he?

Harry Ashworth and an older man, of a similar height, dark hair turning to salt and pepper, whom Connor assumed was Adrian Ashworth, were on the bottom steps of the Hall, Kay Hendrix just behind them. Harry had his hand twisted behind his back, so Kay could hold it. Becca ran over to join them, hugging them tightly, and Connor faltered. Paused between the tree and the steps, unsure where he belonged.

Warren was wearing a dark suit, his hands in his pockets, but his face was tight with anger and he was stuck with all the others under the rowan tree. Connor could feel the buzz of the strong, old magic encircling the tree.

When he met Warren's eye, his boss raised his eyebrow and tilted his chin as though he was taking his time to consider Connor and his presence there. Warren's gaze dipped, assessing him, head to toe, as if he could *see* something different about him. Connor supposed he did look different to the way Warren usually saw him, in the dignified setting of his office. He was rumpled and breathless. There were cuts on his cheek. Becca's blood on his shirt, which he still hadn't got around to cleaning off. Warren shook his head.

'Connor, I wasn't expecting you to pitch up,' Warren said, with a wry smile. 'Especially not with Rebecca Ashworth. I had assumed she'd be too intimidated to work her feminine wiles on you while you were away, considering she knows you are the Abrogator, but perhaps

I shouldn't be so surprised. The Ashworths are ruthless in their pursuit of hiding the truth.'

Connor sucked in a breath as though he'd just been slapped in the face multiple times. Warren casually announcing his status as the Abrogator in practically the same breath as his name – showing that he was not bound by the anonymity charm. Nor did he care to protect Connor's identity in front of at least three witches who hadn't known.

Seeing the reactions of those witches to the news and feeling their immediate apprehension. Adrian Ashworth's sharp look to his niece, his wary assessment of Connor. The two young witches with Warren, paling and darting worried glances at each other. It had been a while since he'd experienced that, and it felt no less demoralising.

And then Warren daring to suggest that about Becca. Immediately trying to drive a wedge between Connor and her. Insulting her, making Connor look like a fool. It turned his stomach. The worst thing was, the suggestion that Becca was only feigning feelings for him might have worked last week. His view of himself as such a monster to other witches could have had him easily convinced that any sign of affection from her was no more than an act. If Warren had planted that seed . . . But he'd tried to plant other, similar seeds instead. Ideas that she was deceptive and not to be trusted.

Connor trusted her with his life.

'It's not like that,' he said, shaking his head and firming his jaw.

'Is that so? I'm relieved to hear it.' Warren gave a small laugh. 'Then be a good chap and remove these wards that are holding your colleagues prisoner, and then go into Ashworth Hall to take Samantha Ashworth into custody for her violation of Worldwide Witching Tenet Number One, and remove the dangerous stolen artefact in her family's possession.'

Connor automatically looked to Becca, not even caring how it might appear to undermine what he'd said earlier, and read the acceptance in the soft half-smile she offered him.

This was like that moment in the car earlier, when he hadn't known what direction to drive in. He'd chosen then to go back to Becca, but this time he couldn't choose that. Not so definitively. Because Sam Ashworth *had* done harm to people with a powerful spell. That much was true. Connor had witnessed it – the people affected could attest to it – and Samantha had even confessed it.

He looked back to Warren. He wouldn't take his side either. Because no investigation had been officially completed. No legal warrant could have been raised in the scant few hours Sam had been home, to sanction her arrest. And she'd not shown herself to be a physical, immediate danger to anyone, so Connor could not exercise his gift to protect others in an emergency.

'I already told you, I won't act without official dispensation.'

Warren's mouth flattened into a thin line. 'She is a dangerous witch.'

'According to who?' Becca spoke up, stepping down from beside her family.

The cold look Warren turned on her had Connor's adrenaline level spiking. 'According to the witnesses who, this afternoon, began to remember parts of their lives that she'd stolen for the last decade.'

'Has it been proven that she was the one to cast the spell?'

'She is famous for her rare gift. In conjunction with the amplifier she stole, boosting her power, she is the only witch who would be able to do something of this magnitude.'

'Debatable.' Becca lifted one shoulder, carelessly deflecting Warren's declaration, then folded her arms. Her eyes narrowed as she enunciated her next words: 'And the spell was in place for *eleven* years. My cousin was *barely* an adult at the time. If she did have anything to do with it, there is a strong possibility she was *coerced*.'

The message seemed to penetrate Warren, who for the first time lost some of his arrogant bearing to tension. The subtle change in body language seemed to be picked up by the Enforcers and younger witches surrounding him, too; the gap widening between them until they realised they were getting closer to Connor.

The growl of an engine and gravel crunching on the driveway drew everyone's attention to the motorcycle pulling up beside Warren's sleek car and Becca's pink van. The rider climbed down, pulling off their helmet to reveal herself as a woman, most likely in her forties, with short black curls. Celestine Murray – the Head of Magical Gifts and Designations for the UK Witches Council.

'Evening, Adrian, Warren . . . Connor,' she said belatedly, noticing him. Connor had only met her a few times, back at Dentwood, when his gift had manifested and they were debating how to test its perimeters. It occurred to him now that it was odd she hadn't been more involved in his mentoring. 'This is an interesting garden party you've invited me to. But then I expect you've had a rather interesting day,' she added, drolly.

'Very much so. Thank you for coming at such short notice. I appreciate it.' Adrian Ashworth's deep voice rolled over the congregated witches. He wasn't using his magic, but Connor could feel it, the potential resting beneath the surface. He didn't know if they'd reinstated the amplifier to their anchor spell yet, but if this was Adrian Ashworth after years of illness and having his magic regularly drained, his power was impressive.

And if the head of the Ashworth family decided to use his gift to influence through speech, opinions could be easily swayed, actions coerced. He could potentially get his family out of trouble with a few magical sentences if the subjects were in any way suggestible – but that would have been a misuse of his power. And he was choosing not to do it.

'You should. I had a glass of cava with my name on it when you called.' Celestine put her helmet down on the seat of her bike and marched closer, unzipping her leather jacket with a decisive tug. 'You're lucky I hadn't drunk it, or I wouldn't have been able to get here. Now, what is all this about?'

'We needed an impartial witness to Warren Barraclough's attempt to gain unsanctioned access to Ashworth Hall and take custody of my daughter and our personal property.'

'Typical Ashworths, bringing in their cronies to get them out of trouble,' Warren muttered.

'I resent the implication, Warren,' Celestine said, putting her hands on her hips. 'Adrian and I are hardly chummy. I've been hankering to get into the library at Ashworth Hall for years to back up my genealogy research and get stonewalled at every turn. I've yet to bring a SWAT team to the door, though.' She eyed Connor with interest, her dark eyes seeming sharp enough to recognise that he was not part of that SWAT team.

'Is that what he's offered you?' Warren asked. 'Access to the library?'

'Are you accusing me of accepting a bribe?' Her voice took on a tone that would have any person knowing they'd overstepped. 'To what end?'

'Corroborating his story. Having the case against them shut down.'

'Is there a case? Adrian just said you're here unsanctioned.'

'There wasn't time. As you probably know, this afternoon it was revealed that Samantha Ashworth stole a dangerous magical artefact and used it to cast a harmful spell over hundreds of people. So, yes, I have brought a team to arrest her. And any other witches who resist.' Warren removed his hands from his pockets, revealing that they were clenched.

'The amplifier wasn't stolen,' Harry Ashworth disputed. 'It's impossible for Sam to have stolen an amplifier that belongs to her, as much as it does to any other member of the Ashworth family.'

'That is true,' Celestine commented, dispassionately, and Connor remembered that she was an empath with the valuable gift of being able to read truth from lies. It had its flaws, because she could only read the truth according to the person speaking it – if they believed it to be true, it wouldn't flag as a lie. But it still made her an excellent judge. And it supported Connor's instinct about Adrian Ashworth not intending to use his influence to manipulate the situation. Celestine's ability to read the truth would make her impervious to influence in the same way Connor was.

'They may be choosing to see it that way now, but if it wasn't stolen, why was the Abrogator in Cornwall for five days tracking it down with Rebecca Ashworth, who was utilising her gift to find lost things?'

'A lost thing does not equal a stolen thing,' Becca said acidly. 'Or are you the type of man who accuses your kids of stealing your keys when you've misplaced them? Is it always someone else's fault?'

Warren threw a scathing look at Becca and then directed his attention back to Celestine. 'Fine. The issue about whether it was stolen is irrelevant. That she used it to cast a dangerous spell is not.'

'There's no proof that she did because there hasn't been an investigation—' Adrian Ashworth began to point out.

'OK, OK.' Celestine's voice rose over the argument. 'This is going to go in circles, and I want to go home at some point tonight. Here are the facts: you do not have any official warrants to pursue this arrest or confiscation, Warren, regardless of your arguments as to whether Samantha Ashworth is a dangerous witch. There is only one person here with the authority to apprehend Samantha Ashworth if he deems her to be an immediate danger. Connor, do you believe that to be the case?'

'He can't be trusted to answer that truthfully,' Warren jumped in, before Connor had the chance to reply. 'He's been compromised by his infatuation with a member of the Ashworth family.'

Connor could have argued that he and Becca walking up to Ashworth Hall together did not constitute an infatuation with her, but he didn't want to deny it. Whether he'd been made insensible by those feelings was another matter. 'If I believed Samantha Ashworth was an immediate threat to anyone, I would not let my feelings for her cousin cloud that judgement,' he said clearly.

'True.' Celestine gave a relieved nod. 'Excellent. So, please give me your professional assessment. I'm all ears—'

'I don't believe she is—' Connor broke off, his confidence shaken for a second by the thought that perhaps Adrian Ashworth *had* bribed Celestine Murray. Because she'd just indicated that she could tell whether *he* was telling the truth, and that wasn't possible. 'Hold on, you

373

can't verify whether what *I* say is a truth or a lie.'

'I can't? That's news to me and my gift.' Her patience was clearly wearing thin.

He lowered his voice, despite knowing it was a lost cause to keep any secrets from all the people congregated. He wasn't even sure he wanted to any more. 'I'm impervious to magic. It can't work upon me.'

Celestine frowned. 'But my gift doesn't work *upon* you. Empathic abilities pick up what is already being put out there by the subject. It's just another level of body language. I can read you just fine, don't you worry. So, you were saying . . .?'

Connor's eyes darted to Warren. 'That's not true, is it?'

'Having doubts about how honest *she* is, Connor?' Warren shook his head. 'I warned you about this.'

'What on earth are you talking about?' Celestine's voice was sharp. 'You know he can be read by empaths. *You're* an empath and you report regularly to the Council on him in that capacity.'

Connor took a step back. 'Since when?' That couldn't be true. Warren had told him empaths *couldn't* read him, just like influencers couldn't influence him, healers couldn't heal him and seers wouldn't have visions of just him.

Warren sighed. 'Since always. I didn't tell you because I didn't want you to feel self-conscious or avoid meeting with me—'

'One lie, one truth,' Celestine said, grimly.

'*What?*' Connor was only talking to Warren. The man who'd just casually admitted to lying to him since he was a teenager.

Becca turned to him, reaching for his hand, and he couldn't help but wrap his fingers around hers tightly. He felt like a puppet whose strings had been cut, and she was the only one who could keep him from collapsing. He didn't want to put that weight on her, but it was so hard to refuse in that moment, and with her offering it so openly.

Warren's eyes narrowed on their linked hands.

'You must appreciate,' Warren said, softly. 'You're a threat to other witches that needs to be monitored. Being able to see what you desire is the best way to assess any risk you pose. You know the drill. It helps me to flag the potential for problematic behaviours.'

'You told me it wasn't possible.' And he'd never been able to spend enough time around other witches to find out any different. Because they were all terrified of him. Because Warren had said it was best for none of them to know about all the other things he could do. That it was best for him never to have a desk at one of the offices . . . best that they never realise he could do more than take their magic.

'I'm sorry. Sometimes I have to navigate around the truth to ensure the safety of many.'

'One lie, one half-truth,' Celestine muttered.

Connor flinched. 'I have to go. You got the answer from me you needed? I don't deem Samantha Ashworth to be an immediate threat to anyone and I won't be apprehending her.' He directed his attention to Celestine, whose irritation had softened somewhat. She nodded. He stroked his thumb over Becca's hand and received a squeeze back in response. She understood. 'Then I'll take my leave—'

'Surely not before you've released your colleagues from this captivity?' Warren's voice was sharp.

'As I understand it, you'll be free to go once you stop having bad intentions towards the Ashworths.'

'Bad intentions towards the Ashworths is seeking justice to other people. Remove the wards.'

Connor shook his head. 'No.'

'Are you refusing an order from the Witches Council, Connor? Be careful how you answer here,' Warren warned. 'You are not above the law yourself and not invulnerable to ordinary methods of detainment.'

'Are you threatening to lock him up for not obeying you?' Harry asked, incredulous.

'He's a dangerous witch. If he doesn't recognise the Witches Council's authority, what kind of havoc do you think he could wreak?'

'It's never been about him being dangerous. It's about you wanting to control him.' Becca pulled away from Connor, rounding on Warren, growing even closer to the circle of grass the tree was on.

He didn't want Warren anywhere near her, and as upsetting as the realisation about him was, it was also freeing. It had finally clicked. Warren was not his friend. He was his jailer. He'd woven a cage around him for years.

Connor stepped forward to wrap his arm around Becca's waist and pull her back against his chest. There was a collective inhale of breath from several of the witches at his movement. One of the Tenet Enforcers lifted a small crossbow, seemingly in a reflex, training it on him. The metal darts in it would drain an ordinary witch as they drew magic into them until they reached capacity. It wouldn't do that to Connor, but aimed at his head the metal would still . . . well, probably kill him.

'Put that down, you idiot,' Becca growled at the Enforcer, laying her own arm on top of Connor's.

His heartbeat was probably crashing against her spine – he was surprised that her teeth weren't rattling from it. Most of these witches were still terrified of him and Warren could use that to his advantage. *Would* use that to his advantage now he knew Connor's eyes had been opened. He had to show himself to be better than the big bad wolf they expected.

He cleared his throat. 'If I understand rightly, that tree is old enough to be afforded protection from the Witches Council's heritage department.' He looked over his shoulder to where Kay was. 'Is that correct, Kay?'

'Yes. Yes, it definitely is,' she said, clearly and calmly. She'd stepped forward now, her arm through Harry's, and it seemed strange that she was the one seemingly reassuring him, considering how nervous she'd been of Connor the other day. And then he realised *she* was an empath, too. One who could see the emotional bonds between people. She could see exactly how he felt for Becca and that he'd never hurt her.

'Thank you. I'm not willing to remove the spell holding you all, Warren, because I know the magic on it is unique enough that it might damage the tree. And given that it's only holding people with bad intentions towards the Ashworth family, you'll be able to walk free and unharmed from it as soon as you realise that the right thing to do in this situation is to turn around and go back to your homes, and when you go into work tomorrow to start a proper, thorough investigation into *all* of this.'

'Truth,' Celestine said. 'Lots and lots of lovely truth. What say you, witches?'

The Tenet Enforcers and two younger witches looked at each other, and then tentatively, one by one, stepped out of the warded area around the tree.

Warren did not attempt to leave.

'This is rather damning, Warren,' Celestine noted. 'And providing me with somewhat of an issue. I hardly want to leave you on Ashworth property under these circumstances.'

'I have a suggestion,' Adrian said. 'The rowan tree is in

tune with magic. It doesn't detain non-magical people, even if they mean harm, since we have an intrinsic advantage over them. He can voluntarily expend his power trying to get free and it will release him once he has exhausted himself.'

'Sounds like it would be fun to watch,' Celestine scoffed, and Warren folded his arms over his chest. 'But we could still be waiting some time.'

Weariness hit Connor in a wave. He didn't think he had it in him to watch his mentor railing ineffectually against the Ashworth magic – poetic as it might be. And what if Warren targeted the tree and the wards failed suddenly? An offensive spell could escape, hitting any of the witches surrounding the tree. He could mitigate that risk. 'Or I could drain his power temporarily?' He looked to Celestine for her approval.

She tilted her head in consideration. '*Just* temporarily?'

'Of course.'

'That sounds like a reasonable course of action under the circumstances.'

Becca turned beneath his arm, slipping her arms around his waist and pressing her chest against his, a wealth of sympathy and understanding in the prettiest eyes he'd ever seen. 'You don't have to do it, if you don't want. We'll throw him a tent and some food until he comes to his senses or wears himself out.'

'You've already got one unwanted house guest from all of this,' he attempted a joke.

She gave him a sad smile because he didn't fool her for a minute. He took her arms gently from around his waist and kissed the back of each of her hands. At Warren's disgusted snort, Connor glared at the man he had once considered a father figure.

The look of betrayal he received threw Connor. Did

Warren truly think this was betrayal? He waited until Connor was stepping through the ward around the rowan tree to speak to him.

'You know, your deepest desire is her. And hers is protecting her family,' Warren said, so quietly it would have been hard for anyone else to hear. 'You are a means to an end for her, at best. I should have known you would be vulnerable to something like this.' And it almost did sound like he cared, until he added: 'I never even *needed* to read your greatest desire when I found you at Dentwood. You reeked of the desperation for someone to care about you. Grateful for any crumb of attention I threw your way.'

'You are a *vile* excuse for a human being.' Becca's voice wavered behind him, and Connor flinched inwardly at the thought that she had heard.

'Good luck piecing the scraps of him back together into something useful.' Warren smirked at her, but as Connor arrived before him, the expression fell from Warren's face.

Connor's heart was heavy, but the grass was soft under his feet, and the hum of the old, beautiful magic wrapped around him like a hug. The tree shifted in a supernatural breeze, its timeless wisdom reaching down from its leaves and up from its roots, soothing him despite the pain in his chest. He recognised the strength in it, the whisper of protection, and realised . . . it wasn't just passing through him, as though he were invisible to it. The magic flowed in and out of him, accepting his presence; not oblivious to it because he was a void. He had his own magic, aside from his gifts; he could cast spells and charms, and if he was a void, that wouldn't have been the case, would it?

He took a slow, deep breath, sensing the magic wrap around him, like it recognised kin and supported him. Trusted him.

He raised his hand and caught the flicker of fear in Warren's eyes, despite all his vicious words.

'Don't worry,' Connor said. 'I promised I'd only drain you temporarily, so that's what I'll do. One of us might be a monster, but it's not me.'

BECCA

Becca literally could have cheered when she heard Connor say that he wasn't a monster. And *then* he pressed the tip of his pinkie finger to the spot between Warren's eyes and within seconds the bastard was out for the count. In *seconds*. With his *pinkie finger*, which she knew was figuratively a *middle finger*. And she was positively gleeful about it.

Connor was so much the bigger person, he didn't even let Warren hit the deck as he lost consciousness. He grabbed a handful of the front of his shirt and eased him down onto the grass and then left Celestine to direct the other Witches Council members to pick him up and load him into one of the cars they'd arrived in.

Becca supposed it was too much to hope that they'd use the car boot to transport Warren, and then they'd drive by a cliff and it would accidentally pop open.

Any thoughts of revenge emptied from her mind when she saw the pinch of Connor's brow, the whiteness of his face in the dimming light. Small signs of strain to anyone else but blaring alarm bells to her that he was suffering. She joined him beneath the tree, wrapping him in a hug, squeezing him tightly, wishing it would fill him up with all the love she felt; that it would flow into the parts Warren had just cut out of spite.

His arms came around her, too, though they didn't lock as firmly as the last time he'd held her. He was stiff, like he was in pain.

'Did absorbing his magic hurt?' she asked, looking up into his face.

'No . . . but it was predictably gross. Bitter.' He rolled one of his shoulders.

'Like Brussels sprouts, I bet. It must be like a magical ice-cream parlour for you, but all the flavours are terrible.'

He laughed and her heart lifted at the sound of it.

Someone cleared their throat next to them and Becca pulled her eyes away from Connor's face to see Harry and Kay standing close by.

Uncle Adrian had gone back inside already, having finished talking to the awesome Celestine – an absolutely inspired choice for their witness, which Kay had suggested. No doubt Uncle Adrian was exhausted and wanted to check on Sam and Aunt Elenor. Becca was glad Sam hadn't come out. There was no doubt she was going to need to answer a lot of questions, face accusations and go over a lot of painful ground over the next few weeks. She didn't need to face Warren, too. Not until she was ready, hopefully.

Harry opened his arms to Becca and she moved away to hug him, too. 'We didn't have a chance to tell you.' He told her when they stepped back and he'd put his arm around Kay again. 'We managed to pull the amplifier back into the spell again.'

'It's all working?' That had been fast, or maybe not – Becca had no actual idea what the time was or how long she and Connor had been . . . busy.

Harry nodded happily and Kay curled herself around him, pressing her face into his chest, the relief on her clear now. And Becca could see the difference in Harry, too, now the tension of Warren's presence had been removed. The lines of fatigue on his face had eased; his skin glowed beneath his freckles.

She let out a shriek of laughter and launched herself at Harry and Kay, squeezing them both in another hug. 'Oh, thank the Goddess.'

'Thank *you*, Becca. And you, Connor.' Harry looked over the top of Becca's head as she stepped back.

'No thanks required,' Connor said, but his voice was strained, his eyes coming to rest on Becca.

'Are you coming in?' Harry asked.

'I think we could all do with a drink,' Kay added.

'Definitely,' Becca nodded.

'And you're welcome to stay after, too.' Harry was very clearly looking at Connor when he said it, because it wasn't like Becca needed an invitation.

'Ermm . . . that's good of you, but . . . I think I should probably not.'

'You can't stay?' Becca asked, her head whipping back to look at him.

'Well, if you change your mind,' Harry said tactfully, and he and Kay walked back inside the Hall, leaving Becca and Connor alone by the tree where they'd first met.

'You're going?' she asked, and she didn't even care that it came out full of all the shock and disappointment she was feeling. 'We don't have to have a drink with my family. We can just go back to my place.'

'You *should* go and be with them.'

'But where will you go?'

'A hotel, and then I think . . . I think I should probably go back to Ireland for a little bit.'

'What?' She stepped back as though the extra distance would enable her to get a better perspective of him. He'd

382

faced Warren, made his position clear. Her family were in full acceptance that there would be an investigation into everything. She'd assumed a lot of the hardest parts between them had been cleared up. 'Why?'

'I think maybe I should take a wee bit of time to sort my head out.' He wiped a hand down his face and sighed. 'I don't *want* to,' he said, his voice earnest and low. 'What I want to do is come back to your oast house and . . . well . . .' His cheeks went adorably pink and he cleared his throat. 'But that wouldn't be fair to you.'

'Judging from earlier, I think you'd be very "fair".'

He raised his eyebrow and caught her hips, sending a thrill through her as he pulled her close again. '*That* would be better than fair,' he pressed his lips to her temple and whispered in her ear. 'I'd be sure to worship you.'

She shivered and ran her hands up his shirt. 'OK, if you're still going after saying things like that, you're just being mean.'

'I'm sorry. I just think it might be for the best.'

She took a breath to stop herself from letting all her frustration and sadness out. He was telling her what he needed. It was the first time probably in his whole adult life that he was thinking about what *he* needed. She couldn't guilt-trip him or make it any harder for him than it probably already was. 'What makes you think that?'

'Because I'm a mess. And I don't want to make you responsible for putting me back together again.'

'Don't listen to that dick—'

'I'm not. It's not because *he* said it, it's because I *know* it. I want to figure myself out – I don't want to risk making you my saviour. You're amazing – generous and forgiving, and you fix problems for people as though it's no big deal and it doesn't cost you anything. But that doesn't mean I should take advantage of that. I want to come back to you with some semblance of self-respect, so you don't have to deal with helping me *all* the time.' He took a deep breath. 'And that being said, I don't expect you to wait for me—'

'Don't be an idiot,' she interrupted, tiptoeing up and cupping his face in both hands. 'Of course I'm going to wait for you.' She pressed a soft kiss to his lips. He leaned into her, sharing the warmth of his mouth tenderly, but lifted away before it could turn into anything more.

'You should go inside,' he repeated, his voice low.

She kept her eyes squeezed shut as she had stern words with herself. If he thought he needed this, then it was for the best. It did make sense. Having his whole world view overturned, and the one person he'd thought he could rely on betray him, must be killing him. And, of course, all that made her want to do was wrap him up in her arms and make everything better. But she wasn't responsible for his happiness, as much as it enriched her soul to make him happy. And the fact that *he* recognised that and didn't want to doom the potential for them before they'd even started . . . it just made her love him all the more. It throbbed through her chest, a painful ache.

She nodded and opened her eyes, meeting his with their beautiful spiky lashes and winter-sky splendour.

'I'm not saying goodbye,' she warned him as she lowered back down to her heels. 'But I will say . . . go on now, go.'

He laughed out loud again and she squirrelled the sound into her heart and locked it up tight. '*Such* a piss-take.'

He kissed her forehead again, and then, as she watched him walk away into the gentle summer night, she decided to make one more wish.

That he would heal enough to come back to her.

Chapter Thirty-three

Celestine Murray turned up on his dad's doorstep two weeks later.

Connor took her out into the garden to sit and talk at the small wooden table his dad had made. It was in the shade, the sun bright overhead but the grass a lush, deep green that smelled of his childhood. Connor had forgotten how much he loved summer in Ireland. For a start, it didn't make him want to peel off his skin.

She faced him from across the small wooden table on the patio, took a sip of the tea his dad had insisted on making and then got down to business.

'I won't beat about the bush, Connor. I'm here to offer an apology on behalf of the UK Witches Council. As you know, over the last couple of weeks a number of investigations have been taking place, one of them into Warren Barraclough and his conduct during his career within the Council. It's become clear that he abused his position in a number of ways, and that the Council has been remiss in its safe-guarding of the welfare of young witches he might have come into contact with in his early role as Educational Liaison.'

Connor shifted on his seat, the wood creaking. He didn't like the thought of other young witches being affected by Warren. He was so isolated from the community, he couldn't even think who that could be, other than Sam

Ashworth, of course. He wished he'd not treated her with so much suspicion. He wished he could speak to Becca about how she was doing.

Honestly, he just wished he could speak to Becca. No one was stopping him. She would take his call. But he knew if he spoke to her, he would want to see her, and then he'd get on a plane or ferry, too soon, and that would be a disservice to both of them.

'Obviously,' Celestine continued, 'this affected you further with regards to the handling of your position as Abrogator, answerable to the UK Witches Council. The parameters of your unique role are no excuse, but they led to a lack of auditing when it came to your assignments and remuneration, as well as the confidentiality of your identity.'

Connor had already had it confirmed to him that Warren had picked and chosen who he would insist on being held by the anonymity charm, depending on how it suited his purpose, like with Edward. That wasn't the reason Connor leaned forward, interrupting her with his heart in his mouth. 'Has there been any evidence that he used me to remove magic from witches who hadn't been investigated and charged?' The thought that Warren might have faked warrants and charge sheets to eliminate his political competition or anyone he'd held a grudge against had been keeping him awake at night.

Celestine shook her head and the sudden release of tension had Connor collapsing back in his chair, air expelling from his lungs in a whoosh, his shoulders relaxing for the first time in days.

'No. Thankfully, so far, we've discovered no such evidence. You've been kept busy enough with the real rogue witches,' she said dryly and not without sympathy. 'Mostly, the abuse of his power in this regard has been

– to put it bluntly and off the record – having the threat of you in his political arsenal, something that was only strengthened by his insidious work to create an atmosphere of fear around you.

'He also broke the terms the Worldwide Witching Councils had agreed to when it came to your remuneration for the dangerous work that you do. The model proposed in the original policies was that of a regular stipend made up of fees from each Council that wished to call upon the services of the Abrogator. This stipend should have been paid directly to you, with administrative expenses going to the Council you'd chosen to report to. Warren . . .' she took a deep breath and shook her head, 'was transferring the stipend to an off-shore account, minus the expenses you required to carry out your duties.

'He also . . .' She looked up to the heavens. 'He also negotiated separate deals with Councils who had not signed up to the stipend agreement at higher one-off rates. All of which is to say, he pimped you out and has been stealing from you for years.' Her professional demeanour collapsed a little under the weight of her disgust. 'While also exercising a form of financial abuse upon you, having an unethical level of control over your money.' It was her turn to sigh. 'On the plus side, once all this has gone through the witching court, you will be receiving an enormous sum that you are quite rightly owed. And, of course, will immediately begin receiving the stipend . . . should you wish to continue your work as the Abrogator.'

'That's a choice, is it, now?' Connor raised his eyebrows, Becca's voice – never far from his mind – echoing inside him.

'It should always have been made clear to you that it was a choice.' Celestine linked her fingers and looked at him solemnly. 'I need to make a personal apology to you, Connor. I should have been more involved in your acclimatisation to your gift. I should have fought for you to come under my remit when you joined the Council at eighteen as well. I will not make excuses for it. I should have done better.'

'I appreciate the apology. I'm not sure it's required, but I do appreciate it.'

'Good.'

'Grand.' Connor stretched his legs out until his feet were in the sunlight and then looked back at the powerful, highly respected witch sitting in the garden where he'd once tried to dig out a trench after watching a First World War documentary, and raced snails along the tiles that bordered the flowerbed. 'Is that everything? You flew out here to confirm to me a bunch a stuff I'd already figured out – with the exception of the stipend. You could have put that in an email. I'm sure you're very busy.'

'A face-to-face apology seemed more appropriate.'

'Right . . . and you need an answer as to whether I'm available for Abrogator duties.'

She looked uncharacteristically uncomfortable.

She needn't. However refreshing it was to be away from the antipathy of the witching community towards him, he knew he wasn't going to step away from it. He may now recognise that Warren had crafted invisible bars to hold him in with all his talk of 'duty' and 'responsibility' for his own ends, so that he could wield the threat of Connor whenever it suited his dubious motives – but Connor couldn't deny the uniqueness of his power and the responsibility he felt to step in should a witch become dangerous. When the magic of the rowan tree at Ashworth Hall whispered to him of protection, his bones agreed. He, too, was made for that. Wanted to provide it.

'The answer is yes, I will make myself available for emergencies. Of course I will. I need to think over the way the rest of the role is structured.'

'Cutting back services?'

'Perhaps some – certainly response time. I'm also . . . I'm also interested in the Educational Liaison role.'

'It's being looked into,' she said, grimly.

'Good. But I mean, I'd like to talk to the – whoever it is – department, Council member, who's in charge of it and put forward some suggestions about integrating kids who don't come from magical backgrounds into their new witching communities.'

Celestine tilted her head. 'I'm sure there will be plenty of people interested in talking to you about that.'

'As Connor Lynch. Not as the Abrogator.' It was both an observation and a request. There was a long way to go to change the idea of the Abrogator from something to fear – he knew some people would never stop.

'Of course. Now, I'll leave you to the rest of your holiday.' She stood, extending her hand to him. Voluntarily. Wonders would never cease.

After he saw her out, his dad caught him in the kitchen. Initially, it had been a little awkward, staying with his dad, what with them having little contact over the last decade, but Connor had also recognised as an adult what he hadn't as a child: that his dad was a quiet man, just like Connor. It was good to sit beside someone who also enjoyed stretches of silence.

'It sounds like I owe you an apology, too,' his dad said as he filled the kettle. Again.

Connor had also noticed that his dad drank far too much tea. Connor wouldn't have cared, but every time the appliance clicked, he was taken back to the honeymoon suite, to the smell of blackcurrant tea, and the vision of Becca sitting on the four-poster bed, sipping from a cup . . .

'Come again?' he roused himself from the memory. From the yearning.

'You've been mistreated.'

Connor harnessed a gentle breeze and redirected it towards the bumble bee that was about to come in the open back door, coaxing the dumpy insect to go find some flowers instead. He closed the door, mission accomplished, and raised his eyebrows at his dad. 'You've been eavesdropping.'

'It's summer; my windows are open.' His dad shrugged. 'Connor, I never realised. I should have made more of an effort to understand this . . .' he waved his hand vaguely, 'world you are a part of. Then I might have been able to protect you better.'

'It's OK, Da,' he told him softly, and made a mental note to add support for non-magical parents and guardians to the list of things he would talk to the educator-whoever about, when the time came.

'And that Warren sounds like a prize wanker.'

'He is that, aye,' Connor agreed, but he wasn't going to be Connor's problem any more. He was free.

Connor had made his own apologies when he came back, for being so absent from his family's lives – particularly his cousin Rory's. And he ended up telling him the truth. About everything – Connor's dad having been the only member of his family to be aware of magic. A situation that, of course, Warren encouraged.

Considering his cousin was seven years his senior and the most level-headed, responsible man Connor had ever known, he took it surprisingly well. Perhaps being the sole carer for two children had made him capable of accepting anything as a possibility.

His main response to Connor's description of the witching world and how those witches feared his ability to remove their magic was to laugh as if it were ridiculous that anyone could be scared of his scrawny little cousin – no matter that Connor was slightly taller these days; Rory had played rugby for years and most people were scrawny next to him.

He also commented dryly: 'I can see how that would be a nightmare, so. To actually have to wash dishes and clean clothes the long, boring way for the rest of your life. Poor bastards. Speaking of, you want to throw some of that magic around in my house to help with the chores? Or finding missing socks? Or to stop my girls arguing about having the fecking pink cup when there are two identical pink cups, but one has become mysteriously superior?'

It was fair to say that it being almost halfway through the school summer holidays was beginning to wear on Rory. Connor found himself offering to help out with babysitting a lot. And not even because he felt guilty about not being there for his cousin after he lost his wife – he enjoyed being with the kids. His birthday present for Meghan had gone down a treat, and the girls were hilarious. The way they wore all their emotions out on display was refreshing.

The only problem with the regular babysitting was that it came with the temptation to use magic, because – as Rory had so quickly pointed out – it made life a lot easier, and whenever you were having to look after kids, an easier life was a good thing. Rory had told him to go for it and explained that he didn't really see how them knowing could be a problem. Kids believed in magic already, so any friends they told wouldn't think it was a big enough deal to tell their parents. And even if they did, their parents would just dismiss it as kids being kids.

Connor started out slowly, using just the odd touch of magic here and there, and then got to experience a wonderful thing: eyes aglow, an eagerness to see him do more, awe at his ability to do simple things, like floating plates with their lunch on. He'd got so used to being feared for his magic that he'd forgotten how fun it could be. It was a balm to his soul. The way it had been whenever Becca had looked at him with her warm gaze and seen whatever he was showing her of himself, rather than just all the preconceived notions about the Abrogator.

And some evenings, when the girls were asleep, he and Rory would sit up talking until late, and Connor would mention Becca. Rory never made him feel like an eejit for walking away from the woman he clearly loved, when Rory would do anything to have his wife, Abby, back – but he did point out that if Connor was waiting to be a perfect person for Becca, he would be waiting forever. And if Becca cared for him, she wouldn't need him to be perfect.

Which Connor already knew. She was the princess who didn't need a knight. But she'd asked him to come and find her when he was ready, all the same.

Chapter Thirty-four

BECCA

It was, without a doubt, the best Lammas festival the Ashworths had held in years.

OK, it was the *only* Lammas festival they had held in years, but still, they had outdone themselves.

With the worry of Uncle Adrian's and Harry's health alleviated, they had been able to go all out. Warren had, of course, flung every piece of mud that he could in the direction of Becca's family as the Witches Council began their investigations, and there had been a hearing about the tattoo and the amplifier as a separate issue to Sam's memory spell and her accusations towards Warren.

For the moment, the family had special dispensation to continue using the spell, due to the detrimental effect it would have on the community to break it, and the stance that the use of the spell was a matter of cultural heritage. But it was all reliant on further confirmation that the spell could not be applied to anyone outside of the Ashworth family, who had not agreed to having the tattoo inked onto them. Becca knew who they were thinking of to provide that information and was trying not to be excited at the prospect of Connor turning up at Ashworth Hall to read the spell. Because she wanted to see him when he was ready, not because he was being used for his gifts.

She was trying so hard not to be impatient about him coming back. As much as she wanted to contact him, she didn't want to put any pressure on him. It was an odd relationship problem, waiting for someone to become more selfish – but that's what he needed. And in some ways, it was selfish from her perspective, too. Because it meant that when he did come back to her, she would know he was truly ready, and the relationship was what he wanted. Which was what she deserved, too.

Thinking about him was something she tried to ration. Like a guilty pleasure. He was the reason she smiled when certain songs came on the radio, or tasted lemon, or woke in the night hugging a pillow, and, Goddess, the way she wanted him there with her made her ache throughout the whole of her body, but she just kept reminding herself that it would pass. Eventually. One way or another.

She'd wondered if Rhiannon had been able to fix the duvet buffer in their bedroom at the inn and asked Sam to apologise for her if they'd had to throw it away.

Sam clearly missed the inn, but wanted to be with her family, too, making up for lost time. She was also on probation with the Witches Council for the mass memory spell, while they figured out if there were any long-term side effects or complaints from the people it had reached with its tendrils. Becca herself had nearly received a slap on the wrist for the unauthorised summoning, which Warren had thrown into his desperate defence as they turned every detail of his life over.

Luckily, all she needed to clear her name was Horatio coming through with a cringe-worthy speech about how he'd always been at Ashworth Hall; they must be mistaken that she'd summoned him; he'd been witness to everything from the introduction of the steam engine to women getting the vote – of all things! As he'd begun to detail his opinion on technological developments since the Industrial Revolution, the Witches Council representatives had all but sprinted from Ashworth Hall.

Becca had woken on the morning of 1 August to watch the sun rise with a peace in her heart that she genuinely hadn't felt for a long time, while her uncle's and cousin's health had hung in the balance, and the endless hustling to try to figure out how to fix it had continued. Connor hadn't been wrong. She did take it upon herself to solve problems, to make the people around her happy, and realising that and where it had got her with her dad – i.e. nowhere – was prompting her to question how often it was her place to step in. She still couldn't help offering assistance if she could see an easy solution – or her gift was literally telling her where something was – and she wasn't going to stop being cheerful and seeing the best in situations, but pushing herself to have all the answers was a trait she recognised she should start detaching herself from.

She helped throughout the morning as the Hall and grounds were filled with stalls bearing food and drink and activities for all the guests. When the gates opened at midday, the sun was shining, a folk band was playing down by the water fountains in the gardens and the air was filled with the smell of fresh bread and berry pies. She wandered with her camera, filling the memory card with snippets of summer fun: bright colours and smiling faces everywhere.

Children ran in and out of the Hall, brandishing corn dolls and cinnamon broomsticks, which Kay and her friend Jaz, the local florist, were demonstrating how to make in the ballroom. Aunt Elenor and Zeynep were manning one of the refreshment stalls, handing out gooseberry cordial, elderberry tonic and iced teas. Harry was helping kids do chalk drawings on the big patio at the back of the house and Kay's brother Joe and her dad were playing football with a bunch of kids on the grass to the side of it. Sam stuck with Uncle Adrian, sitting in the shade, watching the band.

It had to be hard for her. The memory spell being lifted had set a wave of recognition through the witching community without doubt. As well as awe at what she had managed to do, and scandalous whispers as to why she had done it. Becca had heard rumours about her having an affair with Warren, and it made her mad that people's minds would go there first – as though that were something *Sam* should be ashamed of, even if it had happened. *He* was the married one and Sam would have been less than half his age, barely an adult, vulnerable to him. And just because she was a thirty-year-old woman now, people forgot.

But her family would stand by her through it, and Becca's uncle's obvious display of being overjoyed that his daughter was home would go a long way to change the narrative. As would Warren finally being punished for his political manoeuvrings and exploitation of young witches . . . not to mention his theft of the amplifier.

Becca was ready for a short break from taking photographs and just trying to decide whether to fill her stomach with some of the delicious barbecue on offer or skip straight to what she really wanted – a toffee apple – when someone tapped her on the back.

She turned around to find little Aisha from Biddicote Primary looking up at her, Bun Bun clutched tightly under her arm. 'Becca, want to come dance with us?'

'Do I ever?!'

She took the little girl's hand as they walked with Aisha's mum, talking about the latest adventures Bun Bun had been on. They made it to the grass near the band and Aisha pushed Bun Bun into her mother's hands. Becca unlooped her camera from her neck, heading over to one of the tables to ask if she could leave it there while she danced and did a double take when she found her dad sitting there.

'What are you doing here?' she blurted out.

He raised his eyebrows and crossed his arms over his chest. 'Waiting for something good to happen.'

Before Becca could question that any further, Aisha was tugging her arm, ready to show Becca the dance moves. Once they were on the grass with the other dancers, Becca very quickly realised she was out of her league but gamely tried to keep up, much to the little girl's amusement.

'Mind if I cut in?'

Becca swung around at the sound of the low Irish voice she dreamed about each night. And there he was. Connor. Her heart squeezed to the point of pain as every detail she'd remembered, but that looked even better in real life, assaulted her senses. And there was something slightly different about him, too.

His black hair was a little longer, curls still contrasting with the sharp angles of his face; his skin had some actual tan, even though it was basically one shade away from his usual vampirism. He was wearing a shirt and trousers, but the shirt was *short-sleeved*, and *blue*, the colour lightening the grey of his eyes. Her throat tightened, her pulse tripping.

'Hi, Becca,' he spoke again, because she was still just staring at him, probably with her jaw slack. 'Want to dance?'

She blinked, trying to gather herself together so she didn't burst into happy tears, because that would cause a scene and they couldn't be interrupted by people wondering what was wrong. There was nothing wrong. Everything was amazing. He was back. He was back.

She forced herself to look down at Aisha. 'Is that OK with you?'

Aisha shrugged. 'I'm not the boss of you. He's taller even than Mr Herman,' the little girl observed, squinting up at Connor and then turning to dance with two other little girls from her class at school.

Hell yeah, he is. Becca grinned and then bit her lip. Hey, grimoires weren't written in a day – she could keep working on the 'tall is attractive' thing another time, because most importantly: 'You're here.'

'I am.' His mouth crept up at the side and Becca's heart fluttered. 'Harry invited me. Is it OK?'

'Of *course* it's OK.' What a ridiculous question. '*Better* than OK. How are—'

She was cut off by his arms gathering her up in a sudden, fierce hug. All the air was expelled out of her body and replaced with him, his warmth, his smell of oakmoss and rosemary, earthy and comforting, the gentle strength of his long limbs. She wrapped her arms around his neck and squeezed so tightly he was forced to lift her off the ground. She resisted the impulse to wrap her legs around his hips, because there were many children present.

'I'm good. I'm really good.' He spoke into her ear as they pressed their cheeks together. 'But I missed you.'

She laughed because the emotion was bubbling up inside of her, threatening to burst, and it was better that than crying. 'I missed you, too. So much I had to get another man around the house.'

'What?' He leaned back to look at her and she smiled, seeing that he wasn't buying it for a minute by the lift of his dark eyebrow.

'The bed just felt so big without you in it. He's a ginger and Michael isn't super-keen on him yet . . . Maybe you can help me name him?'

'How's about Joker, like his new owner,' he said, dryly, and Becca laughed. He set her down gently on the grass and fitted his big hands to either side of her face, studying her as if he couldn't believe she was real. He leaned in close, his grey eyes burningly intense as he whispered against her lips, 'I've got to offer my apologies to Shakespeare and his Romeo, because I've fallen for you, Becca. Hard and fast.'

Becca's breath stuttered in her throat, and she squeaked out: 'Just how I like it.'

He half groaned and half laughed. 'Have mercy on a socially awkward man trying to confess his feelings.'

She stroked his cheek; the cuts were now healed, just a pink line in their place. 'I take no prisoners . . . but I'll take you, if that's what you're offering. In case it isn't obvious, I've fallen for you, too.'

His eyes lit up with happiness the second before he shut them and kissed her with a sweetness so acute it made her ache. But this was different to the throbbing pain she'd experienced while he was gone; this was the burn of a muscle stretched to make it stronger.

'So, want to come back to my place and meet my new cat?' she whispered when he pulled away.

'I could make a joke about that kind of offer, but I'm too classy,' he said, making her laugh until he scooped up her hair carefully from the back of her neck where it was tangled inside the knot of her halter-neck dress, his long fingers on her nape sending shivers of need down her spine. He caught her heated look and stroked his hands slowly down to her waist. 'When d'you want to go?'

Her libido screamed *now* but her sense of community tragically intervened. 'Well, technically, I'm working,' she admitted. 'D'you mind staying for the festival?'

'No. I don't mind staying.' He looked around them, at the witches and non-magical people dancing and eating and talking, enjoying the festivities together, and he smiled, wide and bright. Then he dipped his head and kissed her again, murmuring against her lips, 'I'm looking forward to it.'

So was she.

Acknowledgements

An absolutely enormous thank you to Sanah, it's always such a pleasure to work with you. To Holly Kayte, my proof-reader. Jessica Hart, the designer, and Lucy Davey, the illustrator, who together created such a gorgeous cover, as well as all the team at Orion. Thank you also to Saskia, my agent.

The fantastic 'Bar Babes': Emma, Kate, Katie, Sandra, Julie, and Jenny. You are all amazing, and your support is, as always, invaluable. All the other wonderful writers who make up the community I couldn't be without, including Lucy Keeling, Leonie Mack, Jaime Admans, Anita Faulkner, Katie Ginger, and Kate Smith, as well as so many others. To Sue, Suzanne, Deirdre, Margaret, Maureen, Liz and Wendy who I still haven't been able to see nearly as much as I would have liked to but are always there.

I can't forget all the bloggers and social media friends I've made over this writing journey too. You are so supportive and kind.

Jessica, my fabulous partner in crime! I shall just say 'Narf' because we know that covers it.

To all my friends and family.

And last but the complete opposite of least, Dan and my two girls. The centre of my universe. I could not do this without you.

'Fun, sexy and sweet' **Sarah Hawley**

Sometimes all you need is a little magic . . .

Kay knows three things to be true: a witch who cannot control their powers is dangerous, she needs to make it home for her brother's wedding, and Harry Ashworth is the last person she ever wants to see . . .

But after visiting the witching community's equivalent of IT support to try to fix her misbehaving magic, a hurricane hits and her flight home is cancelled!

Not only is Kay stranded, but she's stranded with Harry – her infuriatingly handsome and charming childhood friend, who broke her heart when they were teenagers.

Except Harry is a frustratingly powerful witch, so working together might be their only way to get back home. And the more time they spend together, the harder it becomes to ignore what is simmering under the surface.

Soon it becomes clear that Kay's magic isn't the only thing she doesn't have control of . . .

Credits

Emma Jackson and Orion Fiction would like to thank everyone at Orion who worked on the publication of *Careful What You Witch For* in the UK.

Editorial
Sanah Ahmed

Copyeditor
Holly Kyte

Proofreader
Francine Brody

Contracts
Dan Herron
Ellie Bowker

Design
Jess Hart
Morven Davis
Loveday May
Nick Shah

Editorial Management
Charlie Panayiotou

Jane Hughes
Bartley Shaw
Tamara Morriss

Finance
Jasdip Nandra
Nick Gibson
Sue Baker

Marketing
Corinne Jean-Jacques

Production
Ruth Sharvell

Sales
Jen Wilson
Esther Waters
Victoria Laws
Toluwalope Ayo-Ajala
Rachael Hum

Anna Egelstaff
Sinead White
Georgina Cutler

Operations
Jo Jacobs
Sharon Willis